Gerald Seymour was one of the UK's premier television news reporters. He was an eyewitness, up close and on the ground, to some of the epoch-changing events of the last decades. He was on the streets of Londonderry on Bloody Sunday when paratroops clashed with Irish demonstrators. He was at the Munich Olympics and saw the agony of Israeli athletes held hostage by Palestinian gunmen and then the catastrophic failure of the German police to save them. He was in Rome in the cruel days when the Red Brigade captured Aldo Moro, a veteran politician, then savagely murdered him.

His first novel, *Harry's Game*, was an instant bestseller and immediately established Seymour as one of the most cutting-edge and incisive thriller writers in the UK and around the world. Since then, his extraordinary blend of breathtaking storytelling and current-events prescience has held his many readers in his spell.

A LINE IN THE SAND
'Brilliantly written and deserving of the Booker
Prize, if only it wasn't so populist'
Mail on Sunday

THE WAITING TIME
'Seymour is writing at the peak of his powers...in
a class of his own'
The Times

KILLING GROUND
'A tense, taut tale of mounting suspense and
emotional drama. A thriller in the true sense of the
word. Mario Puzo, eat your heart out'
The Times

Also by Gerald Seymour

HARRY'S GAME
THE GLORY BOYS
KINGFISHER
RED FOX (published in the US as THE HARRISON
AFFAIR)
THE CONTRACT
ARCHANGEL
IN HONOUR BOUND
FIELD OF BLOOD
A SONG IN THE MORNING
AT CLOSE QUARTERS
HOME RUN
CONDITION BLACK
THE JOURNEYMAN TAILOR
THE FIGHTING MAN
THE HEART OF DANGER
THE KILLING GROUND
THE WAITING TIME
A LINE IN THE SAND
HOLDING THE ZERO
THE UNTOUCHABLE
TRAITOR'S KISS
THE UNKNOWN SOLDIER
RAT RUN
THE WALKING DEAD

and published by Corgi Books

TIMEBOMB

Gerald Seymour

CORGI BOOKS

TRANSWORLD PUBLISHERS
61–63 Uxbridge Road, London W5 5SA
A Random House Group Company
www.rbooks.co.uk

TIMEBOMB
A CORGI BOOK: 9780552156622

First published in Great Britain
in 2008 by Bantam Press
a division of Transworld Publishers
Corgi edition published 2008

Addresses for Random House Group Ltd companies outside
the UK can be found at: www.randomhouse.co.uk
The Random House Group Ltd Reg. No. 954009

The Random House Group Limited supports The Forest
Stewardship Council (FSC), the leading international forest
certification organisation. All our titles that are printed on
Greenpeace approved FSC certified paper carry the FSC logo.
Our paper procurement policy can be found at
www.rbooks.co.uk/environment

Typeset in 10/11.25 Palatino by
Falcon Oast Graphic Art Ltd.
Printed in the UK by CPI Cox & Wyman, Reading, RG1 8EX.

2 4 6 8 10 9 7 5 3 1

For Gillian

Prologue: 24 March 1993

'Come on, boys, put your backs into it,' he rasped. 'Show some life and push.'

But they wouldn't have heard the anger, or the anxiety, in his voice.

It had been sluicing rain when they had started to move the cart and its load away from the bunker in Area 19. By the time they reached their destination, the sleet would have become a dense shower of snowflakes.

Three conscripts were at the back, gasping with the effort. Their boots slithered and slipped on the metalled surface where thin layers of ice had crusted. Himself, he had his shoulder on the right side of the cart. From there he could use his strength and guide it down the centre of the roadway towards the check-point. They had already passed through the gates in the wire that circled Area 19. In front of them was the entry and exit guard post to the Zone, and another half-kilometre ahead the main security post. Even he, Major Oleg Yashkin – and he had thirty-two years' service with the 12th Directorate – was subject to the bitter cut of the cold in the gale. His uniform, of course, was of far better quality than those of the conscripts, and his greatcoat was heavier and thicker, but he, too, felt the brutality of the weather, coming from the north, sweeping down from the regions of Arkhangelsk or Novaya Zemlya or the Yamal peninsula. It was perfect for his purposes.

Not that he would show the three chosen conscripts that the cold affected him. He was an officer of status and experience, and to these three wretches he was a deity. He drove them on, his tongue lashing them when the speed of the cart sagged. He had chosen them with care. Three kids, none yet beyond their teenage years, none intelligent and able to question what was ordered of them – putty in his hands when he had come to their barracks hut and made the selection. He could reflect, as he strained against the cart, that the quality of the conscript kids was far below – in these times of chaos and confusion – what would have been tolerated in the 12th Directorate in the past, but standards for recruits were disappearing into the abyss . . . That, at least, suited him. These new times of chaos, confusion and betrayal were the source of his anger.

The cart slewed to the left, one of the kids tumbled over, and he had to wrench it back on course. Pain snapped in his shoulders and forearms, but it was merely a minor, irritating distraction from the anger that consumed him.

'Come on, boys, concentrate. Work at it. Do I have to do it all myself?'

At the guard post was a barrier, chipped white paint highlighted by faint diagonal red lines. Another conscript came out of the hut and seemed to rock in the force of the gale. Inside, an NCO sat at a desk and showed no willingness to move into the teeth of the elements. Major Yashkin anticipated no problem, but anxiety lingered in him. It should not have. He had, after all, responsibility – six more days of it – for the perimeter security of Area 19 and the Zone. He commanded the troops, regulars and conscripts, who patrolled the fences and stood sentry on the gates. But anxiety gnawed in him because what he did that late afternoon, in a freezing sleet storm, was more than sufficient to cause him to face a closed, secret court-martial and be sentenced to death – a pistol shot to the back of the neck while kneeling in a prison yard.

At the barrier he told his conscript kids, his donkeys, to stop. Major Yashkin straightened to his full height, thrusting his medals' strips into the sentry's face, and accepted the salute. Beyond the grimed glass in the hut he saw that the NCO stood at attention. He did not have to, as a respected officer, but at least he had made the gesture. He went to the far side of the cart and lifted the protective covering, an olive green sheet of oiled plastic, shook the sleet from it and exposed the ends of two metal filing cabinets each laid lengthways. The sentry had little chance to observe that between them a smaller item was swaddled in black rubbish bags and fastened down with rope. The bar was raised. The NCO was now at the guard-post door: did the major need help? He declined the offer.

Two check-points were now behind him, one remained.

It was that sort of afternoon when the pulse of the huge installation had almost died. Physicists, technicians, engineers, chemists, troops of the 12th Directorate, managers, all those who contributed to the beat of the pulse, were gone to their homes if

11

they did not have duties. The buildings on either side of the road were dark.

Twenty minutes later, the major, the three conscripts and the cart were through the outer gate. If the guards at the final barrier had demanded to search the cart, they would have found a canister, close to a metre in length and two-thirds of a metre in height and width, contained in a dull camouflaged protective bag that had stencilled on it 'Batch No. RA-114' in heavier type than the name of the mechanized-infantry unit to which it had been issued. As it was, they had seen only what was visible, the ends of two filing cabinets, and not the weapon, designated RA-114, which had been returned from Magdeburg as a front-line division packed, sent home its arsenal and stripped out its armoury from a base in eastern Germany.

The previous evening Oleg Yashkin had removed or amended the paperwork that existed around RA-114. He believed that unless a thorough search was made, RA-114 no longer existed and, in fact, had never been manufactured.

The afternoon had become evening. The sleet had become snow. The cart creaked through the suburbs of the city beyond the perimeter fence, its wheels gouging tram lines in its wake. They had left the road behind them and were on a track of rocks and stone chippings. Now he was close to his home. The cart was pushed past clumps of birch and pine trees, past small plots where families would grow vegetables after the thaw, past small houses from which dark smoke bustled out of chimneys to be dispersed in the increasing pitch of the snowstorm . . . If what he had taken out of the bunker in Area 19 had been smaller and more easily handled by a single man of his age, he could have carried it to one of the many holes in the fencing that now existed, where the alarms no longer functioned, and from where the patrols had been withdrawn because of troop shortages.

It was all chaos and confusion at Arzamas-16, the place that had no proper and historic name and went unmarked on any map covering the Nizhny Novgorod *oblast*. He had given his working life, his loyalty, his professionalism to that place. And for what? Major Oleg Yashkin did not see himself as a traitor, nor as a thief, but as a man wronged and betrayed.

His home was single-storey, built up from the foundations with bricks to waist height that gave way to an upper frame of stained wood planking. There was a low picket fence separating a hand-kerchief-sized front garden from the track. A dull light burned inside, where there was a living room, a bedroom, a bathroom and a kitchen. It had been his home for eighteen years, since he and his wife – Mother, as he called her – had moved out from an apartment in a block inside the wire. For years now she had been 'Mother' to him, though they had not been blessed with children. She was not privy to what he had done that afternoon, with the help of the three young conscripts, but he had asked her specifically to cook apple cakes with the last fruit of the previous autumn's harvest and to leave them in the small porch at the front of the house.

He had the kids unload the cart, take off the filing cabinets and the wrapped shape, then gave them the cakes. The following morning, back at his office inside the Zone, he would write the orders that would transfer each of them – with immediate effect – to duties closer to their homes and many hundreds of kilometres distant from Arzamas-16.

Oleg Yashkin had had only four days to make his preparations, but the hours had not been wasted ... In bed, that night, he would tell his wife – Mother – of the betrayal inflicted on him four days earlier.

He watched them push the cart away up the track and disappear into the whirlwind of the snow.

The filing cabinets were heavy, but he was able to drag them past his parked car, on which smoothed snow had settled, to the porch and to stack them on either side of it. Their usefulness was now over. Sweat trickled on his back, under his uniform clothing, as he heaved the wrapped shape, RA-114, round the side of his home to the plot at the back. In a wooden shed, he took off his greatcoat, tunic and trousers and hung them from nails. The cold clawed at him as he put on two sets of workman's overalls, then lifted tools from more nails and went outside into the dusk. A mound of earth confronted him. The previous night his neighbour, who out-ranked him and was a *zampolit* in the community inside the fence, had called 'What are you doing? You'll disappear in there, Oleg. Is it your own grave ... ?' He had been more than a metre down in the pit, and he had yelled back to the political officer a lie about a blocked drain. Then he had heard a gust of laughter, and 'You shit too much, Oleg. Shit less and your drain will flow.' He had heard a door close behind his neighbour. With a spade and a pickaxe he had dug till past midnight by the light of a hurricane lamp. Then he had scrambled out of the hole on his hands and knees, and washed in the kitchen. Mother had not asked why he had dug a pit in the night that was a full two metres deep.

14

He dragged the canister to the pit's rim, paused, then put his boot against its side. It was a weapon. It would have been built to withstand being bumped and rocked across country in an army truck. He pressured the sole of his boot against it and it toppled into the black hole. He heard the squelch as it fell into the muddy pool from the earlier rain, but he could not see it and did not know how it lay – on its side, askew, on its end.

There was lead sheeting at the back of his home, strips of it, which had been there for weeks. He had planned to use it to repair the flashing around his home's single chimney, but now he took the strips and laid them in the pit across the plastic sheeting that he could feel but not see. Then, laboriously, he began to throw back the earth, and cover what he had brought home.

He wanted to be finished by the time his wife came back, wanted it hidden. Inside the Zone, the name they had for the wrapped weapon was Zhukov. The fact that the weapon was called after Georgi Konstantinovich Zhukov, victor at Leningrad and Stalingrad, conqueror of Warsaw and Berlin, the most renowned commander of the Great Patriotic War – dead now for nineteen years – was a reflection of its reputation for awesome power. As an officer of the 12th Directorate, he knew that the giveaway radiation signature of a Zhukov would be masked by the lead sheeting.

He had not thought when the grave he now closed would be opened . . . More pressing among his concerns was how he would explain to his wife what the future held for them. It had to be done that night, could be delayed no longer. She did not know yet that at 16.05 on the afternoon of 20 March he had been summoned to attend the office of a

15

brigadier general in the administration complex, or that he had reached the outer door at 16.11. She did not know that the brigadier general had not asked Oleg Yashkin to sit, or offered him coffee, tea, an alcoholic drink, but had kept his eyes on his desk and a typed list in his hands. He was told that, for financial reasons, the size of the 12th Directorate force at the Arzamas-16 site was being reduced by thirty per cent, that officers of long service whose wages were highest would be the first to face dismissal, and be gone by the end of the month. The sheet of paper was flapped in his face long enough for him to read the names. He had pleaded: what was the position with the pensions of retired officers? The brigadier general had shrugged, held out his hands, implied he had no authority to speak on the matter. He was told again that his last day of service would be at the end of the month, and then – as if this was news of high quality – that the house he occupied would be given him in thanks for his devoted service . . . There would not be a party to see him off after thirty-two years with the Directorate, no speeches and no presentations. He would come to work on the last morning, leave on the last afternoon, and there would be no line of hands for him to shake. He had seen the brigadier general take a pen, scratch out the name of Yashkin, Oleg (Major), then look sharply at his wristwatch, as if to say that the list was long and others waited, and would he, please, double quick, fuck off out of the room.

He had blundered out, across an anteroom, and barely seen those now waiting for an audience because humiliation blurred his vision . . . A man such as Oleg Yashkin believed himself owed the respect of the state and that he was entitled to his dignity. He remembered, of course, all those dismissed the previous year because their wages could not be paid – but such a thing could not happen to a trusted officer charged with the security of warheads. He had been in the room for eight minutes. His lifetime achievement was reduced to an interview with a bureaucrat who had not had the courage to look him in the face.

It wasn't that his job was becoming less important, less busy. Most days, now, weapons came in to be stored haphazardly in the bunker and in wood buildings at the side. There were Zhukovs, and warheads for artillery shells, for torpedoes, for mines. They came to Area 19 to be dismantled – swords to be turned into plough shares – because the state could no longer pay the bills. Receipt of them was scribbled on dockets, abandoned in trays on crowded desks, and they were stacked in readiness for transportation to the workshops used by Decommissioning on the far side of the Area. He had taken one, and it would not be missed.

He had been the servant of a great country, a superpower. But wages could no longer be paid and his reward for loyalty was to be pitched out on the last afternoon of the month. His anger had found purpose, had been channelled. He tossed the last sods on to the slight mound, and in the spring – when the thaw came and the ground loosened – he would plant vegetables around it, would have time to do it. Behind him, a light came on in his home. His wife would have returned from the chapel that was a shrine to St Seraphim where she obsessively cleaned and scrubbed.

He changed back into his uniform. Racked with exhaustion, he went in through the kitchen door. Having washed his hands in tepid water, he poured himself coffee from the pot, laced it with vodka, and wore his best smile to greet her. Later, in bed, when they lay close to pool their body warmth, he would tell her of the betrayal and injustice inflicted on him. And he would tell her – so rare for him to lie to her – that he had repaired the damaged drain in the plot at the back of the house so she could parrot it once more to his neighbour.

He did not know of the grave's future, or when it would be opened. Anger had made him dig it and fill it, but to what purpose he could not have said.

What Oleg Yashkin did know: he hated them for the humiliation piled on him. For the first time in his adult life, hatred governed him, not loyalty.

Outside, the snow fell and disguised the mound of displaced earth. The whiteness gave it cleanness and purity.

Chapter 1: 9 April 2008

He had been embedded in the family since the start of the year. Jonathan Carrick waited at the front door, listened as the children's mother chided them for being late and not hurrying. He heard the scolding and could not help himself. He smiled. Then the clatter of feet on the landing above him, and their mother was leading them down the wide staircase and past two paintings, sixteenth-century Italian, more suitable for hanging in a gallery. She grimaced at him. 'I think, Johnny, that finally we're ready. At last . . .'

'I'm sure we'll make up time, Mrs Goldmann. Won't be a problem.' It was a soft lie, not an important one. The traffic would be building on the streets between the house in Knightsbridge and the school in Kensington that specialized in providing an education to 'international' children from families of great wealth. For Jonathan Carrick, every waking moment of his life was governed by deceit, and each time he spoke, he had to consider whether he risked exposing it. He grinned. 'No, they'll be there for Assembly – I promise, Mrs Goldmann.'

The housekeeper emerged from the door at the back of the hall, the route to the kitchen, holding two plastic lunchboxes containing fruit and sandwiches. It was more of the ritual of the morning departure. The children would take the boxes with them to school, would eat the lunch the school provided, and the boxes would come back in the afternoon, unopened. The sandwiches and fruit would be eaten in the kitchen by Carrick, or Rawlings, who had been his entry point to the family, by Grigori or Viktor.

She called again. 'Please, loved ones, hurry.'

Selma and Peter cascaded down the stairs. The girl was nine and the boy was six. Cheerful and happy, noisy and loved. The children greeted him: 'Good morning, Mr Carrick ... Hi, Johnny ...' It was not right that he should show familiarity in front of their mother, so he assumed a frown of mock-severity, muttered about the time and gazed at his watch. His reaction won shrieks of laughter from the girl and giggles from the boy.

He had the car keys in his hand and stood by the heavy door. Now Grigori had slouched out of the kitchen area, skirted the children, their mother and the housekeeper and come to stand beside Carrick. Their eyes met, a formality of communication. He had little time for the Russian bodyguard, and the bodyguard scarcely hid his dislike for this intruder into the household. Grigori nodded sharply to him. They did not have to discuss the procedures. After three months they were well rehearsed. Carrick's fingertips hit the keypad, unlocked the door, closing down the alarm, then opened it. It was well oiled but heavy, having a steel plate covering its back.

Grigori clattered down the steps, his eyes raking

the street, each car and van. Then he waved, a small, economical gesture. Carrick came next, going awkwardly on the steps. The limp was accentuated. The big Mercedes was parked across the pavement. Carrick went to it, flashed the key, slid into the driver's seat, gunned the engine, then leaned back and opened the rear near-side door. Now the children spilled after him and dived in. As their belts clicked, as the door was slammed shut, he pulled away from the kerb.

He looked back a last time. Mrs Goldmann, Esther, was at the top of the steps and waving, then blowing kisses. If it had interested Carrick, he would have said that she was a good-looking woman, with something slightly feral about her thinness. The way her collarbones and cheekbones protruded from the skin was attractive, as was the blonde hair that the morning sunlight caught. She was dressed quietly, blouse, skirt, a knotted scarf at her throat . . . He thought her as dangerous to his safety as any other adult in the household.

Each morning he drove the children of Josef and Esther Goldmann to the international school. And each afternoon he brought them home. Between the trips to and from the school, he sometimes escorted Mrs Goldmann to an exhibition of furniture or art, to a reception for a charity she supported, to a lunch appointment. After school, sometimes, he took her to a cocktail party, to the theatre or a concert. He would have described her as discreetly prominent in the community of newly rich Russian citizens making their home in the British capital, would also have said she was intelligent and sharp-witted, much more to her husband than a social decoration. He could not have said how much longer he would continue working for the family, maybe weeks but not months. He drove carefully, not fast.

The truth was that high expectations had not been fulfilled; he was inside the family's home, but outside the kernel of the family's existence. He did not know where Josef Goldmann, or Viktor, or indeed Simon Rawlings were that morning. Behind him, the kids were quiet, stamping their small, pudgy fingers on the controls of their GameBoys. Josef Goldmann, Viktor and Simon Rawlings had left the house before Carrick had arrived for the start of his day. It was not that he could be criticized for not knowing where they had gone, but there would be disappointment that an operation involving resources and expenditure was proving much less than fruitful.

Often he looked in the rear-view mirror. He did not know whether a tail was on him, if back-up was close. His employment was to prevent the kidnapping of the kids – they were a worthwhile target, had to be, with a father worth more than a hundred million in sterling. The Mercedes sat low on its tyres because of the armour plating on the doors and the reinforced glass, and he carried an extendable baton with an aerosol can of pepper spray in his suit jacket . . . He was so damned alone, but that was the nature of his work.

Near to the school, he joined a queue of top-of-the-range people-carriers, sports utilities and saloons with privacy windows. He did not let the kids out and on to the pavement short of the school gate, but edged forward till he was level with it and within sight of the school's own security staff. He was not a child-minder, a chauffeur or a door-opener. Jonathan Carrick, Johnny to all who knew him half well, was a serving police officer, Level

One Undercover, a bright star in the firmament of a small and secretive corner of the Metropolitan Police Service that carried the title of Serious Crime Directorate 10. And the high-value target that was Josef Goldmann still eluded him.

He braked and loosed the lock on the rear door, near side. 'OK, guys. Have a good day.'

'And you, Johnny . . . You have a good day, too, Johnny.'

He grimaced. 'And do your work. You work hard.'

One droll answer. 'Of course, Johnny, what else?' And one query: 'Will you be picking us up, Johnny?'

'Yes, lucky me.' He gave an exaggerated wink, and they were gone. As ever, the little beggars didn't bother to close the door behind them, so he had to lean back and do it himself. It would be him who picked them up because he wasn't yet deep enough into the family. To have been deep, to have made the operation worthwhile, he would have been driving Josef Goldmann and Viktor to whatever destination was given him, as Simon Rawlings had that morning.

It was regular, not sophisticated but simple.

It was a procedure that was used twice a month during the spring, summer and autumn.

Sitting in the back, on the leather seat of his 8-series Audi, Josef Goldmann waited for Viktor's return. In front of him, head back and eyes closed, was his driver, Simon Rawlings. He liked the man. Rawlings drove well, never initiated conversation, and seemed to see little. There was a litheness to his movement that came from his pedigree history: Rawlings – why Goldmann had chosen him – was a one-time sergeant in the British Parachute Regiment. It had been Goldmann's opinion, when he emigrated from Moscow to London, that he must have his own men for close protection but British men for the driving. His mind that morning was clouded. Other matters dominated his mind and had for the last two months – since Viktor's return from Sarov in the Nizhny Novgorod *oblast*. He could have refused what had been offered to him, perhaps should have, but had not. Every day of the last week he had checked the Internet for a weather forecast in the region of that *oblast*, with particular reference to the air temperature. What he had learned yesterday and the previous day had warned him to expect the call, and a mobile phone in Viktor's pocket was dedicated solely to receiving it. It was beyond anything that Josef Goldmann had attempted before, and there had been many nights in those two months that he had lain awake on his back, beside Esther while she slept, and his mind had churned with the enormity of it. The business that brought him regularly to the port of Harwich was predictable enough to allow him to be distracted.

Gulls wheeled over the car park, shrieked and yelled. Away to his right were the sheds for arrivals and departures, and above their roofs were the angles of the cranes and the white-painted super-structure of the cruise ship. The *Sea Star* was the first of the season, 950 passengers on board, to have returned from a Baltic sea voyage to St Petersburg. A pair of pensioners, probably using an inside cabin, would be bringing with them two large suit-cases, and would have told Security on the quayside near the Hermitage that they had been so cheap in a street market they could not pass over the opportunity to purchase them . . . Not sophisticated but simple. It was the waiting for the mobile call that chewed in him. A gull, flying a few feet above the car, defecated and the windscreen was spattered. Rawlings jolted into action, swearing softly. He leaped out to clean the glass, wiping it furiously.

Through the windscreen, beyond the smears, Josef saw Viktor pushing in front of him a trolley with two suitcases . . . and then he stopped. He had a mobile phone in his hands, lifted it, had it against his ear – possibly for ten seconds, no more – and then it was back in his pocket, and the trolley was wheeled past the Audi. Goldmann snapped open his door, was out of it and by the boot. If any had watched the parking area, they would have seen a host of cars, large and small, expensive and cheap, into which such suitcases were loaded. At the front of the car Rawlings had finished cleaning the windscreen and was now back in the driver's seat. The man was suitable because he heard nothing and saw nothing, and could drive at speed with a soft touch. And now Rawlings had introduced his friend, brought him to share the workload, to drive the children and Goldmann's wife . . . Waiting to be told of the call's message, he found that his breath came faster.

He stammered his question: 'What-what information?'

Viktor said, calm, 'They have replied to what we sent them. Just one word, difficult to hear, not a good connection, and the one word repeated three times. "Yes . . . *da* . . . *da*." I think I heard their car engine.'

'Just that, nothing more?'

'Just that.'

'So, it has begun.'

'They are on the road,' Viktor said, 'and the schedule is one week.'

As if the enormity of it had struck him a powerful hammer blow, Josef Goldmann gasped. It was a moment before he had collected himself. 'Viktor, tell me, should we have followed this path?'

Viktor said, 'Too late to forget it. The offer was made, the price indicated, they accepted. Arrangements are in place, people are alerted, and they're coming. It has begun and can't be stopped.'

Goldmann winced, then snapped his fingers. He was given the keys to two suitcases. He unlocked two sets of padlocks, unbuckled reinforcing straps, dragged back zips. He rummaged through two thin layers of unwashed clothing, then felt for the catches that released the false bottom of each case. Exposed were hundred-dollar bills. Packages, each bound with elastic bands, of a hundred notes, each package with the value of ten thousand dollars. Fifty packages in the base of each bag. A tidy one million dollars, to be repeated twice a month through April and May, June and July, August and September. He replaced the lids, then the pensioners' clothing, drew the zips tight, fastened the padlocks and slammed down the boot lid. He sighed.

'Maybe twelve million comes out of St Petersburg, maybe seven million out of Tallinn, nine million out of Riga on the boats, and twenty on the roads across the frontiers. I take my cut for washing it, and I have four million, and that's the top of what the market can sustain. Two men are on the road, send a message of one word, repeated three times, and we have negotiated a fee of eleven million.'

26

'Your share is five point five – which means that everything coming from the boats, with expenses, is chicken shit.'

'But what is the danger when you play with chicken shit?'

Viktor had minded Josef Goldmann since 1990. He had been put alongside Josef Goldmann in the city of Perm by Reuven Weissberg. He protected Goldmann on Weissberg's orders. He heard a grim little cackle of laughter. 'Where is the excitement in living when there is no danger, where there is only a carpet of chicken shit?'

'You'll tell him now?'

'I'll call him.'

A call was made. Three or four words. A connection of three or four seconds, and no response gained.

They were driven away at speed, but within the legal limits, to a warehouse in an industrial estate outside the Essex town of Colchester. From habit Simon Rawlings twice employed basic anti-surveillance techniques: circled a roundabout four times on the A12 at Horsley Cross, and slowed on the fast dual carriageway to twenty-five miles per hour. No car had followed them on the roundabout, or slowed to keep pace with them. And the car was clean of tags – it was swept each morning. All routine. Another safe run. Risk minimal. At the warehouse on the industrial estate, the two suitcases containing a million American dollars were to be loaded into a container that would hold, when filled, a cargo of best Staffordshire bone china to be exported to the Greek zone of the island of Cyprus. Reuven Weissberg touted for the business, Josef Goldmann washed the money, and the new millionaires and asset-strippers of the Russian

Federation could rest assured that their nest eggs were safe and well protected.

Josef Goldmann laundered cash and made it clean for legitimate investment, was regarded in the Serious Crime Directorate as a major Organized Crime target, and thought himself safe . . . and wished that time could be turned back, that two old men had not started out on a drive of sixteen hundred kilometres, had stayed in their goddam hovels in the arse-end of Russia. But, and Viktor could have told him this, time was seldom turned back. On the return journey to London, he wondered what progress they had made – two old men and a carload that was worth, to him, a half-share in eleven million dollars – and he knew the clock was ticking.

The departure had been planned with the care and precision expected of former officers. The details of the journey, the route and the distance to be driven each day of that week, had been pored over, analysed, queried, debated and agreed.

But they had left late. Should have been gone as the dawn broke under the low cloud on a spring morning. In two weeks they would be home, his neighbour had said to his wife, with attempts at reassurance: there was enough cut wood for two weeks, they had no need of soup, bread and cheese, bills could wait for two weeks, in the car he would be warm, and what did it matter if he stank in soiled underclothes? It wasn't a posting to Afghanistan, the Chinese border or the Baltic fog fields . . . It was two weeks' journey, there and back.

Then it had struck Igor Molenkov, co-conspirator and neighbour of Oleg Yashkin, that Mother's prolonged goodbye intimated that she had sensed danger he had not considered, or Yashkin spoken of. Pride, self-esteem, had rejected any acknowledgement of danger – as had anger. They were now on the road, and the car rolled along through the sodden forest of the state park, then past great stagnant lakes.

The anger remained as sharp today as when it had been bred, sharp as the talons of a fish-eating eagle circling over the park, sharp as the claws of the bears in its remotest parts. There had been so many days of anger over the betrayal he had endured, and their accumulation had put him in the Polonez car with the road map on his lap, his neighbour beside him, and a destination almost sixteen hundred kilometres to the west.

They had chosen to drive on side roads, and the potholes shook him. Because of the weight at the back of the Polonez, the car jerked with each pitch of the wheels.

But his anger had found a valve through which to escape. It had put him where he now sat, in a weighted-down Polonez whose engine and body-work were a virtual wreck. His wife was now twenty-four years in her grave. Their son, Sasha, had burned to death in an ambushed tank a few kilometres short of the Salang Pass, one of the countless casualties of the failed Afghanistan campaign . . . His son had been the idol of his brother's boy, Viktor. He, Colonel Igor Molenkov, had fast-tracked his nephew's application to enter the ranks of the Committee of State Security. Viktor had left the KGB after only two years' service, and gone to work in the flourishing new industry of 'security', had worked with a criminal gang in the city of Perm, gone abroad, then come back in the last days of that year's February to visit him;

decent of him to do that. That visit had begun it all. Dinner cooked in his neighbour's house by his neighbour's wife, 'Mother': grilled chicken, potatoes grown the previous summer, cabbage stored for six months, and a bottle of vinegar-like wine from Sochi. Hints dropped of the rewards of protection, of the 'roof' for which businessmen paid willingly and heavily or saw their trading opportunities collapse in bankruptcy. A small envelope left on the table when his nephew had driven away in his silver BMW, as if they needed and were deserving not only of thanks but of charity.

And then they had talked. 'Mother' away to her bed. The dregs of the bottle were there to be drunk. His neighbour's confession. Knowing he was the first to be told of a grave dug in the vegetable patch. Looking, as if he needed confirmation, out of the kitchen window and seeing the snow lying smooth on the shaped mound. Shrugging into their coats and stumbling away down icy roads to the hotel where Viktor had stayed the night. Waking him, watching the dismissal of the girl, and waiting for her to dress and leave. Telling him what was buried and offering it for sale, and seeing the wariness on his neighbour's face give way to growing excitement. Telling him their price. Past four in the morning, they had emerged from the room with a new mobile phone each, instructions on what message would reach them, and what message they should send back. The girl had been waiting downstairs in the lobby. As soon as they had passed her she had run to the stairs, her short skirt bouncing on her arse as she had gone back up.

In time, a message had come.

Together, in the dark before the dawn, they had

dug rain-saturated earth from the mound, then pushed aside strips of soil-coated lead, then lifted up – struggling, cursing – the drum still wrapped in rubbish bags. The plastic torn away, they had gazed at the warhead, so clean when exposed to the torchlight that he had been able to read the batch number stencilled on it. He had felt fear at handling it, but not his neighbour. Clean plastic had been put over it and tied with string. They had carried it – a desperate weight – round the side of the house and dumped it in the boot of the Polonez, which had sagged on its rear wheels. They had laid a tarpaulin over it. They had stowed inside their own bags and – a small gesture, but demanded by Molenkov – hung their old dress uniforms across the back doors.

Before they had left, Colonel (Ret'd) Igor Molenkov had walked down the track in front of their homes, found the best place for a mobile transmission and used the phone Viktor had given him to call a pre-programmed number and say the word three times: 'Da . . .da . . . da.'

The car drove along the side road towards the city of Murom.

Molenkov reflected: what had the old fool hunched over the wheel beside him led him into? Wrong, sadly wrong. There were *two* old fools in the Polonez. Two men of equal guilt, two men who had stepped across a threshold and now travelled in the world of extreme criminality, two men who . . . He was thrown forward and his hands went up to protect his head before it hit the windscreen.

They had stopped. He saw Yashkin's yellow teeth bite at a bloodless lower lip. 'Why have we stopped?'

'A puncture.'

'I don't believe it.'

'Rear left. Didn't you feel the bumping as it went down?'

'Have we a spare?'

'Bald, old, yes. I can't afford new tyres.'

'And if the spare is holed?'

He saw Yashkin shrug. They were beside a wide lake. From the map left on his seat, Colonel (Ret'd) Igor Molenkov estimated they had covered no more than forty-eight kilometres, and now they had a holed tyre to be replaced with a bald one, and a further 1552 kilometres before they reached their destination. He could have sworn, cursed or stamped.

They hung on each other's necks, and their laughter pealed out.

There are great white spheres on a Yorkshire moor. There are antennae on the summits of a mountain range running across Cyprus. There are huge tilted dishes on the roofs of the buildings on the edge of the town of Cheltenham. Spread across the United Kingdom, and behind the perimeter fences of a sovereign military base on a Mediterranean island, there are vast computers, some manned by British technicians and some by American personnel from the National Security Agency.

Each day they suck down many millions of phone, fax and email messages from around the northern hemisphere. The majority, of course, are discarded – regarded as of no importance. A tiny minority are stored and transmitted to the desks of analysts at GCHQ, who work below the dishes, in that Gloucestershire town. Triggers determine what reaches the eyes of the analysts. Programmed words, phrases, spoken in a mêlée of languages, will activate a trigger. Specific numbers will attract a trigger if those numbers have been gobbled into the computers' memories. And locations . . . Nominated locations are monitored. If a location registers in the computers, the memory will search back for matches and a trail is established. The men and women who sit in darkened rooms and stare at screens are unlikely to understand the significance of what the triggers throw up. They are a filter, unsung and anonymous.

The city of Sarov, in the Nizhny Novgorod *oblast* of the Russian Federation, trips a trigger. Calls into and out of the city that cross international frontiers are noted, and the location of the receiver or transmitter can be narrowed to a square with a precision of less than a hundred metres.

The calls in question came to the screen of a young woman, a graduate of Russian studies, working on the third floor of the central building at GCHQ in D Wing. Four days before there had been a mobile-telephone connection to another mobile telephone in Sarov, duration eight seconds, from a residential street in the London district of Knightsbridge. That morning, a call was placed from Sarov and answered at the dockside in the East Anglian port town of Harwich, duration four seconds. The same mobile phone from Harwich had then called from the Essex town of Colchester to a location adjacent to the Polish-Belarussian border.

The young woman could not have been aware of the significance of what she learned – priorities were beyond her remit. But she typed in a code on her keyboard, opened a secure electronic link, transmitted the details of the calls and included as an attachment satellite pictures. They showed an unmade road or track in Sarov, running east to west, that was flanked to the north by trees and to the south by small detached single-storey homes. Another showed the car park at Harwich, another identified an industrial park on the outskirts of Colchester, and another a Knightsbridge street. There was a final image of a forest of pines and birches where a wide circle filled the only cleared space, to the right side of the picture, and a railway track ran close to it . . . It was all so easy.

She left her desk and went to the coffee machine. A spider's web of trails had been made.

If, *if*, the call to Sarov had been answered as few as twenty-five kilometres from the city, the triggers would not have reacted . . . Mistakes had been made. The young woman's messages and attachments were now inside a building in London of monstrous ugliness on the south side of the river Thames, VBX to all who worked there.

The trees moved with the wind. The pines had been planted in regimented lines and filled rectangular shapes, apparently the work of a woodsman with a character of parade-ground orderliness, and they grew ram-rod straight. Among them, making a defiant chaos, were wild birches that lacked the strength of the pines, and were forced to grow tall and too fast if they were to find natural light. They were spindly and many had been bent almost double by the winter snow. The canopies of the pines wavered, moved with that wind, but they were planted sufficiently close to diminish the daylight on the floor of needles. Reuven Weissberg sat quietly among the trees, awaiting the call.

A light rain fell, but the wind was from the east,

from across the river, and the tight canopies deflected the dribbling water. Little cascades came down among the birches, but where he sat his head and the shoulders of his jacket stayed dry. It was a small matter to him whether he was soaked, merely damp or dry, and his mind was far from considerations of his personal comfort. His thoughts were of what had happened here more than six decades ago, and the stories he had been told, which he knew by heart. He heard the bright songs of small birds, and the cry of an owl . . . That was no surprise to him because the place had long been known – before the events that had made the stories he could recite – as the Forest of the Owls. The surprise was only that the owl had called, perhaps to its mate, during the day, in the morning. That small birds sang was a surprise too. It was said, he had been told, that birds did not come, refused to nest and breed in a place with a history such as this. They flew between the lower branches of the birches, perched precariously and called for company, then flew again; he watched them. It was strange to him that they should show such joy here, as if they had no sense of where they were, did not understand that the misery of mass death haunted this place.

Behind him, a mobile phone had rung, had been answered. Then the silence had cloaked him and the trees again.

In that quiet, he could imagine. Not imagine Mikhail, who was fifty metres clear of him and would be standing against the trunk of the broadest pine he could find, a pile of littered cigarette stubs at his feet. Or imagine the screams and struggles of the Albanian Mikhail would bring to the warehouse the next afternoon. Or imagine the consequences of the call that Mikhail had taken.

He seemed to see them, figments of his thoughts that came to life. They were in flight. The heroism of some and the panic of many had shaped his existence. He was their creature. Figures drifted, either fast or painfully slowly, between the steady trunks of the pines and the wavering stems of the birches. They were clear in his eyes. He thought he could have reached out, touched them. The sight of them was agony to him. In the peace around him, he could hear also the guns, the dogs and the sirens.

This was Reuven Weissberg's heritage, here, in the Forest of the Owls. He did not know that a satellite photograph of this mess of farmed and wild trees had been sent as part of an attachment to a building known as VBX, and that the photograph had picked out a grey-white shallow mound. Such a mound was in front of him, perhaps eighty metres across, but near-hidden from his view by the pines and birches. To him, a story that has a beginning is only of value if it has an end. He knew that story from its start to its finish.

He had been told it so many times. It was the blood that ran in his veins. He was the child of that story, knew each word, each line and each episode. As a small boy he had wept on his grandmother's shoulder as she had told it to him.

Now he told it to himself, as she would have done, from the beginning. The trees rustled above him, the rain fell and the birds sang. It was Anna's story, and in his lifetime he would never be free of it, or want to be.

It was early in the morning of a summer day in 1942 that we were ordered to be ready to move from Wlodawa.

36

Most of our people had already been taken in the previous four months, but we did not know where they had gone. We no longer had access to our homes, but had been made to live inside and around the synagogue. That area was fenced off and we were separated from the Polish people – already I had learned that we were Jews, were different, were subhuman.

I did not know where we were going . . . If there were any among us who did, they did not share it. I believed everything I was told. We were told that we could bring one bag with us, and in the last hour before our departure each of us – young and old, man and woman – filled a bag or a case, and some of the older men sewed gold coins into the linings of their overcoats and some of the older women stitched diamonds or other jewels from bracelets, necklaces and brooches into slits they had made in their clothing.

Always there was little food at the synagogue, and that morning I do not remember whether we ate. I think we started off hungry. Yes, hungry and already tired.

When we were formed up and counted, about a hundred of us, the officer said that we were going to walk to a transit camp. There, selections would be made, and then we would move to new homes in the east – in the Ukraine part of Russia. We walked, and left behind our synagogue. As we went through the town we passed the houses where some of our people had lived. Washed sheets hung from windows and the doors on to the street were open, and we realized that our homes had been occupied by Polish people while we had been kept at the synagogue.

I walked near the back of our group. I was with my father and mother, my two younger brothers and my elder sister, with my father's parents, my mother's father, three uncles and two aunts. We wore the best clothes we still had. At the front of us was an officer on

37

a horse. I remember it – a white horse. Alongside us were Ukrainian soldiers who walked, but there were Germans at the back on horses. We crossed the bridge over the Wlodawka, near to where it flows into the Bug river, and then we came to the village of Orchowek. The reaction of the villagers, as we passed them, was a great shock to me . . . but for many months we had been confined inside the wood fences around the synagogue, and it was nearly two years since I had seen Polish people.

People were lined on either side of the road, as if they had been warned that we were coming. They abused us, threw mud and rocks at us, spat on us. When I was a child, before the war had started, before we were sent to the synagogue, I had worked often when there was no school in my father's shop where he repaired clocks and watches. Among those on the side of the road, I recognized some who had come to my father's shop. They had thanked him for the work he had done, or had begged him to accept late payment. I did not understand why now they hated us. A bucket of waste and urine was hurled at my father. Some of it splashed the silk scarf I had been given for my eighteenth birthday, two weeks before. I looked at the Germans on their horses, hoping they would give us protection, but they were laughing.

Beyond Orchowek, where the road goes east and towards Sobibor village, the officer on the white horse led us on to a forest track close to the railway line, the one that goes south to Chelm. I remember also that in the late summer of 1942 it had rained heavily. The track we were now on was a river of mud. I was one of many women and girls who had worn their best shoes and one of many who lost a shoe and had to walk barefoot through big puddles.

There were older people who could not keep up with the pace of the white horse, so those who were younger and stronger carried them or supported them, but the bags of the infirm and weak were left beside the track. I helped my father's parents, and my younger brothers helped my mother's father, while my elder sister – it was hard for her because she had had polio and walked with difficulty herself – helped my two aunts. If the speed of our march dropped, we were shouted at by the Germans, and a few of our men were hit with whips.

A train came past, and our guards waved to the crew. The engine pulled many closed cars. I thought they were for animals and had not been cleaned because the smell was disgusting, like a place for pigs. It stayed in the forest after the train had gone on towards Wlodawa. I said to my father that I hoped we would have a different train when we went to the east: it was intended to be funny, but my father did not laugh. Usually it was easy to make him laugh, even when we were kept in the synagogue.

And we were there.

I think we had been walking for two hours on the forest track when we came to the place. The officer on the white horse was shouting orders, the Ukrainians were pushing us together, close, using their rifles. I thought we had arrived at the transit camp. It was huge, but so quiet. As far as I could see there was fencing, but it was strange because the branches of fir trees had been woven into the wire strands, and I couldn't see what was on the far side, except the roofs of some buildings and a great high watchtower. At the corners of the fencing and by a gate there were more towers on stilts with guards in them and machine-guns, and I saw that the barrel of one of those guns followed us. What threat were we – old men and old women, girls and children? How could we hurt soldiers?

I was so innocent. Perhaps I should thank God for my innocence.

We were lined up outside a gate. We were in twenty

ranks, five in each rank. Women to the front, with the children, men at the back. I saw my mother leave my father's side and she tried to kiss his cheek, but a Ukrainian put his rifle between them and forced her back. I saw my father shrug, and his lips moved as if to mouth a word, but I did not hear it . . . and it happened very suddenly.

The officer on the white horse surveyed us, as if he was a kaiser or an emperor, and he pointed to me with his whip. A guard moved forward, grabbed my shoulder and dragged me out. Why? Why me? I was eighteen and my elder sister had said enviously that I was beautiful, that my hair had the sheen of a raven's feathers. I had heard men in the synagogue speak of me and praise the shape of my body – but my mother had not spoken to me of such things. I, I alone, was taken out of the group.

I was led to another gate. I thought then it was a more important gate, the main gate, and I stopped, twisted and tried to look back, tried to see my parents, my younger brothers, my elder sister, my father's parents, my mother's father, my aunts and uncles. But I was kicked hard in the back of my legs, a boot against the skin. I never saw them.

I was brought through a maze of paths and on either side of them were the fences with the fir branches slotted on them. Then I became aware of sounds – the shuffling movement of men at the end of their strength, low, muttering voices, hacking coughs and sharply issued orders. More gates opened ahead of me, and I was escorted through. Then they closed behind me. There was the smell, and the men who shuffled, the women who coughed, the Germans who strutted with whips or guns did not seem to notice the overwhelming stench around them, of decay and burning . . . did not seem aware of it.

Inside a compound, I was met by a Jewess. She led me towards a long, low, wooden hut. She told me she was a

40

capo, that I should obey her at all times. I heard then a new sound. Shots were fired, individual shots and many together. I asked the capo who was shooting and why, but she did not answer.

Later, at the end of the afternoon, I learned that I was in Camp 1, that in the morning I would be given work. The sinking sunlight was then obscured and the compound darkened by a black cloud of smoke that was carried from beyond the woven fences. The pall hung over me, and fine ash coated my hair and face.

I did not understand and was blessed briefly with ignorance. The innocent do not know evil. But innocence cannot last, cannot continue to protect against evil.

'You going to be all right tonight, Corp?'

'Not a problem, Sarge.'

'Don't want me to hold your hand?'

'Can manage without.'

It was their banter, to use the old ranks of their army service. Simon Rawlings had been a Parachute Regiment sergeant when he had come out to try his hand in the civilian workplace, with a Military Medal on his record, and Carrick had been a corporal. Each would have said that any man, at his peril, ignored the value of an old, proven friendship. Their friendship had been combat-tested on the streets of Iraq: when the bomb had detonated, catapulting the Land Rover off the banked-up roadway, when Corporal Carrick had been wounded, bad, in the leg and bleeding, close to unconscious, Sergeant Rawlings had been two vehicles behind in the patrol. He had taken the decisive actions, had staunched the casualty's injuries and organized the defence of the ambush site, had sanitized a perimeter big enough to accept an evacuation helicopter, had seen his corporal

41

lifted off to the trauma theatre of the hospital at the base out in the desert from Basra. Sergeant Rawlings had come to visit him while he had waited for shipment out and treatment back in UK. 'I tell you what, Corp, I don't think you'll be doing too many more jumps, or wearing that pretty beret much longer . . . Nor me. I'm thinking it's time to ease into the slow lane. Had an offer last leave of bodyguard work – plenty of holes to be filled by Special Forces, marines and Paras, and you don't get your butt shot off or your leg mashed. Keep in touch, and I hope it mends.' He'd been given a scrap of paper with Rawlings's number on it, and he'd been flown home. The leg had looked worse in the devastated Land Rover than after it had been cleaned. Skill from surgeons and physios had put him back on his feet, crutches and shaky at first, but then he'd walked, the torn muscles had knitted and the bones had fused, leaving him with only a slight limp.

Paratroopers weren't permitted to limp, but policemen were. He'd come out of the army four years back, and within three months a West of England force had accepted him. Then he had been thirty-two, and had a leg that was a mass of blotched, grafted skin but serviceable. Time had moved on. Change of workplace and change of specialization, a target in his new unit that was being evaluated for a crack or weakness in its defences. A surveillance photograph showed Josef Goldmann, Russian national and launderer of dirty money, on the steps of his London home, two Russian hoods escorting him, and a springy, slightly built guy holding open the door of an armour-plated, 8-series Audi saloon. 'I know him – God, saved my life in Iraq. That's Rawlings, my sergeant in recce platoon, Zulu Company, of 2 Para . . .' An engineered meeting had led to an interview with Josef Goldmann. Rawlings must have spoken up for him, and the Bossman must have felt the threat level around him and his family rising – could be rivals after his cake slices or could be government agents from back home. Anyway, Carrick had been offered employment. His controller had said that after three months 'on the plot', the operation would be reassessed. His cover officer had said that three months would give them an idea whether the investment was good, indifferent, or cash down the drain.

It wasn't going well. Carrick drove the children to school, drove Esther Goldmann to shops and parties, watched the security of the house, and spent most days in a basement ready room, watching security screens and waiting to be called upstairs. Most hours of most days he sat with Grigori and most hours of most days the heavier honcho, Viktor, was closer to the family and up close to the Bossman – and Simon Rawlings had the Bossman's trust, drove him, and never talked about him. Simon Rawlings was a model of a limpet shell: closed down and gave nothing, didn't even do small-talk about his employer.

'Haven't had a night off in a fortnight, about damn time.'

'Not going down the pub to get bladdered, Sarge?' Carrick grinned because he knew the response.

'Cheeky sod. When did I last have a drink? Eh, tell me.'

'Have to say it, not while I've been here – haven't seen you.'

'Not since I walked in the door here, not one.

43

That's three years, five months and two weeks. Go down my pub, but no alcohol. Get pissed up, chuck this lot away, you've got to be joking.'

'You have a good evening. You going to call by, late?'

'Maybe, depends whether I've a promise . . . That's a joke, Johnny. Most likely I'll call by.'

Carrick understood the pecking order and, also, that nothing could be done to alter precedence. The family, the Bossman in particular, depended on Simon Rawlings because of the man's bloody dedication and reliability. He was always there for them, their doormat. And he doubted that Simon Rawlings knew, or cared to know, the first basics of cleaning, washing and rinsing money. 'Have a good evening, then . . .'

He watched Rawlings take his coat and go out through the ready-room door. Grigori looked up from the TV home-improvements show and waved a languid hand. Carrick checked his watch. He went to the hooks, took down the Mercedes' keys. Time to get the kids from school.

He was the most disliked man in the building. With the exception of two people – his director general and his personal assistant – he had no friends, no soul-mates, no confidants inside the massive edifice beside the river. Every weekday morning upwards of two thousand people streamed through the main gates and out again every evening, and more came for night shifts and more for weekend work. Other than Francis Pettigrew and Lucy, none of them knew him well or even had a slightly complimentary word for him. The dislike ran like a virus through all floors of VBX, from heads of department and heads of section, via

44

heads of desks, and down to chauffeurs and analysts, typists and human-resources clerks, archivists, security guards and canteen staff. The dislike was based on his keen rudeness, his refusal to gild lilies when most would have applied a brush of sensitivity, his short-fuse impatience, and a boorish refusal to accept diminished standards. Those who knew his domestic situation best gossiped that his wife treated him as an unwelcome stranger in the marital home and that the only child of the union now lived on the other side of the world. They also said that he cared not a ha'penny damn for their feelings.

Christopher Lawson was sixty-one, had been an officer of the Secret Intelligence Service for thirty-eight years – never had and never would answer to 'Chris', would ignore any man or woman who addressed him with a comrade's familiarity. But somehow, aloof, awkward and prickly, he survived. His most recent ultimatum had been accepted; his seniors had caved in the face of his demand. His most frequent heresy was ignored. Other men and women of similar decades of experience had issued ultimatums on where in the building they would work and where not, in what fields they were prepared to operate and what they would refuse: they had been politely given their premature pensions and had their swipe cards summarily removed. Other men and women who had voiced the ultimate heresy – that the 'war against terror' was being lost, was unwinnable, that the tectonic plates of global power had shifted irreversibly – had been labelled defeatist and had gone by the end of the next Friday.

His survival was based on his success as an intelligence-gatherer. Without it, Christopher

Lawson would have been put out to grass years ago, like the rest of them. The director general had told him, 'The vultures may hover above but I'm not letting them get to your bones, Christopher. I'm not losing you. About as far from Arab matters as I can shunt you is Non-Proliferation. You'll do the Russian section there. I remind you, but I'm not hopeful you'll remember it, that blood on the carpet leaves a permanent stain. I value you, and by doing so I expose myself – I urge you not to abuse my support.' And his personal assistant, Lucy, had said: 'I don't care what people say about you, Mr Lawson. I'm staying put and not asking for a transfer. I'm running your office, at your desk, and the legs of my chair are set in concrete.' And he hadn't even thought to thank either of them.

He was, to be sure, a much disliked man. He was also a man who had respect, however grudging. Respect came from success. Success came from his ability to isolate and identify seemingly trivial items of information, then ruthlessly focus upon them. It was not a talent that could be taught by the Service's instructors and was in rare supply. Christopher Lawson was blessed with it, knew it, and was arrogantly dismissive of colleagues lacking his nose. It was on his screen that the detail of calls from and to the Russian town of Sarov arrived.

It had been a quiet week. He had gutted a couple of papers on arms reduction, and Lucy had worked on the improvement of his computer files . . . Then he had read the word 'Sarov'. He knew where the town was, what work was done there, what name the town had had in Soviet times . . . Papers were flung aside, the filing abandoned. The scent of a trail was established, and his eyes gleamed.

Chapter 2: 9 April 2008

He was aware of more phone calls than usual coming to the house.

Flowers were delivered that afternoon, a massive bouquet that filled Carrick's arms when he took them from the van driver. An hour after the flowers, another van had brought a dress from the shop in the High Street that Mrs Goldmann patronized. Both had come to the main door so Carrick had escorted the housekeeper, Irena, up from the basement, had done the checks through the spy-hole, opened the door and signed the dockets with a scrawl.

And he was aware of greater activity upstairs in the reception rooms, had heard an unfamiliar pace in the movement there of Josef Goldmann.

Carrick had sensed the changed mood and had heard phones when he had gone up the front stairs – the formal rooms used when they entertained were on the ground floor and off the hallway, but the family's rooms where they ate, watched the TV and lived their lives were on the first floor, bedrooms above. Under the roof and reached by narrow back stairs were the cramped attic rooms where the Russian minders and the housekeeper slept. It was unspoken but understood that Carrick was not permitted up the stairs unless by invitation or unless he was accompanied. The housekeeper was with him and he trailed behind her, first with the bouquet, then with the dress box.

An atmosphere of urgency penetrated the house. He couldn't isolate it, or make sense of it . . . A problem for Johnny Carrick, one that went with the job, was to lead two lives – to act like a civilian, and to retain the suspicion and prying wariness of a police officer . . . Something was different, strange, as it had not been before.

When he had brought up Mrs Goldmann's flowers, had hovered behind the housekeeper, had heard the lady of the house exclaim with extravagant delight, had watched her rip open the little accompanying envelope, had listened as she had read out a note of gratitude for the generosity of her donation from the organizing committee of a charity raising funds for Chernobyl children, he had seen through an opened inner door that Viktor spoke on a mobile and that Josef Goldmann was close enough to him to take in both sides of a conversation. On the way back down the stairs he had heard two telephones ring. Returning with the dress in the box, through that same inner door, Carrick had seen Josef Goldmann and Viktor in deep whispered conversation. Then his view had been masked by the lady holding a cocktail frock across her body and twirling in circles. Her eyes had met his, a flash of the briefest flirtation, and he had mouthed silently, as if it were expected of him, 'It's very fine, ma'am, very suitable.'

It had been hoped, of course, that the presence in the Goldmann house of a skilled police officer – one with the talent and nerve to reach level one in the small, closed society of SCD10 – would open up the hidden secrets of the launderer's existence.

He had assumed, as weeks went by and as the family and the minders became more used to him, that he would be increasingly accepted. It hadn't been that way. Truth was, Johnny Carrick knew little more about the life and criminality of his employer than when Katie had put the file into his hand for him to speed read, than when George, his controller, had done the 'big picture' briefing, than when Rob, his cover officer, had talked through the details of communications for routine reports and for a crisis moment. He dealt with the children and with Mrs Goldmann. He lived alongside the housekeeper, Irena, who either did not have English or cared not to use it. He shared the ready room, off the kitchen and in the basement, with Grigori, who spoke only when he needed to and slept in a recliner chair, smoked or watched football on the satellite channels. Simon Rawlings had the access to the Bossman, and was a gossip-free zone.

With Rawlings, when they were together, the talk was of forgotten wars – a tour of Northern Ireland, down by the border, as the ceasefire was shaking down, the advance into Kosovo, the fire-fights and bombs in southern Iraq – but nothing that had meat on it. He did not believe himself to be suspected by either of the minders, but they seemed to live by a code of total secrecy and silence. In honesty, Carrick could say that he had not learned one item of intelligence that could have been presented as evidence of criminality in the Central Criminal Court.

The target, Josef Goldmann, seemed indifferent

to him. Always polite, but always distant. They met rarely – on the stairs, in the hallway – and then the Bossman was remote. Carrick would be asked how he was, how the school drive had gone, how he liked the Mercedes. He was no closer to the man than he had been on the day he had arrived. Always he was greeted with a smile, but behind the smile and the quiet voice was a wall. Light on his feet, almost dapper in his walk, slim and slight, with styled hair cut short on his scalp, the best suits on his back, fashionable stubble on his cheeks and chin, the Bossman appeared like a host of other immigrant businessmen making their names, and fortunes, in London . . . The frustration of failure gnawed in Carrick when he reflected on his lack of success. It was worst when he had the meetings with his cover officer and his controller. Then he saw the disappointment on their faces. It would be the same the next evening, on the narrowboat, when he told George, the DCI, and Rob, the DS, that he had learned – frankly – fuck-all. There was no bug in the house, and no tag on the big Audi car. Grigori swept the house every other day, and the car each morning.

But for the first time something in the pulse of the household had stirred that day. It beat faster and harder. He didn't know what it was, only that it was *something*.

He killed time before the drive to collect the kids. He sat in the ready room, read a paper for the third time and watched the security screens.

It stood to reason: if it didn't improve – and fast – George and Rob would be hacking at the old calculator, Katie would be offering up an inventory of cost against effectiveness and they'd be cutting the cable. Too damn soon he'd be going to

Rawlings and saying, 'I'm really sorry, Sarge, and it was good of you to get me this little number, but actually I don't think it's for me. Reckon I'll be going, busted leg and all, for protection work overseas. But thanks for what you did for me.' Simon Rawlings was a good guy, straight. He would be devastated and disappointed. Carrick did not know of an alternative to him coming out, operation abandoned. He might be told of it as soon as the next debrief session on the narrowboat. It bloody hurt, failure did.

Josef Goldmann was taken back in time. He had heard the voice of Mikhail, and later that of Reuven Weissberg, and memories had flooded him.

An ethnic Russian Jew, Goldmann was from the city of Perm, twenty hours by the fast *firmeny* train south-east from Moscow. It was the city used by Chekhov as the inspiration for his *Three Sisters*, and its name had been stolen to identify the 'special regime' prison camp of Perm-36. A few, today, would have delighted in the city's association with a considerable man of letters, but many more would have acknowledged the links with an archipelago of gaols where politicals and criminals had been held and had laboured.

From the age of ten, on his entry to secondary school, Josef Goldmann had known Reuven Weissberg. Jews, the minority in the city, either stood together or were bullied, abused, beaten. From its birth, it had been a relationship based on mutual need. Reuven, four years the older, had recognized that Josef possessed an extraordinary ability to understand money, its value and the use to which it might be put, and was sharp with figures that were to become balance sheets: Josef had accepted the need for protection and the source where it could be found. They had become inseparable.

Reuven Weissberg had built little roofs over the heads of schoolkids whose parents were in the *nomenklatura* of the city's life. A father was a noted physician in the central hospital, a factory manager or a senior police officer. The roof, the *krysha*, offered protection not from the snow and the springtime rain, but from the thugs who stalked school corridors and playgrounds. When it was known that Reuven Weissberg provided the roof for a kid, and was paid for it, the thugs had learned quickly to back off. There were fights. Knives flashed. Along with the knives there were clubs with leaded ends. A culture of premeditated and exceptional violence had swept through a school that was in a concrete jungle wasteland behind the Tchaikovsky Theatre of Opera and Ballet, and then the calm had descended.

The head teacher and her department heads had been shocked, horrified, at the sight of scarred and bruised kids attending classes, then had marvelled as peace had fallen across the complex. That head teacher, a perceptive woman, had realized the cause of the violence and the cause of the calm and had, herself, bought a roof from the Jew teenager, Weissberg. For three more years there had been no hospitalization of students, and the pilfering of school property had ended. The head teacher, of course, had never written down in any report for the Education Committee why, for a brief period, the statistics of violence in her school had soared, or why, almost as suddenly as conflict ended on a battlefield, the statistics of property stolen from her students and her school had ebbed away, like water into sand. The conclusion of such a report, which remained unwritten, would have mirrored the judgement of another Jew kid, Goldmann. The provider of the roof had no fear, was a beast of ruthless cruelty, was a man-child capable of inflicting horrific injuries without losing sleep. From the age of eleven to just past his thirteenth birthday, Josef Goldmann was the banker.

He had had no training in investment, no background in economics, no tuition in finance. With a squeaky, not yet broken voice, he told Reuven Weissberg where the fees for the roofs should be put, what should be bought and how the money could be hidden. In the city of Perm, a portfolio had built and a treasure chest of bicycles, leather jackets and alcohol had gone into store for selling on when shortages dictated there was demand for the unobtainable. The new business had broken out of the perimeter walls of the school and had moved on to the city's streets. Kiosk-holders had received visits from the hugely muscled Weissberg, who had explained the risks of fire engulfing a kiosk, and from Josef Goldmann – with a pimpled face and large spectacles perched on a shallow nose – who made fast estimations of what a kiosk business should take in a month and therefore what should be the cost of protection. Where there was refusal, there followed fire. Where there were rivals and a roof already in place, there were skirmishes. Reuven Weissberg was never bested.

Defectors came. Tongue-tied and awkward, kids from other teenage gangs pleaded to be allowed to join the Weissberg *brigada*. Loyalties shifted. At eighteen, in one of the toughest cities in the Soviet Union, Weissberg was acknowledged as an *avoritet*, and Goldmann as a *brigadir*, and there were more than twenty gofers, couriers and hooligans behind them who were at the level of a *boevik* in the expanding *banditskaya krysha*. Then Weissberg was gone.

More memories. With Weissberg a conscript into the army, Josef Goldmann, only thirteen, had no roof. Power shifting. The *banditskaya krysha* collapsing. The city of Perm, without the roof over him, was a frightening, threatening place. He had lain low, had concerned himself with his studies and with the money accumulated before Weissberg had left. Three times, in the following two years, he had been beaten – clothes ripped, spectacles smashed – and had thought himself lucky not to have been tied at the wrists and ankles and thrown into the waters of the Kama river.

Two years later, Reuven Weissberg had returned to Perm – harder, fitter, leaner – and Josef Goldmann's roof was once more in place. He owed everything to the man. In the shadow of the *krysha*, they had climbed together. Goldmann owed Weissberg his town house in Knightsbridge, his villa outside Albufeira on the Algarve coast, his penthouse in Cannes, where the motor yacht was moored, and his stature as a multi-millionaire who required bodyguards for his and his family's protection.

He dressed. In the adjacent room, his wife slipped over her head the little black dress that had been delivered that afternoon. They were due in the early evening at a reception for the launch of a new collection at a Cork Street gallery, and probably he would bid in the auction for a watercolour landscape, go to a quarter of a million and be applauded for his generosity – because half of the work's fee would go to a charity. Esther came to him. He smelled the scent on her, kissed her shoulder and made to fasten the clasp of her necklace. But his fingers – normally so certain – fumbled with the clasp because his mind was distracted, and he heard his wife's brittle intake of breath when he pinched her nape. Why?

Because Viktor, on family business, had travelled to Sarov two months before. Because an offer of an item to be sold had been made. Because, via a courier, Josef Goldmann had told Reuven Weissberg of the item that was for sale, and a price had been agreed. Because a purchaser had been found for it, and the process of the sale was in place. Because the item was beyond the limits of anything ever handled before. Because he and his colleague could make vast sums, even though neither had need of money. Because money was power, was confirmation of power.

Because two old men had set off, that morning, on a journey.

He could not see the reddened pinch mark at the back of Esther's neck. He said they would take Viktor and Grigori to such a public place as a gallery on Cork Street, and that Johnny would stay at home with the children.

'Is Simon not coming?' she asked.

'He's off duty tonight. It's not a problem ... Johnny's all right for the children.'

'They like him. I like him.'

He said, as if it were of no importance, 'Simon is best for us. Johnny will do the children.'

Offered the item, Reuven Weissberg had snatched at it, as if the risk didn't concern him. Perhaps, today, Josef Goldmann saw too little of his protector and was too far distanced from the aura of confidence Weissberg provided. The deal terrified him.

55

Esther frowned. 'Are you all right, Josef?'

'I'm fine.'

'Is it because Simon has to have a night off? He's—'

He spat, 'Forget Simon, forget Johnny, think only of looking *pretty* tonight. Do what you do well, and I'll do what I do well.'

'You don't bust your balls when there's no need, Christopher. Sit and scratch them, let the world go by. Then when the need comes out of a clear sky, you go after it and get frantic.'

The sayings of Clipper Reade, if written down, would have made a Bible for Lawson, but he had had no need to write them down because he remembered them, each emphasis and inflection.

He had gone after it, was frantic. And Lucy with him. Sarov, its importance, was not a problem; he knew all about Sarov. Any veteran, laced with Cold War experience, and any desk officer in Non-Proliferation was familiar with it. His screen and hers had pumped up a map of Knightsbridge, a particular street and a particular trio of properties. Number twelve was the workplace of a practice of architects with studios below and the senior partner occupying the top floor. Number fourteen was leasehold, forty-nine years to run, in the name of Josef Shlomo Goldmann and lived in by his family and staff. Number sixteen was a freehold property in the name of a charitable trust that aided 'gentlewomen' who had fallen on 'hard times'. Lucy had led with the matching of mobile-telephone calls into one of those terraced, fat-cat houses, and the links splayed out to Sarov and to the forest wilderness by the Bug river. He knew about the Bug river, knew almost everything about where the Red Army had been in former times. He had gone past her, as if he had his chest out and the tape loomed, and had identified the ownership of the three.

Clipper Reade had said, 'Better believe me, Christopher. You may get, in this business, a small window that's ajar. It's criminal not to jump through it. Windows, in my experience, slam shut if you're too finicky to take the opportunity of advantage. Don't call for a committee to sit – just jump.'

He doubted, profoundly, that a firm of architects had links to Sarov or to a marshy and forgotten corner of eastern Poland; beside him, Lucy had scratched out the charitable organization from the list of three. She had been with him since 1980. If he had been sacked when he'd refused to work any longer on Middle East associated desks, she would have left on that same Friday evening. She lived in a tiny apartment across the river in Victoria and spent her evenings in the company of a long-haired blue Norwegian Forest cat. She did not ask a question when she knew the answer, did not speak unless to make a necessary contribution: she was rewarded. Christopher Lawson had never barked at her, and he had never criticized her work or contradicted her opinions. On other desks it was suggested by some that he shagged her, but a more general opinion was that she loved only her cat and he loved only his work . . . yet they were soul-mates.

Lawson went now for the liaison officer from 'that shambles across the river' to demand from the Box 500 building on the north side of the Thames a detailed breakdown of the occupants of number fourteen – Josef Shlomo Goldmann and everyone living under his roof – and he snarled into the phone that he wanted it 'yesterday' and would not accept delay. Lucy tracked, with greater politeness, to a source in Special Branch at Scotland Yard. She had never remonstrated with Lawson for his rudeness to others, and those who had felt the whip of his tongue, then seen him speak with her were astonished to find him capable of minimal pleasantries.

Clipper Reade had said, in the dry drawl of a broad Texan accent, 'Things that matter don't hang about and wait for you, Christopher. Sort of float by you, maybe gossamer, like a butterfly on the wing. You have to snatch or the moment's gone and it does not – believe me – return. Snatch and hold hard.'

Twenty-six years of Christopher Lawson's career had slid by since he had last been with the American, learning and listening. Special Branch came back to Lucy before the Security Service liaison. She scribbled a list of names and he grabbed it from her. He read the names of Joseph Shlomo Goldmann, Esther Goldmann and her children, then the retinue, Viktor and Grigori, a woman whose occupation was given as 'housekeeper', Simon Rawlings and Jonathan Carrick. He told her he wanted more on all of them, and that he was off to the upper-floor suite of the director general.

She would have known he had no appointment, but on that afternoon of the week the director general always hosted a meeting of political figures who concerned themselves with the intricacies of intelligence-gathering and were allies.

Clipper Reade had said, 'At first sight, Christopher, the skeins don't seem to have a shape and make patterns. But it's the art of our trade to give them shape. Men and women now are coming into view, and some don't know each other and some do. Some are connected and some have never met. You watch those skeins and the tangle they make until the patterns unravel the chaos. Then you have success. You have an open mind but you go where the skeins take you, however dense that chaos.'

On the upper floor, in an outer office of the suite – politicians left to sip coffee and nibble biscuits – he clattered through the situation to the director general at machine-gun speed. 'It's because of Sarov, Francis. I cannot ignore anything involving that place. Ask me where I'm currently heading and I'll respond that I haven't the faintest idea, but Sarov is not something I ignore. I don't know yet who I'm dealing with, but I expect to very soon, by the end of the day. I have the feeling that once the chatter starts there may not be much time. Trust me, anything to do with Sarov means the involvement of serious people.'

From far back in the trees he watched the house. He waited for a man to show himself. But for a dog, the house was empty.

Darkness had gathered around him and the canopies of the pines were inadequate as cover in the heavy rain. Incessantly, water dripped from on high on to Reuven Weissberg's hair and shoulders, protected by his thick leather jacket. Only rarely did he wipe the rainwater from his face. More often he reached inside his coat and under his shirt to scratch a small indent in his upper arm where there was dark scar tissue.

He knew the man was named Tadeuz Komiski,

knew that he was now seventy-one, knew that he had been born in that house. A priest, a schoolteacher and a social worker had given him that information. He knew the story because his grandmother had told it to him, and he had hoped that evening to be told what he wished to know . . . He doubted that information would be gained by conversation – more likely in the aftermath of a beating or the extraction of fingernails or the placing of a lit cheroot cigar on the testicles. But the house was empty.

Behind him, Mikhail would be waiting, arms folded, never impatient. Reuven Weissberg stared at the house and his eyes were long accustomed to the gloom. If it had not been built in a clearing, with a patch for vegetables at the front, if it had been surrounded by pines and birches, he would not have been able to see it. He could, just, make out its silhouette. There was no lamp lit inside. Light, had it been there, would have peeped from cracks round the door or windows. No fire had been started or he would have seen the smoke spill from the brick chimney-stack. He looked past a small flat-top lorry from whose body the engine had been removed, and past a stable block where the doors hung off their hinges. It was a place, he thought, that had once been cared for but now decayed. He sensed already that he had stayed too long.

The dog inside knew he was there.

How it knew, Reuven Weissberg could not have said.

From the pitch of the barking, he had identified it as a big dog, and reckoned it would have to be slaughtered if he were to get past and ask the question he wished to put to Tadeuz Komiski. He would think nothing of shooting a dog. Neither would Mikhail. It was the fourth time he had come for

60

Komiski and he had never found him – but he would.

Reuven Weissberg had come to the forest to locate a grave. There was a monument half a kilometre away through the trees, along a track made by the woodmen's lorries, a circular and precise mound of ashes. It could have been said to be a grave. In the trees there were the mass graves that might hold a thousand skeletons or a hundred; they were buried deep under layers of pine needles and composted birch leaves. No stone or indentation marked their resting-place. He had come, again as on those times before, to learn of the place where one corpse was buried, and Tadeuz Komiski would tell him. But the man did not come.

An owl called, as it would have done on the night that a grave was filled.

He was far away but Tadeuz Komiski's sight was as keen as it had been during his childhood.

There were deer in the forest and wild boar, and sometimes the small and protected pack of wolves strayed over from the national park that straddled the marshes west of the Lublin road. He heard the cry of the short-eared owl that hunted close to his home. The deer, the boar, the wolf and the owl had no better sight than Tadeuz Komiski, nor the lesser-spotted eagle that would now be perched close to its high nest in a pine.

All through that day and that evening, he had watched the man in the heavy leather jacket. All of his life, from the age of six, he had known that a man would come, sit and watch . . . It was because of what his father had done that he knew a man would come. He did not dare go back to his house in the clearing where his dog had not been fed. The

61

dog had told him that the man had moved in the late afternoon from a place close to the monument and had taken a new position, seated, close to the house. Throughout his life he had carried the burden of knowing that a man would come – the thought had been easier to bear when he was younger. He could not remember now whether it was the third or fourth time that he had seen the man, sitting in the forest, so patient, and whether it was three or four years since he had first seen him.

Every summer visitors came. They walked on the weed-free raked path from the parking area, past where the foundations of the tower were to the mound of ashes. They circled it, paused by the monument and sometimes laid sprigs of flowers there. A few walked a little way into the forest, on the woodsmen's tracks, and paused, heard the birdsong and gazed round, seeming frightened at the density of the trees. Then they hurried away.

He was now seventy-one. His father, who had made the burden for his life, had been dead more than forty years, and his mother a year longer; both had breathed a last gasping cry in the wooden house that the man watched. Perhaps he should have burned it to the ground, put petrol in it and razed it. It was cursed. He had married Maria in 1964, and she had died eleven months later in childbirth, in the same bed in which his father and mother had died. His wife was buried, the stillborn baby with her, in a crudely cut pine coffin in the churchyard at Orchowek. If he stood beside the stone he could see over a low wall to the trees that lined the banks of the Bug river and the cemetery but it was many years since he had been there. Because of what his father had done, the house was cursed. The curse had killed his mother, his wife and the girl-child who had never lived. The curse had remained alive.

For the evil done by his father a punishment had been handed down to him. It was never out of the mind of Tadeuz Komiski. And he was responsible. It was him, the six-year-old, who had run back to the house, fleet-footed, and told his father what he had seen. And perhaps then his father had not believed him because he had hesitated, but his mother had spoken of the reward on offer. He had led his father back into the forest, and the evil was done in the hope of gaining that reward: two kilos of sugar. That day the curse had been set in place as the rain fell softly in the forest.

He could see the shape of the man's shoulders, and if he moved his head there was a suspicion of his pale skin colour. The man never coughed, never fidgeted, except to scratch one place on his arm below the right shoulder – but insects from the forest floor would by now have found him and would be crawling over him. He never stretched or cracked his finger joints. Earlier, he had seen him walk slowly, carefully, weighing his steps, on the needle and compost carpet, and Tadeuz Komiski believed he searched for the grave that was the mark of the evil done and the cause of the curse . . . And his father had never been given the reward.

Behind the man, sitting against the tree trunk, there was another. Two hundred metres back towards the monument, another watched and listened but lit cigarettes.

Only the owl shouted and only the rain fell, and he waited for them to leave. But the lesson of the curse told Tadeuz Komiski that if they left he would still find no peace – they would return. He thought the grave cried to them . . . The curse had maddened him, made hallucinations . . . What he had done at the age of six had destroyed his life.

Now they moved on.

'Your car, *Major*, is like the story of our lives.'

'Our lives, *Colonel*, are shit. I accept it, my car's the same.'

'A broken car and broken lives – agreed. Both shit.'

'When I first took possession of a Polonez, in 1986, I thought it an accolade, like the award of a medal. A car driven by a man of importance, a mark of personal success. Four cylinders, 1500cc version, top-of-the-range, four-speed transmission, the quality of Fiat technology. When I first had it, and drove through the main gate each morning – forgive me the indulgence, my friend – I was proud to be the owner of such a vehicle.'

'It's still a piece of shit.'

They had lost four hours, and it was only the first day of the journey.

Halfway up, the punctured tyre not yet clear of the road, the jack had collapsed, corroded by the same rust that afflicted the coachwork and doors. The car had subsided on to the flat rear left tyre. Molenkov had dragged the jack clear, Yashkin had hurled it into the lake and it had disappeared into a reed bed. They had sat together beside the tilted Polonez, on the spare tyre, and had waited for help. Each vehicle that came they greeted with shouts, waved arms and pleas for help. The first four had ignored them. The fifth was a van, and had stopped, but the driver had commented immediately on the weight the Polonez carried under the tarpaulin and the bags, and had seemed curious to know what two old fools carried that was so heavy;

they'd sent him on his way. It was nearly dark when a saloon car had pulled up behind them. A schoolteacher, with a life history to be told but also a jack that fitted the Polonez. By the time they knew his name, and where he taught, the names of his wife and children, the success of his pupils at indoor soccer and his hobbies, the spare was in place. They'd waved him on his way, both exhausted from the effort of listening . . . and four hours had been lost.

'There are winners in this world and losers, Igor, and . . .'

'A profound psychological analysis of the state of society, Oleg, and of the quality I would expect from a retired political officer. A *zampolit* would be expected to demonstrate such insights.'

'You sarcastic bastard – and it was your tyre that was shit, and your car. I would have said that winners and losers have little contact in our state today. A very few win, a great many lose . . . We're in a particularly rare situation. We've been losers, dismissed from our work after years of dedicated service, the victims of total disrespect. Our pensions are at best erratic and at worst unpaid, shit identical to your car. But we leap a chasm to a new world, to that of the winners. Doesn't that cheer you? It should.'

Yashkin frowned, pondered, then asked the question that had long been in his mind. 'Is it greed that motivates me – pure greed and envy of others?'

The former *zampolit* was certain. 'No, not greed and not envy. I was a judge of men – the political officer's work. I looked for weakness, but with you I never found such a base condition. They betrayed us. *They* made a state that is criminalized, corrupt, riddled with disgusting disease, a state in which loyalty is no longer recognized. You have done nothing to feel ashamed of, or me . . . I remember the night you told me what lay buried in your garden, and you were nervous of confiding your secret. I thought then how greatly I admired your skill at removing it from the Zone and your opportunism. Now we have set off. The talking's done.'

Yashkin grinned and turned to his friend. He saw his tired, worn features and the long greying hair caught at the back of his neck with an elastic band, the worry lines at his eyes and the stubble on his cheeks. He knew the hardship of his friend's life as it ticked towards its close and remained un-rewarded – as his did. The grin split his face wider. 'I have a feeling that the Polonez – as shit as we are – will get us there.'

They clasped hands. The headlights speared the road running past wide lakes, over rattling wood bridges and through forests. Behind them was the cargo they would deliver, shielded by the tarpaulin and their bags. Two old, thin, calloused hands were held tight, and the road was clear in front of them.

She had been warned about the man she would meet. Her line manager had said that Christopher Lawson had a reputation for verbal violence on an unacceptable scale. With the cardboard file-holder close to her chest, she'd walked down Millbank, along the north side of the river, past the high tower, the Tate Gallery and the Army Medical School, then strode across the bridge. In front of her she saw the hideous floodlit mass of the sister organization.

The main crowds, commuters going home at the

end of their day and spilling towards Vauxhall station, had thinned. She saw him easily. Not particularly tall, without horns growing from his forehead. She smiled to herself because he looked twice at his watch and it did not concern her: she knew she would make the rendezvous a full thirty seconds before the scheduled time.

He was looking over her shoulder, maybe expecting someone older, a man, peering down the length of the bridge. She'd been told he'd be wearing a raincoat and a trilby – as if he'd been dug out of the Ark, her line manager had said – and it was, truth to tell, damn strange to meet face to face on a bloody cold bridge when the age of email communication had arrived and there were closet rooms for shielded meetings back at the Box and at his place. But it was where she had been told to come, and she thought this was the way that unreconstructed veterans did their business.

She wasn't tall, she was young, and probably fitted no stereotype he'd made – which cheered her. She walked up to his shoulder, saw a thin aquiline face and the growth from a careless early-morning shave. 'Mr Lawson? It's Mr Lawson, isn't it?'

He glanced down, a reflex, at his wristwatch.

She shook his hand, gave it a good squeeze. 'Myself, Mr Lawson, I love getting drenched, turning my feet into frozen lumps, screwing up my hair. I love everything, Mr Lawson, about meetings *al fresco*. So, before I drown and before I get blown away, let's do our business.'

They did. She was led down the steps at the end of the bridge to a bench that the wet wind hit.

A plastic bag from her pocket covered the file, and the bullet point digests with the accompanying photographs had been laminated – thoughtfully –

as protection against the rain. The full-length biographies stayed in the dry file.

The liaison officer, rather enjoying the daftness of the setting, said, 'I'm only doing thumbnails. Right? Top of the tree is Josef Goldmann, Russian national, born in Perm. Serial criminal, expertise in money laundering . . . Believed associate, try junior partner, of Reuven Weissberg, major-league Mafia, who bases himself in Berlin. It's all in there, and lines for you to follow . . .'

She was not interrupted. She thought he listened closely, but his eyes roved across the river and, maybe, took in the river traffic – tugs and barges – and, maybe, he gazed at the floodlit seat of government. The big clock chimed.

With the photographs, the rain dripping off them, she identified Esther Goldmann, complete with shopping bags, and the children with their private-school satchels. Still he did not speak and nothing was queried. She thought of all those in the Box who would have chipped in with questions designed to demonstrate keenness or authority; many would have stamped on her fingers. Only the twitch in his mouth showed his interest. The minders' pictures were displayed, and an indistinct image of the housekeeper. Then a man's photograph, moderately expensive suit, with severely cut hair.

'He's Simon Rawlings – ex-sergeant, ex-paratrooper – the factotum. Drives and fixes. No criminal record and never in trouble – has the Military Medal from Iraq. Probably straight as a telegraph pole, and heavily trusted by his employer. I would say, from what I've read, that he walks through life with blinkers over his eyes and plugs in his ears. He's adjacent to Goldmann, but

68

not alongside him, if you know what I mean ... and he's muscle. Doesn't want trouble and is unlikely to be part of any criminality. A duty man. There's one more.'

She lit a cigarette. The tobacco Fascists ruled in the Box, but if she was going to sit in the cold and wet she'd damn well enjoy the luxury. The smoke floated by his nose, but there was no curled lip, annoyance. She warmed to him. She held the final photograph on her lap and damp ash fell on it.

'This one's as interesting as it gets. Jonathan Carrick, aged thirty-six but only possibly ... more of that. He's the junior bodyguard, takes the lady shopping and socializing and the kids to school, a dogsbody. He, too, is a one-time paratrooper but was injured in Iraq and invalided out. He's a phoney. Mr Lawson, put it this way, he's not what he seems. Seems to be a professional bodyguard, but our computers show that the DVLA, Social Security and National Insurance records for that name, and that military background, were erased and replaced three months ago. It's what they do for policemen, those going undercover. You might have the clout – national security and all that – to break open SCD10 because that's where I think he comes from. Do you understand me?'

There was a quiet growl beside her. 'Understood.'

'So, Goldmann is a Serious Crime Directorate target, of sufficient importance for an undercover to be introduced, but he's pretty far down the line. That's all I can give you. Of any use?'

'Possibly.'

She passed him the folder in its protective cover. Stood. Rather formally, he thanked her, but she sensed awkwardness as if that were unfamiliar territory to him.

Boldness took her, a degree of recklessness. 'So, what do you think? Are we talking of imminent danger?'

'Possibly.'

'Where are we on a scale of one to ten, Mr Lawson?'

She saw that his eyes had fastened on her. In the dreary evening light thrown down by the dull lamps, they glistened, startling her. He seemed to be assessing her question . . . The eyes now were mesmerizing, and the voice had changed to a scraping intensity.

He said, 'None of your business, and unlikely to be in the future. I compliment you on your briefing. Very adequate . . . A scale of one to ten? Probably between twelve and thirteen. Goodnight.'

She walked back over the bridge, into the teeth of the wind and rain, and was alone with the implications of her naming Jonathan Carrick, an undercover.

Back in his office, feeling pressure and knowing that action was demanded, Christopher Lawson scanned the files. The programme for proceeding was instinctive. There was a number on the file, and he rang it. He asked for a name and was told the man he wished to speak to was off duty. Would he find the man of that name at home? He might. He had spoken to a voice that had a firm, decisive tone, and a hint of a Scots accent. He shuffled the picture that went with the voice to the top of the heap and gazed at it. He thought a key had been found – and, damned obvious, keys were for opening doors. He always followed his instinct, because that way had been taught him by Clipper Reade. He called to Lucy, 'Get into that increments list.'

'Any special skills?'

'God alone knows, I don't. "General skills", thinks on his feet – whoever's available. To meet me in the Prince Albert, back bar, half an hour.'

'Will do.'

He left his desk, went to the floor safe and tapped in the combination numbers. There were cardboard shoeboxes in there, taking three of the four shelves, all brimful of equipment that had been standard in Cold War times, the times when he had learned a trade from Clipper Reade – pens that fired a single bullet, bottles of invisible ink, hollowed *papier-mâché* rocks that could hold a microphone, little Minox cameras, the detritus of a life that few recognized as having contemporary value. He rummaged through cartons of pills, each labelled, and made his selection.

He'd rather liked the girl, the liaison from the plodders across the river. Bizarre that. Nice girl, yes – and able. And . . . Lucy, who never raised her voice, murmured from the outer office that he would be met, in twenty-eight minutes, at the Prince Albert, in the back bar, by an increment.

A doorbell was rung. The man whose finger pressed down the button was a freelancer employed by the Secret Intelligence Service at an hourly rate of fifty pounds, and expenses. He did work, on a casual basis, that was either too mundane for a full-time staffer or was too dirty for a staffer to be involved in. A host of increments waited for their phones to ring and meeting points to be fixed, and the work made for a reasonable living . . . Above all else, an increment was deniable.

A woman came to the door, holding a screaming child in its nightclothes. 'Yes?'

'Sorry to bother you. My problem, my memory's like a sieve. Simon said I was to meet him, but I've clean forgotten where or if it's here.'

'You on the team . . . darts?'

It was his skill that he could react at speed to whatever presented itself, was worth fifty pounds an hour, cash and no paperwork. 'That's right – well, if they're still short.'

'He's already gone.' She hugged the baby, stilled its crying. Might have been attractive once.

'I'm a right clown – help me. Forget my own name next. Where's the game?'

'They're at that one down off the Balls Pond Road, on the right, before the mini-mart. Across Essex Road, along Englefield Road, turn left into Beauvoir – can't miss it. There'll be a green Golf, 04 plate, parked there. His.'

'Thanks so much. You've been a real help.'

The increment was smiling as he backed away, and the baby had begun to bawl again.

A photograph was glanced at, studied long enough for recognition. The door of a public house was pushed open and a wall of noise – music, raised voices and laughter – bounced into a man's face.

A voice shouted, 'Come on, Sim, you're next up. Double top, ten and a five, and we're in.'

A second voice shouted, 'Your Coke's on the table, Sim.'

And Simon Rawlings, a former paratroop sergeant who was now bodyguard to a Russian-born launderer and integral to a pub darts team, glanced sideways, saw his drink put on the table among filled and empty glasses, and walked to the line in front of the floodlit board. He gazed at his personal arrows and readied his concentration. His team, and the opposition, crowded behind him. The first arrow was the double top, neat. His people cheered and the others groaned, and he prepared to throw his second dart . . . and nobody had a view of the table and the Coke glass on it . . . and nobody saw the miniature bottle of pure alcohol – tasteless – tipped into it.

Simon Rawlings had the ten, and elation coursed in him. He eyed the segment of the five . . . and nobody saw the intruder slip from the pub, or heard the door close after him.

A quiet evening, as it always was. He sat alone in the basement ready room. Viktor and Grigori were gone with the Bossman and the Bosswoman. The housekeeper had finished the washing-up, the clearing and stacking of dishes in the kitchen, and had gone up the stairs to her comfortable chair on the landing outside the kids' rooms. She would spend her evening there.

He didn't like the quiet. It made for complacency, and complacency was a killer in Johnny Carrick's work.

The television was off and he had read the news-paper, had completed two of the puzzles.

Two lives were his existence. They merged, then separated. Carrick would have said that any human being who had not experienced twin lives could not contemplate the stress of deceit. Of the two, one was factual biography, and one was *legend*. That night, on the settee, in front of the security screens, he thought factual – which was safe, as *legend* was not – and childhood.

On his birth certificate was his mother's name, Agnes Carrick, and the address given was of his grandparents, David and Maggie Carrick, both with the listed occupation of schoolteacher. Where his father's name and details could have been entered there was a blank space, free of the registrar's copperplate pen. The certificate was still in place, could be referenced by a thug or a private detective or launderer who checked out his name and his story.

The screens showed the front porch, the rear gardens, the back basement door, the front hall, the landing and the top of the stairs outside the family's bedrooms. Only the one on the front porch moved, traversing slowly. If there was duller work than watching screens in the late evening, Carrick hadn't experienced it.

The address on the certificate was a road in the village of Kingston where a bungalow overlooked the mouth of the Spey river. It was Scotland's premier salmon water then and now, and the kid's earliest recollections were in spate time when the flow drove melted snow off the Cairngorms, carried their great fallen boulders and rolled them on its course towards the grey North Sea. Spectacular for a kid. Not so special was learning, as a kid, that his mother had gone to London for work, aged twenty, had had a fling – older man, married – and returned to bear the baby in her parents' home. Then she had gone to work in the food factory at Mosstodloch. Hard, that, for a kid ... Hard also that his grandparents were high on the church, went twice every Sunday, tried to love their daughter's bastard but couldn't hide from young eyes the difficulty of giving that love. On the kid's learning curve had been the origin of his name, biblical, and an old man gripping his wrists and whispering, breath on his face: *I am distressed for thee, my brother Jonathan: very pleasant hast thou been unto me: thy love for me was wonderful, passing*

74

the love of women. II Samuel, I:26. His grandfather had been David, and it was like they were inseparable friends, and it was suffocating, and he was kept in view and watched. Couldn't go down on to the riverbanks and scramble on the stones, watch otters or seals and have the ospreys swooping over him without the eyes of his grandfather on his back. For all those childhood years, the factual life and the *legend* were merged. He had left school, in the big market town of Elgin, on a June morning, had taken a bus in the afternoon to the recruiting office in Inverness, had been there ten minutes before the doors had closed, had requested to join the Parachute Regiment – that regiment because David Carrick, his grandfather, suffered vertigo nightmares, was terrified of heights. It was safe for him to relive childhood.

A telephone rang.

He jerked alert. His eyes went to the screens, then to the telephone, on a side shelf, that was linked to the ready room. Those that the family used, and the line into the Bossman's office, did not ring in the basement. It was for him to answer, and he did. The telephone was from the world of his *legend*, was where safety ended.

He gave the number curtly.

'Christ, that you, Corp? It is you?'

He recognized the voice of Simon Rawlings, but unreal and strained, hoarse. He asked what had happened.

'Bloody life's fallen in on me, that's what. I can hardly believe this. They've given me one call, and it's to you. I'm throwing darts. I'm not, you know me, on the piss. Finish the game, get in the car, drive off. Gone a hundred yards, not even round the corner, and I'm pulled over – I'm breathalysed, positive, way over. If it hadn't happened, I wouldn't have believed it. "Must have been spiked," I say, and the copper says everyone uses that line. I say the kit must be defective, and the custody sergeant says it's never the kit's fault. I'm going into the cells overnight, that's routine. I'm drunk in charge, I'm going to lose my licence for twelve months. Corp, I'm fucked . . . I'm just telling you, there's nothing you can do . . . You'll have to tell the Bossman. Don't know whether I'll see you again, Corp, because I don't think my feet'll touch the ground when the Bossman hears—'

The call was cut and the phone purred in his ear.

Chapter 3: 9 April 2008

Viktor had told him.

Esther said, 'It is just not possible. There has to be a mistake.'

They were back from their evening, and Viktor had gone down to the basement area. It had been a good evening, the sort that reminded Josef Goldmann of the success of his new life in London, where he was accepted and respected. He had bought a picture, and paid too much for it, but rich applause had rung round the gallery when the gavel had come down, and many had congratulated him on his generosity, while the organizers of the charity for the Chernobyl children, who had thyroid cancer, leukaemia and kidney tumours, had wrung his hand in gratitude ... and Esther had flushed with pleasure. They had returned to their home, and Johnny had opened the front door seeming ill at ease, but Josef Goldmann had barely noticed it. Viktor had gone down to the basement to make himself coffee, Grigori with him. Coats off, himself flopped in a low chair, Esther perched on the arm and working her fingers on the muscles of her husband's shoulder, relaxing him, until Viktor had come back to report on what he had been told.

'I can't believe it of Simon. It's impossible.'

Viktor had told him what was 'impossible' in a voice that carried no emotion. Brief and factual. Nothing in the words he used betrayed Viktor's feelings on the matter, but his eyes were not so utterly controlled. In them, not hidden, was his contempt for a foreign worker allowed so close to the family. Viktor was not Josef Goldmann's man. Two low-ranking officers in the apparatus of State Security, working in Perm – once with responsibility for political dissent, later in a department operating alongside the criminal police and offering protection to businessmen during the great sell-off of national assets – had realized they worked from the wrong side of the fence. One had been Viktor, the other Mikhail. One had been outwardly sophisticated, the other outwardly a thug. They had resigned from State Security and had climbed the fence – stepped across the ditch, whatever – and gone to an apartment in a tower block. They had been admitted by the old lady, had stood in the presence of Reuven Weissberg and offered themselves to him. They had brought with them a degree of respectability in the provision of protective roofs, a deep knowledge of the work practices of their former employers and a network of contacts. They had stayed together when Reuven had tired of Perm and moved to Moscow with his financial adviser and launderer, but had split when Goldmann had transferred his office to London, and Weissberg had relocated to Berlin. In Josef's mind, and he had seen nothing to dislodge the thought, Viktor's loyalty was first to Reuven Weissberg, second to the Goldmann family. In Berlin, Reuven Weissberg lived the life almost of a peasant, and employed no foreigners . . . Not Josef Goldmann's way.

'I don't believe it.' Esther slapped her hands on her thighs in frustration. 'He doesn't drink. It's ridiculous.'

Was it a big or small matter? That was the confusion. Viktor had brought back from Russia the offer of the deal. It had gone through the fingers of Josef Goldmann and been referred to Reuven Weissberg. He, Josef Goldmann, would have turned it down the day it was presented to him, but the decision had not lain with him. He remembered his surprise on being told that a deal was to be made, and a market found for what was on sale, and arrangements for delivery concluded. It was beyond the scope of his experience – but he would not have dared gainsay Reuven Weissberg. It was, now, close to completion, and his trusted British-born driver was locked in a common police cell, accused of driving while above the legal limit of alcohol consumption.

'You should do something. Arrange a lawyer. Get him out.' She waved her arms, an actress on a stage, across furniture, at artwork, over carpets and drapes. 'What's all this for if you can do nothing? Are you powerless?'

Esther was beautiful to him. She was admired in company, was a honey-pot to men, satisfied him in bed to the limits of his vanity, and asked little of him. When her arms waved and her throat was thrown back, the diamonds mounted in rings, bracelets and necklaces flashed. He refused her nothing. His frown deepened. He was not in Perm or Moscow where a phone call, quoting his relationship to Reuven Weissberg, could be made to a police official. He was beyond the immediate reach of his patron. The satisfaction of the evening

79

was gone, because a goddam driver was drunk and in a police cell, because she challenged him and he couldn't rise to it.

'So, tell me, what are you going to do?'

He stood and pushed her aside, went to the table by the door, lifted a telephone and dialled the internal number. It was the mark of the worry hovering over him – two men were driving the merchandise towards a pick-up and exchange point, an onward purchaser was in place, and the verifier of the merchandise's integrity had been approached – that he wanted only to be in his bed, to sleep and lose the weight of the cloud. He asked Viktor to bring Johnny Carrick up. He had liked Simon. He had trusted him, within limits – there was never business talk in the car when Simon drove. He had thought Simon grateful for the inflated salary paid him, and that gratitude dictated self-discipline. He put the telephone down heavily. Was Viktor right? Should there be no foreigners in the house? But there was need of them, a goddam proven need. He heard the knock on the door.

'Come.'

Carrick stood, was not asked to sit. Viktor was behind him.

Josef Goldmann paced. 'Is there anything I can do, Johnny? Anything I should do?'

Carrick thought of the man who had pulled him from the wreckage of an under-protected Land Rover, who had put a tourniquet on his leg that might have been the sole reason it was not amputated, who had stayed with him, held his hand and told him bad jokes until the casevac chopper had come in. He thought of the man who

80

had visited him in the field hospital before his flight home.

'Straight up, sir, I wouldn't have thought so. Send a top-flight lawyer down there and all you do is draw attention to yourself.'

He thought of an engineered meeting. The pub that surveillance had identified – better than an 'accidental' recognition in the street. He saw himself going through the door and seeing Simon Rawlings throwing darts, waiting his turn, then expressing all the crap, his surprise, and mouthing off that it was a bloody small world.

Esther Goldmann sat upright in the chair. 'We should do anything possible. What is possible?'

He thought of himself going to the bar and calling back, asking what his sarge would have: being told it was the usual, Coke, ice, lemon. Had ordered a lime and soda for himself, had lied, not with difficulty, that he himself no longer touched alcohol, didn't miss it and felt better for it. Had been asked, with the noise of the pub bar flowing round them, the obvious and banal question – what was he up to now?

'There isn't anything, ma'am. It has to take its course. Forgive me if this sounds brutal, sir, but he put himself into that situation and he'll have to get himself out of it. Nothing you can do will take him out of that cell tonight.'

He thought of the lies and deceit that had tripped off his tongue in the pub. First a fact, then into *legend*. The fact was that he could have stayed in the army – just not the Parachute Regiment – in one of the support corps: signals, intelligence, logistics, ordnance. They weren't for him. Then into the *legend*. Joined a firm that did bodyguard work, a firm that couldn't get their hands on enough ex-Para guys. The acquired biography – the *legend* in

SCD10-speak – was, of course, checkable and would stand examination, and there was a bogus CV available from a front address up in Leeds: an office in Leeds, run by a guy and two girls, supplied proof to the legends of maybe half a dozen undercovers. All lies from then on, up damn near to closing time, and the run of them broken only when Simon Rawlings was called up to throw darts at the board.

Josef Goldmann turned on his heel, as if this was a crux moment. 'What are the consequences of this for Simon?'

He saw the Bossman's mix of anxiety and irritation. The legend said he had gone on the bodyguard courses, checkable, and had escorted starlets and millionaires, checkable. All a lie. Johnny Carrick had left the army on a medical discharge, had gone before an interview board at the headquarters of the Avon and Somerset Police, had been lucky enough to have a former naval officer – now doing human resources – on the board, who had taken a shine to him, who had remarked that he was probably, duff leg and all, a damn sight fitter than most they recruited. He had sailed through a probationary half-year, then been posted to the inner-city station at the Bridewell, had found himself the oldest among the juniors and realized he did not fit easily with them; he had badly missed the buzz of active service with a front-line regiment.

It had happened by chance. Crown Court security had been beefed up to protect an under-cover officer whose evidence was going to send away a drugs-importation syndicate. Police had crawled through the court complex, been on every landing, every lift, every door. He'd heard the chatter among the full-time court staff about the undercover – life at risk, wormed inside a gang of serious people, had laid a finger on untouchables – had known it was for him. He'd gone to see the officer who had supported him at the interview board and been encouraged: 'Why not? They can only turn you down. My advice, give it a thrash.' Before the trial had ended he had sent in his application to join the Serious Crime Directorate, Section 10, and when the letter had gone into the box he'd rated himself able to live with lies.

'I would assume, sir – but, of course, I don't know, because courts and the police are outside my experience – that Simon will be released, then summonsed to appear in court. He'll end up with a criminal record and a driving ban for something between a year and eighteen months.'

'For definite?' she asked.

'Yes, ma'am. Only in the most exceptional circumstances would there be – I assume – an acquittal and no criminal record, or just a fine and no driving ban.'

'I like you, Johnny.'

'Thank you, sir.'

'We have both found your work satisfactory, and the children like you.'

'Thank you, ma'am.'

He saw Josef Goldmann look at his wife, and he saw her, almost imperceptibly, nod agreement. The Bossman's eyes lifted, would have focused on Viktor, who was behind him. Then the hesitation . . . Carrick thought he had taken advantage of a situation – dumped on Simon Rawlings, whom he had never seen drink alcohol and whose breath had never smelled of it . . . who had been the saviour of his life, possibly, and his leg, probably. Then the hesitation was wiped.

'You will take his place, Johnny. I offer you his position.'

'That's very kind, sir. I am very happy to accept. Only thing, sir, I've a family matter tomorrow evening that's important to me. I'd be grateful if I could be excused duty then – Simon was covering for me. Thank you, sir, thank you, ma'am. Goodnight.'

He was gone. Viktor watched him go through the door, but Carrick didn't meet his eye. A cell door had slammed shut, but for Carrick another had opened wide – he couldn't fathom it, just couldn't. But climbing the ladder would make life harder, would demand more care on the legend's preservation, would expose him to more thorough inspection.

He wiped the mud, clods of it, from his boots. Then he took the sheet of old newspaper, passed to him by Mikhail, and cleaned the leather. If there had been a stream nearby, or a pond in the trees, he would have washed them. It was not the interior of the car that should be protected, but his grandmother would scold him if he came back to their home and tramped dirt on the floors. He worked hard at the sides, soles and uppers of his boots and did not finish until he was certain they would leave no mess on the carpets. Mikhail watched him. Satisfied, Reuven Weissberg put his boots back on, laced them loosely and opened the car door.

He never used the rear seat when Mikhail drove him and they were alone. They rode together always, in silence if he wished it and in conversation if he did not. Sometimes he would give Mikhail the role of sounding-board and demand his opinion, and sometimes he would ignore him.

The former KGB officer would not have dreamed, or dared, to take the liberty of commenting on plans and intentions unless requested to do so. Two differences existed. Nobody paid Reuven Weissberg. He paid Mikhail. He was a Jew and Mikhail was not. But, other than his grandmother, no one was closer to him than his minder. And such a man as Reuven Weissberg, who was now in his fortieth year, needed protection. He could provide it, could put a secure *krysha* above the head of a businessman, a politician or an oil man, but his success required that an altogether more carefully built roof covered his own scalp. Once, that cover had slipped. Mikhail carried a Makharov in his belt and a PPK in the glove compartment, and he would have said that Mikhail's loyalty to him could not be doubted. Once, Mikhail had been tested. It came at a price.

It would take them six hours to drive to the apartment. They would be back in the early morning, before the dawn washed thinly over the city, but his grandmother would be up and dressed, waiting for him.

Mikhail would take a route carrying them first due south to the town of Chelm, which they would skirt, then reach the feeder road for the highway to Lublin. Lublin to Warsaw, and Warsaw to Poznan. After Poznan they would join the best road in Poland, then cross the frontier. An hour after negotiating Immigration and Customs, when staff were either in their huts or asleep, he would be back at the door of his home, and his grandmother would greet him, and he would hold her frail, aged body in his arms.

He paid many men for their services, drivers and couriers, thieves and killers, but none was allowed to be as close to him as Mikhail, who slept in the next room and carried the weapons, and who could scent danger. He'd always had that skill, which had failed him only once – and had many times served him well. Weissberg tolerated minimal familiarity from this one man, a degree more than he would have accepted from Josef Goldmann, whose talent was in the manipulation of money.

The car pulled away, left the parking area empty behind them. The lights swept over the trees where, buried from sight, was the house built of wood planks – and inside a barking dog but not its owner. The beams flared back from the tree trunks.

'You don't believe I'll find the grave.'

Mikhail went at speed on the forest road and perhaps did not care to taunt him. 'If you want to find it, I believe you will. I understand why you search.'

Ahead, an owl flew low, was caught by the lights, veered from them and was lost in the trees. He had promised his grandmother that he would find it, and her life was ebbing.

'When we come back . . . How many days?'

'Five.'

'Then I'll look again.' He let his hand rest lightly on Mikhail's arm, near to the wrist and the fist that held the wheel. 'It is demanded of me.'

He closed his eyes and shut out the view of trees, pines and birches, racing past, and in his mind he heard the story of what had been done to Jews in the forest.

Innocence is gone. I think I was lucky – or stupid – to have known innocence for a whole week.

I am in Camp 1. I sleep in the top bunk of three in a dormitory barracks for women, and I am the youngest there, more a girl than a woman. The first nights I cried myself to sleep and the women around me cursed and said I disturbed them. I cried because I wanted to be with my family, close to my father and mother, everyone else. 'Why are you making such a noise?' I was asked, many times in the first night and the second. Each time I told the questioner I wanted to be reunited with my family, that I was fearful they would be shipped on to the east, to the new settlements, and that I wouldn't be with them. Some women swore at me, and others tittered . . . but it was a week before I was told, and innocence was lost.

In the first week I did not go out of Camp 1. All I saw of the world was the sky. I saw clouds, rain, and for two days there was fierce sunshine. There were men in Camp 1 but we were forbidden to speak to them, and the open ground inside the wire was patrolled by Ukrainians under the supervision of German officers. On the third day, a male prisoner was shot by an officer. He was in the ranks lined up for roll-call. It was dawn. He was sick. Those on either side of him tried to hold him upright, but he slipped from their grasp and fell in front of the officer. Then he vomited on the officer's boots. The officer moved his boot from under the man's head and away from his mouth, and took a pistol from the leather holster that was on his leather belt. He cocked it, aimed for the man's head and fired. The bullet broke open the man's skull, and there was blood with the vomit on the boot. He lay where he had been killed through the roll-call, and he was taken away only when we were sent to the workplaces. I couldn't believe it, but he was dragged to the gate of Camp 1 by the same men who had tried to support him. They each had a leg and dragged his body as if it were a sack of rubbish.

Later that day, the third, I saw through the window of the hut where I worked a prisoner carry a pair of boots into Camp 1. He cleaned them for an hour. He used his

87

tunic to wipe off the vomit and blood, then spat on them and polished them with his undershirt. Of course, I cannot be exact in the time because there were no clocks in the hut, but I thought from the sun and the shadows beyond the window that it took him an hour to clean them.

Inside Camp 1 there were places for work, but some of the men were escorted outside to the forest to cut timber. Some of the women were taken out to the officers' compound for cleaning. Inside Camp 1 there were workshops for tailors, who cut and sewed uniforms for the Germans, a shoemaker's shop, where leather saddles were made for the Germans' horses, a place for mechanics and for carpenters, a hut where paints were stored, and the kitchen.

I was sent to work in the kitchen within an hour of being separated from my family.

We mixed soup for the men and for the women. We provided the food for all, except the officers, in Camp 1. What we made was foul, and only hunger prevented us vomiting or refusing it. In that week I wondered where my family was, and whether they had the same food as us, and whether it was as awful, and where the kitchen was that made it. It is important to understand that the camp was a cage, and I knew nothing of life beyond the fences that were interwoven with dead pine branches. When the needles fell from them and it became almost possible to see out, the men brought more and repaired the gaps.

It was a miracle that my innocence lasted a whole week. It ended so suddenly.

We were heating soup on the seventh day – it was in old metal dustbins that were on bricks above chopped logs that made the fire, and we stirred it with lengths of wood that had been stripped of bark.

The capo was behind me and supervised an older woman who put potatoes into the water, and some

88

turnips, but no meat. The capo was from Chelm and did not have to work; she was a Jewess but was privileged and carried a short whip. She was feared. I had forgotten she was behind me, I think tiredness and the ache in my stomach had made me forget her. Her name was Miriam.

I said to the woman beside me, 'My elder sister won't eat this. She has a delicate stomach.'

Because of the heat from the open fires under the soup, we had the window slats open, and I heard the clank of a train behind our fence and beyond the officers' compound, the howl of its wheels as it stopped.

The woman looked away and did not meet my eyes.

The capo, Miriam, flicked my buttocks with her whip so that I should turn and face her. She said, 'We live here by sound. We exist by hearing – our ears are our eyes. A train comes. Musicians play. We hear those sounds. Our ears pick up the shouts of the Germans. After that there are screams, which are drowned, but not completely, by an engine starting. Then we hear geese. A prisoner goes into a little place where geese are kept, not to be eaten. He has a stick and chases them. The squawking means we can't hear the screams and the engine. It is very short, this process. A train coming, an orchestra playing, orders, screams, an engine and the geese – it is what we hear every day. We heard it on the afternoon you came . . . You should not worry about your sister's stomach because she was dead before dusk. All those you came with were dead before the light failed that afternoon . . . Stir harder, or the taste of the potato and turnip will not get into the water.'

I found that innocence lost is never regained.

They crossed the bridge over the Oka river and ahead were the ancient streets.

Yashkin said, 'They boast here that Murom is the prettiest town in all Russia.'

'They talk shit.' Molenkov yawned, could not stifle it.

'Gorky wrote, "Whoever has not seen Murom from the Oka river has not seen Russian beauty." '

'Fuck him.'

'It's the birthplace of the *bogatyr*, the epic hero, Ilya Muromets. Look, there's the statue of him . . .' Yashkin had his hand off the wheel and pointed from his window. A knight in armour, a cloak across his shoulders and a battle sword held high, triple the size of a man, was floodlit on a plinth. 'It's very fine.'

'Another fucker.'

'You know there are monasteries here that were founded nearly a thousand years ago. I think that's the roof of the Monastery of Our Saviour.'

'I don't give a shit for a monastery.'

'I read all this in guidebooks. It's where the *kalatchi* bread comes from. Yes, we knew that.'

'I don't need to know about heroes, monasteries or bread. It's ten to midnight. I'm exhausted and I want to know where we'll sleep, that's all.'

Yashkin grimaced. 'I was only talking to keep myself awake.'

He heard the yawn again, then a groan, blinked and tried to keep his eyes open. At night in Sarov when he drove the Polonez as a taxi he always slept in the afternoon, at least four hours. At the thought of it, an officer of the 12th Directorate forced to ply for trade with his old car to put food on his table and light in his home, bitterness surged in him. Such a long day. He would have collapsed on his bed now if he'd had the chance.

And again Molenkov, beside him, wheezed his yawn. 'I need to sleep.'

Yashkin took the Polonez down narrow streets,

past the square that had the illuminated Cathedral of Our Saviour and Transfiguration – he'd read of it – and saw the scaffolding climbing towards the dome. They had money to rebuild old and useless monuments, but not to pay the pension of an officer who had given his life to the 12th Directorate. They reached the doors, closed, of a hotel. He parked. His friend was asleep, but he shook him hard.

They went together up the steps and hammered on the door, a tattoo of their fists. There was the muffled shuffle of feet, then a chain rattled and a bolt scraped. Light flooded them. Was a room available? A porter's eyes raked over them. His head shook decisively. There was an inner door of glass behind him. Yashkin saw, through it, the reception desk, the line of hooks and keys hanging from the majority . . . and he saw his face and Molenkov's reflected in the glass. The door was shut, the chain replaced and the bolt pushed home.

They went to two more hotels. At the last, they gained admittance to the desk, but were turned away. They were told by a girl, challenged but evading, that the rooms with the keys on hooks were undergoing 'refurbishment' and not available. There was a mirror behind her head, and it showed two old men, unshaven, with dirt and grease on their faces, and he remembered how they had struggled with the spare tyre before the jack had broken.

Beside the Polonez, Yashkin said, 'It's because of how we look. Did you see us?'

'What do we do?'

He was pleased that the colonel (retired) deferred to the major (retired). Yashkin shrugged. 'We must wash, but I'm not going to the Oka river

91

to get clean at this time of night. We'll find a park and sleep in the car.'

Under old elm trees, Molenkov lay across the front seats with the gear stick wedged in his crotch and snored. Yashkin was on his back, his spine pressed against the tarpaulin and what it hid.

'Are you all right? You're not ill or anything, are you?'

Sak's head jolted up off his hands, which were on the table, and the sudden movement tipped sideways a pile of books. He saw the cleaning woman, anxiety cutting across her face. He stammered that he was fine.

'Don't mind me saying so, but you don't look it – you look like you've seen a ghost.'

He opened a book but barely glanced at the pages. She started close to him, as if to emphasize her displeasure at finding someone studying in the school's sixth-form library, and not a pupil or teacher but in the white coat of a laboratory technician. He ignored her, did not flinch when the vacuum-cleaner thumped against his feet under the table – no apology – and did not move a centimetre when a damp cloth was wiped hard on the table surface. Their eyes never met, and she moved away with her vacuum-cleaner and cloth. He called himself Sak. The name was bred from his split life, his split cultures and split races. To his mother, British born, he was Steven Arthur King, her maiden surname. To his father he was Siddique Ahmed Khatab. With his mother's family he was anglicized; when he had visited his father's relations in the Pakistani city of Quetta he was Asian . . . A racial hermaphrodite, a college guy had called him. Now the name Sak suited him, and the kids he worked alongside were rather taken by it, as if it had uniqueness. It was his position as a laboratory technician that was unique.

He had left Imperial College at London University in the summer of 1997, at the age of twenty-two, with an upper second-class degree in nuclear physics, to the huge delight of the one-time Miss King, now Mrs Khatab, and his father. Eleven years later, bruised by what had happened to him, and harbouring the secret, he was a laboratory technician in a comprehensive school on the edge of the West Midlands. The work was humiliatingly easy, barely taxed him. But since his world had collapsed, Sak had allowed himself to be recruited. If he had had a confidant, which he did not, he might have admitted to *offering* himself for recruitment. He had two attractions for the recruiting sergeants operating from a villa on the northern outskirts of Quetta.

He thought himself rejected and betrayed.

He had worked from '97 until his dismissal in '02 in the secret world of nuclear weapons.

Sak was gobbled and sent back to the UK to wait and sleep.

He was a dour man, and as he approached early middle age, with receding hair to prove it, there was little about him that was romantic, and such fantasies were rarely in his mind. A brush contact that morning, walking the last couple of hundred yards to the school gates, not seeing the man whose shoulder had hit him – couldn't have said what he was wearing, what his skin colour was – and Sak had realized that a minutely folded piece of paper was in his hand. Had looked round, had seen only droves of kids coming to school.

Sak was ordered to be ready to travel; the details would follow.

He had not gone home. He had stayed in the library, and the story, in minutiae, of what had been done to him ran over and over in his mind.

High above the port of Dubai, the wind off the Gulf rocked the crane driver's cabin – not yet as high as the Dubai World Trade Centre, which had thirty-seven floors, but climbing.

Not a bird but a man, the Crow could look down on the lights of the creek, the ruler's office, the yacht club and the docks, and far out to sea where the container ships and tankers were anchored, all brightly lit.

He was squashed into the small space behind the heavily padded chair in which the crane driver sat. The name 'the Crow' came from the pitch of his voice, which croaked when he spoke. His vocal cords had been minimally damaged in Afghanistan twenty-one years before by the shrapnel of shell-casing fired from a Soviet 122mm howitzer artillery piece. That period of his life was hidden, and those who needed to have the scars explained were told of an operation, successful, for throat cancer. He was known as the Crow across the construction sites of Dubai.

The Crow's responsibility was to keep teams, from labourers to skilled craftsmen, working efficiently on the developments along the coast. He was supreme at his work, in demand and a trusted friend of architects and quantity surveyors. He was admired by potential purchasers of property. He had been hauled up by the hydraulic winch, in a secure basket, to the cabin because the driver had reported stress on the cables running the length of the crane's arm, and to see for himself the shake. That he went himself, in the middle of the night, was a mark – so the professionals who relied on him said – of his dedication to the projects on which he worked.

They knew nothing.

The crane's driver had returned the previous day from a month's rest in his home town of Peshawar, on the fringe of the North-West Frontier of Pakistan, and a slim, rolled piece of paper had been retrieved from a tiny pocket sewn inside the waist of his trousers. The Crow had thanked him gutturally, then read the message sent in answer to a note he had sent with the driver when he had gone home. There were no bugs and no cameras in a crane cabin that rolled in the blustery wind some two hundred and fifty feet above the Gulf shore-line. He read it, digested it, then methodically tore the paper into myriad tiny pieces, then let his hand go to the window and opened his fingers. The pieces scattered and gulls chased them.

He was asked by the driver if it was good.

The Crow growled, 'As good as the cables under your crane arm.'

They laughed. High over the harbour, above the dhows and yachts, a ripple of laughter, a meld of shrill and a black crow's call, spilled down. The driver radioed for the basket to be made ready.

The Crow stepped over the void between the cabin and the basket floor, feeling it pitch. He waved at the driver, then was lowered at speed.

Then – because such men did not sleep – he went in search of the *hawaldar* in his home beyond the Fish Roundabout. The *hawaldar* had prepared for the Crow the details of the transaction that had been taken back to Peshawar, passed on and moved forward until it had reached a compound hugging the foothills of a mountain range. The answer, by a similarly complicated route, cut-outs, blocks and checks, had returned in the lining of the driver's trousers. The *hawaldar* whom the Crow would see had in the financial world connections dedicated to the Islamic faith who could guarantee great sums of money, coffers and treasuries of it, with no electronic trace and beyond the reach of investigators.

The Crow would tell him to make the arrangements, then wait to be told of his own travel schedule.

He climbed from the basket, did not need a hand to help him. The wind ripped his hair, and he was smiling. He said to the site's night foreman, 'There's no problem with the cable. The driver's an old woman, frightened of his own shadow. The cable is fine . . . Everything is fine.'

Once a fortnight, Luke Davies did the late evening shift.

The girl who was doing night duty was away down the corridor, would have been getting chocolate out of a machine, or a coffee. The area, open plan, around his desk was empty and the ceiling lights were dimmed. The girl would be looking after a dozen desks during the night and would not be relieved till after six in the morning. He rather envied the quiet and the peace she would experience after he'd gone and she had the area to herself. He tidied his desk a last time, dumped a final file in the small floor safe beside his knees, closed its door and flicked the combination to random numbers.

The desk told little of Luke Davies. Years before, the staff of the Secret Intelligence Service had been uprooted from a shabby tower block, Century House, and shifted a few hundred yards west along the Albert Embankment to a green and yellow angular building on the east side of the bridge that ended in the junction of Vauxhall Bridge Cross. It was a monument to a modern architect, derided by many and loved by a few. Luke Davies was among the few, thought it magnificent and reckoned it a fitting home for the Service that he was proud to belong to. But the architects' remit reached inside the outer walls and windows, and carefully drawn-out colour schemes ruled the interiors. They had been chosen, after expensive advice from consultants, to provide the best working environment; walls and partitions were not to be cluttered with calendars, pictures, personal photographs, printouts of joke emails, Post-it reminders or the images of targets. Discreetly shown on the partition dividing the desks of the juniors of this section of the Russia Desk (Baltic), close to his mouse-pad, screen and keyboard, were three snapshot photographs: himself in mortarboard and gown, holding the rolled degree certificate – first-class honours from the School of East European and Slavonic Studies; himself again in front of the little bridge over the Miljacka river, standing on the spot where Gavrilo Princep had fired the shots that launched the First World War and made Sarajevo famous – his first, only, overseas posting had been to Bosnia-Herzegovina; and a smiling girl with a blue UN helmet rakish on her head, pouting as if she was blowing a kiss. Around her was desert and behind her were huts of dead branches and thorn hedges and by her knee was a child, African, with a ribcage showing semi-starvation. He called her his girlfriend but she was in Darfur, or Lebanon, or Afghanistan, and the photograph was two years old. Most of the story of Luke Davies's life was captured in three photographs. He left his desk, went to the far wall and the line of lockers, and opened his.

He had his back to the door at the far side of the room – and did not see it open. He pulled out the waterproofs he had worn when he'd come to work, and lifted the cycling helmet off the locker floor. He heard, 'It's Luke Davies, isn't it? You are Luke Davies?'

'That's me – I'm him.' He had a soft south-Yorkshire accent, had tried to lose it and failed, was stuck with it. He thought his accent, at VBX, counted more against him than his degree – rated 'outstanding' by his tutor – benefited him.

'Good thing I caught you. I'm Wilmot, Duggie, Human Resources. Just going off, I see. Sorry and all that. Cycling, eh? Not much of a night for that ... You're to be seconded for a week or two, immediate effect. I was called by Pam Bertrand – she's your desk chief, yes? She said it should be you.'

Something evasive about the guy, as if that was only half the story. He asked, 'Where am I going?'

'It's Non-Proliferation, Mr Lawson. You're to be seconded indefinitely, but not for ever, to Mr *Christopher* Lawson in Non-Proliferation and—'

Eyes closed, hugging the waterproofs and the helmet, sucking in breath. 'I'm not hearing this.'

'Authorized by Pam, not in my hands.'

'That man is a Class A shite.'

'Pam said you'd not be happy. Came to her from above. I'm afraid it's set in dried concrete.'

'Should have been put out to grass a decade ago.' He felt the sweat on his back and his voice was louder than it should have been. The night-duty girl was back, had stopped eating her chocolate to watch his display. Didn't care. 'What if I go sick?'

He saw a smile spread. 'You'd get dragged out of bed – wouldn't wash. Suicide might do it.'

'He's the most unpleasant man known to exist in this building, an antique and—'

'And you're seconded to him. Non-Proliferation, third floor west, room seventy-one. Got that?'

He subsided. 'Right. I'll be off home and into my bathroom cabinet to count the painkillers, see if I've enough and—'

'He's waiting for you, *Mr* Lawson is . . .' a little laugh '. . . expecting you. Oh, Pam said – I nearly forgot – it's sanctioned by the DG. Good luck.'

Davies threw the waterproofs back into his locker with the helmet, then slammed its door. He stomped past the night-duty girl and out to the corridor.

At the end of the corridor he banged his fist against the lift's call button. Lawson was one of those who harked back in time to when everything was fucking perfect, talked of the Good Old Days. In the Good Old Days of the fifties, sixties and seventies, Cold War era, everything worked a fucking treat. Unlike today, which, to a god, was useless, pathetic, and the new intakes were crap. Davies had been five years in the Service, and other gods had been pointed out to him before his Sarajevo posting – red-faced old bastards, mumbling about the time when the Ark floated off – but they'd gone by the time he'd returned from the Balkans. Only one remained. Didn't matter if every seat in the canteen was taken except at one table, he would be left to eat alone. Stories of his rudeness were legion. Davies came out of the lift. He swore and his voice was spirited down the corridor, then bounced back in an echo to him, as if his efforts were mocked.

He knocked.

A woman came out, glanced at the laminated ID he offered, pointed towards an open door.

Lawson's back was to him. Had a phone against his ear. Shouted at it. 'If I say I want two increments and that gear at seven tomorrow morning, it's what I mean. Pretty clear to me, and should be clear to anyone who's not an imbecile or obstinate. I want them where I said at seven – not a minute later – and the gear.'

The phone went down and the chair spun.

'Are you Davies – Luke Davies?'

'Yes.'

'How many years with the Service?'

'Five.'

'Oh, time enough to know it all, be an expert. Do you know it all?'

'I'm sure when you were told I was being seconded to you that you'd had sight of my file. You'll have read what my line managers have reported on my abilities and—'

'If I want a speech I'll ask for it. When I don't want a speech I should be given answers of one word, two or three . . . Sarov, what does that name mean to you?'

He blustered. 'Excuse me – is that a person's name or a place name?'

'I hadn't been with the Service a year – let alone five – before I knew *what* Arzamas-16 was and *where* Sarov was, but the sort of people inducted into the Service then were of a different quality . . . Six thirty, here, in the morning. Don't stand around, go away and learn.'

Luke Davies was flushed and his cheeks burned as he spun. He went out, past the woman, and into the corridor. He had never heard of Arzamas-16 or a place called Sarov, but had six hours and twenty-six minutes to discover them.

After the bus ride Carrick walked the last mile. It was a routine for him since he had gone on the plot and into the household of Josef Goldmann. Hadn't used his mobile. The worst place for an undercover, a level one, to call in to his case officer was on the street. Couldn't say there whether he was under surveillance. Worst thing was to get away from the work location, then be seen to use a mobile. Back in the first weeks after being embedded he had had a back-up car tracking him during work hours, and sometimes a back-up walking behind him when he'd finished his duties, but nothing had happened in the last month, the threat assessment had been reduced and back-up guys had been deployed for other undercovers. If he had taken the risk and used his mobile – to report the arrest of Simon Rawlings, drunk in charge, and the invitation to go a small step up the ladder and replace the sarge – he would have found, probably, Katie at the end of the call, not Rob, who was his cover officer, and not George, the controller. Not a risk worth taking. Everything could keep till the evening of the day already started. Couldn't say, when they met for the debrief, whether the promotion was enough to keep the operation going. Neither could he have said that he was now guaranteed greater access than before.

He felt flat, washed through. Simon Rawlings had done him well, too damn well to have deserved betrayal and deceit. But that was the world of an undercover, level one. Everything exploited, and every man. No relationships allowed to count.

It had been the question at the interview board. 'Let's put this pretty crudely, Johnny – and my colleague will forgive me the vulgarity. You get to like people in the target area, you get a bit fond of them, you get to see the better sides of them, but the job says you have to fuck their lives. Screw them down, fuck them and walk away . . . Up for that, are you?'

The board had been a superintendent from the Murder Squad – it had been his question – a divisional commander, a woman in a starched blouse and a well-pressed uniform, and a psychologist, middle-aged, intense stare, not speaking but watching.

He'd said, 'I would regard myself first and foremost as a police officer. My duty as a serving officer is to obtain evidence of criminal activity. It's paramount. I'd do my job.'

The friend down in Bristol, the older man, had told him before he headed for London and the interview that he should not flannel his answers, should keep them brief and focused, that he should display honesty at all times, that he should be his own man.

The woman had asked, 'Can you live on your own, Johnny? Can you survive in an environment that is a lie? Can you field the solitariness of the work, which is demanded by the deception? I promise you, it's not easy.'

They had been the two big questions and they had stayed in his mind, with his reply: 'I had a sort of childhood that wasn't dependent on company. Left to myself, valued my own scene. Didn't need a shoulder to cry on when I was a kid, and I haven't been home since I walked out on them and joined up . . . I did two months in hospital, a convalescent, and I didn't have a visitor. I'm fine on my own, doesn't frighten me.' He had set out his stall, had done it pithily, and his interview before the board had lasted only ninety-two minutes – those of others had lasted in excess of three hours. He'd known he was accepted. Brave words: *I'd do my job . . . I'm fine on my own, doesn't frighten me*. More questions about his ability to live among druggies, alongside prostitutes, close up with paedophiles . . . Gutsy words spoken, but in the easy times and before they were tested.

He remembered a final statement from the Murder Squad man, who leaned back, sort of avuncular. 'You, with your background, will reckon to be able to take care of yourself. With us, I'd like to emphasize, you'll never be beyond the reach of help. We take the safety of our people very, very seriously. We ask them, after due consideration of realities, to go into unpleasant and dangerous situations, but we're there all the time, close by. And if a situation deteriorates unexpectedly we're not in the market for heroes. We expect our man to cut and run.'

He reached the steps of the house. He had moved into the room upstairs two weeks before joining the household of Josef Goldmann.

He unlocked the front door, picked up some circulars and started on the stairs.

Ahead of him, as he climbed, was a barely furnished top-floor conversion into a one-bedroom apartment: his home. Where he was alone, where no one needed his lies.

Chapter 4: 10 April 2008

Maybe it was because of his new status, but that morning he fancied he was more clearly watched.

An instructor had said during the training period, 'The deeper you go into the organization, the more access you have, the closer you will be observed. The natural suspicion they harbour for an outsider cannot, ever, be totally erased. Each step up means greater care must be taken.' They had done role-play at the start of the training, simple stuff: buying Class A drugs, dumping counterfeit money on a bureau de change, drinking till late, then they'd been quizzed abruptly about an area and the specifics of the legend, had been tested on their ability to lose the police ethic.

The front door had been opened for him by Grigori. Carrick was eyed, as if he was meat on a slab, no greeting or welcome offered. He could not have said whether his advance in the household made him, now, a competitor for Grigori's position. He smiled warmly, but the gesture was not returned – and it was strange to him because it was hard to believe in danger when the whoops and shouts of the children billowed down the staircase, there was the smell of cooking from the basement kitchen and of fresh coffee. He'd gone down to the ready room.

An instructor had said, 'You'll think you can handle the isolation of the lie, but we don't know, none of us does. Role-play is useful but it's a poor substitute for actuality. If you're going to crack, feel yourself slipping, then for God's sake come out. Don't take it as a failure of the macho-man you want to be. There's no disgrace in not being able to field the pressure.' They did sleep-deprivation, and slap-around questioning that left small bruises – and had lessons in the use of bugs, where to hide them, and the fixing of tags to cars. Seven of his intake had passed, but two had dropped out and never been referred to again. He'd done as well in his training as he had on his appearance before the selection board, and had told himself that pressure didn't faze him, or stress.

The internal phone rang.

Viktor for him, to go upstairs. Grigori's eyes were locked on him till he had gone out through the door. The briefing papers said that Grigori and Viktor were from Perm – wherever that was. They were believed to be former officers in a security police unit and were thought of as long-term associates, providing muscle for the family.

Viktor met him on the first floor. Hard, piercing eyes gazed into Carrick's. Just the glance, nothing said. The look in the eyes gave Carrick certainty: nothing that he had done so far in the household had yet clinched trust. He wondered, a snap thought, what weapon Viktor had used in his past when he was enforcing protection. A pistol? Unlikely, too clean. A pickaxe handle was more likely. Fire, or power drills and cutters would have been the best and would have given him a rare thrill – like a jerk-off. He smiled again. His aim was to appear simple and straightforward, not stupid, to be a piece of furniture that was there and unnoticed. He reckoned Viktor would have loathed the very idea of employing foreign nationals in the house, but Viktor had only halting English, Grigori less, and the family needed to have around them men who were both reliable and familiar with roads, traffic, driving and . . . Viktor did not answer his smile.

'You wanted me up here.'

Viktor jerked his thumb at a door. 'Mr Goldmann waits you.'

He went through to the salon, used for entertaining, where the drapes were still drawn. The kids' shouts, behind him and up another flight, were in Russian, but it was just kids' noise and he sensed nothing of importance; but there had been nothing of importance. If the legend of Johnny Carrick had marked the actual limits of his life, and he had been a bodyguard, handyman, chauffeur to a Russian *émigré* businessman, who was clean and legitimate, he would have liked them. Nothing to complain about. But he had read a briefing paper, with an attachment, and lived a lie in the house. The family sitting room was at the end of the salon, and beside it was the door to the little office area that Josef Goldmann used. Maybe there was a tickle in Carrick's throat, a cough he didn't register, maybe there was a floorboard below the pile that was loose enough to creak. Whichever, the Bossman was alerted, and was in the office door, and he held two tickets – airline style – in one hand.

'Ah, Johnny . . .'

'You asked for me, sir.' Carrick could do the

corporal-to-middle-ranking-officer act well. No impertinence, no cheek.

'It is incredible to me, what happened last night.'

'Difficult to understand, sir.'

'You have to take the place of Simon, of Rawlings, as I said last night.'

'Yes, sir. If that's what you want, sir.'

He saw the tickets, noted the logo of the agency on Kensington High Street. He stood, feet slightly apart, straight-backed, hands clasped behind him, as if he was the corporal and he faced his officer.

'You do the school drive.'

'Yes, sir.'

'Then you take me to the City. Viktor does not drive well in the City.'

'Yes, sir.'

'And you bring me back, and you collect the children.'

'Of course, sir. I apologize, sir, but I mentioned last night a family commitment.'

'You did.'

'And I would need to be away by six, sir. In the future, in the new circumstances, I would not make any commitments without checking with you first.'

'That is satisfactory.'

He thought his Bossman was worn down, at the edge of exhaustion. Josef Goldmann was pale, looked not to have slept, seemed burdened. Wouldn't be from the loss of Rawlings, no way . . . The fingers fidgeted with the two tickets. The instructors had said that an undercover should press for information only in exceptional circumstances: 'I see you've got two tickets there, sir. Are you going somewhere interesting?' would have been about as bad tradecraft as was possible. To

107

push for information, hurry it, was flawed practice.

'I'll be off, sir, on the kids' run, then.'

'Yes, Johnny, thank you. Then we go to the City, late morning.'

'Yes, sir.'

'I don't have time to mess about. You either have an officer in that household or you do not. Which?'

It was a few minutes past eight. Lawson was in charge and gloried in it. An hour and a few minutes earlier, at one minute after seven, there had been the rap on his office door, room seventy-one on third floor west, and he had admitted – Lucy not yet at her desk – the young man, Davies. He had asked if the detail of Sarov had been learned, had seen a half-awake nod. Had asked if the history of Arzamas-16 had been studied, again the nod. He had not asked a clever or trick question to assess Davies's reading of the history. The young man's face had fallen when he'd realized he was not about to be tested on his work. Then he had told him he was late and received a sulking apology. A good start to the day. All in good time, the young man would be told the codename of the operation and shown the file – it would be done later, if time allowed. He had led and Davies had followed. They had crossed Vauxhall Bridge, had not headed for Scotland Yard but had branched away into Pimlico, had found the door of a tatty, tacky office block and had rung a bell. When their business was asked by a porter, Lawson had given the name of who he had come to see, though not his own, and they had been escorted up two flights.

'I'd have thought it a pretty simple question, requiring a pretty simple answer: yes or no. So, I repeat – which?'

He was in a room that had not recently been

decorated, and the iron window frames had traces of rust where he could see them through the open slats of the dropped blind. There was a tidy desk, a pair of filing cabinets, a plastic-coated board on the main wall with a cover draped over it to prevent a visitor reading what was displayed on it, the compulsory mounted photographs of senior police posing and a family shot. He thought that in the moments before his arrival, with Davies in tow, the room had been sanitized. He had introduced himself only by his first name, and Davies's. The other men had been George and Rob – and George had said, 'Why don't you take a pew, and tell me how I can be of help, Chris—'

And he had snapped back, with venom and interest, 'It's *Christopher*, thank you.' He had not come to negotiate, or to be deflected.

'I'm a busy man – yes or no?'

He watched George fidget and shift on his chair, and his fingers cracked together as he clasped them. His companion, Rob, peered out through the blind's gaps. George drew air into his lungs, then let it hiss out.

'I'm waiting.'

George bit his lower lip, whitened it. 'Would this be a matter of national security?'

'I raised from his bed, at three this morning, a deputy assistant commissioner. I am assuming, or I would not have breached your front door, that you were instructed, *ordered*, to give me your full co-operation. Are you going to obstruct me? In which case I guarantee you will be spending rather more time with your family. Yes or no?'

Lawson thought George turned as if seeking support from his colleague, but the head was averted. No comfort to be gained there. The man

109

caved: they usually did if kicked hard enough. Clipper Reade had preached that public servants when threatened with an early pension inevitably crumpled. He had found little, from thirty years back, in the creed of Clipper Reade that he could fault.

A small voice, as if the habit of a professional lifetime had been ditched: 'Yes.'

'Thank you, and I don't know why we spent so long getting there.'

'I confirm, with extreme reluctance, that we have an officer inside the home of Josef Goldmann. He is there as part of a criminal investigation into the laundering of money, an investigation mounted by the Serious Crime Directorate. I have never seen, or heard of, anything in the investigation that involves national security.'

'Do you have bugs in the house?'

'Is that question in the interests of national security?'

'Bugs or no bugs?'

Again the lip was bitten, and the fingers now unwound the shape of a metal paperclip. 'There are no audio or visual devices in the house. It is swept most days, and – for the same reason – there are no tags on the cars.'

Lawson leaned back, as if he owned the room, tilted himself, as if he was on home territory. He took pleasure from the obvious intimation that he was detested inside that office. Clipper Reade had said that an intelligence officer could never be loved, should not seek to be . . . He remembered that huge figure, a beast of a man, the battered hat, the crumpled raincoat, the cheroot, the wisecracks and the homilies . . . He thought rudeness created domination, and it was needed, and he believed time raced.

'How well has your man done since his insertion?'

'Not as well as we'd hoped.'

'What's working against him?'

'The circumstances.'

It was like drawing teeth, but Christopher Lawson – if need be – could wield pliers and drag out a back wisdom. When he rasped his voice, and the police officer, George, winced under attack, he heard slight gasps from behind him, where Davies sat, as if in reaction to the directness of the frontal assault. No, it was not about negotiation.

'I seldom make idle threats, so listen carefully. If you do not provide me with complete co-operation I give you my solemn promise that you will be clearing your desk and on a lunchtime train home – not to return. Prevarication with me is not an option. So, what circumstances are working against him?'

George swallowed hard, as if discussing an undercover was a personal hurt to him, and against every instinct. 'Right, he is the junior in the house-hold. He does school runs and drives the lady – both she and the kids would be possible kidnap targets so he escorts them. He has little to do with Josef Goldmann. Alongside the subject – we don't call them 'targets' any longer, it infringes their human rights – alongside our *subject* are two Russian-born thugs who do close protection. Then there is Rawlings—'

'Poor old Rawlings.' Lawson grimaced a smile.

'Rawlings – I don't understand your comment – is unlikely to be a member of a criminal conspiracy. He's outside the loop of confidences, but has access and has never shown any sign of utilizing it. I don't understand what you find amusing. These are serious matters. Officers take considerable risks. This is dangerous and delicate work, no laughing matter.'

From his briefcase, Christopher Lawson took a sheet of photocopied paper and passed it. It was taken and read. It listed the offence of driving a vehicle with excess alcohol in the blood, and gave the name of the accused.

George shook his head, pushed the sheet to his sidekick. Lawson saw their frowns, shaken heads, disbelief.

'That's extraordinary. He doesn't touch it. This doesn't make sense.'

Lawson said, 'Might provide an opportunity for promotion, something of advantage to us . . . When is your next scheduled meeting?'

He was told where and when. He asked, without an explanation as to the use it would be put to, for a fast sight of the undercover's file. With no good grace George lifted the telephone, sent for the file. Nothing more to say. Lawson went further back on his chair legs. George chewed a nail and his lips seemed to move as if he was rehearsing what he should have said but had not. Rob was following the flight of gulls between the blind's slats, and had the look of a man who has lost something as precious as faith. The file was brought in. The girl was boot-faced, as if she confronted an enemy. Quite a pretty girl, made prettier by the un-disguised anger at her mouth. Lawson assessed her as the girl Friday. She reached out with the file, to pass it to her superior, but Lawson stretched out his arm, the quickness of a snake's strike, and his fingers intercepted it. For a moment he and the girl had hold of it, then it was loosed.

Lawson held it high, above his shoulder. It was

taken behind him, a relay baton. He imagined it would be speed read. Silence fell. He thought that little would be left of the man's nails, and that every seagull traversing the skyline of SW1 had been tracked. There was the rustle of papers behind him. The file was passed back and, without comment, he handed it on to the girl, and thought she hated him. He stood.

Of course, there would be a final throw. George said, 'This is a very professional and dedicated officer, currently working in a difficult environment. Nothing should be done that puts his safety at risk.'

Lawson smiled, the enigmatic one that betrayed nothing of his aspirations. Clipper Reade had always referred to agents as the *mushrooms* of intelligence officers in the field. 'You know it, Christopher, they're best kept in the dark and fed on shit.' Lawson had always chuckled when the Texan growled out his mushroom bit.

'I've matters to deal with, gentlemen – and young lady. Thank you for your time . . . Yes, matters are coming to a head and I believe they involve dangerous men.'

Rain lashed down. Flooding on the road between Poznan and the frontier had delayed them, and the approach to the bridge had been slow. They had been in single-line queues of heavy lorries. A six-hour journey had taken ten, but the last run had been faster, on the *autobahn*.

Mikhail brought Reuven Weissberg down the wide street, past the grey mass of the Russian embassy, took the diversion around the Gate, then went left. He skirted the memorial to the killed Jews – a great open space of rectangular dark stone blocks, like rows of different-sized coffins – flashed the code on the zapper, then drove down into the basement parking area and into the numbered slot. The jolt woke Weissberg.

He was home.

He took the lift up, Mikhail with him. It was standard duty for the bodyguard to escort him from the car to the lift, and from the lift to the penthouse door. Mikhail, from his past, knew the theory of close protection and put it into practice. A man who could be a target was most vulnerable when arriving at a destination. He put his key into the door's lock, and the sound of it turning would have alerted her. She would have been waiting for him, and he rehearsed in his mind what he would say about the delay through flooding west of Poznan because she would scold him for his lateness. Had barely turned the key when he heard the shuffle of feet. Mikhail always waited with him until he was inside, then would go down and clean the car, take it out and top up its fuel tank. Mikhail always left him alone when he came back, was greeted by his grandmother.

He held her.

She was tiny in his arms, but his bear-hug was gentle, and he was careful not to hurt her. She offered him each cheek in turn and he kissed the lined skin. He saw clouded opaque colours in her eyes and wetness. The damp was from the infection, not tears. He had never seen her weep. He was now in his fortieth year, and for the last thirty-five – as a child, a teenager and as a man – he had lived with her, been cared for by her and had loved her. She stood on tiptoe in his embrace. Had her heels been on the floor, her height would have been 1.61 metres, and her weight was a fraction under forty-eight kilos. As always she was dressed in black: flat black shoes, thick black stockings, a black skirt and a black blouse, and because winter had not yet passed for her, she had a black cardigan over her shoulders. She wore no jewellery, had no cosmetics on her face, but her hair was pure white. As he held her, his fingers were in the hair at the back of her head, and it had been white – with the purity of fresh-fallen snow – from his earliest memories. He loosed her and she stood back to gaze up at him.

She did scold him. 'You're late. I've been waiting for you. I cooked and it's ruined.'

He told her about the flood on the road west of Poznan, the delays near the frontier bridge across the Odra river.

'Have you eaten?'

He said he had not.

'Then I'll cook for you – but you smell. First wash yourself, and when you're clean come to the kitchen and your food will be ready.'

He did not tell her that although his belly was empty he had no appetite.

'What did you find?'

He told her he had searched for a whole morning in the forest but had not found the dip in the ground that might have marked the disturbance needed for a single grave, that he had sat for a whole afternoon with his back against a tree and had heard the songs of small birds, that he had watched a house built of wood planks for a whole evening.

'Did you not see the bastard who was then a child?'

He told her that Tadeuz Komiski had not been at the house, but that the dog had barked, warning the bastard, who had hidden.

His grandmother held his hand tight. 'But one day you will find him and the place?'

He promised he would. He stared into her eyes, and thought the colour was that of a little milk in water. But there were no tears . . . He said that the two men were coming, that their journey had started, that it was beyond recall.

'Is it too great a risk? I don't think so.'

He leaned forward and kissed her forehead and murmured that it didn't compare with the risk she had faced.

'You smell bad. Go and wash.'

Reuven Weissberg, who had been an *avoritet* in Perm at the age of twenty-one and had then outgrown the city, having taken control of the roofs of the fruit and vegetable market, who had ruled a gang's empire in Moscow, providing protection for foreign business enterprises by the age of twenty-eight, who now controlled an octopus enterprise in the German capital city and was five days from the biggest and most hazardous deal of his life, went for his shower. He took it because his grandmother had told him to.

He had never refused her, and never would. Had never contradicted her – water splashed over his head – and would not have gone for the deal if she had opposed it.

'Did you sleep?'

'Until you woke me.'

'Did you sleep through the night, or just now? I ask because of the time. I thought we were to start early.'

Molenkov watched as Major Oleg Yashkin tried to push himself up from the contorted position in which he had slept, then wiped his eyes. Himself, he felt good, had already been down to the river, knelt close to the water, cupped it over his face and rubbed hard to remove dirt. He had washed without soap, then come back to the car. There had been two elderly fishermen close to him but he had not spoken to them, or they to him: old habits of former times dictated that citizens did not interfere or pass comment on the actions of others. They saw nothing and remembered nothing. And when he was clean and had dried his face with his handkerchief he had gone to a stall at the far end of the park and bought two *kalatchi* rolls, fresh baked.

'You shouldn't have let me sleep so long. We have so far to go today. It's three hundred and twenty kilometres to—'

'Just now, you slept like a mother holding her baby.'

'Fuck you, Molenkov.'

'You had your arm over it, as if it was a baby. Is it alive?'

He saw that Yashkin blinked, then smiled, then ran his filthy hand across the tarpaulin, and said, 'In a fashion, yes.'

'It has a pulse, a beat, does it breathe?'

Yashkin wriggled out stiffly from the hatch of the Polonez. He stood and stretched – his breath was foul – then jabbed a finger at Molenkov. 'What do you want to know?'

'I want something to eat, but first I want to know what it is, have more understanding of it.'

'Why now? Why not last week or last month?'

'I regret nothing, I just ask. Some detail, what is it?'

'I need to piss.'

He followed Yashkin towards the riverbank, where he sheltered Yashkin from the view of the fishermen while he urinated against a tree trunk – with the weak flow of the old – and listened.

'I'll tell you once more and not again. We call it a Small Atomic Demolition Munition. I do not know exactly, but it would have been assembled at some date between 'sixty-nine and 'seventy-four, and it would have gone to the Special Forces who were attached to the mechanized divisions. But every six months it would have come back for maintenance work. They came back for the last time, to be dismantled, in 'ninety-two and 'ninety-three . . . and it was called the peace dividend. This one had been returned a week before I took it. Right, now I'm going to wash.'

Molenkov steadied him as he went down to the edge. Water splashed across his face and there was a gulped curse at its cold. He spat to clear his mouth.

'I didn't see this one's inside, but a similar batch had been brought to Arzamas-16 two weeks before from Ukraine. As a security officer I could be anywhere. I was shown the process of breaking up the weapon. You ask what's there. It's very simple. The complication's in the engineering, but the principle is basic – that's what I was told. First, there's a canvas bag round it, with carrying straps and handles. Open that and you expose something that looks like a small oil drum, which has hatches in it, screwed down tight. You undo the screws and you see moulded shapes to hold materials in place. A tangle of wires, inside and out. Then conventional military explosive is packed into a sphere, but when the detonator system is removed it's not dangerous. There is engineering sophistication that I was not told of, and would not have understood – I can only tell you what I saw.'

Again and again, Yashkin had poured the river

118

water over his face and across his short hair. Now he cleaned his hands. Molenkov watched, and tried to build pictures from what was described.

'Inside the explosive is the "pit" – that's what the engineers call it. It's very small. A little bigger than a tennis ball, the size of an ordinary orange, and a perfect sphere. That ball, the pit, is heavy, weighs perhaps four and a half kilos and is plutonium. To go for highly enriched uranium is a different process, but ours is plutonium. It is known in scientific terms as Pu-239. Actually, I held a pit in my hand.'

Wonderment, and a tinge of horror. 'You *held* it?'

'With a glove, but I was told that wasn't necessary. They say the pit – Pu-239 – is benign. Most extraordinary. It was warm.'

Molenkov closed his eyes, squeezed them shut, pondered, opened them and saw Yashkin shake his hands vigorously to dry them. 'Warm?'

'Not hot, but not with the chill of any metal. You asked me if it was alive. Perhaps. It has a natural warmth, not the cold of the dead.'

Molenkov turned to walk back towards the Polonez. A fisherman had a rod that bent over the water. He called, excited, to his friend to come. Over his shoulder, Molenkov shouted to Yashkin that he had new bread rolls in the car, and that they should start out for Kolomna, on the second stage of their journey. And as he walked he gazed down at his open palm and tried to imagine that he held in it a *warm* orange, which lived.

'Don't I get to see Mr Goldmann? For God's sake—'

'Mr Goldmann is busy. He is not to be disturbed,' Viktor said.

Hanging back, half in the shadow of the hall, Carrick watched. It had been predictable that the scene would happen, and it played out predictably. His sarge, Simon Rawlings, was on the top step but blocked by Viktor in the doorway, with Grigori at his side. Carrick thought he hadn't slept last night, looked washed out. His eyes were bagged and his face stubbled.

'I want to see him, or I want to see Mrs Goldmann!' His sarge's voice rose.

'It is not possible, and Mrs Goldmann, too, is busy. I am asked to give you an envelope, and it is the finish of your work here.'

Carrick saw it passed, saw it ripped open. It was packed with banknotes, fifties. One flew clear and floated in the wind that came up the street, but his sarge didn't grovel and didn't scrabble on the lower steps for it. He stood his ground, but had pocketed the envelope and the remaining notes. 'So, that's it. That's the end.'

'It is the finish of your work. Please, I require the keys.'

'I was spiked. Don't you know that? I was set up. Doesn't that interest you?'

'Please, the keys.'

The hand went into the pocket, emerging with the keys. The keys on the ring were thrown forward and caught low down by Grigori. Carrick thought his sarge was losing it – fast.

A snarl: 'I have clothes downstairs. I want them.'

Viktor, beside the seam of his trousers, flicked his fingers. That was predictable and had been planned for. From behind him, Grigori picked up and passed forward a black bin-liner. Carrick had packed it: spare suit, spare underwear, spare pair of shirts, socks, shoes and – junk items that went with

120

the job – overalls for car maintenance, heavy-duty gloves, torches, pepper-spray canister and a truncheon, a couple of well-thumbed books. Carrick thought it was because of the disrespect shown to Grigori, the chucked keys, that the bag was heaved forward, landed close to his sarge's feet.

'You aren't listening to me. The drink was spiked. Aren't you interested?' There was froth on his sarge's lips. He seemed to look up and his jaw clenched. 'You all right, then, Corp? You look all right. Hot-bedding already, are we? Not got a voice? You moved into my space? I'm listening, and I've not heard you speak up. I suppose it's a good bloody career move for you, me being set up. Well, listen to your old sarge. Listen hard. If they fuck me, they'll fuck you. Remember who told you.'

His sarge had turned, had bent and trapped the one dropped note and it went into a pocket. Then he hitched the bin-bag on to his shoulder and stood straight. 'Don't worry about me. I'm not going to make trouble and I won't be looking for a reference. You won't hear of me and I'll have forgotten you. Go steady, guys – and don't trip in your own shit.'

Carrick thought it well done, but there was a month's money in the envelope and it was clever to let the steam fly, then walk. His sarge went off the bottom step and never looked back. Carrick edged towards the door, watched him go. His sarge had most likely saved his life, and had later remembered a friend and had tried to help with work. Now he was gone. He heard the shout of his Bossman from behind him, up the stairs: 'In five minutes I am ready to go, Johnny.'

Viktor pushed the door shut, and Carrick lost sight of the lone man, bag on his back, walking away with a sort of hard-won dignity.

* * *

At least he was soothed by Johnny's smooth driving. He could be a nervous passenger in the back of the Audi if the car wove through traffic and accelerated past obstacles. Simon Rawlings attacked the road ahead, not Johnny. Josef Goldmann had more on his mind, and his progress towards the City was far back in his thoughts.

The image of Reuven Weissberg overwhelmed him. He could not back out. He saw himself as having little more importance in the schemes of the master, the leader, than any of the men who had the rank of *brigadir* in Perm or *boevik* in Moscow. He was a junior, a handler of money. His opinions were not asked for and his loyalty was assumed to be automatically given. They were on new territory here, faced new dangers, moved in new circles, but no exit route presented itself. The next day, when he travelled with Viktor, the quagmire under his feet would be deeper, more cloying . . . He realized it, he shivered, and the papers he tried to read quivered in his hands. He shook his head sharply, an attempt to break the image's hold.

Josef Goldmann said, 'You drive well, Johnny. You are very relaxing.'

'Thank you, sir.'

'If it's not too much trouble, could you tell me, *please*, what we are doing here, and why?'

'You'd best stand, not wave a flag or make yourself conspicuous, and observe.'

He didn't do Davies the courtesy of turning to face him, but spoke from the side of his mouth and stared down the street at the entrance to the building. Christopher Lawson had long believed that courtesies and explanations were usually a waste of breath.

'What am I supposed to observe?'

'It will all, I hope, become apparent – and chattering will not accelerate it.'

Pretty much the same thing had been said to Lawson, all those years ago, when he was new in the company of Clipper Reade. Waiting on a dark night, a breeze rippling the surface of the Landwehr canal, the floodlights on the Wall. A hissed flood of questions asked, the second time he had been out with the heavy-built American, and the sharp rejoinder that silence was a better virtue than blather. 'More valuable in this trade to keep quiet, watch, wait and observe, Christopher, than make useless talk.' Chastened by the reprimand, he had stayed silent and watched the water, had heard ducks and radios playing beyond the Wall's height. The name 'Clipper' was already in place when he'd met the Texan on his first posting abroad to the British headquarters at the old Olympic park. 'Clipper' was a British accolade: had come from the UK's station chief in Berlin at a meeting when, apparently, the American had downed four mugs of tea, then asked for another pot to be brought him, and an hour later another. The station chief had remarked, drily, the story said, that they'd have to run a particular tea-clipper up the Spree river to satisfy the guest's needs; then five minutes had been lost in descriptions of nineteenth-century trading vessels. It had stuck: from then, Charlton A. Reade Jnr was Clipper Reade. The name had had legs and had been accepted by the Americans out at their place in the Grunewald forest. He was Clipper Reade to all who met him, and his trademark was a vacuum flask in the leather bag he carried on his shoulder, which had hot water in it, a little plastic box of teabags and a Bakelite mug. The last time they'd met, Lawson had given him a present, gift wrapped, that he'd had sent from the shop at the museum in Greenwich, and he'd watched as it was opened, paper discarded, a cardboard container pulled apart and the mug with the tea-clipper on it, under full sail, had been revealed. Clipper Reade had smiled grimly at his *protégé* and his voice had had the pitch of pebbles under a boot, 'Don't ever get sentimental about friendships. Don't. Be your own man, and fuck the rest of them.' Most of his professional life had been governed by the teachings of Clipper Reade, an icon of the Agency.

'Right, I'm watching and observing and—'

'And you're talking, which you shouldn't be. You may scratch your bum or pick your nose if you have to, but don't talk. Just wait and watch.'

A man in a heavy windcheater, black, without a distinguishing logo, idled past them. Lawson had no eye contact with him, had no need to ... and he doubted that Davies had noticed him.

It was one of those City streets that the sun rarely penetrated. Too narrow, with too many high buildings lining it, this street had a built-in greyness. The old stonework on either side was stained dark from a near-century of fuel emissions. And it was empty. Wouldn't be empty in three-quarters of an hour when the City workers spilled out of the doors, came to smoke or buy a sandwich or elbow into the wine bars, but the time for the exodus had not yet come.

Damn all to watch and precious nothing to observe. Yes, there was the newspaper-seller with his small portable stall, and a van had drawn up,

dumped an early-edition bundle on the pavement,
then sped off, and a man in a black anorak, who
wore a fleece under it and had its hood up, had
bought a copy and was now leaning against a wall,
studying the pages intently – wouldn't have been
the stock-market indices but the dogs running that
night at Catford or the horses that afternoon, wherever . . . But his attention was on a dark doorway
that hardly showed in the street's shadow and
which was on the far side from the newspaper stall
and the guy who examined runners. A commissionaire, in uniform, with old medal ribbons,
had come out of that door briefly and smoked half
of a rolled fag, then pinched it out, replaced what
was left in a tin box and retreated back inside.

Luke Davies – because the awkward, rude
bastard had starved him of information – did not
know how long he would be left stuck on the pavement like a scarecrow in a field. Another
three-quarters of an hour and the workers would
be flushed out of the buildings, and he reckoned it
a fair chance that a hand would clamp on his
shoulder and he'd hear, 'Hello, Luke, how're you
doing?' and he'd be confronted with someone who
had been at East European and Slavonic Studies
or had sat the civil-service entry papers with
him or the Foreign and Commonwealth exam. 'Did
you stay in? I didn't. This is where the money is.
Afraid the money was where I went – but good to
see you.' At least there would be no one from
school. A comprehensive sink school in Sheffield
did not supply ambitious recruits to the City, and
those of his year were on building sites, driving
white vans, or squaddies in some God-forsaken
desert. If money had been Luke Davies's target he
would not have been a civil servant, a junior officer

125

in the Secret Intelligence Service and living in Camden Town in what was little more than a student bed-sit. He shared a terrace house with two teachers, a junior at Revenue & Customs, a trainee Tesco manager and a guy from the Probation Service, and didn't see much of them. He heard a sharp hiss of breath behind him. God's.

Funny thing, he hadn't seen the black Audi saloon with the smoked windows come towards them on the street, then pull in outside that office door, flush up to the pavement and over double yellow lines – and hadn't seen the man in the black windcheater with the hood up abandon his study of the horses' form, and drift forward. Had seen damn all. Blinked, looked around. They hadn't been in the street when the car had arrived. Their call had come, directing them to the location, after the car's passenger had been dropped, and then the Audi must have headed away to find a place to wait until telephoned for the pick-up. He recognized the driver, who came round the back of the car, opened the rear door and left it ajar. The engine was running.

In Luke Davies's ear: 'Don't bloody move. Move and I'll kick you.'

He recognized the driver from the photograph in the file he had been shown that morning. Then he saw that the black windcheater was in the next doorway and had the newspaper half across his face, but it was held in only one hand and the other was deep in a pocket.

Grigori came out first from the plate-glass inner door, crossed the pavement, stood at the Audi's rear door and held it wide open. Carrick had done a crash bodyguard course, two weeks' residential from people who specialized in the private-sector market, and it had cost SCD10 more than two thousand of their budget. He thought then that Grigori would have failed the course, was listless and bored and didn't do the drills. He had his head down, as if he was examining the shine of his shoes.

The Bossman followed, came through the door, then hesitated, maybe said something to whoever had escorted him down to the building's lobby, as if it was a final exchange in whatever business had been done. Carrick was at the driver's door, had only to drop into the seat, do the gears and they'd be moving. The Bossman was on the pavement, but still talking . . . then coming for the car.

Carrick saw the man, black against the grey stonework, emerge from the next doorway, and he wasn't right. He was dressed casual and shabby, a layabout's gear, and had a wino's stubble where the cheeks and chin were not hidden by the hood, but he moved lightly on his feet, as if in an athlete's dance, and closed on his Bossman.

Damn, damn – fuck – Carrick saw the pistol in the man's hand. Short, stubby, a black barrel, same as the sleeve of the windcheater. Tried to shout and hadn't a voice.

The arm came up, the pistol raised. The Bossman saw the man, gaped. Carrick came from the car. Where was the lump – where was fucking Grigori? Saw Grigori, saw him cringing. Saw Grigori pressed back against the car body, and his hands were up at his mouth; he heard Grigori's shrill little cry. The pistol wavered in its aim.

Carrick charged. No thoughts in his mind. He made no evaluation. Went on instinct. Ran. Carrick came round the car's bonnet, half tripped on the kerb and launched. Was brain-empty. As he hit the man, shoulder against stomach, he heard the first shot fired.

Was deafened, couldn't hear. He might have shouted, might not. The second shot was fired and his head was a few centimetres from the barrel. Realized then that he wasn't the target, that his Bossman was.

The man went down. They were on the pavement together. A first sensation, Carrick smelled cordite, sharp, from the pistol and fast food, chilli, on the breath. He heard the grunt, and knew it was an older man because the stubble was greying, pepperpot colours.

Turned him over halfway, fists grabbing the windcheater, then smashed his right knee up into the man's groin. Did it hard, and heard the gasp. Heard the clatter as the pistol was dropped. Dared to look away, raked a glance, and saw Grigori still frozen, the Bossman on his knees, his hands over his head, in the middle of the pavement.

One hand holding the windcheater, the other clenched. Punched a short-arm jab into the man's face and felt the impact of his knuckles on the nose bone. Carrick scrabbled with his leg. The pistol went off the pavement, skidding across the slabs, and disappeared under the Audi.

He pushed himself up. The man groaned. His hands were over his privates, and he seemed to sing out his breath.

Carrick wasn't a policeman. He was in the employ of Josef Goldmann. The play-act had been automatic. He lifted the Bossman up, held him almost as if he was a child, shifted him, legs trailing, to the car, and threw him inside and slammed the door. Was at Grigori's side, had a fist in his jacket, by the neck, and flung him into the front passenger seat.

He ran to the driver's door, dropped inside. Went into gear, surged, felt the slight bump and knew they'd gone over the pistol in the gutter. Realized that Grigori hadn't closed his door, reached across and shut it.

Carrick drove away.

At the end of the street, alert from the adrenaline rush, his eyes went up to the mirror. He was ready for a following car, for a second stage in the attack, but he saw the man crawling on the pavement and then it looked as if he put two things, Carrick didn't know what, into his pocket. Then he was in the gutter where the pistol had been, then shambling away. He swung his eyes down, saw the street junction clear and powered right.

His heart pounded. His arms were leaden and he clung to the wheel. He felt the Bossman's fingers on his jacket and on his flesh, as if he was reassurance, but he couldn't hear what his Bossman tried to say.

He drove away from the City. Beside him, Grigori trembled and was ashen pale. Behind him the fist held his jacket and would not release him.

It had all been reflex, and Carrick could not have explained it.

The street was empty except for the newspaper-seller. Then the commissionaire came down the same steps, stood on the same pavement, opened his tin, took out the rest of the cigarette and lit it, puffed, dropped it and ground it out where two men had struggled, then kicked it over the kerb.

It was as if, Luke Davies thought, *nothing* had happened. He could make no sense of it. There were no gawpers at upper windows, no crowds gathering and no sound of sirens. A woman had appeared, he did not know from where, and bought a newspaper. A delivery lorry had pulled up and was unloading and had its hazard lights flashing. The man in the black windcheater and the hood had disappeared from the far end of the street. He was trained to retain in his mind, with clarity, what he had seen, but he doubted himself.

He heard the snigger, then: 'Come on, the show's over.'

'Excuse me, *Mr* Lawson . . . At the risk of sounding a complete idiot, did I see an armed attack on Josef Goldmann? Did I see Carrick?'

'No names – highly unprofessional to use names. He's November.'

'Did I see Carrick fight off an assassin?'

'I told you to observe. It's all a matter of perception.'

'And I did observe, and would have run to help him if you hadn't stopped me.' His arm had been held in a vice grip, more strength in it than he would have reckoned on Lawson's having.

'If you had broken free of me I'd have kicked you – as I promised – and you wouldn't have walked for a week.'

'What did I see?'

'Decide for yourself. I don't do twenty-four seven nannying.'

Lawson had gone, walked away, and Luke Davies had to skip along to catch him. Confusion reigned because he didn't know what he'd seen – what should have been clear was misted.

'Without him I was dead. I have no doubt of it – dead.'

In short, darting steps, Josef Goldmann paced the salon carpet. His wife watched him and knew better than to interrupt at a crisis moment.

'You see it, your life – it's as they tell you – at that one moment. You're about to go to Heaven, Hell, wherever one goes, and you see your life. It's extraordinary that you see so much. I was in Perm, in Moscow, I was with you, with the children. All of it went by me when I was low on the pavement and I was looking at a pistol and its aim was coming down to the line of my head. I could see the finger on the trigger. Believe me, the finger on the trigger was white from the pressure. The whiter the skin, the greater the pressure. The greater the pressure, the sooner he shoots, and I am dead – but Johnny hit him.'

He babbled, was incoherent, and dabbed his forehead with a handkerchief to clear off the sweat from the fear he had felt. The profits of violence had never come close enough to touch him before.

'Do I understand that I have enemies? Of course. Understand that you, loved one, or the children should be targets? Of course. I never quite understood that I could be shot – kidnapped for ransom, yes, but not killed like a stray dog, put down in the street – and it was so close. A half-second more . . . He came like a lion.'

He stopped abruptly, thought his legs would no longer support him, slumped into a chair. Many times in the past, in Perm and in Moscow, he had reported to Reuven that a client had defaulted on payment or used fraudulent bank drafts in settlement of debt and in two days, three, a week, the photograph would be in the paper of a body splayed out among bloodstains, of a car destroyed by explosives, of a petrol drum with a man's legs protruding as it was winched from a river. But he, the launderer, had almost – in London – believed himself immune from danger.

'Last evening we were among sophisticates. This morning I was with men who deal in money, have villas, play tennis, have . . . Then I am dead, but for Johnny. I tell you, I wasn't brave, I cowered and waited for the shot. Almost I was screaming for him to hurry, to end the agony. Grigori, useless imbecile, has legs of lead – he didn't move. I think he was crying, and he's supposed to protect me! Johnny did that. From this moment, this very moment, I tell you that I'll go nowhere without Johnny. Johnny beside me, in front and behind me. He will be with me.'

He leaned forward, reached across the coffee-table, the fashion magazines and hospitality brochures for Henley and Ascot, took his wife's hand and held it tight.

'Would Viktor have done better? Would Reuven's man, Mikhail? I doubt it. When Reuven was shot, Mikhail killed the man, but it was *after* Reuven was hit. Johnny dedicated himself to me, me. I am only his employer, not of his blood. He might have been shot himself. I asked him, in the car, why he had – almost – sacrificed himself to protect me. He said, very simply, "It's what I'm paid to do, *sir*." That's the man he is. Incredible. I owe him my life.'

She bent her head and kissed his hand.

'He will go everywhere with me. *Everywhere*. He goes with me tomorrow.'

Chapter 5: 10 April 2008

'Mrs Goldmann requires to see you upstairs,' Viktor said.

He couldn't read Viktor, impassive, unemotional and masked. Grigori was different. Grigori had sat in the ready room all afternoon, and hadn't spoken, just sat with sullen, blurred, glazed eyes focused on the middle distance. He seemed to see and note nothing. Grigori did not have to speak to betray his feelings. Grigori was a failure and Carrick assumed he was spoiled goods, would be replaced at a time of convenience, never again trusted. The older and more senior man, Viktor, had been closeted with the Bossman and the Bossman's wife upstairs, and Carrick assumed the crisis would have been thrashed out. Sitting in the ready room off the kitchen, with Grigori not speaking to him, Carrick had calmed, had lost the knots in his arm muscles and the slackness at his chin, had felt strong enough to get the kids from school.

He pushed himself up from the chair. 'Yes, of course.'

Viktor held the door open for him. It was not a gesture of respect but an indication that the summons was immediate. Two things had happened, and he understood neither. Simon Rawlings should have been at the wheel of the Audi going into the City; had been removed on a drink-driving charge, but did not use alcohol. An armed attack had taken place, an attempt to kill: nothing in the atmosphere of the household or from the body language of his employer had shown him to be fearful of a killing strike.

He went up the main staircase, with its gold-leaf paint, with the softly lit pictures at eye level. He paused to rub hard with the heel of his hand at the stain on his knee from the pavement, then at the smear on his elbow.

When he had come off the training course, had won his admittance to SCD10, Carrick had been told: 'We think we're going to like what we're getting from you. What we appreciate most is that you're not painted over with police procedures – you are still, at heart, a squaddie. We reckon you behave more in the old military characteristics than police stereotypes. It's a good legend you have, the paratroop background, and it's checkable. We can use you as a contract hit guy, as a muscle doorman and as protection. It'll go fine. Welcome to the team.' The controller, George, had been allocated to run him, Rob had been the cover officer on his first job and Katie sorted out the office. Katie had told him, shouldn't have, that his first rating had had a handwritten paragraph in the margin: '. . . has common sense, is down to earth, above all has bottle'. On his first job, he had been assigned to a team of north London detectives, with club owners as a target.

Ahead of him, Viktor knocked at the door, didn't wait for an answer, and opened it. He saw the family on the settee. Josef Goldmann had Peter sitting astride his knees and Esther Goldmann had Selma cuddled close to her. He was ushered forward.

The club owners were Jed and Baz – brothers. They had a place off Green Lanes, in Haringey, had made an alliance with the Turks there, and were careful, clever and did Class A stuff. A Chis had done the digging to get him in. The Chis was a Covert Human Intelligence Source, a low-life rag, and he'd made introductions, then been paid to fuck off up north, and was looking at a tenner inside if he reneged on the deal.

For seven months, Carrick had been on the door and inside, but he'd taken a night off when the uniforms did the raid. Wasn't there to rubberneck, and enough Class A stuff was on the premises – as he'd said it would be, and where – for him not to be needed as a prosecution witness: that was about as good as it got. If an undercover could do the business, and not have to go into court and give evidence, it was big-bonus time. After the raid and the arrests, he'd had one drink with the detectives, just the one, and he'd gone off into the night, leaving them to get well pissed up. They'd never know his name, only the bogus identity he'd assumed. They'd never see or hear of him again. About three months ago, he'd read in the evening paper that Jed and Baz had gone down for fifteen years each. Not bad blokes, actually, for company, quite amusing but over-greedy.

The Goldmanns were in shock. It was one thing for the family to have the trappings of protection, men in the house to drive them, scan pavements when they were dropped and open doors for them, another thing to have a snub-nose pistol waved in the face, and two shots fired before an aim could be drawn. The Bossman looked small against the cushions of the settee and the boy on his lap had his arms round his father's neck. The Bossman's wife sat upright, but had her arm close round the daughter. Not every day that a husband and father came home from work to report survival from a killing effort, but there again it wasn't everyone's husband and father who laundered big money out of eastern and central Europe.

The Bossman's wife said, 'We would like to thank you, Johnny.'

He, of course, collecting the kids had said nothing. He'd seen them into the hall, had watched them bolt upstairs, then gone down into the ready room. He wondered what they had said. 'Daddy's had a difficult day' didn't really do it. Esther gave her daughter a sharp nudge, as if something was planned, and the child came off the settee, skipped behind it and emerged with a big, like *big*, bouquet of flowers. More red roses than Carrick had ever seen in a bouquet. He didn't care who knew it, he liked the kids. George knew he liked them, and Rob. He saw awe on the child's face, as if she'd been told that this man had offered his own safety in the protection of her father, and there was sweetness and sincerity there, and she seemed to do a little bob curtsy, what she would have learned in a nine-year-old's dance class at a private school, and the flowers were given him, and he realized how great his fondness was for those children, with the gentle banter they gave him in the car and their innocence.

He blushed, felt the heat in his cheeks. No one had given Johnny Carrick flowers before. Esther Goldmann said, in a brittle voice, 'For you, with our thanks, Johnny. Perhaps you will pass them to someone precious to you.'

The flowers were in the crook of his arm. He assumed, always, that Esther was not the shrinking violet who knew nothing of her husband's trade, but it was the part she played. She took the children past him, past Viktor, through the door. He hadn't realized that Viktor was there – silent, watching, arms folded across his chest.

Josef Goldmann sat upright now, as if energized, the haggardness of his face gone, and said briskly, 'I am, Johnny, a businessman who buys and sells, who trades on his expertise, who is successful and therefore attracts envy. I am also an immigrant to your country, and I am a Jew . . . I do not seek to attract attention. You will be surprised that I have not contacted the police and reported this attempted murder. It is not, Johnny, in my interests to parade myself. Neither is it in the interests of Esther or our children. My work involves discretion and would be harmed if I were to be written about in sensational terms in newspapers. The police have not been told of what happened, or of your heroic defence of me. Is that understood?'

'Yes, sir.'

'Do you have, Johnny, a problem with my attitude to the police and my wish to avoid the spotlight of publicity?'

'No problem, sir.'

'That street, I have learned this in the past from those I visit there – in casual conversation – is not covered by security cameras, one of the few in the City. This afternoon Viktor went there, met the newspaper-seller, who assured him he had seen nothing of what happened. Does that, Johnny, make a difficulty for you?'

'No difficulty, sir.' Carrick wondered how much money had been passed, and whether the seller had now abandoned his pitch and retired to a bar to consider his good fortune.

'You are recovered from this morning?'

'Quite recovered, sir.' He could look back, could try to piece together each moment of the confrontation. He could feel in his knee the jarred blow into the man's groin and could feel in his fist a rawness from the punch to the bridge of the man's nose.

'You will be rewarded for what you have done today – and I hope you will feel that the reward is generous – and your terms of employment will be reviewed. In the future, Johnny, I want you close to me.'

'Whatever you say, sir.'

'You have, of course, a valid passport?'

'Yes, sir.'

'With Viktor, I travel abroad tomorrow. You have a family occasion tonight, yes? You should be here by seven in the morning, and you go with us. You will be away for perhaps a week. Johnny, the events of this morning have gone by and will not again be referred to. I have avenues that I will use to learn who was responsible for the attack on me, and I will use them. Thank you, Johnny, and I will see you in the morning.'

Not asked whether it was convenient, not asked whether it suited his plans, but Carrick did not expect to be asked. He realized he had stepped higher up a ladder, that luck and good fortune had pushed him there. Felt, almost, a pride in the trust now placed in him.

He nodded, turned. Viktor opened the door for him.

He watched. Josef Goldmann stood back from the window but his finger hitched aside the net curtain.

He saw Johnny Carrick go down the steps from the front door.

He asked of Viktor, 'Is the trust justified?'

'You said that two shots were fired, and Grigori says so too. He did not stop, think and debate. He acted. Grigori's reaction, to freeze, was the more normal in close protection when an attack is made. He did not.'

'Which tells you?'

He heard a slight chuckle, but it had no humour. 'Perhaps that he lacks intelligence or imagination, and that he was a soldier. Only a corporal – with intelligence and imagination he would have been an officer. He can be given limited trust.'

Josef Goldmann saw his saviour pause on the step and against the grey of his suit was the great bundle of roses he held to his chest. Then his man walked away at a fast pace.

'What I like about him is that he is limited in what he looks to know of us. Like a machine, robotic. He asks no questions. I do not see him listening. Neither is he where I do not expect to find him in the house. He gives me no surprises. Yes, limited trust.'

Now the chuckle had faint, grim humour. 'If you take him you will expose him to Reuven. To win Reuven's trust, as much trust as can be held between thumb and forefinger, a pinch of trust, that will be harder for him. Perhaps he will be turned out on to the street and sent home.'

The pavement was clear, and the brightness of the flowers gone.

'If you had been there, Viktor, and had seen what I saw, you would understand my trust in him.'

* * *

He was in the outer office, sharing the woman's workbench. She did not speak to him, but nothing, any longer, surprised Luke Davies.

The file contained sheets of paper, every one a printout. He could have challenged her, could have said that he had, until that afternoon, been unaware that the Stone Age was alive and well at Vauxhall Bridge Cross, but he'd noted the sharp darts of her glances at him while he scanned the pages, and reckoned her defensive. He had not heard of any other floor, corner or cranny of the building where paper still existed. If he had challenged he believed he would have embarrassed her and won an evasive reply, something about *Mr* Lawson's preferences.

He'd been back to his old territory, Russia Desk (Baltic), had endured a volley of quips. He'd told them to wrap it, belt up, get lost, and then he'd had to laugh. He'd hacked into his computer and downloaded maps. They were now on his desk.

Fastening the map sheets together with Sellotape, he'd made an extended montage that went from London in the west to the city of Sarov in the east. And her ruler had been within reach.

The lines made a pattern, were as concise as a web left by spiders on a morning when hoar frost had formed. Had to admit that the pattern made a shape . . . and he had read about Sarov, home of St Seraphim, who had been canonized by the Orthodox church in 1903, and about Arzamas-16, home of the team that had built Joe One, the first of their tested atomic weapons, and Joe Four, the first of their tested hydrogen warheads. Lines on his map were traced between Sarov and London, to Colchester in Essex, to the east of Poland and Berlin. More lines ran to the Gulf. His

pleasure, at understanding gained, was stabbed.
'What's that?'

Must have looked like a startled rabbit: spun on his chair, thwacked his knee against the bench edge, hadn't heard the entry. Hated himself for it, but stammered, 'It's to show the linkage of the calls.'

'I know what the linkage is.'

Feebly, 'I thought it might help.'

'How can it help me to understand what I already know? Do you think we're children and idiots? Waste of time. What's not a waste of time is that we have a name. I had it last night, and for the agent, but the DG's sanctioned it. You know, there are some people here, modernists and work-makers, who sit on a committee that thinks up operational codenames. True. You can't credit it. All damn Greek stuff, mythology and that self-serving military nonsense, "Shock and Awe". The DG, and I'm not arguing, said I was thin on facts, and that if I was right I'd be looking for a . . .'

He paused theatrically.

Davies said, 'You'd be looking for a *needle* . . .'

'So we have an "N", which is tidy. The agent is the needle, is the "N", is November. Where is the needle?'

'In a bloody haystack.'

'Language, please.' He was chastised but then – rarer than winter sunshine in Sheffield – God smiled. 'That's our operational title.'

And Lawson reached across him, almost elbowed him, took up a thick marker pen from a tray in front of the woman, and scrawled across the face of the cardboard file Davies was reading the one word 'HAYSTACK'. Then he seemed to do a little jig, one foot to the other, as if the name excited him, as if, with it, they were launched.

141

Luke Davies asked, so softly: 'Will it be that difficult to find, even with November, a "needle in a haystack"? Will it?'

Lawson said, 'Yes, it will be that difficult, if it exists.'

Nothing said between them for four hours.

It irritated Yashkin. He was better able to concentrate on the road, but the quiet of his passenger, the navigator, annoyed him. And nothing said when they were at a road junction, only a gesture of the hand – right or left or straight ahead. On each hour, he steadied himself to ask the direct question. He had put it, he thought, with sufficient force beside the river at Murom, and had not been answered.

He was tired, had driven more than three hundred kilometres, always on the back roads. He was hungry, had eaten nothing cooked, only a sliced-meat sandwich from a stall in a village. He was thirsty, only one coffee in the middle of the day. He was a security officer by training, not a *zampolit*, but Oleg Yashkin, retired major of the 12th Directorate, had the talent to realize that the question must be confronted. The retired political officer must answer it.

A signpost showed up in the gloom: twenty more kilometres to Kolomna. Better it was settled now, dealt with. Yashkin thought the political officer would have been more skilled in probing for an answer, more polished, able to extract a tooth without pain. Too little time left on that day's leg for it to be put off any longer.

'I have to know it, your answer . . . Do you *regret* it?'

'Honestly?'

'Yes. Do you regret what we've done?'

'A little, yes. When you talked about it, described it, I thought then, does this thing, the Zhukov, which you sleep against, which you say has warmth, does it work? Is it effective? No, no, another time, not now. Some of me regrets it.'

Yashkin said, 'In half an hour we'll be in Kolomna. In Kolomna there are trains and buses. You can go home. There, you can lean over the fence, near to where the hole was excavated, and you can tell Mother that her man is crazy, a lunatic, without a brain in his head.'

'And you?'

'I'll go on alone to the Bug. I'll stop when I'm at the river.'

'Why?'

Yashkin said, 'I can tell you each word used at my dismissal. I can tell you about each minute I spent in my office on my last day, and each step of my last walk from my office to the car, with no gratitude offered me. I can tell you about near-starvation through winters when my pension was not paid, the hunger, and about driving drunks, addicts, those diseased creatures in my car, of scavenging for charity rates in the market, and of selling for a pittance what little Mother and I had that was precious to us. Whatever happens, I'll go on to the Bug river.'

'Fuck you again, Yashkin. Alone, you wouldn't find it.'

'I would – and when you've gone, I *will* find it.'

'I doubt – fuck you again and again – you'd find Belarus. I see you driving in circles inside Ukraine, or perhaps still inside our glorious country. I couldn't.'

'A political officer may speak in riddles, but a

security officer hasn't the education to understand. What does "I couldn't" mean?'

'I couldn't, Yashkin – you are my friend and a fucking idiot – leave you to get lost, which you would. Without me, my knowledge of the maps, you're lost.'

'Where, then, is *regret*?'

The voice beside him dropped, was a whisper, a murmur, and he had to lean towards the other man to hear. 'I don't ask, "Does it work?" because then I increase the guilt for what I'm doing, what you're doing ... Perhaps I believe it doesn't work, is harmless and of value only as a relic, which mitigates the guilt. And it isn't entirely to avenge myself, for what was done to you and me ... It's the money. I've dreamed of that money. I spend it again and again. Should I feel shame? I don't ... It's for the money. Fuck! We should have turned right.'

'Molenkov, you talk too much.'

'I've forgotten the regret.'

'You talk too much so you missed the turning.'

The Polonez was reversed, then put into a three-point turn. The back wheels went up off the roadway, and a stone wedged under the chassis. The weight of the Zhukov was responsible, but Yashkin revved hard and cleared it.

He was coming into the town of Kolomna, and his eyelid flickered with exhaustion. To stay awake he had to talk.

'I read about this town. A population of one hundred and fifty thousand, at the last census, is resident here. The town was founded in the year 1177 and had strategic significance because the Moskva and Oka rivers merge there. It is important today as a rail junction.'

He yawned, his eyes closed and he felt the wheel go before he righted the Polonez. Traffic flowed round him and oncoming lights dazzled him.

'It matters not a fuck to me.'

At that moment, Yashkin was about to explain his need to talk – so tired, the strain caused by his belief that his friend regretted participating in the venture, or was a coward, or was afflicted by moral doubt, whichever was worse – and relief flooded him because, together, they would reach the Bug. There was a road junction as they approached the main bridge and too many headlights bouncing in his eyes.

He hit the car in front, a BMW 3 series, shining and new. The old rusted bumper of the Polonez hit a glancing blow to the metallic silver BMW. Glass spewed out from the tail-lights. Brakes screamed. A young man in a black leather jacket – the damned uniform of trouble – climbed out, saw the wreckage and his fist clenched.

Yashkin did not hesitate. From driving on minor roads all that day and the one before, mud would be plastered over his registration plates. He swung out. He thought he missed the young man by no more than half a metre, and he heard a fist thumped on the roof of the Polonez. As he turned, he saw that Molenkov gave the young man a finger. He sped off, drove like a madman in the traffic. He stopped as soon as he believed it safe, got out and bent to examine the plates. He reckoned it possible to read them, difficult but possible. Would the collision be reported to the police? Would they respond and look for a red Polonez that had left the scene of an accident?

They went through Kolomna, and on the far side of the citadel they found a decaying roadhouse, with the virtue of secure parking at the rear, and booked a room.

A minicab pulled up beside him.

Most of the drivers working that part of Dudley, in the West Midlands, were known to Sak, but he didn't recognize this driver.

The window was wound down. He was asked his name by the driver, whom Sak thought to be north African, perhaps from Algeria or Morocco. At the school where he worked as a laboratory technician he was Steven King. The name he gave to the minicab driver was Siddique Khatab.

'Repeat that.'

'Siddique Ahmed Khatab.'

'And your father's name?'

He gave it. The light was failing and the street was a crowded bustle of kids and parents surging away from the school's gates towards the estate. On the far side of the estate was the guesthouse his father and mother owned. It was used by sales representatives and lorry drivers on long hauls and those coming to the town for weddings or funerals. He understood the wariness of the approach, as careful as the message that had woken him: the arrests of the last two years had shown the futility of using telephones, analogue or digital, and email links. The driver accepted what he was told, grinned as if he enjoyed the sense of conspiracy, and reached into the glove compartment. An envelope was passed to Sak.

He took it, folded it quickly, thrust it into his hip pocket. He gulped. The minicab drove away. It would have seemed to any who hurried by him on the pavement that he had given a driver instructions on a destination.

Where there were longer shadows, and the crowds walking with him had thinned, Sak took out the envelope. He examined the tickets and the dates on them, returned them to their envelope and the envelope to his pocket.

There was a reason for him having been woken.

From university, in 1997, he had gone to work in the Atomic Weapons Research Establishment at Aldermaston. There, he was Steven Arthur King, BSc, involved in low-level work but it had interested him. He had felt a part of a great team involved in the far frontiers of science. He had lived in a hostel for single professional and qualified staff. He had revelled in it, had taken time to read in the library of the early giants of the laboratories and test-beds, and had felt he belonged to an élite. After five years, he was outside the main gate for the last time – no appeal permitted – his access card withdrawn.

On the train home, returning in ignominy to the West Midlands, he had dropped his head on to his arms and wept, such was the humiliation he felt.

The anger had been born.

A man came to the Portakabin where the Crow worked. The door was rapped. He opened it. A package was given him. He closed the door. He had not seen the courier's face, and was confident that once the man had left the site, under the huge crane, the entry pass given to him would be destroyed.

Inside the package he found airline tickets, a passport issued by a Canadian agency and a map of the rendezvous point where he would meet a brother and the criminals. There was a contact address for the *hawaldar* in the German city of

Hamburg. He would provide the funds to be paid to the criminals. He had no love of such people, but times were hard and survival ever harder.

Too many were now arrested, were in the gaols of the Americans. Too many networks had been broken into, too many plans, near to execution, had been disrupted. But this would be a great strike, the greatest, and the Crow's part in it – though small – was of prime importance. He must work and deal with criminals, pay them for what they delivered in American dollars supplied by the *hawaldar*, though they were *kaffirs*. It was necessary to buy from whoever could supply, even from unbelievers.

The hate in his heart was undiminished by the years that had gone by, was fresh and keen. He locked the package and its contents in his floor safe. To work with unbelievers – to achieve a great strike – was justified, as it was to buy from criminals.

He returned to his work and quantified how many tons of cement mix were needed for the coming week, but he would not be in Dubai to oversee its delivery. He would be with *mafiya* men whom he despised.

Reuven sat quietly in the shadows. This part of the warehouse was Mikhail's territory.

Back in Perm, in the early days, he and Mikhail had owned expensive pedigree dogs, two Rottweilers and a German Shepherd. They were vicious beasts and controlled only by Mikhail and him, but gentle with his grandmother. She could handle them and they slobbered at her whisper, all of them, but the dogs created terror. Reuven thought Mikhail more violent and more sadistically cruel than the dogs at their worst. When they had left Perm, moved to Moscow, he had asked his grandmother what should be done with the dogs, to whom they might be given. She had said, 'Shoot them. You want a dog, put a collar on Mikhail.' She had walked away and the dogs were not spoken of again, but she had stroked their heads, had bent her small head low so that they could lick her face, and she had condemned them.

Two weeks before, the chair had been taken by a Bulgarian who had tried to muscle into the Kurfürstendamm trade in girls. The stains were still on the concrete floor, with the dirt that had been thrown over the wet blood. Those who already ran strings of girls on the Kurfürstendamm paid for the protection of their businesses, and two weeks before, the competition had been removed. They would have thought their investment in a roof was money well spent, and they would have seen the reports in the *Morgenpost* newspaper and on television after the Bulgarian's body was discovered on the banks of the Tegeler See. Reuven had been away, reconnoitring the Bug river, but he had seen what Mikhail had done, and what his clients would have read and watched, and knew they would be satisfied.

In the chair now was an Albanian.

The Albanian, an immigrant from the Kosovo city of Priština, had tried to sell passports. Not good passports, inadequately forged ones, but they competed with those sold to non-European Union men who had come across frontiers to Germany and needed legitimacy, and who would pay ten thousand dollars for a passport, however poor. But Reuven Weissberg provided the roofs for a Russian and a Romanian who sold better passports. The day before he went to Poland he had visited the Albanian and had spoken calmly of the need for this man to transfer his business to Dresden, Rostock or Leipzig, anywhere other than Berlin, but the man had spat in his face.

That evening the Albanian was brought – having been lifted off the street when walking his daughter, the child abandoned to find her own way home – to the old warehouse in the Kreuzberg district between the canal and the Spree. Tied down in the chair, where the Bulgarian had been, the Albanian had again spat defiance, but then had seen what was his fate.

A cable brought the power from the wall. Among the multiple plugs at its end was the lead for a power drill. On a table beside the drill was a small chain-saw, a welding burner, lit, and a loaded pistol. A message was about to be sent to the two traders in passports who would read the *Morgenpost* and see the city news on television.

The chair was screwed down to the floor. The Albanian was tied fast to it. His shirt was pulled back and the marks of the flame disfigured his body. He was not gagged and not blindfolded. He could see what would be used on him next, and could scream, but no one came to that warehouse. It was as it had been in Perm, to enforce the roofs, and in Moscow . . . This, of course, was only minor business in the empire of Reuven Weissberg. He had links in Sicily and Milan; he could arrange protection for any American business looking to exploit the new wealth of Russia; he could transfer cash sums, suitcases and boxes of it, to London where it was handled by Josef Goldmann. But the small detail of insignificant contracts – the protection of men running girls or selling passports – excited him.

The screams expired in the dark steel joists high

above the Albanian. The purr of the drill was drowned by them. The needlepoint went for the kneecaps. He watched.

He had survived beatings as a conscript in the army, and a killing attempt when shot in the arm in Moscow. He knew pain, but not fear. In two years in the army, stationed at the Kaliningrad base, he had been thrashed by NCOs and officers for selling off military equipment pilfered from stores, and for organizing the shipment of Afghan heroin out through the docks, but he had never cried out. After the fourth beating he had cut his infantry colonel into a share of his profits, then been left free to trade. His ability to endure what was handed out to him, with boots and clubs, by the NCOs and officers had made Reuven Weissberg, the Jew, a hero among the conscripts. He had never howled for the pain to be stopped. Had he done so, he would have disgraced his grandmother.

It was enough. The Albanian was burned, his knees were pierced and he had fainted with the pain.

Mikhail shot him. Stood behind the chair, held the pistol and fired one bullet. He thought he heard the cry of geese. If the Albanian had not fainted, Mikhail might have started up the chain-saw. The geese squawked and the shot seemed a faint retort. Blood spattered the concrete floor and the plastic hooded cloak that Mikhail wore.

Then the silence came, and the geese did not call. Weissberg sat for a moment, then glanced at his wristwatch. He told Mikhail they must hurry or be late. A body was to be moved, taken to open ground by the Teltow canal, and the plastic clothing disposed of, the chain-saw, the drill and the welding burner put away in the concealed safe.

151

The warehouse was returned to the pigeons that nested on its roof beams. He and Mikhail worked fast, then dragged the body away, leaving a thin smear of blood across the concrete.

I learned it, every detail. I could have walked each step of it. I knew how long it took from beginning to end.

The women on the bunks at either side of me, level with me, in the barracks said I had no right to ignorance. I think they were jealous that it had protected me and not them. I was told what happened.

They came by train. If they were Polish Jews or Jews from the east, they expected to be murdered so they were controlled with extreme violence. They were so terrorized that they had no idea of how to resist, and they were exhausted from their journey. From the Germans, there was no pretence of a new life awaiting those Jews. It was different for those who came from the west, from Holland or France.

The western Jews, and there might be a thousand in the train transport, were greeted with deceit. Often they came in the best carriages with upholstered seats, had brought luggage with them and wore their best clothes. They came to this small station in the centre of a forest and had no idea where they were, or what awaited them. Their carriages were detached from the engine, then shunted to the siding. From the windows they saw flowers in pots, an orchestra played, and young Jews, who were dressed in railway uniforms, waited on the platform. They were helped down from the train and their heavy bags lifted for them.

They were escorted first to a building where they were asked – it is correct, asked – to leave their luggage, and ladies' bags. Then they went through the gate into Camp 2. When that gate closed behind them, they were dead, but they did not yet know it. They were separated, man from woman, but the children stayed with the women. And they were moved on to a covered but open area. Already the bags were being searched for valuables and money by the Pakettentragers, Jewish men who could do this work and live a week or a month longer. The Jews from the train were now addressed by SS Scharführer Hermann Michel: not an old man, a little more than thirty, with a smooth face, a baby's. From a low balcony, he would say that he was sorry about the hardship of the journey from Holland or France, that he welcomed them, that because of extraordinary sanitary conditions at this transit camp – their home only for a short while before they moved to settlements in the east – everyone must be washed and disinfected. Then he would tell them in glowing words of the life that awaited them after they rejoined their men or women. He spoke so sympathetically, was so pleasant, that often at the end he was applauded.

An officer in a white jacket, appearing to be a doctor, then led these west European Jews into the yard and requested they undress. There were Ukrainian guards with guns, and the Germans with whips, but still the deception succeeded and the Jews retained their innocence. They undressed. It might be snowing or raining, or the sun shining, they might be young or old, with perfect bodies or ugly ones, but they had to undress to complete nakedness. They were led into the Tube.

The Germans called it the Himmelfahrtstrasse, that is the Road to Heaven, the Heavenly Way. It was about a hundred and fifty metres to the far gate, and the surface of the track was sand, and wide enough for three to walk abreast, and they could not see what was beyond the Tube because of the pine branches placed in the wire. Guards were behind them to hurry them, and 'the doctor' led at a brisk pace. Before they reached the end they came to the Barbers' House. Here, the hair of the women was cut short – but the men were led straight past it. A few more yards and there was one more gate.

The officer, the 'doctor', worked now with great skill. He would make jokes, and talk, and then, abruptly, this gate was opened, and beyond it were the doors of the chambers that awaited them, and the sign above them was 'Bathhouse'. They were pressed in, forced close. The chambers were four metres long and four metres wide, and they put many more than a hundred people in each. Six chambers could contain a thousand souls. Then the doors were shut.

Now, they did not have to be Polish, Ukrainian or Belarussian Jews to know the deception: the French and Dutch Jews, too, understood . . . By now the next train transport would have arrived at the station platform, the orchestra would be playing, the jewellery and money was gone from the bags, and the clothes moved to sorting sheds – it was a production line.

Many would sing in the last moment before the engine was switched on. Schma Israel! Adonai Elohaynu! Adonai Ehad. The voices would rise. 'Hear, O Israel! The Lord is good! The Lord is One.' The engine killed the noise.

A German, Erich Bauer, was responsible for the good functioning of the engine, which had been stripped from a heavy Russian lorry. He was the Gasmeister, and his assistant was a Ukrainian, Emil Kostenko. Only once did I hear that the engine failed and the Jews were in the chambers for four hours before it was repaired. Then they were gassed with the carbon monoxide that was piped from the engine's exhaust into the six chambers. There would be great screaming, but the engine and the walls made it seem like the rumble of artillery guns, and a Jew was always in place to chase after the geese and make them squawk. They sang, in the last moments of their lives, 'God, my God, why have You forsaken me?'

154

The engine of the Gasmeister and his assistant could kill a thousand men and women and children in twenty minutes.

When the engine was switched off, the geese were left to run free and there was silence in the chambers, the far-end doors were opened and a Jewish Kommando started work to clear out the bodies and make the chambers available for the next transport – perhaps already listening to sweet words of reassurance or stripping naked or walking along the Tube. Most of the bodies still stood because there was not room for them to fall when they died.

Twenty minutes, crushed in the chambers, to die. Two hours from the shunting of a train to the opening of wide doors and the escape of the poison.

Once, naked women fought the Germans and Ukrainians in the Tube and were machine-gunned. Those who lived were driven at bayonet point into the chambers.

Once, an old Jew threw sand from the Tube into the face of a German and told him that his Reich would vanish as dust and smoke. He was shot dead.

Most went to their deaths in ignorance or terror. Few had the opportunity or the strength of will to fight ... We did. We who lived and serviced the camp and knew its purpose, and knew our own fate when our usefulness was exhausted, demanded to live – and did not know how to achieve it. If we had not wanted to survive, clung to life, worked in the camp, Sobibor could not have existed. We, the living, enabled it to function.

I knew. I had lost the protection of innocence and ignorance. I wanted to live.

The darkness was over the forest. Tadeuz Komiski sat by a grave. The place where he had dug it, beside which trees, the distance from his home, was his secret.

The summer of 2004, four years ago, had been spoken of on the radio as the worst in a half-century. Torrential rain had caused the Bug to break its banks, fields to flood, tracks to be blocked and the roots of trees to be washed away. A grave had been opened and a skeleton exposed. The layers of needles, composted leaves and shallow sand had shifted under the incessant rain.

He remembered the young man and the woman. The bones still wore the uniform of the camp. He had moved the remains. The uniform had disintegrated and the bones had come apart, but he had tried to do it with dignity. He had dug a new grave, deeper than she could have, with his long-handled spade. His life was cursed by this man, but he had buried him again and had mumbled a prayer before filling in the earth.

If it had not been for his fear of watchers in the forest, as there had been the day before, he would have put posies of wild flowers on this spot. He could not. They would be seen. A crime would be uncovered.

He knew of no one else who lived under such a curse, with such guilt.

Alone, Tadeuz Komiski watched the grave.

He picked blackberries. Little Jonathan. Ignored by his grandparents and left to roam while his mother was at work in the food factory. Below him, in mid-stream and on a spur of submerged rocks, an angler wielded a great salmon rod and cast a many-coloured fly, with big hackles, towards the top of a wide pool. He picked the fruit and dropped the berries into a plastic bowl.

He was not asleep, but dozed. Sometimes he was the child who heard the thin cry of the osprey over the Spey near its mouth. Sometimes he was the man and there was the clatter of ducks on the river outside the narrowboat's hull. He was too tired to sleep.

Only in a few early autumns had there been enough sunshine to bring on the blackberries in the last days before term started. He might have been eight or nine, but he remembered everything of that afternoon, and he had searched the banks for the bramble clumps among the gorse on the banks.

The narrowboat was the *Summer Queen* and she was moored at another bank, of another river, was held by two ropes and two iron pins hammered into the grass. He had been there three hours, and Katie had been waiting for him. She had cooked for him but he had only toyed with the food and he knew she had expected to get into bed with him, but he had pleaded exhaustion so she'd left him. Still dressed, his shoes kicked off, he had stretched out on the bed. In his mind was his weakness that evening. He had left the house, had walked away down the street with the family's bouquet in his arms, had turned the corner – only reached it by extreme willpower – and had known he was out of their sight, and had damn near collapsed against an iron railing. He had realized how weakened he was. He had leaned on the railings and shivered.

The child, Jonathan, picked and filled the bowl. The little cry of excitement from the river, an arching rod, then the silver flash in the water as the fish was brought to the net. He had seen that, and its clean execution with a hammer blow to the head. A tear had welled at the killing of the fish but he had wiped it away. The fish's death was not important. It was not why he recalled that afternoon above the Spey.

If he had not recaptured a moment of his youth, Carrick would have been overwhelmed by the suddenness of the gunfire in the street and by the long stress of living the lie. He would have seen again the family's gratitude, the perfect brilliance of the flowers given him. It had taken a toll of him, he recognized. By now he should have written up the Book: it was obligatory for an undercover level one to take the first secure opportunity to write up the Book in which all matters of potential evidence and interest were listed. The Book was too sensitive an item for him to keep. Katie had brought it. He should have written up the events of the last several days – the routine, the confusion over the arrest of Simon Rawlings and his own promotion on the household's ladder, the chaos of gunfire in a City street, major material, and the promise of Josef Goldmann that Johnny would, in future, be at his side. It should all have been in the Book, but it was not.

Why did a grown man remember seeing a salmon killed, and picking a full bowl of blackberries? He had gone home to the bungalow, let himself in quietly, had put the brimming bowl beside the sink, had not told his grandparents of what he had done – or of the killing of something as beautiful as the salmon – and had gone to his room. He had waited there for praise and thanks. He had heard his mother return from the factory, had heard her in the kitchen, then her trill of pleasure, and she had gone to the sitting room to thank her parents for picking the blackberries – had never thought it might have been him. They had accepted her thanks, had not disclaimed them. A pretty small matter in the life of a child, the denial of gratitude for picking a bowl of blackberries, but it had cut him off from the adults who had reared him – a never-forgotten memory, never erased. He had thought then, as a child, he could live alone and without company.

And he was alone. Katie had abandoned him. She was in the sitting area, waiting for them to come. He was alone and suffering: she knew it, no one else in the team did. Quite deliberately, Carrick hit his forehead against the varnished planks beside the pillow, as if that would clear bloody melancholy. He pushed himself up, shook his head hard, as if that would expel demons. The *Summer Queen* was owned by Katie's parents, and through the months of August and September they would take extended leave from work and navigate at snail's pace through the networks of canals in the South and West Midlands. For the rest of the year it was available to Katie and she used it as a safe-house where an officer, in deep cover, could come to be debriefed, write up his Book and crash out from his stress. Every month, for a weekend, her parents would come to the *Summer Queen*, get the old Ford Escort engine coughing and alive, then move her to another branch of a canal or to the Thames. It was good, and secure, and no pattern of its movements existed.

Most times when they came to the narrowboat, they had sex on the bed – not wonderful but good and adequate – and they'd roll away, feeling the better for it. Not that evening. When he'd turned her down, with her blouse nearly unbuttoned, her shoes off and the zip on her skirt undone, he'd glimpsed her hurt, and had twisted to face the varnished wood and the porthole window. Most times, when George and Rob came, she had to scamper after their warning shout to get herself half decent for them. Always the Book was written up before they went down on to the bed. It was bad that he'd hurt her, but the gunfire was still in his head, and he lived with greater deception. All the guys in the SCD10 team had bad days when they screamed to be let free. Rob understood, and George, and they soothed the scratches. God . . . God . . . There was a whistle from the field.

Rob's voice: 'You there, Katie?'

A torchbeam scudded past the porthole. Maybe it was what they all needed, an ego massage. Rob, the cover officer, was expert at lifting the bloody dark clouds of an undercover's doubts. George, the controller, could lift a level one's self-esteem. Carrick wasn't the first, wouldn't be the last, to need them. He cursed himself that he had wounded Katie, had treated her like a tart.

'I'm here. Come aboard.'

Then George's voice, 'Half Oxfordshire's bloody cattle seem to be in this field, and I've walked in three heaps of their shit. What's wrong with the marina?'

'Marina's full. Exercise does you good, sir.'

He had never worked alongside Katie on a plot. She'd had two runs as an undercover. She'd played at being a prostitute in an investigation of the call-girl trade in the Kings Cross area of London, had had her face scratched by rivals for the pitch, and had learned to accept volleys of abuse each time she found an excuse not to get into a punter's car. Armed back-up had never been more than a hundred yards down the street. She had played the role of an undercover's girlfriend up in Manchester, tracking the import of Croatian firearms, to give the officer his get-out excuse for refusing to screw girls and drink all night. She'd given evidence in the Manchester case, at the Crown Court, and it was thought she was compromised. She hadn't wanted to go back to uniform routines and had been taken on as a desk worker in the Pimlico office George used. Carrick thought her the best girl he'd known – natural, easy, without ceremony, honest and, most of all, with a bucketful of loyalty – and that evening he'd failed her. He swung his legs off the bed.

And heard a voice he didn't know: 'Don't mind me saying it, but a pretty stupid place to choose. I wouldn't have.'

Feet hit the deck, then the steps down. Carrick smoothed his hair, tucked his shirt into the waist of his trousers, pushed on his shoes and knotted the laces.

Rob's voice, chuckling: 'Nice flowers, Katie – rather grander than my lady's used to.'

'He brought them.'

George's voice, serious: 'In my experience, the more lavish the expenditure on flowers, the more abject the apology it's intended to cover. You got a problem with him?'

'Just that he's knackered, hasn't talked much. It's the biggest armful I've ever had.'

The voice of an unknown: 'Very pretty, very charming. My colleague and I have not travelled to listen to your little soap opera. Can we get down to business? And I'd like coffee.'

He slid the door back, came out, pushed it shut behind him, walked past the kitchenette and into the living area.

Carrick nodded to George, took Rob's hand and held it tightly for a moment, then saw the other two. One was older and suited, had neat grey hair, the other was younger than himself, wore a loose

161

anorak over a crumpled checked shirt, faded jeans, and had tousled red hair. The flowers he had brought for Katie were still in the wrapping-paper but filled a plastic bucket on the screwed-down table.

The older man said briskly, 'I haven't yet worked out my name, or my colleague's, but you're N for November. Of course, I know your correct name, but it will no longer be used. You're November.'

George said, 'I'm afraid things have moved a bit quickly, and—'

Rob said, 'Just what I'm looking at, sorry, but you seem shattered. Everything all right, old boy?'

Carrick grimaced. 'Yes, I'm all right – not by much. Two things. First, Rawlings is done for drink-driving last night, and as far as I've ever known is teetotal, like a priest's celibate, and is sacked. I get to drive the Bossman. Second, a hood tries to kill the Bossman down in the City today, two shots fired – God knows how they missed him and me. It's not been reported. I'm now the Bossman's flavour, and we're travelling in the morning – don't know where to. Shattered, yes. Dead, no. Otherwise, everything's all right. Who are these gentlemen?'

George looked down, evasive. 'Don't know much more than I said. What I said was that things have moved a bit quickly.'

'Meaning?'

Rob said, 'These gentlemen are from the intelligence services.'

'What? Dirty raincoats in the shadows? Spooks?'

George said, 'I am hardly, as has been made clear to me, inside the need-to-know loop. Josef Goldmann is now of interest in a matter of national security.'

162

'Nothing I've seen adds up to that.' Carrick shrugged theatrically.

The older man rasped, 'Then perhaps you haven't been looking, November, where you should have.'

He bridled. 'That's rubbish. If it was there, I would have—'

'And haven't been listening. I'd appreciate coffee, soonest, but appreciate more that we conclude the preamble.'

'Excuse me, I was damn nearly killed. If you didn't hear me, two shots, bloody near on a slab – so don't, whoever you are, tell me I'm not doing my job. Got me?'

'These "gentlemen", and it has authority from on high, require you to be seconded to their control.' George looked at the carpet on the floor and the mud and shit he had brought on to it.

'It's out of our hands – sorry and all that.' Rob fidgeted his fingertips aimlessly against his palms.

'You washing your hands of me?'

Neither answered. Neither George nor Rob met Carrick's gaze.

'Right. Can we now get to work?' the older man said, with a studied calmness. 'Matinée performance over – and the coffee, please.'

'Might just be premature, going to work . . .'

The older man sighed, not from exasperation or annoyance but from a reckoning that time was being wasted and it was a commodity of value.

'What if I refuse? What if I tell you to look elsewhere? What if I say I'm not interested in your invitation?' Carrick felt a chill around him, not the heat of anger, and it settled on his skin.

The older man beaded his eyes on him. 'Three

very fair questions, November, and deserving of very brief answers. Do I have to make that coffee myself?'

Katie caved. As she went past Carrick she gave his hand a momentary squeeze – but she couldn't help him and he knew it.

'To the point. Refusal is not an option. Do I want you? Not particularly. Would I prefer to substitute for you an officer from my own organization? Most certainly. You alone have the access I need . . . Just pause for a moment, November, and think. Having thought, I imagine you wouldn't believe I come lightly. It is not for some minimal personal amusement . . . I'm taking you over, and into an area that I predict will be of maximum danger, in the clear knowledge that national security may be involved. I will have a team with me, behind you, whose job will be to ensure – if possible – your personal safety . . . I tend to find morale-boosting speeches boring and usually irrelevant to the matter at hand. At last. Thank you.'

He was given by Katie, who glowered at him, a mug of instant coffee.

'I'm not in the business of concessions, but the role of the young lady has been explained to me, and her detailed knowledge of the files associated with Josef Goldmann. She, too, I am co-opting. I suggest we sit down. Oh, gentlemen, goodnight.'

He had dismissed Rob and George. He saw the senior bite his lip, the junior shrug, as if this was a force beyond their remit. Embarrassment wreathed them, as if neither knew of anything apposite to add. Carrick realized that the transfer of an undercover, mid-investigation, to different masters was beyond their experience, would conventionally be regarded as disastrous and unprofessional.

164

They left, tramped out and up the steps, and the narrowboat shook as they jumped off.

The younger man slapped his briefcase on the table, pushed the flowers aside, and said to the older man, 'I suggest that you're now Golf, and I think it would be appropriate if I were Delta. That all right with you?'

At that moment, Carrick believed the older man – Golf – betrayed confusion, as if he wondered whether the piss was taken but couldn't be sure of it, and he thought Delta an ally of sorts, but it passed.

Carrick listened, and Katie stood behind him, her fingers gripping the muscles of his neck, and the man, Golf, said, 'You will be told the minimum of what we have. Bluntly, the more you know the greater is the potential compromise to the operation – it's called Haystack – in the event of you being suspected, then tortured. And you would be tortured . . . The stakes, for us and for those we regard as the potential enemy, are very high.'

He flicked his fingers. Delta opened the briefcase, and took out a map. Its sheets were Sellotaped together, and lines were drawn across it. Then photographs spilled out and he saw the images of Josef Goldmann, Viktor, and a bull of a man, with dead and chilling eyes. Delta's finger stayed on that picture.

The man, Golf, said, 'Where they lead you, you go. I imagine it will be to him. I don't gild it, November. This man, Reuven Weissberg, will be as ruthless as a ferret in a rabbit warren, and if you fail with him – though we will try, bloody hard, to save you – you are, without question, dead. So, no misunderstandings. Dead.'

Chapter 6: 11 April 2008

Carrick checked his bag again, had done it three times.

The first time he had gone through it, when tension had tightened his arms and made them clumsy, he had invented an excuse. He had said to Viktor he had no toothpaste so he'd walk down to the arcade and buy some. He'd thought there might be a brush contact or a casual approach – he'd be asked for directions or a light for a cigarette – and he had walked the three hundred yards to the chemist, had lingered inside and let the queue stay in front of him, then sauntered back, but no one had stopped him. He had been unable to report at first hand his flight and destination details, so had texted the information through. It was a shadow world he lived in, and needed lights shining bright, and those lights were brush contacts and approaches. Unless an undercover believed that support was close, he was alone . . . which festered.

He had not felt like this before, since coming to SCD10 and working with George and Rob. He sensed his isolation, and hated it. Could, of course, have turned them down. Was within his rights, and would have been backed by the Police Federation. It hurt that they had not attempted to talk him round and build his ego, but had taken his acquiescence for granted. Now the clock had moved on, and the chance to quit had gone. Viktor shouted from the staircase to the ready room that they were to move in five minutes.

He didn't get a remark from Grigori, or from the housekeeper. Carrick did not belong in that household – their view, not hidden. He wore his best suit with his raincoat, and carried no weapon. The only protection he would offer Josef Goldmann was his body and a repetition of the instinct that had caused him to charge across the pavement and tackle a man. It would be his reputation, a bullet-catcher. The housekeeper was in the kitchen preparing food and Grigori was watching the satellite. Carrick went upstairs and dumped his bag by the front door.

The trust factor had been like a backbone to the operation of entrapment against Wayne in Mallorca, George had said, and the senior detective in charge of the investigation had nodded vigorously. 'I can't demand trust, or loyalty, I have to earn it.' The handlers had been close and had lifted him . . . He had worn a wire woven into the waistband of his trousers, and the microphone was in the central button – had to be there because it was so damned hot. He'd had to plead a skin allergy as a reason for not joining Wayne and his associates in the pool below the villa's patio, and for staying in the shade with his shirt on. They were brilliant guys who had nailed Wayne and his associates in Rotterdam when they'd taken delivery of the container from the docks. But it was history, and history had no place in the bloody present and the bloody future.

Grigori had come up the stairs, was behind him.

And the Bossman descended from the first floor with the family, kissed the kids and hugged his wife.

Viktor went down the front steps first, did the checks. Carrick had already brought the car to the door and Grigori had swept it. He thought the Bossman appeared pale, strained, the wife was distracted and the kids seemed to have caught something of their parents' mood: they clung to their father's arm.

Viktor nodded and had the rear door open for Goldmann; the boot lid was raised. Carrick threw in his own bag, the Bossman's soft leather one and Viktor's, then ran for the driver's door.

He pulled away from the kerb.

He glanced in his mirror, saw the road behind was clear, saw the preoccupied gaze of the Bossman, as if he stared at nothing.

Viktor watched Carrick.

He thought Viktor's eyes were locked on his face, studied it. Carrick did not know what the man thought he could learn from watching a driver's expressions, movements, twitches, blinks. It was as though Viktor searched for a truth about him. He sensed no acceptance there . . . He took the car out on to the main route going west towards Heathrow. He played the part of the careful driver and often looked up to the mirror, but could find no car or motorcycle tailing them. Should have been able to see them if they were there, because that was Carrick's trade. Almost shivered, felt the aloneness.

Remembered that cold, emotionless voice from

the narrowboat: *Where they lead you, you will go.*

Felt he was on soft ground, sinking, and that nothing familiar remained to cling to.

'Good of you to call by, Christopher . . . ah, and this is Luke – Luke Davies. I'm sorry our paths haven't crossed before, Luke. I hear good things of you . . . Run it all past me, Christopher.'

It was the first occasion, in the five years and three months since he had joined the Service, that Luke Davies had been in the restricted-access lift to the top floor, east wing, of VBX, and the suite of the director general. He regarded himself as a creature of independence, a free and liberated thinker, and it annoyed him that he felt pangs of nervousness. He nodded in reply – and perhaps there was a trace of something surly at his face, but Francis Pettigrew's glance lingered the fractional moment longer than necessary. He disliked himself for it, but smiled and did the head bob again, adopted a servile pose. He had not spoken as that would have betrayed his origins: a housing estate in the Yorkshire city of Sheffield, where his father was, the last he'd heard more than three years back and closer to four, a window cleaner, his mother did school lunches and his brothers were a lorry driver, a plumber and a struggling motor-repair mechanic. He felt disadvantaged. There were two cricket bats, autographed and mounted on the wall, but Luke Davies didn't play. On another wall was a panoramic photograph of a villa with a backdrop of Tuscan hills, but Luke Davies lived like a pauper in Camden Town. On a side table, in a silver frame, was the photograph of a wife and three children, but Luke Davies was not even in a stable relationship. There was a friendship between the two older

169

men. And Luke Davies was outside and felt awkward . . . and listened.

'I've read your summary – God, what time did you write it? Have you had any sleep? Your stamina amazes me – and I find a welter of innuendo, supposition, hunch and instinct that I can hardly offer up to the Joint Intelligence Committee. There's barely a hard fact in it.'

Davies let himself turn his head fractionally away from the director general and fastened on Lawson. Seemed pretty damning to Davies, and he thought Lawson might bluster, but he didn't. He was indifferent to the assessment.

'Some would say, Christopher, that there's barely enough to run with – even jog with . . . Some would say we should aim for something more detailed, with provenance, then scatter it far and wide, let others share. But that's not your conclusion. You're asking me to back Haystack, and to keep the business close inside the Service. "Inside" means that if the alarm call wasn't justified we don't face the titters behind the hands of colleagues in other services, who would dearly love to see us fall on our faces – but "inside" also means that if your suppositions are justified we're going after a problem with minimal resources, and if we fail we won't easily be forgiven. It's an interesting dilemma you present me with.'

Spoken as if the matter in hand was before the chair of the golf club entertainments committee – except that Luke Davies was not a member of any golf club.

'Very frankly, Christopher, if this didn't have your name on it, it would be a non-starter. But it does have your name. You've listed the resources and time parameters on Haystack, and I accept

170

them. My caveat is that you must promise to call the cavalry if you acquire proof of this conspiracy. I suppose this is all down to Clipper, his legacy.'

There was then, and Luke Davies saw it, a brief smile on Lawson's mouth, small cracks at the sides where the upper and lower lips met. Then it was gone. He had no idea *who* or *what* was Clipper.

'So, you have met the agent, whom you call November, recruited him, and fought off the opposition of his current handlers. You've run more men than I have, Christopher, but I'd be failing in my capacity as leader of the Service if I didn't point out that you are asking much of this young man. You are putting a huge weight on his shoulders – is that justified? Is November capable of achieving what is asked of him?'

They had been in the cramped living space of the narrowboat for an hour. He had watched November, hardly ever contributing, and the man had seemed to Davies to go through the gamut of reactions. Anger, hostility, then weakening, as if accepting the inevitable, on towards a modicum of pride that he was called out, and finally the clear-cut vision of November's exhaustion. The girl had done well. Her eyes had blazed antagonism and her hands, through the long hour, had never left November's shoulders. She had sustained their man.

Lawson said, 'I think Clipper, from what I recall, was clear on such a situation . . . As I said, he's what we have.'

'I hear you, but the burden he'll carry is considerable.'

Lawson stood. 'In such times, you use what's available. As I said, he's what we have . . . I'll be in touch.'

171

'And you won't forget the cavalry?'

'Not if the moment is appropriate.'

'God speed, Christopher. I have to hope, of course, that you're wrong, and it's a chase after wild geese. If you're right, we face a situation that is quite appalling in its implications, but you know that. Good to have met you, Luke.'

Lawson hadn't waited. Was gone out through the door, and his long stride already crossed the outer office. As he turned to close that door after him, Davies saw the director general staring out of the plate-glass – might have been examining the city skyline and the great public buildings, might have been thinking of the 'quite appalling' implications. He could have sworn it, with a hand on the Bible, that the mouth moved and said silently: *He's what we have.* Davies had entered new territory, was beyond his experience.

He closed the door, hurried after Lawson. He thought the Good Old Days had returned and that the bastard revelled in their resurrection. And the bastard had a plaything to toy with, an undercover to manipulate. He fell in, a pace behind, as they went to the lift, and instructions were given him about a meeting.

They had left early, as the dawn was coming up.

They were gone, without breakfast, from Kolomna. The schedule for the day, as laid down by Igor Molenkov, called for them to cover a hundred and sixty kilometres, and their destination was the town of Kaluga. He had reckoned they would achieve only a short leg because the route he had mapped was on the side roads south of the Oka river, which were too narrow to permit the Polonez to pass a tractor and trailer, or a horse and a cart, without risking going on to the grass verges. They were overgrown with dead grass and weeds that might hide a drainage ditch. There were many pot-holes in the road, but he could not fault the care his friend took in avoiding them.

It was nearly an hour since they had slipped away from the hotel, retrieved the Polonez from the lock-up car park. They had not seen a police patrol, but there had been tension in the car. A BMW, new, 3 series, with metallic silver paint, would belong to an individual of status in that town. The damage caused in an accident would have been reported, and the subsequent flight of the perpetrators. Molenkov had the map across his knee. Beside him, his friend hummed a tune, again and again, but he did not recognize it.

The countryside was flat, dull, unremarkable. There were small farm settlements, wooden homes from which smoke belched, and little yards beside them in which cattle or pigs were corralled. There were birch forests, and the open fields between them were not yet ploughed. And it rained, always, and the river, when they saw it, was high, near to breaking its banks. He noted on the map that three kilometres ahead was the big junction where the back road they used crossed under the meeting point of the M6 road from Volgograd to Moscow and the M4 that ran to Moscow from Rostov-on-Don, two great roads merging.

At the end of that day, wherever they slept and midnight chimed on a municipal clock, it would be his son's birthday. Sasha, had he not burned to death inside the hull of a tank, would have celebrated his forty-first birthday; would have been a man of middle age, in all likelihood would have had a family, receding hair and a paunch; would

173

have been his father's confidant. His son had been snatched from him, a forgotten statistic in the folly of a conflict far from home. There had been no coffin shipped first to Dushanbe and the base over the frontier from that shithole place and that shit war. No commander had had the time to retrieve burned bacon from a wrecked tank in an ambush site. It would have been bulldozed off the road and abandoned. His son's body would have been left to crows, rats and the scavenging bandits who had taken his life. Because of his son's one great friendship, with the younger Viktor, he had gone with his friend to a hotel in Sarov in the early hours of a winter morning.

More thoughts cavorted in his mind, and he barely saw the great overpass constructions where the M4 and the M6 came together. Saw instead the shock on the one-time State Security official's face when he was told of merchandise for sale. Recalled the handing over of two mobile phones. Remembered the code that he had been told for when the first phone was used, before it was to be thrown far out into the river that ran through Sarov. It had come – ###****51332365 – and two old fools, forgetful, trembling with excitement, had deciphered it: ### was confirmation that a deal was accepted, and each asterisk represented a quarter of a million American dollars, which would be paid them on delivery, and the numbers were a grid reference, longitude east and latitude north, where the delivery should be made. That phone was in the river, the second phone – also discarded – had made the one call and given their date of departure. They went under the great roads that carried traffic from the south and south-east on into Moscow. Lorries thundered above. He saw the wry smile on his friend's face and grimaced because he had forgotten to give the direction. Yashkin punched him. They went past a parked patrol car. Yashkin, peering over his wheel, read the signs and avoided being transported to Moscow, in a roaring traffic line from which there was no escape, or to Rostov or Volgograd. He heard the siren, and his dreaming ended.

He looked behind, but the view from the central mirror was blocked by the shape hidden under the tarpaulin. He leaned forward, saw the flash of blue lights in the wing mirror and heard the siren. He said, a hiss, 'Fuck.'

Beside him: 'What?'

Exasperation. 'Are you deaf? Can't you hear?'

A shrug. 'I'm old. What should I hear?'

Molenkov wound down his window, felt the rain spatter on his face.

'Now you hear it?'

'We broke no speed restrictions.'

'We broke, friend, the tail end of a fine BMW car.'

'What to do?'

It closed on them. The siren screamed, the lights blazed. It was a new saloon, and could have outrun them, probably on three fucking wheels. Molenkov swore again. He noted the reaction, immediate, of Oleg Yashkin: foot on the accelerator, chin closer to the wheel, forehead nearer to the windscreen. For what? Futile. The police vehicle came up beside them, bucked on the verge, then was spewing back mud and rainwater from its tyres and was past them. No contest. He had seen two grinning faces under wide peaked caps, and a hand had gestured for them to pull over. Just a scrape of paint off a fucking BMW, and a broken tail-light or two. What exercised the mind of Colonel (Ret'd) Igor

Molenkov, as the police vehicle slowed in front and blocked them, was the item covered with an old tarpaulin behind him. He reached back. Old ways died hard and old lessons stayed learned. He groped in the side pocket of his bag, found what he needed, set his face – and thought he looked at a half-share of a million American dollars, or the rest of his life in a strict-regime penal camp.

He said, 'Stop the car, and don't open your mouth.'

Defiance. 'I can ram them.'

'Stop the car – for once do as I fucking say – and don't open your mouth.'

He was pitched forward, almost lost them, but the safety-pin mounted on them caught his trousers. He pinned them to his chest. The Polonez stopped. It was the only tactic he could think of using.

They came out of the police car. The bigger man had a cigarette hooked to his lips, at the side of his mouth, and the buttons of his uniform shirt were undone. The smaller man, younger, had his tie loosened and was lighting a cigarette. Both wore side arms in holsters. They sauntered. On Molenkov's chest, hidden by his arm, were three rows of medals, mounted on a plastic frame. He saw the smirks on their faces. They came to the window, his side, and ash from the bigger officer's cigarette fell on to the Polonez's bonnet.

He heard a practised routine: 'You were speeding.'

And, 'In a restricted zone you were exceeding the limit.'

'Without the payment of a spot fine, you are liable to arrest.'

He understood the procedures of extortion. His arm still concealed the medals because he was not yet ready to display them. Neither officer had in his hand the official notepad from which a receipt could be given in return for the payment of a fine. He wondered if they were near the end of their shift. The bigger man's cigarette was now ground out on the bonnet. The younger man blew smoke into Molenkov's face.

'What are you carrying, old man?'

'Open the boot. Show us what you have there.'

He climbed out of the car and snapped upright. At full height, with the rain falling lightly on him, his shoulders back and his medals now in their faces, he surveyed them. The medals glinted. Anyone of a colonel's rank had three rows – a medal for long service, short service, passing promotion exams, taking part in Kremlin parades, party membership, for wiping his arse with his left hand, first class, and wiping his arse with his right hand, second class, for staying alive – and they rattled as he confronted them.

He spat, 'You are a *disgrace*.'

The smirks faded.

'A disgrace to your uniform and your country. You are criminals.'

He forgot his situation, relived his past. 'You are *khuligany*, the scum that steal from kiosk-owners.'

Two sets of clenched fists, then the hands went into the pockets.

'You think that I, with my service, do not know the senior officers responsible for policing this *oblast*? Try me – and get your fucking hands out of your pockets.'

Hesitation creeping over them. The hands came out of the pockets, hung limp against the trousers.

'Your appearance is shameful. You, your buttons, do them up.'

Eyes blinked, then dropped.

And again, with cold contempt: 'Do them up.'

Fingers at buttons.

'And you, your tie. Are you a police officer, serving society, or are you a gypsy thief? It is for the neck, not the navel.'

The knot of the tie was raised.

'Your shirt is filthy. I would not have my dog sleep on it. Stand straight when I address you!'

They stiffened, stood taller. The bigger officer dragged in his belly and his lip quivered.

'I have given a lifetime of service to Russia. My son gave his life for Russia, and my friend's father died for Russia to make a place safe for shites like you to steal and besmirch the honour of the police. Put that cigarette out.'

It was dropped and burned out in the rainwater.

'Now your vehicle. What state is your vehicle in? Don't shuffle!'

He led them to the patrol car. There were sandwich wrappers, drinks cans and discarded cigarette packets in the two foot wells, and magazines across the back seat.

'You go to work like that? You shame the whole of your force. You shame your uniform and your profession. Have I worked to preserve the safety of crap like you? Get that car clean.'

They did. Rubbish filled a plastic bag. When it was nearly done, Molenkov ordered that the patrol car be moved on to the grass verge, but his prayer for a ditch went unanswered. It was moved. He made a small gesture, hidden to them, and Yashkin started the Polonez. He climbed in beside his friend and shouted through the window that they should, both of them, consider themselves fortunate that he would not report them in person to his friend, a senior police official in the municipality of Kolomna. The two policemen stood stiffly at attention as they passed ... and the breath sighed out of Igor Molenkov's throat. All bluff, nothing but bluff, and if bluff was called ... Yashkin gripped his arm.

'I have seen everything. They saluted. Really. They were kids on parade, and they saluted as we drove away. I think they expressed gratitude that you will not report them.'

They laughed. Not mirth, not amusement, but hysterical cackling. They laughed without control, veering right and left on the road, then back again, and Molenkov buried his head in Yashkin's chest, and had to be pushed away so that his friend could steer.

Yashkin said, 'You were supreme. If ever I doubted we would get to the Bug, the doubt is gone. Nothing can stop us, nothing and no one.'

They sat in a horseshoe round Christopher Lawson, who had the bench, and listened, while a brisk wind whipped them. 'What you have to understand, gentlemen, is that disparate personalities are called together, and have only one common character defect. They will arrive on the scene of events from many directions that appear to have no link. It is the defect that governs them. All harbour a grievance against their society. Now it rules them. No love, no loyalty is permitted to gain supremacy over the grievance. I offer up a supposition – and I do not idly "suppose". A warhead from the arsenal at what was once Arzamas-16 is being transported out of Russian territory. A further supposition. It will be bought, or has already been purchased, by criminal elements. More supposition. It will be sold

179

on to those who wish to detonate the warhead. I believe in supposition. Without doubt, a clear and unmistakable danger exists, has many arms, but all of the participants are chained together by the factor of grievance. Find the origins of the grievances and we will find the men. We stun the beast, then stand with a boot on its throat and cut off its head. So, gentlemen, lady, welcome to Haystack, and I will do the introductions.'

Including Katie, there were eight of them. Luke Davies sat at Lawson's side on a folded edition of a morning paper to keep the mud off his backside. They were on the Embankment, beyond the VBX perimeter. His people, on Russia Desk, would have done the presentation in a darkened auditorium, with maps projected on to a screen and photographs. He had suggested one of those small rooms on the ground floor, where increments were permitted to go under escort, and where the equipment was permanently stored, but the glance had been steely, enough to state that it would be done Lawson's way, tried and tested disciplines, as in the old days. In the open, Davies understood the thinking, there could be no hidden microphones in walls or ceiling, no hostages given if an inquest was called for.

'Names first. I am, don't know why, G for Golf. My young colleague is D for Delta. We have a cuckoo in our midst, foisted on us, but whom we will attempt to welcome, so she will be C for Charlie: you will remember she is not one of us. Our man, of whom we expect great things, is N for November. The targets, the opposition, will be allocated numbers as appropriate. Target One is Josef Goldmann, and so to the rest of you. I gather the names are baggage picked up over the years. We'll start with Bugsy.'

He was a dapper little man, tidy in appearance, and all that was remarkable about him was the size of his spectacles, the thick weight of the lenses across the bridge of the nose. He was squatted on the grass and seemed hardly to have heard Lawson's words.

'He does the electronics, and has been in my teams since he left college. My advice to the rest of you is never to complain of foreign food, or you'll start him off and wish you hadn't. He'll also bore you half to death on the subject of racing pigeons. He will do visual and audio surveillance, bugs and tags, and if November ever gets to wearing a wire it will be under the guidance of Bugsy. Then it's Adrian and Dennis.'

They sat on the railings with their backs to the river. One would have been late forties and the other was early fifties. They were so similar, could have come from any high-street shopping precinct, any football crowd or any business conference for low-level management. In every respect, they were average – average height, average weight, average build – were dressed in the average clothes that men of their age wore. They sat close, as if they were a partnership.

'Not the faintest idea where those names come from. You'll find them rather ordinary, but that's their trade and they do it well. They represent the mobile and foot surveillance element of our team. They will have particular responsibility for tracking November and reporting on where he leads us. They have the additional responsibility of checking, by counter-surveillance, whether November is under suspicion and tailed – "dry-cleaning", in their jargon. From my experience of them, they're seldom satisfied with the resources available, and will bleat they need a dozen operatives, not two. We cut our cloth according to our budget and the practicality of Haystack. There are two of them. Next, Shrinks.'

A man grinned, waved a fist in an airy gesture. Davies thought him only three years or four older than himself. There was a buzz of confidence about him, he didn't have to talk to demonstrate it. He was squatting easily on his haunches in the walkway. The chill off the river did not seem to affect him: sleeves rolled up, a safari-style waistcoat worn loosely, a wooden imitation of an animal tooth hung from a leather thong at his throat, and his hair was a messy tangle, coming down on to his collar.

'He's always been Shrinks since he started to work with us. He tediously protests that a "shrink" is a psychiatrist and that he is a psychologist. Ignore this. It seems standard today that such a profession is regarded as necessary on a field operation . . . We seemed to manage in the past pretty well without one, but I must live with it. He will evaluate, as best he can, the morale and state of mind of November as Haystack progresses, and whether he is capable of continuing to operate effectively. Whether I take a jot of notice of his opinions remains to be seen. Then, we have Deadeye.'

He was rather small and sat cross-legged on the walkway, eyes roving. Davies had noted the facial wound and the halting way in which he had walked to the Embankment. It had taken him several minutes, well into Lawson's introduction of the electronics guy, to recall where he had seen him before, where he could place the jacket and the hooded sweatshirt.

'He's been Deadeye as long as I've known him.

He's responsible for the protection of our backs. We may get to a stage where we believe a solitary individual is inadequate for that purpose. Then we'll swallow the complaint and make do. He is to be listened to at all times and his word, alongside mine, is law. You will find him at the best of times to be sour and ill-tempered, as he is now. The degree of animosity arises from his injured nose – suffered in Haystack's cause – and, should he drop his trousers and underpants, you would see that his testicles are quite severely bruised . . . He is an experienced marksman, shoots straight.'

Davies recalled the charge, the scuffled struggle, the crack of the pistol, the knee going into the groin, the clatter of the weapon into the gutter, and the roar of the car powering away down the street. Saw everything, but struggled to comprehend its meaning . . . then realized his mouth gaped open at the implication.

'Now, the *Miss* in our ranks, C for cuckoo, so she is Charlie.'

She was apart from them and her frown seemed chiselled on her forehead. She had dressed that morning in jeans, layers of sweatshirts, and tough hiking boots. To Davies, it seemed that nothing about her was designed to attract, as if she had forsworn sensuality, and he thought that made her prettier than she intended, but not beautiful. He remembered how her fingers had worked at November's muscles, to lift him. He thought her stronger than November, and hard.

'I didn't ask for Charlie, but her presence with us was a small compromise I felt obliged to make. In gaining control of November, and ditching the people who formerly looked after his case, it was *suggested* I take her on board. She knows

183

November, his capabilities and weaknesses, and has worked from its inception on the police investigation that deals with the money-launderer – our Target One, Josef Goldmann. If she steps over the line I've drawn for her, she'll be on the plane home without time to blow her nose. That's it.'

There were no questions. Luke Davies thought these the sort of professional operatives who did not need to hear their own voices. He would have admitted it, Christopher Lawson – prize shit and alpha-grade bully – had done it well and had achieved domination expertly.

'In conclusion, they fly this morning to Berlin, and we follow. My colleague Delta has dipped into a travel agent's computer and learned where they have booked accommodation. My assessment is that Berlin is a staging post. Where they, and we, move to, I don't know. Where an end game *may* be played out I simply do not know, but wherever it is, I promise we'll be there.'

The Bug river swelled and its level rose. That week, the rainfall over the Volhynian-Podolian hills in the central regions of the Ukraine was at record levels, and the sluice gates of the canal that linked the Bug to the Dnieper river were opened in the hope that the huge volume of surplus water could be taken up the Bug's flow. With an angry, mud-laden power, the Bug spewed out of the heartlands of the Ukraine, then took its course along the frontier with south-east Poland, and its route swung north.

The river, rising by the hour, formed a new, more formidable frontier where it separated Poland from Ukraine and from Belarus. Other great European rivers had done that work before, but politics and alliances had changed. The Elbe was no longer the boundary between East and West as it had been for forty years. Briefly, the Odra river that divided the recent greater Germany from western Poland had acted as a fault across the northern area of the continent. The most recent realignment of cultures and regimes gave that role to the Bug.

At a United-Nations-sponsored conference to draw up a framework for the Protection and Use of Transboundary Watercourses, a scientist said to a colleague, 'To swim in the Bug is pretty near to suicide. Personally, I'd eat nothing grown within several kilometres of it. That foul water spills out over the agricultural plains.'

Where it meets the Polish border, the Bug is a filthy drain. Too high now for a fisherman going with a pole rod after carp for food. But in late summer when the Bug is at normal height, a fisherman would be insane, or near starvation, to eat his catch. The river carries extreme levels of pesticides and herbicides from agriculture, toxic chemicals that include heavy metals and phosphorus from industrial wastelands, and the untreated sewage from many of the three million people living within its basin. The Bug's strength, as it approached the moment when the banks would break, was awesome – a power without mercy.

The scientist finished his coffee. 'I don't know whether you've heard the forecasts – no? Particularly severe rain over Ukraine. Floods by the end of the week.'

The Bug marked barriers that were clear to the eye and obvious to the mind: the Catholic faith of Poland divided from the Orthodox of Ukraine and Belarus; the democracy of western Europe and the Russian-dominated society of the neighbours. Old enemies squared up on that river, and old enmities were kept alive by it, but apart. As the waters rose, lapping at defence walls, the river Bug – had it a living soul – seemed to have taken on a brooding, resentful anger, as if it dared men to challenge its thrust.

The colleague finished a last cake. 'And the floods distribute more of the filth. Don't quote me, I never want to see that place again. To me, it's damned and dangerous.'

Reuven Weissberg asked, 'Who is it? Who's he bringing?'

Mikhail answered, 'A minder. An English minder.'

'Is Viktor not with him?'

'He is, and an English minder – a new man.'

'Why?'

'There was an incident yesterday. He was impressed by the reaction of the new man.'

She moved, like a wraith, into and out of the room. His grandmother listened but did not contribute.

Reuven asked, 'What did Viktor say?'

Mikhail answered, 'I haven't spoken to him.'

'I'm perplexed as to why Josef would bring a new man with him, at this time. Where is the sense of it?'

'There was not the opportunity for explanations.'

His grandmother was at the door, watched him. Her head was cocked forward to hear better and a wisp of hair, pure white, lay across the lobe of her right ear. She would not comment unless her opinion was asked. He did not ask: it had been dinned into Reuven Weissberg since he was a child at her knee that trust should rarely be given and then only with great caution. Her mind was moulded, he knew, by a place where trust had not existed.

'Josef lives in London, the life of the fat *pig*. Has his mind softened? Could he be mistaken?'

'Perhaps, but it would surprise me if Viktor was. It's what Viktor is for – to prevent mistakes.'

Reuven Weissberg exploited the mistakes of others. When he was still a teenager, an *avoritet* had agreed to share the pickings from a part of Perm's taxi trade, and before his nineteenth birthday he had pushed aside that *avoritet* and had answered the man's protests by beating him unconscious. Back from the military, he had sensed the weakness of an *avoritet* who was losing control against rivals for the meat stalls of the open market. He had put in his own boys – Mikhail and Viktor among them – seen off the rivals at gunpoint, and put that *avoritet* in the Kama river. Mistakes had made openings for him in Moscow, and more mistakes in Berlin had given advantage. Mistakes stripped men of their status, left them on a pavement in a blood pool, or in an oil drum, with hardening concrete, bouncing on the bed of a great river.

'Did you say to Josef that he shouldn't bring a stranger?'

'He said he was coming, and that it was not for discussion.'

It did not have to be said – his grandmother eyed him from the door, suspicion in her eyes – but a mistake brought every *avoritet* down. And concern had settled on Mikhail's face: no *avoritet* chose a time to walk away from the power, influence, status, wealth. It all lasted until a mistake was made. So much to plan for in the days ahead, and the talk among them – time wasted – was of a minder his launderer brought with him.

'When the stranger comes, before business is done,' Reuven had the smile of a stalking cat, 'we will look at him, and if we like him it will be good for him, and if we do not . . .'

The increments and the policewoman were in a Transit ahead of them.

A pecking order of seniority was clear to Luke Davies. He and Lawson were chauffeured by a driver from the Service's pool. About fifty questions had rampaged in his mind, but his silence was governed by the need to choose where to start. They were on the motorway, going west, and had passed the first sign for the airport turn-off. He had wondered how it would be in the Transit, had imagined a quiet murmur of voices as the team bonded to the necessary level of effective cooperation. He reckoned bonding would have low priority for Lawson, but those questions jarred in his head. He had, finally, determined where to start.

I suppose this is all down to Clipper, his legacy, the director general had said.

Lawson had said, *I think Clipper, from what I recall, was clear on such a situation . . . You use what's available. As I said, he's what we have . . .*

'Do you take questions, Mr Lawson?'

A word puzzle on the back page of a newspaper was interrupted. 'I do, yes, if they're relevant.'

He could have asked about the lack of liaison with friendly agencies, the lack of provenance in the Haystack operation, the lack of planning and the rush to action. Instead he asked, 'Who is he? I believe I've the right to know. Seems he's a bit of an oracle, put on a pedestal by you and the DG. Who's Clipper?'

Looking into those clear eyes, he saw what he imagined were minute cogs turning as if an apparatus was at work; what should he be told, how much need a junior know? Then, remarkable, there seemed to be a softening in Lawson's face – as if he'd forgotten himself. He let his jaw sag from the normal aggressive jut – and a limp smile spread.

'He was from the Agency. He was Clipper Reade. He did central Europe out of Berlin.'

'What did he look like?'

'Big, what we would today call obese, and tall with it. Had a fine shock of hair but it was mostly under a trilby. Smoked cheroots. Had a voice that could be a whisper or a foghorn. He was pretty well known throughout the seventies and—'

'How does he get to stand on the pedestal?'

The chauffeur took them on to the airport's feeder road.

'Don't interrupt, just listen. When kids interrupt I fancy it's to hear their own voices. He did a cover of being a salesman for spare parts in Czechoslovakian-made tractors. Could produce anything for the Romanians, Bulgarians, Poles or Democratic Germans when their tractor fleets packed up. We never quite knew how he'd landed the contract, but he had and it was a miracle of achievement. Amazing how many collectivized farms with broken tractors seemed to be on the edge of a runway used by the Soviet's bomber fleets and interceptor aircraft, and how many farms on the Baltic coast overlooked their naval facilities. For almost ten years he swanned through those countries with officials from economic-development or agriculture ministries eating out of his hand. If you knew your history of the Service, had read it up in the archive, you wouldn't need to be told. He was a genius at suborning agents, but most of all he had a nose for his work. Got me? A nose that sensed the frailties of men, and how they could be used. It permitted him to second-guess opponents, to anticipate, to act when others would hang back. I was privileged to work alongside Clipper Reade, and for nine months my junior was Pettigrew. In your modern jargon, Davies, "icon" is an overused word, but Clipper Reade was truly iconic. Of his generation, he was the finest intelligence officer.'

'And he handed down words of wisdom that you cling to.' Said tersely as a statement, not as a question.

'Because you don't understand your response is sarcasm. The DG and I know otherwise. Clipper was of an age before the computers you rely on, before analysis of El Int ruled. In his day, and mine – and the DG's – officers were happy to get their feet and hands dirty. They were prepared to exist at the sharp end. Does that give you an idea of who Clipper was?'

Luke Davies pursed his lips, looked hard at him, and thought he hacked at the coal face of the Good Old Days, bloody days that were long gone. 'Not quite finished – what happened to him?'

'Busted, of course. Inevitable. Scrambled clear from Budapest not more than a dozen hours before he was due to be picked up, made it over the Austrian border, incredible in itself. Couldn't last for ever, but was pretty damn good while it did.'

'And drinks all round, back in Berlin?'

'A few taken, yes—'

He interrupted. 'But not party time for the networks left behind. Tell me. Arrested, tortured, imprisoned, shot?'

There was the roar of aircraft on the runway. They went down into the Heathrow approach tunnel and dead yellow light bathed them.

The softness was gone, the hardness returned and the jaw protruded. Lawson said coldly, 'They were agents. Volunteers. They chose their own road. Agents never last, never can. Months if they're lucky, weeks if not. Agents don't last if they're where you want them, at the heart of the matter – you've much to learn. They get burned.'

Carrick was jolted, shaken. The cabin shuddered and rattled. He remembered those landings at Basra when the transport aircraft had come down in a corkscrew approach, then flattened out and hit the runway hard – but it was Berlin, which was not a combat zone.

He turned to Josef Goldmann and smiled politely but ruefully, as if to say he understood and sympathized. His Bossman had one fist clinging to Carrick's sleeve and the other to Viktor's, his skin was milky pale and bore a sheen of sweat. His Bossman was, the file Katie had prepared said, a major player in international crime. He laundered money for Russian *mafiya* gangs, among others. He was a target for intelligence guys defending national security – and was shit scared of flying. He had bad shakes if there was turbulence. Carrick did not have that fear: he could jump from a moving aircraft with a 'chute on his back, or from a tethered balloon that was eight hundred feet up. For him, the fear was of being on the plot and alone.

Viktor pushed Josef Goldmann's hand off his sleeve, while Carrick let the other stay. For the flight out of Heathrow, the Bossman had been wedged between them.

They went through Customs, then to Immigration. It wasn't Josef Goldmann's name on the passport he offered, but his photograph was there.

Carrick did not know where the back-up people were, how close or how far. He carried his own bag, as Viktor did, and he had said that Josef Goldmann should carry his so the minders would each be free to react.

A man met them, heavy, muscled, and hugged Viktor. They were led to a Mercedes. He thought of his own world as having been tipped on to the floor of the narrowboat by the men who had corralled him. Everyone said, when they were volunteered, that the moment never came to spin on a heel and walk in the other direction.

They were driven towards Berlin. Carrick tried to act out his role, the bodyguard's, but found himself staring listlessly at the streets of a city he did not know.

Chapter 7: 11 April 2008

Carrick was first out. He did the routine. The car braked, the doorman advanced, but he was out and checked both ways on the pavement. Had reason to. How had the bastard missed at that range, so close? But the routine took his attention, not the events of a previous day. He would work out how the bastard had failed in the hit some other time. He stood across the car door.

The street was clear of dawdling vehicles and he did not identify a loiterer, just people, nothing to show that their business was in any way extraordinary or threatened him. The only gawpers were on the far pavement, separated from the hotel entrance by the traffic flow. Trouble was, Carrick had to act out the part of a man with more than two years' active experience of bodyguard work, not the two weeks that had been allocated him. On the bodyguard course, more trouble: the teaching was for mob-handed protection, maybe seven or eight men deployed, maybe with an outer screen of police officers. Carrick knew nothing of what to expect. Maybe at that hour of the day everyone – old men in suits, young men in jeans and sweats or hoods, women with shopping bags and women with pushchairs, kids skiving off school, the elderly wrapped against the cold – hurried in Berlin, except two men on the far side of a six-lane street who watched indifferently.

'Right, Mr Goldmann, let's move – please – and quickly.'

He saw, could not miss, the worry lines knitted across his Bossman's face, and also the gratitude shown him. 'Out of the car, Mr Goldmann, and straight to the door.'

Everything happening to him was distorted, as if mirrors were bent, throwing up images that were grotesque and malformed. *Concentrate,* he told himself, *and cut the shit.* He reached down, took his Bossman's arm at the wrist and levered him up from the depths of the car seat. Realized the dependence, could feel it, the way the man's fist clawed into his sleeve.

'That's it, Mr Goldmann, and let's go.'

The role-play consumed him, filled his thoughts. He looked round, saw that Viktor was behind the Bossman, strode for the swing doors and a man materialized. Hadn't seen him coming. He came fast in a line, shambled and swayed. Might have been a drunk or a druggie. He was unshaven, dressed in clothes that had been slept in. A junkie's young body but aged and haggard, his hair a dank tangle.

Carrick dropped his shoulder, and nudged him clear of them in one brutal, sharp action. The man crumpled. Carrick glanced down and saw a grimy face that pleaded. He knew the man was harmless, that he had reacted beyond a level that was necessary. He had thrown aside a beggar or a derelict, and the door was held open for him.

He saw hostility on the doorman's face, and there was a jumble of words, German.

'I don't speak German,' Carrick said, and walked towards the lift at the far side of the lobby.

The doorman called after him, in angry English, 'He scavenges from the kitchen, is harmless, *sir*. For what he is, *sir*, we give him some respect.'

Carrick ignored him. He did the role-play well. He saw his Bossman and Viktor into the lift, stepped in with them and pressed the button. It was a glass-sided lift and he saw the doorman stalk away. He had known his ground or would not have spoken out so forcefully to the bodyguard of a guest, Carrick reckoned. The doorman went out now through the swing doors, on to the pavement, bent and lifted the man off the pavement, then seemed to slip something – money? – into his hand. Beside him, Viktor was impassive, but he thought Josef Goldmann's mood had lightened, calmed by the display of force. They came to the reception floor.

A girl behind a desk said, 'You are very welcome, gentlemen. It is three rooms now, not two, and one is a superior suite, yes? The reservations are for two nights – it is for departure on the thirteenth of April, correct? Just your signatures, please.'

His Bossman's scrawl was unrecognizable. Carrick just did his initials.

They were given key cards. Carrick led back to the lift and they went up six more floors. Along a silent corridor. He stood aside as his Bossman worked the lock and opened a door.

Viktor said to Carrick. 'I work out the rosters, which you will accept. Now get the bags.'

He was dismissed, as if he was low-life.

195

He went back down. Had to make peace, of a sort, with the doorman because he needed him to organize the parking of the prebooked hire car, arranged by a Berlin contact – but Carrick hadn't been told a name – in the basement under the hotel. A good-size euro note was passed, not acknowledged as it was pocketed. The doorman, now, had that aloof look, and Carrick reckoned it was to show his contempt for the hirelings of a Russian Jew mobster who needed the swagger of protection. He took the three bags out of the boot. He didn't know where they were moving on to – *It is for departure on the thirteenth of April, correct?* – whether they had enough clothes or would buy more. The man who had come to the narrowboat, who had invaded the *Summer Queen*, had said that the risk against him, in Berlin, increased to the level of . . . *dead, so there are no misunderstandings. Dead.* He hitched a bag on to each shoulder and picked up the third. Across the road he saw, in a doorway, the hunched shape of the derelict he had thrown on to the pavement. A stream of lorries passed on the street and in a gap between them he noted that two men still lingered on the far side.

He took the bags through the swing doors. He thought his life depended on how well he played the role. And, here, Carrick understood nothing.

He brought the bags to the rooms, was told what hours were his to rest, and what hours were for duty stretches.

In his room, stretched out, he slept.

They waited till a uniformed porter took away the hire car.

'What did you think?' Reuven Weissberg asked.

'I thought it peculiar. The little boy held his

196

father's hand as if it were dark and he was frightened.'

'And scum was pushed away.'

'Harmless scum.'

Reuven Weissberg turned away from the place where they had watched the front entrance of the hotel on the Joachimstaler, and began to walk towards the U-bahn. There was a question he did not ask Mikhail. In fact, many questions were in his mind and he asked none. Did the man, shown on the reservation as Carrick, demonstrate his qualities as a professional bodyguard when pushing scum aside? Was the man merely professional or was he also loyal? The questions floated with him as he walked. Was a bodyguard ever loyal? How far would a bodyguard risk his own skin in defence of his paymaster? Was any bodyguard to be trusted? Should Carrick, on the word of the launderer, be trusted? Had his own Mikhail earned trust? That last question, never answered, was like a stone in the shoe of Reuven Weissberg. When guarded by Mikhail he had himself been shot.

They walked to the Uhlandstrasse station and went down the steps. He had been shot in Moscow. In the hectic days when he had battered his way into territory where other groups had believed themselves supreme, when he had snatched clients and given them new roofs, when he had recruited from State Security and Special Forces to enforce the roofs, he had made enemies of stature. In Moscow he had not used restaurants because that was where men such as himself were most vulnerable – and where he chose to attack rivals.

He had lived with the fever of the bunker, had surrounded the villa where his grandmother cooked and cared for him with high walls, electronic alarms and guards. He did not display himself at the wheel of a high-grade Mercedes, but drove old cars that could disappear on the streets and stay unrecognized. But he had been shot on the steps of a bank after depositing money. He could count few mistakes in his life, but it had been a mistake to visit that bank on three consecutive Fridays. He had come out into the sunlight, had paused because the snow had not been cleared adequately off the steps, and looked for a sure footing. Mikhail had been behind him – not in front – and the pistol had come from a pocket. He had seen the recoil and had dived to his left. There he would have made a good secondary target had the impetus of his fall on to the icy step not caused him to slide two steps lower. The second shot had missed him. Then Mikhail had reacted.

One shot into the chest and two into the head. Mikhail had identified the getaway driver, whose panic had caused the wheels to spin, and shot him, a bullet in the head. They had fled. They had slithered away to their car. Mikhail had made it plain he thought himself a hero. He, Reuven, had congratulated him, had found the words as the pain reached beyond the numbness in his arm. They had not gone to hospital. At the villa, his grandmother had cleaned the wound, then had boiled water and used the scissors from her needlework box, tweezers and a knife to take out the debris of his coat that the bullet had forced into the cavity. She had not stitched the holes. He knew it was long ago, during times in the Forest of the Owls, that she had learned to treat wounds. He had never cried out when she had probed for debris, would not have dared to. Within the next week, six more men had died from weapons fired by Mikhail and Viktor, and a new business roof was successfully taken under his control. It had been his first step into the multi-billion-rouble death industry, and the killings made his control of an entrepreneur's roof absolute.

Of Mikhail, his grandmother had said to him, 'Why was he behind you, not in front? Why did he only shoot when two shots had been fired at you? What did he risk? Trust only yourself. Never put your life into the hands of another. Guard your own body.'

He stood on the platform and waited for a train, Mikhail a pace behind him. He thought of the man, Carrick, whom he had seen barge aside scum, and the trust written large on the face of Josef Goldmann as he held the man's arm.

The train came, clattered alongside the platform.

His grandmother had told him that survival was in his own hands, as it had been in hers, in her stories that he knew by heart.

How much did I want to live? How often did I wish I was dead?

Always, I wanted to live.

In Camps 1 and 2, where the Jews were whose work made Sobibor function, there were few who did not wish to live. Only twice do I remember that a prisoner ran at the wire and started to climb, in the certain knowledge that the Ukrainians in the guard tower would shoot and kill. I learned that life is the flame of a candle. Whatever the gale of misery, we shelter it and try to protect it. Those who knew their fate, understood that they were condemned, would – not often – fight the guards as they were herded from the train. They would be shot on the platform or clubbed, then dragged down the Tube. Most of those close to death spent their last minutes in prayer.

For us, in Camps 1 and 2, however awful the experiences, there was little thought of death as a release. Few believed liberty came with it. To survive, to wake at first light the next morning, was the goal. Some claimed it was their duty to survive in the hope they would become a witness to the atrocity of Sobibor. For most it was the simple glory of breathing that next morning, the freshness of the air, the scent of the pines, and forgetting the foulness of the smoke from the burning pits.

There was a brothel for the Ukrainian guards outside the perimeter. The girls there, at first, were not Jews but prostitutes from Lublin. I heard it said that they were ugly, old, diseased . . . It was even said that a farmer from Zlobec sent his twelve-year-old daughter there for money because the Ukrainians wanted younger girls.

There were no prostitutes from Lublin for the SS, the Germans. They used Jewesses. For a month after I had learned this I waited for it to be my turn to be taken to the Forester House, which the Germans called the Swallow's Nest. I knew I would be taken one evening. In the days of waiting, I could have killed myself. I could have eaten glass, I could have spat in the face of an officer and been beaten to death, I could have run at the wire and been shot. Instead I waited.

Three days before I was taken, I knew it would be soon. The Germans relied on the capos to bring Jewish girls to the SS house. The capo who supervised us in the sewing room came and stood behind me. She reached over my shoulder and held my breast. Her fingers seemed to weigh it, as if it were fruit in the Wlodawa market, and then she reached lower, poked at my stomach as if to learn whether I was slim under the loose smock I wore. I endured, after that, three days of waiting because I wanted to live.

It was the late afternoon, a Friday. It was February. It was cold. We were in the barracks. I was on my bunk

200

when the capo came for me. She stood in the door, pointed to me and beckoned. In the month since I had known about the Forester House, I had seen six Jewesses taken out of our camp, and only one had returned. I did not think about five, but of one. She sat, always alone, in a corner of the compound, or apart from the rest of us at a bench in the workshop, or she lay on her bunk hunched up and cried without sound. She did not talk of it.

As she took me out into the dark and the night chill, towards the lights of the internal fence and the gate, the capo said to me, 'If you want to see the light of the morning, be alive. Don't fight them but appear to enjoy it.'

There was music in their house, from a gramophone. The capo escorted me through the gate into their compound, and in through the back entrance to their house. I heard the music, very loud, and their shouting. In the kitchen I was told to strip by the capo, then a tin bath was produced from a cupboard. I stood in it and she poured water over me from a jug. I was soaped, then dried with a towel. I was given underclothes with French labels, and I thought they had belonged to a lady who had been brought from France in the Pullman cars, who had been innocent of the purpose of Sobibor and had worn her best underwear and silk stockings for the journey to her 'new home in the east'. The clothes would have been left in a neat little pile, then the lady would have run down the Tube, thinking of the cleansing shower ahead and the chance to dress again. I wore the brassiere, the knickers, the suspender belt and the silk stockings of the dead. My hair was smoothed, and perfume – I was disgusted by it – squirted over me. The capo took me to the door, and said, 'Show you enjoy it and please them. Then you may live. Show you hate it, and you will die. You decide.' She opened the door, pushed me through it, and I heard it slam behind me. A wall of noise, their music and shouting hit me, and all their eyes were on me.

They wanted me to dance. I wasn't a whore, I was a girl whose father repaired clocks in the town of Wlodawa. I didn't know how to dance other than to the folk music of our people. They clapped to the beat, and I tried to dance. I'm not ashamed that I tried, because it was for survival.

They were drunk.

They weren't young – not as old as my father but far older than I was.

Perhaps I didn't dance well enough. Perhaps it was the urge in them.

I was pushed from behind and tripped from the side.

I was on the carpet. The underclothes were torn off me. One made a bandanna of a silk stocking, and I recognized him as being in charge of Ukrainian guards. I was naked. But my mother and my grandmother had been naked when they had been taken down the Tube, and they had not had the chance to live. I could accept my nakedness, and their eyes on me, as the price paid.

I bled when it started. The first grunted and pushed, swore and heaved. He had taken off none of his uniform, had only unbuttoned his trousers, and his boots forced apart my ankles. They would have seen the blood, and they cheered. Glasses were thrown into the fire, and I screamed at the pain, which excited them still more. The first hadn't finished when he was pulled off, because others wanted to feel my blood. By the third, I moved. I did it to live. I let my hips rise when they thrust and drop when they withdrew. One was sick on me, and it was wiped away with their handkerchiefs. They all did it to me, except the senior officer. All – except SS Scharführer Helmut Schwarz, who usually commanded and supervised the men's work parties outside the compound – penetrated me, and then they came round a second time.

I was on the carpet till they staggered back from me, exhausted and limp.

He took me upstairs. They cheered Scharführer Schwarz when he led me out through the door. He took me to his room and hung a dressing-gown over my shoulders. I understood. There was a photograph of his family beside his bed. A father in full uniform stood and his hand rested on the shoulder of a girl, his daughter, and a mother gazed proudly at her man and her growing child. He thought me like his daughter. He sat on the bed and held my hand. He was near to tears, and if I had had a knife I could have slit his throat, but then I would not have lived.

I became his. I was the property of Scharführer Helmut Schwarz, and in his room I acted the part of his daughter and the bastard stroked me each time I was brought to him. Did not come into me, but stroked me, and I would pant and groan as if I took pleasure from him. There was danger. An SS man, Groth, fell in love with a Jewish girl, and softened in his attitude towards us – animals, a subhuman species – and when he was on leave the girl was taken down the Tube and shot. Other girls, Austrian Jewesses called Ruth and Gisela, who had been actresses in Vienna and were far more beautiful than I, were taken to the Forester House, then shot the next morning. I did not know if I would live.

He went on leave, went back to Munich to see his wife and stroke his daughter. The women helped me. I had no protection. They put ash on my face so that I looked older. I shuffled with bent shoulders so that my bosom was hidden. New girls came, younger girls, and were taken to the Forester Hut, but I never went back. I was forgotten, and I lived.

Never in that night when they struggled with each other to be the next, or came into me with violence, did I wish I was dead. I knew that only God, good fortune and

*I could save myself. I thought love forgotten and had
learned to hate.*

'I don't understand – why are we here?'

He had been brought to the zoological garden.
Luke Davies was baffled.

He was answered, 'That you understand better
where we are and what we're doing.'

'Mr Lawson, I haven't been in a zoo since I was a
kid.'

It was ridiculous. They had been met at the airport by the deputy station chief, Berlin. All of them
had fitted snugly, or squashed, into a minibus, and
the deputy station chief had driven them into the
city. The vehicle had stopped in a side-street near to
the old Zoo Hauptbahnhof. Lawson had climbed
out, had gestured for Davies to follow him. They'd
taken their bags from the tailgate and walked
to the door of a small, perhaps discreet, hotel.
Inside, Lawson had been greeted by an elderly
porter as if a prodigal had returned. Then an old
lady had come through an inner door and Lawson,
with full formality, had kissed her hand. The bags
were dumped and they were gone without even
checking in. He had asked where the minibus was
and everyone else. He had been told that Lawson
never stayed at the same hotel as his team. And
enigmatically, 'They'll take on the transport,
and they'll go to work. We're going for a walk.'
They had been hit by a shower, and had sheltered
under the arch outside the zoological garden, then
Lawson – in fluent German – had bought the two
tickets, an age concession on his own, and they'd
gone inside.

There was a smell about the place. Luke Davies
had never been inside a gaol, but men he knew had

always spoken about the distinctive stench, like a zoo. Might have been the fodder, the bedding, the stale, green-tinted water in the pools, or the creatures' droppings. The zoo's smell was in his nostrils, and was worse when they went inside the big cats' house. He focused on one cage. A lioness had just been fed. A great joint of pink-fleshed bloody meat was between her huge front paws, and her eyes were malevolent as she licked the meat. He could have asked a hundred trite questions. Didn't, held his peace – and wondered what was so important about the zoo that it took priority over checking in to the hotel ... He wondered too what the team, with its disparate characters and daft identification codes, were doing.

They reached the hippopotamus house. It was closed – was being refurbished – and would not open for another week. He saw a flash of annoyance pass over Lawson's face.

'Right,' Davies said. 'Can we move on along the agenda, please? I think it's going to rain, and I don't want to get soaked again. I've much enjoyed our jaunt but ...'

Lawson headed for the aviary and beyond it were the penguins.

Lawson said, 'You are in the heart of Europe, young man, not on an offshore island. Everything here is governed by the last war. Boundaries, attitudes, loyalties, all are affected. This was the finest zoo in Europe, but we bombed it to destruction. The lions had to be shot by the keepers or they would have been free to roam the streets and attack people. Elephants were crushed by the collapsed concrete of their enclosures. Deer and birds were slaughtered by citizens desperate for food. It irritates me that the hippopotamus house is shut. One great beast – Knautschke – survived the bombing and hid in the mud of its pool. It was resurrected, fed back to health, and its sperm started a new hippopotamus collection. Of five thousand animals here at the start of hostilities only ninety-one were alive when the white flag went up.'

'What's your point?' Davies could see none.

'I would have thought it apparent even to an idiot. This city breathes history. The past cannot be discarded, is a ball and chain. You must sniff at the history here if you are to comprehend the present. Is that disrespectful to the *genius* of youth? Are you so arrogant that you cannot find room for history, are fearful that it will dull the lustre of your glory? When you know history you will know, too, the motivation of men. A sense, warped, of history will drive forward those we attempt to challenge.'

'Were you here with Clipper?'

'A good place. No microphones, difficult for counter-surveillance. We met people here, talked about things . . . Yes, we were often here. Come on.'

'Can't I go to the hotel and put on dry socks?'

'You cannot.'

They walked out of the zoological garden. Lawson set a brisk pace. They went past modern embassy constructions, where the Japanese were and the Saudis, the Mexicans, Malaysians and Indians. He asked why they walked and was told that atmosphere was gained by walking on a city's streets, not by sitting in a car. He presumed that Clipper Reade had walked in Berlin, and Christopher Lawson merely imitated him slavishly. He resented his treatment. They reached a building faced with clean-cut grey stones. Through an open archway there was a wide courtyard, with leafless young trees in a line at the far end, and a shallow plinth in the centre with a charcoal grey statue, larger than life, of a naked man. Against the left wall, level with the statue, was a plaque and below it were a wreath and a bouquet of fresh yellow flowers.

'You realize, of course, who this statue commemorates?'

'No idea.'

'Claus von Stauffenberg.'

'Never heard of him. Sorry and all that,' Davies said.

'God, the ignorance of the young. At the Wolf's Lair, he put the bomb under the briefing table. He tried and failed to assassinate his Führer, on the twentieth of July 1944. Hitler lived and von Stauffenberg, who had returned by air to Berlin and had seen his *coup d'état* fail, was shot by firing squad where the plaque is. I'm trying to show you the confusions under which we operate. To most, even in those dark days when defeat loomed, he was a traitor. To almost none was he a hero. Today, the best that can be said for him is that he is – now, at this late hour – respected. Myself, young man, I make no judgements. I am no crusader for democracy, not a champion of our concept of freedom, merely an observer. Very little in our world is clear cut, and that is best remembered.'

Davies wondered whose words they were, guessed they were spoken first by Clipper Reade. He tried to imagine the two of them, the gross, overweight Texan and a young Englishman feeding from an American hand. He snapped back, 'Is there not *right* and *wrong*? Don't we make that choice?'

'You are, or you purport to be, an intelligence officer. Look for sugar or saccharin and you'll be boring and pompous. Come on. More for you to see. I'll fight my opponents tooth and nail, but I will not have judged them.'

There had been no talk in the Polonez, merely laughter puncturing the quiet, but now his old friend was silent. Yashkin drove, and wondered what new demon tormented the former *zampolit*. They had turned off the minor road to a village, had purchased bread at a shop and then pressed on. A range of low hills blocked their view of the Oka river, but they would meet it again when they came to Kaluga. There, the third stage of their journey would be complete and four more would remain. He saw the black soil of the fields, too wet to be ploughed yet, and his speed was seldom above forty-five kilometres per hour – and then they were behind a tractor that pulled a trailer loaded with cattle dung. An old man – older than himself – drove it, and a teenage boy was perched beside him. He thought he watched Russia, his Russia, as he slowed and tucked in behind them, and the manure stench wafted to him. They were the peasants of Russia, obstinate and stubborn, exploited and deceived. The tractor coughed fumes. If he made a victim of the peasant – as he was a victim – he could ally himself to the tractor driver.

It must have welled inside Molenkov, but whatever had been dammed now burst out. 'Yashkin, have you seen one?'

'Seen what?'

'An explosion.'

'What explosion? What are you talking about?'

'Have you seen a nuclear explosion? With your own eyes?'

Had Major (Ret'd) Oleg Yashkin ever lied to his friend, Colonel (Ret'd) Igor Molenkov? He couldn't remember having done so.

'I have not.'

'I thought you had, at Semipalatinsk-21.'

'I have never seen a nuclear explosion, big or small.'

He couldn't remember offering even the most trifling untruth to his friend. If his friend had asked him, after they had gone their separate ways in the fruit and vegetable market at Sarov, in the late afternoon when prices were lowest, whether he had found potatoes, cabbage or turnips at what could be afforded, and he had enough for Mother and himself, he would have said what he had bought – and then he would have shared. If he were down to the last bucket of coal, needed as a base under wood for the kitchen stove, and his friend came to the door to ask if he could spare some, he would not have denied that he had it. He had always shared the truth with his friend.

'In your papers, do I not remember seeing you had the security clearance to accompany weapons to Semipalatinsk-21 and for the test site?'

'I did the escort but didn't visit the test site.' He lied again.

'You passed up that opportunity?'

'I have never seen an explosion, and have never visited a test site, so let it go.'

The weapon had been taken from Arzamas-16 by road to Kazakhstan. The journey had lasted five days, and Yashkin – then a lieutenant – had been third in command of the detachment of 12th Directorate troops. The device, and he did not know its power or the delivery system intended for it, was to be exploded deep underground. There would be no mushroom cloud and no flash, as there had been in earlier years when First Lightning was detonated, and the RDS-37 hydrogen bomb. The one he had seen was called Project 7. He could not have described it honestly. If he had, his friend would have abandoned him. He did not yet believe fully in Molenkov's commitment. At the edge of the Semipalatinsk-21 test site was the dry bed of the Chagan river, and a shaft had been sunk among the stones. Kilometres back, safe in a bunker with reinforced-glass slits to view through, he had waited, heard the countdown and had not known what to expect. First the movement of the riverbed, then a towering column of stones, mud, earth and rock as strata and layers from far down were thrown up. The noise had pierced the bunker, a rumbling roar that he couldn't describe adequately. The concrete floor had shaken, men had clung to walls and chairs, and coffee cups had fallen from the table. The cloud had surged into a clear sky and darkened the sunlight. It had reached its height but had not dispersed for many hours, and dirt from the far down subsoils coated the ground. He had been among those permitted, the next day, to go forward. He had seen a crater that was a hundred metres deep and four hundred wide, and the ground's contours had changed. He had heard, the next year, that the explosion had formed a dam that would block the flow of the Chagan river in spring when the winter snows melted, and would make a new lake. He had heard, also, the year before his dismissal, that Lake Chagan was dead and polluted, contaminated by radiation. He could not have told his friend what he had seen.

'If you say so.'

He pulled out recklessly and hooted. The tractor driver slewed to the side, and the Polonez had enough room, barely, to squeeze past. He had to mount the verge and the car bucked, but he had silenced the questions and would not have to lie again. Molenkov grabbed the dashboard and braced himself.

The most incredible sight Oleg Yashkin had witnessed in his life was the eruption in the bed of the Chagan river, and no man or child in Russia would live long enough for it to be safe to walk where the spring waters had made a lake.

He said, 'I think we've made good time. We've earned a bath and good food tonight.' He talked then, with his friend, of the beers they would drink, and how many, and what was the local brewery in the Kaluga district, how often they would need to get up to piss in the night, and the laughter returned.

The *hawaldar* told the Crow – and sighed, holding out his hands as if to mark the dimensions of the sum – that a huge amount of money was guaranteed.

The Crow told him that the guarantee was from the Base, whose word had never faltered, and was not an advance of one-tenth already made in Dubai.

The *hawaldar* told the Crow that the necessary messages had been sent by courier to a German city, that confirmation had been received of the courier's arrival, and the acceptance by a colleague and trusted friend to make payment.

The Crow told the *hawaldar* that he would be gone from the Gulf in the morning, would fly to Damascus, and from there the trail of his movements would be lost.

A construction-site foreman and a banker of the Islamic faith prayed together. Then they hugged. The *hawaldar* had prayed fiercely and hugged tightly. He had thought the Crow to be a man of the greatest importance if he was entrusted with purchasing an item for ten million American dollars. He showed the Crow out of his villa and asked if he would ever return to the harbour-front skeletons at Dubai. His answer was a non-committal shrug. So the *hawaldar* asked a question that had concerned him since he had met this man: how was it possible that the giant crane stayed stable when the winds blew in from the Gulf? Patiently, the Crow detailed the science of cantilever weights, and he found the answer fascinating. He watched the Crow walk to his car, climb into it and drive away. He thought he was a small part in a great network, one of the many wheels turning behind a clock face, and that so many others, of whom he would never know, were also wheels in the clock.

'I'm going to be away for a few days,' he announced, breaking the silence at the evening meal.

'How is that possible?' Sak's father asked. 'There are three more days of term.'

'The classroom laboratory is now closed. A school trip is planned to Europe in the autumn, but if it is to be successful it must be reconnoitred now.' He was fluent at deception, had been taught well.

'That will be nice for you,' his mother said.

He saw on their faces – in the dark chestnut eyes of his father, the pale blue ones of his mother – relief. They did not know the full reason why, that afternoon in January 2002, he had arrived at the front door of the guesthouse as they prepared for their evening's clients. He had had two bulging suitcases of his possessions from the hostel room at Aldermaston. From the West Midlands, he had lethargically chased some work opportunities in academic research under the name of Steven Arthur King and with hospital trusts, but he had gone for a job with police forensic investigation when hoping for ethnic discrimination with the name of Siddique Ahmed Khatab. He had always been turned down, or his applications had gone unanswered, so he had worked for his father and had helped his mother to clean the guest bedrooms. In the last summer he had gone to his father's relatives in Pakistan and had stayed seven weeks. He had returned revitalized – his parents had noticed the change in him and rejoiced at it – and had been offered a job at the nearby comprehensive school. 'Not important work, not yet,' his father had told a friend, 'but steady, with security.' He had presumed the role of laboratory technician was too lowly to feature in the computer checks where he had failed on previous applications.

'Only for a few days,' he said, shrugged, and ate.

It had been the start of a day like any other. He had bicycled from the hostel to his workbench. Before going to the centrifuge unit, he had been enjoying a mug of coffee and light gossip with colleagues, and a call had come for him to go, *immediately*, to the headquarters/administration block. He was given a room number to ask for. There had been three men. He had recognized Summers, who was CSO for the Aldermaston complex: everyone knew the chief security officer who obstinately smoked a big pipe when he was outside a building. Another was introduced as a sergeant in Special Branch. The third man was not introduced by name or occupation – Sak now believed him to be from the Security Service – and in front of him was the folder with Sak's personal file. There was little preamble. Summers had awkwardly revolved the bowl of his filled but unlit pipe, and had spoken.

'This is not easy for any of us – for you or me. You understand that the world was turned upside-down in New York four months ago. The aircraft into the Towers, and all that, altered perspectives. We have gone with painstaking care through your record and note family links with the Tribal Areas of Pakistan. We are making no accusations concerning your loyalty to all of us at Aldermaston, nor is there a criticism of your work. However, security and the safety of the nation demand, in these difficult times, that we make hard decisions. You will be "let go". This is not a dismissal, you are not sacked, but your clearance to work here is, with effect today, withdrawn. In conditions of confidentiality, your union has been informed that your employment is terminated, and I have their guarantee that they will not, repeat not, support legal action by you against us. You have been with us for five years, but you will receive six months salary in lieu of notice, which I consider generous, but it will be in staggered payments. Should you, in the vernacular, "go public" on this matter the payments will be halted. Also, don't take this as a threat, we would counter any public statement you made with accusations concerning the quality of your work and your fitness to be employed here.

You are a casualty of this war. Your family in Pakistan ensure that. I am very sorry but that is the situation, and no appeal procedure exists. I wish you well in finding other work that does not involve nuclear weapons and materials. Do you have any questions?'

He had had none.

A cousin of his father, living in West Bromwich, would do the redecoration of Room 2, it was decided, in the summer when the guesthouse business was slackest. A new shower unit, an upgrading, would be fitted in the bathroom outside Room 3, by a nephew of his father who lived in Brierley Hill. To his parents these were matters of importance weightier than Sak's travelling to Europe on school business.

It was the last boat of the day. They had walked all afternoon on the streets of the new Berlin, Lawson's voice dripping in Davies's ear. On looking out at a panorama of huge glass-and-concrete constructions that seemed to trumpet corporate wealth: 'It is a mirage of affluence and the comfort zone does not exist. Grand façades, but not backed by reality. An attempt to plaster over the history of this city, but it cannot – not while the grandfathers still live. It's skin deep, and society is raddled with high-level corruption.' Going past the designer benches in public parks and seeing the drunks, destitutes and druggies sprawled out on them: 'The money's run out. The economic miracle was a mirage and is no longer even pretended. This city is a place where the rats with the sharpest claws and the biggest teeth survive. Do you see charm? Anything attractive? This city is a sack where rats fight – and it's where Clipper taught me my trade.

There were rats here then, and little is different now.'

It was a big pleasure-boat. It was raining hard now and the open seats on the deck were empty. They sat in the lounge cabin, and only one other couple – talking French but more interested in kissing than the sights – was there. Three girls lounged at the bar, but Lawson had waved them away when they had offered coffee or drinks. Luke Davies endured it, and did not know the journey's purpose.

They had walked past the great buildings, recreated, of the war where Bormann and Speer, Hess and von Ribbentrop had had their offices, where the Gestapo had been – and their sunken holding cells: 'The past dominates, cannot be escaped from. Know the past and you can fight the modern danger. Ignore the past and you're defenceless.' And past a building where a sign indicated there was a Stasi museum, and outside it bronze statues of a uniformed man from the Democratic Republic's security police, and civilian workers who symbolized the network of informers used by the regime: 'The mentality still lives. The mentality was bugs and microphones, friend denouncing friend, a daughter betraying a father. The mentality is now pushed further to the east, beyond the Bug. It is alive in Ukraine, Belarus and Russia. The men who bred it still have their desks in Warsaw, Budapest and Prague. That's why we don't share. Here, they even collected smells. In glass jars, hermetically sealed – the sort of jars your mother would have used to store beetroot in vinegar – there were handkerchiefs, socks and underwear for a dog to track. A jar stored in the basement of Normannenstrasse held a crushed cigar end. Clipper Reade's.'

They had walked past a section of the Wall. Seventeen years since it had been breached, and the Cold War, the war of the gods, had been wound down. Yes, certain of it, in Luke Davies's book, but not Lawson's . . . 'They regret now that they took down so much of it. Should have left it up. A good, clear, understandable world then, not the confused quagmire we now thrash around in. Look at the end of this section, how narrow it is, just the width of a concrete block, but it defined cultures as clearly as if it had been a chasm a mile wide. It's where I was with Clipper Reade. I yearn for those days again when ideology was the battleground, not this damn faith business.' They had gone to the boarding point for the boat trip at the Potsdamerplatz, had waited by the pontoon. He had thought Lawson mad, certifiable. At least they had a shrink with them. He would broach it with the guy.

The voice over the loudspeakers urged him to look forward. Now Lawson reacted. He had been slumped in the plastic chair, not peering out of the windows on which the rain dribbled. He jerked upright, light in his eyes.

The voice spoke of the approaching Oberbaumbrücke, completed in 1896, the finest bridge construction in nineteenth-century Berlin and . . .

Lawson said, 'This is why I brought you. You needed to feel the width of the river, not just to stand on a bank and look across. We were on the left side, Clipper and I, and Foxglove was on the right where the Wall was. He worked in the east sector's central telephone exchange. It was always difficult to debrief him, and the tractor-salesman cover was getting thin – about six weeks before

217

Clipper was blown in Budapest. He was useful, and we used exchange students, military people who had the right of access to East Berlin and tourists – anyone with a visa – to bring back tapes, logs and lists of ministry numbers, but he wasn't important enough for us to mount a full-dress exfiltration operation. You see, he was of no use to us afterwards, only when he was in place. Foxglove was a good agent, but not priceless, and his shelf life was gone.'

The bridge was misted by the low cloud and the rain dropping from it. Luke Davies's head was at the window. It had seven low arches of brick with stone facings. A U-bahn train was crossing its top deck, but a lower one seemed empty. There were twin towers in the centre and they straddled the central arch, which their boat headed for. The voice said that the Oberbaumbrücke had been dynamited in 1945 to prevent Soviet troops using it, then rebuilt after Berlin was joined again; the central arch was from the design of a Spanish architect.

Lawson said, 'He was on his own, really, Foxglove was. We told the police on this side that "someone" was trying to come that night. They had an inflatable ready and an ambulance was on stand-by, but he had to get halfway. I suppose we'd been running him for six months, Clipper and I, and we'd reckoned him a decent young man. No dinghy available to him, of course, but we'd suggested to Foxglove that he try to get hold of an inner tube to keep himself up, then kick like hell. There were booms and barrage nets on their side, and we didn't know how he'd cope with them, but that was his problem. We didn't see him go into the water.'

The boat splashed foam aside, then slowed in front of the bridge. Davies thought that later in the season, when it was loaded and the sun shone, this would give a better photo opportunity to those wishing to recall a sight of the Oberbaumbrücke. The wake died, and the boat idled. He looked down into the dark depth of the water, and sensed the terror of a man in flight.

'We knew he was in the water only when the searchlight found him. It locked on him. He was on an inner tube, as we'd suggested. Then there was tracer, one round in four, red lines of it. He must have been hit but not badly by one of these first shots. He screamed. Had no chance then. There was concentrated fire on him, not only the machine-gun but from rifles. Then the searchlight lost him, which meant he'd gone under and the tube had been holed. We waited, owed him that. Next time we saw him he was tangled in one of the barrage nets, dead. I was young, a bit cut up about it.'

He looked across at the left bank, saw old buildings that now seemed derelict, and wondered where Lawson had stood, and the American, where the boat crew had waited and the ambulance people, and seemed to hear the sirens, the crack of the guns, and the lights seemed to dazzle him.

'Clipper didn't do emotion. Clipper said to me, "Let's go get a beer." We went off to a bar, and did just that. Four or five beers, actually, and a half-bottle of schnapps. Spent the small hours in a bar with drunks and pimps, and I learned the creed of the agent-runner from Clipper Reade. He said, "Lose an agent and you go find another." And he said, "Get close and sentimental to an agent and you get to be useless." And the dawn was coming up, and he said, "Treat them like dirt in the gutter, and when you've finished throw them back there." We went out into the dawn light, and he said, "Agents are just means to an end, and you owe them nothing." I brought you here, young man, so you'd know where I'm coming from and where I'm intending to go.'

They left the boat at the next stop, at the Jannowitzbrücke. Luke Davies no longer thought of Christopher Lawson as mad but reckoned him brutal, cold and utterly detestable. And there was an agent out there who was owed a damn sight more than Foxglove had been given. It was damnable, what was asked of November, the agent of today, not a bloody ghost from the past.

Carrick was on four-hour turns. Slept for four hours, then sat on a hard upright chair just inside the suite's outer door, which had the chain fastened.

Thought of it as pretty much a wasted day because he had learned little, if anything.

One visitor. A Russian, in a uniform of shaven head, worn leather jacket and boots laced up over the ankle, as if they were required for his role. Must have come when he'd slept and Viktor had done the guard turn. Josef Goldmann had brought the Russian out of the inner room, had escorted him to the outer door and the hotel corridor. Carrick had watched the man amble away, then gone back inside and secured the chain again. He'd noted the face of his Bossman. If he had been filling in the Book, he would have written: 'Target One had a meeting of at least two hours with unidentified male (Russian) and appeared anxious and under major psychological pressure at the end of it.' His Bossman lingered in the outer room, lips writhing and throat heaving, as if he weighed the consequences of confiding – did not, but let his hand rest on Carrick's sleeve, clutched it, then broke the grip and went to the inner room. He looked, Carrick reckoned, more pressured than when he had been chucked into the car after two shots had been fired. Carrick wondered if chickens had come back to roost, but knew no more than what was in front of him to see.

Chapter 8: 12 April 2008

Carrick was beside Viktor, who drove. They had left the wide avenues of the city and the squares of the Charlottenburg district behind them. They were on a highway going west. He had not been told their destination, only that at all times he was to be close to his Bossman. He'd nodded, and had been told that they drove to meet his Bossman's associate, Reuven Weissberg. Words had seared in his mind: *Reuven Weissberg will be as ruthless as a ferret in a rabbit warren, and if you fail with him – though we will try, bloody hard, to save you – you are, without question, dead. So, no misunderstandings. Dead.* They went between wide forests of birch, and the roofs and walls of fine houses were masked by the trees. Discreet lanes led to them and bore security notices at the junctions with the highway. He could stare at the houses between the trees because it was his job to be wary and to scan outside the windows of the car.

He felt the hand settle on his shoulder. Josef Goldmann asked him, 'Do you own property, Johnny?'

'No, sir. 'Fraid not, sir.'

'Why not?'

'Been moving around. Not really settled enough, sir.'

'This is good property, here. Better down the road. We go to view property.'

'Right, sir.'

'You know, Johnny, it is always better to buy than to rent.'

'I'm sure I'll get round to it, sir.'

There were digits spinning in his mind. He estimated what a half-decent apartment cost in central London, and how far beyond the reach it was of a police constable – with the capital city's allowance – who had to repay into an SCD10 bank account every pound, every damn penny, he was paid by the family. He had no place of his own. He was rootless. He flitted between bed-sits and mini-flats that were, most likely, either in a basement without a view or under the eaves in an attic conversion with a view of chimneys and TV aerials. The nearest Johnny Carrick had to home ground was the desk in the Pimlico building that had been allocated him after coming off the importation case and before moving on to the Josef Goldmann investigation. In none of the properties where he had lived since joining SCD10 had there been anything personal to him. He did not do family photographs, or holiday baubles, but lived on sanitized territory, could close a door behind him and feel neither loss nor emptiness. It was right to be bland, noncommittal, with answers. Every detail given, if a part of a legend, offered hostages to fortune and could be checked: the instructors preached that criminals survived on a diet of suspicion. Carrick sensed that the time had come when he would be challenged to maintain his postured identity. He wrapped the duty of the job, like an enveloping cloak, tighter round him. He peered out through the car windows, tilted his head to see into the driver's mirror and played the part of the bodyguard – had reason to. A man had been close enough to fire two shots, point-blank, and— He saw a bridge ahead, built from heavy steel girders.

Now his Bossman spoke softly into Viktor's ear, in Russian. The car was driven into a parking area. Brakes on, a smooth stop. Two lakes here came into a narrow channel that the bridge spanned. At the far side he could see houses half hidden by trees not yet in leaf. At their side, behind them, was a renovated palace.

His Bossman said, as Carrick opened the door for him, 'Now we will meet Reuven, an associate in business of mine – stay close – and then he shows me property which I may invest in.'

'I'll be close, sir.'

They walked. There was a pavement on each side of the bridge and heavy traffic surged past. He had noted that for part of the journey out from central Berlin, Viktor had driven fast, then glanced at his watch face and slowed for, maybe, five kilometres, as if he were ahead of schedule. They crossed the bridge, and when Carrick looked out over the water he saw small boats with raised sails, swans, grebes and coots. He thought the place pretty and calm.

Two men approached, both leather-coated, one to the knees, the other to the hips. Both had short-cut hair and hard faces. Carrick, his Bossman and Viktor walked towards them. Carrick was more than halfway across the bridge when he thought of the photograph he had been shown in the narrow-boat, of the near-silent movement of a ferret's pads in a dark, stinking tunnel, and of the cowering

224

rabbits trapped in a cul-de-sac of their warren. He recognized Reuven Weissberg from the photograph that the younger man, Delta, had produced from the file. He seemed to hear every word, and the inflections, of the older man, Golf. Reuven Weissberg wore the shorter leather coat, which was older and frayed, and Carrick assumed it a less prized possession than that of the man standing a couple of paces in front. He did not do stereotypes. The prejudices of allocating men and women to pigeon-holes was dangerous to the culture of an undercover, level one. A prejudice, stereotyped, would have made him look for caricature Jewish features. There were none.

They came off the bridge. Behind the waiting men was a large villa that had decades-old bullet pocks in its walls. Its windows were boarded, and skirting it was a wide path for cyclists and those promenading beside the lake. He saw the villa, the walkers and a cyclist who pulled a mini-trailer in which a child was perched, because it was his role as a bodyguard to scan.

Over his shoulder, 'Johnny, you should meet my associate, Reuven Weissberg.'

The man in the long leather jacket, which had more status and was obviously the more expensive, took a half-pace forward, as if he had heard what the Bossman said.

So easy . . . Carrick's mind raced. He had not done this exercise in role-play during his training. So simple and therefore so easy to make the mistake. He had been shown the photograph of Reuven Weissberg and it was a good likeness, would have been taken by the German police, an organized-crime unit, within the last six months. As his legs went leaden, Carrick absorbed the extent of the trick offered him. If he went a half-stride beyond the long leather coat and greeted the man in the hip-length coat, he demonstrated that he had been shown an identifying photograph.

Carrick reached out his hand to the man in the long coat, whom he knew was not Weissberg. He tried a brief smile and his heart pounded. He said, 'I'm Johnny – pleased to meet you, sir.'

There was laughter, not warm but cold, and no hand was pushed forward.

His Bossman said, 'No, that is not Reuven. That is his friend.'

The one he knew to be Reuven Weissberg now came a step closer. The hand was extended. Carrick flushed, as if he had made an error. There was an exchange, in German, as his hand was held in a vice grip, between Reuven Weissberg and Josef Goldmann. Then Carrick's hand was freed and the two men hugged. Carrick did not understand what was said.

His Bossman turned to him. 'My associate wants to know, Johnny, why I have brought you with me. I said you were here because you had saved my life, and that is a good enough reason.'

Good enough? Carrick saw that Reuven Weissberg pondered on it, frowned fractionally, then turned to walk. He also saw huge properties, masked by trees, and thought them to be the ones that might be purchased to facilitate laundering, for investment.

He believed he had passed a test, did not delude himself that it was the last – and felt the sting of vomit in his throat.

'It is the Glienicker bridge,' Lawson said. 'Two hundred metres across, and it's where we did the

226

big prisoner exchanges. Did it when they had someone to trade, and we did. Incredibly exciting, with a choreography all of its own. Two men starting to walk from either end when the second hand of synchronized watches reached the hour, and crossing in the centre – they never seemed to look at each other as they passed. See that building on the other side, young man? That used to be stuffed tight with the East's security people, a sardine tin of armed men. Took months to set an exchange up, and it could all go down at the last moment. It was the American sector, of course, but Clipper used to bring me here for the theatre of it – and we'd go across there, the *Schloss* built as a hunting lodge for Prince Karl, the brother of Friedrich Wilhelm the Third, and there was a café and—'

'Don't tell me, Mr Lawson. You'd have a pot of tea together.'

'Yes, we did – most times.'

He was staring across the expanse of the bridge, and on the far side was Königstrasse and the wide road on into Potsdam. Lawson felt, almost, joyous, reckoned himself blessed to have been brought here. They had travelled, again, in two vehicles. The woman, codename Charlie, had driven the car carrying himself and Davies, following the minibus, Deadeye at its wheel. They were mob-handed that morning. Deadeye had now pulled off at the approach to the bridge over the Wannsee, and had stayed in the minibus with Bugsy and Shrinks. On either side of the bridge, on the pavements, were Adrian and Dennis, the stalkers. Lawson found it hard, at that distance, and with the bridge's slight hump, to follow the targets but they'd had a good view of November and Target One crossing, a reasonable glimpse of

227

the meeting, and that had gone well. He was wired, from a transmitter on a harness on his back, a microphone in his sleeve at the wrist and a button for speech in his pocket and a moulded earpiece, to Bugsy.

Lawson raised his arm and his cufflink brushed his mouth. His finger, in the pocket, held down the button. 'Golf here. Move off, maintain visual contact. Out.'

Heard a little chuckle. 'Best you stay with the trade talk, Golf. We call it eyeball. Will do, out.'

The sun was on his face. He thought years were propelled off his shoulders: age was shed like a snake's skin. The minibus came past and headed on to the bridge.

Then something was nagging at him. 'I suppose you had to be pretty high up the pecking order to get a Glienicker swap – assuming he'd been arrested, higher than Foxglove was. What counted for an acceptable swap?'

'If the man in their cells was one of our high fliers or, indeed, if he was one of us.'

'Is November "one of us"?'

'That is a provocative and pointless question.'

'I just wanted to know whether I should keep a couple of beers handy in my kit, and a few teabags . . . just in case.'

The car pulled up.

Lawson said, 'If you believe that Haystack depends on your presence – the participation of a junior – you delude yourself. I would imagine there is a flight for Heathrow out of Tempelhof every two hours, and I'm sure there are seats available.'

The young man slipped, sullen, into the back of the car, and Lawson took the front seat. He anticipated now that the pace of events would quicken.

Charlie, his cuckoo, drove over the bridge, and at its highest point he could see Adrian and Dennis on different sides of the path to the right, meandering. Ahead of them was the little group with the agent – he thought Luke Davies decent enough but lacking spine and needing to learn, fast, the realities of the trade – and they had stopped in front of a villa that had scaffolding across its façade. The agent stood away to the left, as though isolated.

Now money had usurped – the talk of money.

'Ten million euros each, paid through the Caymans or the Bahamas. That is the price we should be looking to pay, Reuven. Pay too much too quickly and the vendor worries. Pay too little, haggle too much, and the vendor goes elsewhere. A total of twenty million euros, which is available on call. That's a decent price for the two properties.'

Reuven Weissberg stood alongside Josef Goldmann. He listened to Josef when the talk was of money. Viktor, Mikhail and the young Englishman, who walked with an awkward limp, were away from them and could not have heard their conversation. It was a residential street without residents. Reuven Weissberg had no interest in the investments that Josef Goldmann placed in his name, or in using the profits that Josef Goldmann fashioned for him. He thought he sensed excitement in the man, as if the opportunity to trade gripped him with pleasure. Reuven thought the houses gaudy and pretentious, and he believed they would attract attention from the revenue authorities. He had many such investments, and his identity was hidden in the paperwork by the names of the nominees Josef Goldmann created for him.

'Yes, I can do that. You leave it with me and I'll do it. I think, Reuven, they're very suitable for you, and there isn't a better part of Berlin for return on capital investment. This area, off Königstrasse, between the lake and Potsdam, will become the new residence of the capital's élite. Consider it done.'

He thought that Josef Goldmann would have chosen either of the houses – if he should ever move from London to Berlin – as a home for himself, Esther and his children. Goldmann believed an address made a statement. The statement that Reuven Weissberg made was an apartment in the city centre that was small, adequate for himself and his grandmother, enough. Josef Goldmann had said he would not move without the young man, Carrick, at his side. He had babbled about an attack. Reuven had heard the story, but had interrupted once to put a single question: had there been warning of an attempt on Josef's life? 'No warning. Nothing has ever happened in London that gave me to believe I might be a target for assassination. I tell you, I had one piece of luck, one, but it was sufficient. My English driver, an idiot, was caught by the police while off-duty with excess of alcohol in his blood. I upgraded Johnny. I let him drive me into the City. I was leaving a meeting, coming on to the pavement, and was attacked and Grigori, whom you chose for me, froze and was useless. I would have been dead but for Johnny, his courage. He risked his own life to save mine, and it was lucky he was with me.' Then they had come to the houses and the talk had changed to money.

'But the reason I'm here, is that in place?'

Reuven nodded.

A breathy hiss. 'You risk so much for all of us . . . On my side, all is prepared.'

230

Reuven cuffed his launderer's arm.

'If you had asked my advice, I wouldn't have suggested . . .'

He walked away.

'. . . that you proceed. But you didn't ask it.'

He quickened his stride, turned his back on the two houses he would buy. First, Josef Goldmann scurried to keep pace with him, then the three other men – Mikhail, Viktor and the Englishman – jogged to catch up. He thought the one called Johnny had a good face, perhaps an honest face . . . It was three days away, and two old men drove from Sarov to deliver it, and he did not take advice on the matter – would not . . . He remembered that his own man, Mikhail, had not reacted with sufficient speed to block the gunmen who had shot him in the arm, had not risked his own life. It was an honest face.

In the car park, Bugsy circled the vehicle. Back when he had started his career, an electronic tracking device had been the size of a house brick and had needed clamps and supports to hold it in place – always more reliable than the magnets police forces used. Graduating out of the workshops – in the secure lock-ups of what had seemed, to a casual eye, a small industrial estate in Kennington – he had reckoned ETDs to be high risk. Then they had called the brick-scale metal boxes 'tags', still did.

He only needed one circuit of the car that had driven Target One and November to the lakeside and the car park at the near end of the iron bridge. It was a perfunctory check. In his steel case in the back of the minibus, Bugsy had a selection of tags that ranged in bulk from a cigarette packet to a matchbox. Easy enough to attach one – and easy enough to blow the whole show away.

231

He turned away from the car. He understood the importance of getting a tag under or into it, but shook his head – to himself – ruefully as he calculated the risk factors. In the ideal world that, as a professional, he hankered for, Bugsy would have identified the make and series of a vehicle, then called the showroom that sold it and a demonstration model would have been delivered. It would then have been driven into the lock-ups and lifted up on a ramp. He would have crawled under, over and through it to learn where was the best chance of secreting a tag, then the tag would have been activated and Bugsy would have checked the quality of the signal. He prided himself on that professionalism, and on his ability to make the decision as to where in a car the most satisfactory hiding place equated with minimum interference in the signal the tag emitted.

If they were organized crime – which the guv'nor, Mr Lawson, said they were – then it stood to reason they would have access, and frequently, to the best gear. Trouble was, their gear was usually better than that issued to Bugsy from the industrial-estate workshops. The trick that high-level organized crime employed, in Bugsy's experience, was to drive a few kilometres, stop, deploy with the detector, then sweep. Good tactics. The batteries of a tag had a life of no more than twenty hours and were activated by remote. A target car drove away and the tag was switched to transmit, but the chances were pretty damn near certain that there would not be time to cut the transmission bleep before the detector had registered the signal – even if it was on 'deep snore', the weakest – and that was a show blown away.

Bugsy reached the minibus and went past it to the car to report.

He thought that the guv'nor might be dozing but an eye was opened when he climbed in. The girl they called Charlie watched him keenly.

Bugsy said, 'Wouldn't be possible to lodge a tag and maintain integrity. Sorry, but we have to do without.'

The guv'nor nodded, didn't seem disappointed.

Bugsy said, 'Not the circumstances where I could do the business and feel satisfied. Just have to be the eyeball stuff.'

The girl, Charlie, reacted – blazed. 'Brilliant. Left out on his own, is he? Aren't you aware of the shit he's facing? How do we keep close if there's no bug on his wheels? Have you a better description, or is this cutting him adrift? I thought you were supposed to be the bloody expert.'

Bugsy said, 'If you didn't know it, Miss, putting our November in a vehicle with a tag in it, and the tag's found, puts him at higher risk. And I am the bloody expert and that's my assessment. Oh, and putting a wire on him adds to a greater risk. When it's possible I'll do it, and when it's not I won't. Got me, Miss?'

He went back to the minibus, unlocked it, climbed in. He settled on the back seat. He was alone. The others, his travelling companions, were all across the far side of the bridge, putting the eyeball on November. Adrian and Dennis would be up front and closest. He'd seen November walking away over the bridge that spanned the narrow point and had thought the man pale-faced, shoulders hunched, as if his confidence ebbed . . . Well, it would, wouldn't it? He was alone, cut off from them. He thought of the meal he had toyed

233

with last night in their hotel, foreign food that he couldn't abide, and he yearned for what he would have had the previous evening if he'd been at home – a village in the Surrey hills near Guildford – a plate of butcher's sausages, the chips his wife cooked and sharp brown sauce in a puddle across them.

The undercover man, November, was isolated – might be lost, might be taken beyond eyeball capability, might be beyond reach – but anything was better than a show blown away. Reputations didn't survive failure.

She attacked. 'Have you done, Mr Lawson, any sort of risk assessment on this?'

His eyes were on her, clear and unwavering in their gaze.

The absence of response stoked her anger. 'Don't you know there's legislation on health and safety that applies to him as much as to a roofer on your house?'

He seemed to smile, cold, and little cracks appeared at the edge of the thin lips.

Katie Jennings's voice rose, battered the interior of the car. 'So, no risk assessment, no acknowledgement of health and safety, and you reckon that *satisfactory*. Not where I'm coming from, it isn't.'

He tilted his head and stared out through the windscreen, looked down the length of the bridge.

'Has this gone through the Office of Surveillance Commissioners? Does it have their approval?'

A quick frown had nudged on to his forehead, as if she was a fly that annoyed him and needed swatting away.

She persisted, 'What about duty of care? Does

234

duty of care to an undercover not exist in your bloody games?'

'Before your tone develops to hysteria, understand, please, you are now operating in a different world. Learn that, and quickly.'

He had jerked upright. Now she was ignored. He was out of the car, went to the bonnet and settled his weight on it. She looked past him. They were coming back across the bridge. She saw Johnny Carrick and he seemed to walk slowly, leaden, behind Josef Goldmann. The Russian minder was ahead . . . There was no tag in the car. If the eyeball was lost, he was alone. They had no bloody right to ask it of him – but it was a *different world*, the man had said.

The nice guy, the best of all of them, Luke, was a clear fifty yards in front of the little group on the pavement of the Glienicker bridge and strode fast, had a good athletic walk, and never looked behind. She saw Bugsy come sharply out of the minibus and trot forward to intercept him at the point where the bridge met the bank, and he seemed to point to a distant part of the lake, in an innocent way, and was talking. Would have been telling Luke there was to be no tag in the car. She swore, and felt no better for it.

'Excuse me, Mr Goldmann, I need to use the toilet.'

'What, Johnny?'

'There's one down there.' Carrick pointed to a concrete block beside a café complex. 'Be as quick as I can.'

The toilets were next to the walkway that led alongside the lakeshore. Couldn't think of anywhere better. He had been aware of the tall guy, codename Delta, on the bridge in front of him. Just had to hope ... Carrick had gone two days, or three, since he'd been on the plot and in the Goldmann household without contact with his cover officer, and it hadn't seemed to matter. Once he had gone a full week without filling in the Book with the log of events – so bloody much to report. Would only have confessed it to himself, but he had felt lifted by the sight of the man ahead of him on the bridge. Also, would not have confessed, except to himself, that the associate – Reuven Weissberg – oozed threat. Thought he had come through the trick played on him. Hadn't slept on his breaks in the guard roster, was damn near knackered. Knew he was under a new level of scrutiny.

There were steps down to the toilet and they had a railing for older people. He had to hold it. Could remember former certainties – at the interview board, and saying he had believed he could cope well with the stress of going undercover.

He pushed open the door. Had no change in his pocket, so dropped a five-euro note into the saucer on the table in front of the attendant. It won no gratitude from the old guy sitting there. Went inside and into the *Herren* section, then to a stall, unzipped and tried to piss. Could not. A man was beside him and a child. The man eyed him. He had opened his fly but couldn't do it. Stood there. Willed himself. The man left with the child. He looked at the cubicles, saw the three doors were ajar, that he was alone. It came in a dribble. The door opened behind him but Carrick didn't turn.

He heard – soft Yorkshire accent and quiet-spoken, 'Don't know how long you have ... As much as anything to let you know we're here and close.'

'Fuck that – try something important.'

236

'Easy, friend. We have you on eyeball, and—'

'I don't have time now – has the car a tag?'

A hesitation. 'No.'

'Why the fuck not?'

'Absence of time and opportunity. What are you learning?'

'What am I learning? That's good. I'm learning that I'm regarded here with the fondness, and trust, of a live rat. Weissberg and his hood are suspicious – suspicious times ten – and—'

'We're staying close, guaranteed.'

'That's a fucking comfort. I'm not a Russian speaker, not a German speaker. I don't know where I'm being led. It's like I'm blindfolded.'

'You lead, we follow.'

'Great – how far behind?

He heard the footsteps, then the squeal of the door. He lost the whisper. Spoke loudly, 'Sorry, can't help you, don't speak German.'

Carrick pulled up his zip. Viktor was in the doorway. He tapped his wristwatch. Carrick said, 'Apologies if I've kept you waiting.'

He followed Viktor out of the public lavatory.

Yashkin peered over the wheel, eyes never off the centre of the road as he spoke: 'As we are now in the Bryansk *oblast* there are things about this place you should know. The total number of hectares is three and a half million, of which half is agricultural land, a third is forested—'

'Do you talk this crap because you think I'm interested, or so that you stay awake?' Molenkov yawned, and did not hold up his hand to shield his mouth. His teeth were exposed, the gaps in the upper and lower sets.

'It's education. Education is an important part of

our lives. Even at the end we should strive to learn. I've read a great deal about the economy and history of the Bryansk *oblast*. Did you know, my friend, that a monk, his name was Peresvet, challenged and defeated the giant enemy, Chelubey, at Kulikovo? I learned that.'

'Was it raining that day?'

'How should I know? You should demonstrate greater respect. We're near now to Borodino where Napoleon vanquished the Tsarist army but weakened himself so much that he failed in his march on Moscow. That was in 1812, on September the seventh, and he won only half a victory, which contributed to a whole defeat.'

'And was it raining on September the seventh, 1812?'

'What's your problem, Molenkov?'

They were crossing a land of flat fields and forests. The Bryansk *oblast*, cut by swollen rivers, was featureless as far as Yashkin's vision reached. A mist was brought down by the rain, not falling hard but with the blurring persistence sufficient to make every pothole a small lake. Yashkin did not dare go fast, and his speedometer showed a constant forty kilometres per hour; had he driven faster he would have risked plunging any of his tyres into a rainwater pool that had formed above a pothole and he would not have known its depth. Greater speed risked the tyres.

'It's like you merely recite pages from a book.'

'I'll ask again, what's your problem?'

'I have no interest in the slaying of Chelubey, or the half-victory of Napoleon in this *oblast*. I think, my friend, we're embarked on a journey of greater importance than the trivia you offer me.'

'Are you answering me? Is that your problem?'

Yashkin would not have described himself, or his

friend, as a man given to sentiment or nostalgia, but as they crossed the rain-sodden roads, bisecting the flooded fields and dripping forestry, each hour he travelled and each kilometre he covered seemed to increase the risk of a soul searched and determination weakened. He imagined the questions bouncing in Molenkov's mind. What would be its target? Who would carry it to the target? Did not know. Over all lay the question, *would it work?* Here, he could absolve himself. He had not the faintest idea. He was not a Kurchatov, a Khariton or a Sakharov. He was not an academician or a scientific leader of the old community of Arzamas-16. He was Major (Ret'd) Oleg Yashkin, forcibly removed, with a pension that went unpaid, driver of a taxi for drunks and addicts. He thought trivia would work well for them.

'Will you talk about it?' Molenkov asked of him.

'No.'

'You refuse to talk about it?'

'Yes.'

'We carry that fucking thing, and you won't talk about it?'

Yashkin said, 'We've done the talking.'

Again he heard the sigh. Had he spoken, before his dismissal, with that cutting whip in his voice to a ranking colonel, and a *zampolit*, he could have expected savage disciplinary sanctions, demotion, perhaps a posting to the Far East or the Arctic cold of the northern test sites at the island of Zemlya, which was close to the eightieth parallel. But the old days were dead and buried.

Molenkov asked him, 'Do you know what day this is?'

'No.'

'Do you know what happened on this day?'

He knew it wasn't the anniversary of the death of his friend's son, Sasha, in the furnace of an armoured vehicle by the entrance of the Salang tunnel in Afghanistan, or his boy's birthday. He knew too that it wasn't the date on which his friend's wife had died, or the date on which his friend had come to his office and confided his shock at seeing a physicist, a man of science who was spoken of as a director of a research zone at Arzamas-16, in a field digging for potatoes.

'I don't know what happened on this day – I apologize because I'm an ignorant bastard, and know very little.'

'On this day, I ran the fifteen-hundred metres.'

'At what level?'

'The final of the Olympic trial. The first three were to represent the Soviet Union, go to the Seventeenth Olympiad, at Rome in Italy. Had I been in the first three, and had I gone on, to Rome, to the Olympic final, I would have competed against the great Herb Elliot who was to take the gold medal. In the trial, on this day, I achieved a personal best. I was twenty-one, and reaching the final of the Olympic trial was enough to gain my entry to State Security . . . I can still see it, the stadium, the crowd, us lined up and the starter with his gun held high.'

'In the trial, friend, where did you finish?'

'Last – where else?'

Yashkin swerved. Laughter convulsed him. He had one hand on the wheel and the other gripped his friend's sleeve. He felt his stomach rise and his eyes were wet with tears. His friend laughed with him. Yashkin did not know how he missed a puddle as big as a lake – his view of the road and the fields was misted. His friend looped an arm round his shoulders and pulled him close. The Polonez rang with their laughter, spittle was on their lips and chins, and his chest hurt. Then they were coughing and spluttering.

Molenkov said, 'I promise I'll try not to talk about it.'

Yashkin said, 'It would be good to see the trotting horses stabled in the Bryansk *oblast*. I believe they're fine animals.'

The rain hammered on the tin roof of the woodsman's home. Water leaked from the ceiling and pattered to the floor, but a steady, firmer dribble splashed on to the table where he sat. His shotgun was down from its wall hooks, broken on the table, but loaded. His dog was alongside his chair and its head rested on his lap. The only movement that Tadeuz Komiski made was to ruffle the fur below the dog's collar. He should have been outside, in the rain, at work.

When the forestry men had cleared a rectangle of planted pines, they had taken only the best, the straightest, trunks and had sliced off the lower branches and upper sprigs. The trunks were hauled away to the depot at the village and there they were cut into lengths to be used as props in coal mines far to the south-west. They were loaded on to rail wagons that were stopped in a line beside the raised platform, then shunted on to the tracks of the main line out of the village. It was the same raised platform that had been used when he was a child . . . and he could not escape from the memories of those long-ago days.

The work he took for himself was to go into the forest on his ancient tractor, with his chain-saw on

241

the trailer and his axe, and drive to one of the rectangles that had been cleared most recently for props. He had few skills and was devoid of sophistication, but could keep the tractor's engine maintained, and the chain-saw. The tractor had been his father-in-law's, given to him as a present in 1965 on the day he had married Maria. To have let the tractor rust, to have abandoned it, would have been the equivalent of disowning the memory of his wife, who had died from the curse with her stillborn child. It was from the tractor's seat that he had first found the old grave where the flood rains had washed earth and compost from the body's bones. Because of that grave, and the curse it had brought down on him, he believed himself watched.

When he went to those cleared rectangles he could find enough of the pine trunks, left by the foresters, to cut into rings and split. With a day's work behind him, he would have a trailer-load of fresh pine logs, with the resin still sticky in them. They spat and crackled in a fire, but threw off good heat. He would drive his load away down the forest tracks, then come to the road and dart across it – because he had no licence or insurance. He would approach the village from a rutted farm path, and reach the priest's home. There he would throw out the logs, by hand, into a loose heap, and they would be used in the church boiler, the priest's house and in the homes of parishioners too enfeebled to gather their own wood. He would be paid, not much but something. Enough to go to the shop in the village and buy bread, milk, and sugar, if it had been a big load, and the noodles that came in plastic packets, broth for soup, and a sack of dried meal for his dog.

A man had sat in the forest with his back against a tree. A man had disturbed the dog. A man had waited silently for a sight of him . . . and he thought the curse revisited his life. He had gathered no wood.

His stomach growled. His own hunger he could accept, but there was only one more day's food in the sack for the dog.

Tadeuz Komiski knew it: it would be the dog's hunger that drove him from his home into the forest, where the curse waited for him, and there was a grave, and a man watched for him.

'And then we have something we've called Haystack which is in the bailiwick of *dear* Christopher Lawson, who is currently up and running in Germany . . .'

As a junior liaison officer, she had never before attended such an august meeting. It was held once a week. Officers of the Secret Intelligence Service and the Security Service came together to brief, with a mutual minimum of detail, those of the sister organization. But her line manager, who would ordinarily have gone to such a meeting with his deputy, had that morning entered hospital for a keyhole hernia operation and would be off for four days, so she had been taken along by the deputy. The Security Service had already completed their description of current operations that had relevance to matters overseas, and the Secret Intelligence Service now listed their work that 'might/could' have 'possible/probable' implications for her people.

'. . . and I understand we've had contact with you concerning a *mafiya* player, Russian, named Josef Goldmann and living in London. Don't get me wrong, anything involving *dear* Christopher Lawson must be of the greatest importance to national security, and of course he has Pettigrew's full backing, but the name "Haystack" must tell us something. You know, needles and that. My impression is that haystacks are seldom successfully searched . . .'

This was a colleague talking. Mistrust between VBX on the south side of the river and Thames House on the north bank was legendary. To SIS, the men and women of her Service were plodding bureaucrats who were fit for not much more than washing dishes; to her Service, SIS were arrogant pedants with a consistent but not admitted record of under-achievement. So, little of value was exchanged at the weekly sessions. They were, that week, on VBX territory – well, not actually inside that citadel of appalling architectural ugliness but in an anteroom off the building's main lobby. The meetings were a leftover, a knee-jerk, from the catastrophe of the seven-seven explosions in the capital, when it had been convenient for both parties to blame the other for non-cooperation as an excuse for the failure to identify four suicide attackers.

'What I can say of Haystack's pedigree is that we're not trumpeting this with allies and friends, and you may draw your own conclusions. Anyway, that's Haystack, and that concludes what we have. Of much greater importance are Sapphire and Nineveh. I'm sure you'd like to take coffee with us before going back over the river.'

Operation Sapphire involved the movement of small-arms weapons from the Balkans into the UK, and Operation Nineveh followed the killing of a Manchester-reared Muslim by American troops in a gunfight in southern Baghdad. The meeting broke up. A series of thoughts flooded her. The man she had met in the tipping rain at the end of the bridge, his responses of brusque courtesy, his compliments on her briefing, and what she had asked him: *Imminent danger? . . . Where are we on a scale of one to ten, Mr Lawson?* And gazing into those eyes, seeing nothing manic in them, listening to his answer, hearing nothing blurted in it: *A scale of one to ten? Probably between twelve and thirteen.* She had believed him – utterly, totally. And he was rubbished by his own.

She went to the side table where a coffee percolator bubbled. She poured herself a cupful.

From behind her, 'Haven't seen you here before – hope you didn't find it too crushingly dull.'

She said that, in fact, she had found it interesting and informative – and that her superior was in hospital for surgery so she had been pressed into service.

'Good to come mob-handed, and I noticed you took a shorthand note, as we did, so there can't be any misunderstandings on who said what and when. That's the damn scene today, inquests and blame passing. I'm Tony, and you are?'

She said she was Alison, and that she had found the report on Haystack particularly interesting and informative.

'Ah, the missing needle.'

She said she had ferried information on Josef Goldmann across the river, and had met Mr Lawson.

'And what did you think of *dear* Christopher Lawson, the originator of Haystack?'

She shrugged, and said she was only a courier.

'Well, Alison, you might just be one of life's

favoured fortunates. Christopher Lawson is a shit –
an alpha-grade, gold-medal shit. In this building,
from top to bottom, he is cordially detested.
Delights in putting people down, belittling them
where it hurts most, which is in front of their peers,
gets some sort of perverse pleasure from serving up
humiliation.'

She saw the colour rise in his cheeks when he
remembered what Christopher Lawson had visited
on him.

'I was late, easy enough mistake. My first trip to
Berlin – anyone could have made it. The rendezvous with an agent was for fourteen hundred hours
in a café in the Moabit district. I had it in my mind
that it was for four o'clock, not fourteen hundred.
Of course, at four o'clock the agent had stopped
waiting. He treated it, fucking Lawson did, as if I'd
farted at a Palace reception, bawled me out in front
of all the section, was just vicious. The next morning he presented me with a gift-wrapped package.
I had to open it, everyone watching, and it was a
Mickey Mouse wristwatch, and he said, "When the
little hand points to Mickey's left ear it's fourteen
hundred." Never let me forget it. Every damn time
he came into the section he'd remind me . . . People
don't matter to him. He uses them.'

She didn't recognize from this the man at the end
of the bridge . . . and she thought of the water
running on the plastic sheeting protecting a photograph, and what she had said: *This one's as
interesting as it gets. Jonathan Carrick . . . he's a phoney
. . . personal records . . . erased and replaced . . . what
they do for policemen, those going undercover.* And
words just told her that had chilled her: *People don't
matter to him. He uses them.* Two faces bounced in
her mind, the one older, features shielded from the

elements by the brim of a trilby hat, and the other quiet and unremarkable, but with a determined and almost bloody-minded jut to the jaw, but with the rainwater washing little streams over it. She had wanted to please so had offered the name and detail of Jonathan Carrick.

She and her colleague were let out through Security and walked up on to the bridge. She glanced down, saw the place where photographs had been shown. She blinked, was responsible, had given the name of Jonathan Carrick . . . God.

He looked around him. The overhead lighting was from low-wattage bulbs, and the furniture was heavy, dark wood. The doors ahead and behind him were painted a deep brown matt. It seemed a place of shadows.

At the door, Mikhail had hugged Viktor perfunctorily. Inside the hall, his Bossman had bear-hugged Reuven Weissberg. At the entrance to the kitchen, his Bossman had kissed the cheeks of a frail elderly lady, who was dressed in black and who would have merged into the gloom but for the brilliance of her short-cropped white hair. Then he was introduced to her.

He held her hand formally, loosely, as if frightened he might hurt someone so fragile, but her response was to grip him and he thought of her fingers as bent wire lengths that were tight on his hand. She did not speak to him but looked up into his eyes. He saw great depth and could not plumb it. He thought she stripped him, and all the while she held his hand he was aware that, from behind his shoulders, his Bossman and Reuven Weissberg spoke to her in tandem. He assumed his presence was explained. Was she satisfied with what she was told? He couldn't say, but his hand was released.

She beckoned him. He followed. She led him into a kitchen. Again, the lights were dulled. He thought it was a modern kitchen with the best work surfaces and a touch-button cooker, but an old, chipped, stained table and two scraped chairs with unravelling raffia seats competed with the smart units. On the cooker, water riffled at simmering point in dented saucepans. Carrick reckoned an old life had been inserted into a luxury modern apartment. On the table a single place was laid, but on a unit there was a pile of plates, all faded and each with broken edges. She pointed to the chair.

Carrick sat.

The woman had brought with her the baggage of her life. He understood that. The Bossman had told him, as they had crossed Berlin in the car, that she was the grandmother of Reuven Weissberg. He could see the night panorama of inner Berlin from the kitchen window. It was an apartment – he grinned to himself and nothing of it crossed his mouth – that a woman would die for and a man would kill for. But what he had seen was furniture and a kitchen that a charity shop, back home, wouldn't have accepted. It was gear that would have gone unsold at a car-boot job. He had seen the deference with which his Bossman treated Reuven Weissberg; stood to reason that Reuven Weissberg was bigger, higher up the damn ladder, than his man.

Carrick turned.

She put four filled plates on to a tray, and there were four glasses. He thought from the cooking smells that she had prepared boiled pork, boiled potato and boiled cabbage. Carrick stood. He assumed it was right for him to carry the tray, but she waved him away. He sensed that her authority, an imperious and short-armed wave for him to stay seated, had been handed down to her grandson. She lifted the tray and shuffled out of the kitchen.

He should never have agreed to being part of it, should have thrown it back in their faces.

He saw the painting. Johnny Carrick knew nothing of art. He went into a gallery only when he escorted Esther Goldmann. He reckoned the picture had class but the frame was junk-shop stuff – it would have gone into a bin at the back of any of the galleries his Bossman's wife patronized. The painting, though, was different. It was not that Johnny Carrick was inarticulate, or stupid, but looking at the picture that hung between a wall cabinet and the spokes for drying washing, he could not have explained its quality. Very simple. An impression of depth. The soft ochre colours of old leaves that the winter had not taken off birch trees, the darkness of pines making a canopy, the gold of rotted compost on the ground, and the trunks stretching into infinity. He pushed up from the chair, scraped its legs back on the vinyl floor, went closer to it. He gazed at the heart of it and wondered where it was, what it meant, and why it was the only thing of beauty he had seen in the apartment. There was also a photograph in a little cheap wood frame, faded and with broken lines across it as if it had been folded for a long time. It was set inside the wall cabinet, behind the glass. He had lingered on the painting, but he glanced at the monochrome photograph that would not have measured more than two inches by one. Another forest. A young woman holding a baby. She had pure white hair that showed against the darkness of the black tree trunks. She held the baby close.

He should have quit. Should have made the excuse and refused to get on the aircraft, should have walked to the Pimlico office and confessed his fear.

Fingers were on his shoulder, as sharp as bent wire. He spun, startled, a kid caught out gawping. She pointed to his chair. He sat.

Should have cut and run – maybe would.

The plate was put in front of him. Boiled meat, potatoes and cabbage steamed into his eyes. She stood in front of the painting, thin arms folded, and blocked it from his view. Her shoulder covered the photograph of a young woman with snow-white hair who held a baby.

Carrick ate. She watched him, and he could read nothing of her mind.

Chapter 9: 12 April 2008

There were four hours available to him. Carrick did not recognize himself. Should have gone back into his room, locked the door, then set the small alarm beside his bed. He did not recognize himself because he had never before felt such uncertainty and loss of purpose.

He did a part of what he should have done, was inside his room, had locked the door and armed the alarm, but he did not strip and crawl under the counterpane. Dressed, he sat on the end of the bed. The room's walls seemed to press close, as if they intended to suffocate him. He could hear vague sounds seeping down the corridor, televisions, voices and footsteps, but they were nothing to him. At the heart of it was his feeling, deep held, that he wasn't progressing in the infiltration. He had sat for nearly three hours in the kitchen, and the old woman had worked round him but had not acknowledged him. He might not have been there. No communication. His thanks for his meal, in English and understandable to an imbecile, had not been accepted. An offer to go with the empty tray to collect the four plates had been ignored, and she had done it. He had sensed, though, when his back was to her, that her eyes were on him and their force had seemed to burn his neck. But if he turned and sought to meet them they had snapped off him. When they had left, when he had held out his hand, she had kept hers behind her back. He knew nothing of what had been discussed. The dilemma was clear to him: if he did not push for inclusion his time was wasted and he would learn nothing; if he pushed, he attracted greater attention and risked greater suspicion.

Carrick left his room. He tiptoed down the corridor and past the doors to the anteroom, where Viktor would be in an easy chair, and to Josef Goldmann's bedroom.

Carrick took the lift down, rocking with its motion, and held the bars at the glass sides as it plunged. He could feel the weakness in his legs.

He walked past the darkened reception desk, and past the night porter. The door was locked and he tried to force it. Panic rose. The night porter came to him and produced the key. Cold air hit him and chilled the sweat on his forehead, at his neck and groin. He had only his jacket on, no coat.

Beyond the canopy above the door, rain fell on the pavement. He went out and heard the door closed behind him.

Before him was the great edifice of a church, a ruin that was a monument. The orange lights from the street-lamps illuminated the rain on old stones still dark from the scorching of incendiaries. He did not know its name or history. He ducked his head and walked faster, skirting the square round the ruin. As he passed the church, a clock chimed – a mournful, doom-laden note – but Carrick did not recognize whether it struck the hour or a half. Dribbles of rain ran down his cheeks and forehead. He saw a cluster of drunks with bottles tilted to their mouths. One called to him and another started to lurch towards him but was pulled back, and he went on, left them behind. A girl beckoned to him. She had blonde hair that the rain disfigured and he thought the wet washed out the dye. He saw her heavy thighs below a short skirt, and went on, leaving her behind too. For much of his walk, though, there were no cars on the streets, and no winos, tarts or druggies on the pavement, only emptiness and the sound of his squelching shoes. He was off a main drag and crossed the side-streets between Kleiststrasse and Hohenstaufenstrasse where apartments were blacked out for the night and offices were charcoal-grey caverns behind their windows.

If Carrick had hoped that by walking through a strange city he might again recognize himself, he had failed.

He was sodden, cold, confused.

The sign on the corner of the block above him said he had come on to Fuggerstrasse. So damn tired . . . Another clock chimed, and he did not look down at his wristwatch to see how much of a four-hour window remained open. There was a doorway with a high step, and a door of heavy wood that was closed – probably chained, bolted and barred against the pariahs of the night. There was a polished brass plate beside the bell button, but he didn't bother to read who worked, at what, in the building.

Carrick slumped down. Wet came off the mat and soaked the seat of his trousers. He wedged himself into the corner and had one shoulder against the wall below the bell and the bright plate, the other against the door. He drew up his knees so that they were against his chest, wrapped his arms round his upper shins and rocked. He couldn't have made himself smaller or more insignificant, and his mind had clouded. He was beyond, now, any evaluation of the consequences of not being in a hotel room when a small alarm bleeped on a bedside table. Nobody cared. Not fucking Katie, not fucking George, who had cut him adrift and handed him over, not the fucking man who called himself Golf. What did they know of goddam Viktor, goddam Mikhail, goddam Weissberg, and the goddam old woman who was a grandmother? And what did they know of being alone? Not a living soul cared. He had no responsibility for missing the call of the clock beside the bed. A man passed, was across the street, walking briskly under an umbrella, but the rain must have blown into his face because he, too, had a drip on his nose. No, he didn't recognize himself.

Johnny Carrick was huddled in the doorway, his head on the arms that were round his legs, and his resolve leached away.

'What do you reckon?' Adrian asked.

'He's gone,' Dennis said.

'Can't argue with that.'

'Ready to chuck in the towel, because he's – like I said – gone.'

They were at the far end of Fuggerstrasse, where it joined Motzstrasse. Dennis had led down the street and identified the doorway in which their man, November, was sitting. They were contrasting personalities, with dissimilar hobbies when not working as increments for VBX, but in matters of their trade they shared skills. Dennis claimed peripheral vision of 140 degrees, and Adrian rated his at up to 160 degrees. When they were not being used as increments, they lectured on the National Surveillance Course for recruits and there they taught the necessity of 'third-party awareness', which meant scanning from the corners of their eyes without shifting their heads – peripheral vision. Neither had had to twist his head to see November in the doorway.

'You happy that he hasn't a tail?'

'Would have showed if he had, but it hasn't.'

'Well, seeing the state of him, we'll have to call the gaffer.'

'If he's a goner, the whole thing's down the tube.'

By touch, Dennis activated his mobile, which was bulky in his anorak pocket because of its built-in encryption devices, tapped the keys, waited for his call to be answered. He was in his fifty-third year, married but without children, and found relaxation in an apron in front of his cooking range where he did serious French cuisine. He would have described his colleague – standing with him on the junction of Fuggerstrasse and Motzstrasse in the damn rain – as the best partner it was possible to acquire, but he did not take their professionalism to social levels and had never cooked for Adrian. What was common with them was a mastery of surveillance, being seen without being noticed.

'That you, Mr Lawson? . . . Right, sorry and all that. Bit of a problem with your November. We were kipping in the wheels by the hotel when he came out. I was doing watch, woke Adrian. He was just shambling about, walking but going nowhere. The rain's been pissing down on him but he has no

coat. He's drenched. Right now, he's in a doorway
. . . Hold on.'

Adrian tugged Dennis's sleeve, said softly, 'Lay it
on a bit thicker, give it some juice. He's about to cop
out.'

'You should get here, Mr Lawson, and quick.
From the body language of him, we're about to lose
him . . . Right, right. It's the junction of Fugger and
Motz . . . Mr Lawson, don't hang about.' Dennis
dropped his wrist from his mouth, and his hand in
his pocket closed the call. 'How was that?'

'Had to be said – wasn't the time for mucking
about.'

If they had been thrown together on a train or
in a bar, and they had not been linked by their
skills in surveillance, they would have had little
in common. Their creed was to pose the question:
'Can I be remembered, recognized or described?'
Dennis did not think so. Neither did Adrian.
But, his opinion, the anticipated hard stretch was
still ahead of them if the agent – November – put
his act together and insinuated further into a
conspiracy . . . got his act together and quick.
Many times before Dennis had trailed in the
wake of undercovers, had watched them from a
remote distance, been unseen and unheard; had
seen the stress on them, like they smelled of it,
and had thanked his good God it wasn't asked
of him.

'Did the gaffer say how long?'

'Did not.'

'Bringing the whole gang?'

Dennis grimaced. 'Wouldn't you, if it's all going
down the bloody drain? Without his access, we're
dead in the water.'

* * *

'We trusted nobody,' she had said, in her thin, whistling voice, as if she blew through a reed when she spoke. 'To seek trust is to look for comfort where there is none.'

He lay on a Spartan, institutional, steel-framed bed. Under Reuven Weissberg the old mattress had lumps and did not protect him from the sharpness of the coiled metal springs. He had slept in that bed, on that mattress, since he was a child. It had been given him on the first night he had spent in his grandmother's care. He had been four years old and his feet had barely reached halfway down the bed. Now his bare toes stretched beyond its end. He knew it was her belief that the bed would harden him.

She had gazed down at him as she said it, and had put on the wood slats of the chair beside the bed the chipped china mug of warm milk. The same mug had been brought him every night that he had slept under the same roof as her, and every night he would wait for the quiet to fall on her room and listen for the faint rhythm of her snoring. Then he would go to the lavatory, tip the warm milk into the bowl and flush it away. He hated its taste, and would not have dared tell her. She had voiced her doubts on the wisdom of *trust*, and her eyes – as they always did on this matter – had screwed and blinked as if the word was an obscenity.

'If you trust, you make yourself weak,' she had said.

He had spoken of Goldmann's trust in the young soldier.

'When you trust, you depend on another. You should trust only yourself, as we did.'

He had spoken of Goldmann's trust in the young soldier who had saved his employer's life without thought of himself.

'Trust is softness, tenderness and pity. They did not exist where I was, except with the dead.'

He had spoken of Mikhail, who had been late on a reaction. His fingers had massaged the gouge in his upper arm where a bullet had hit. He had spoken of the young man he believed worthy of trust.

'Believed? Only *believed*? Do nothing until you have tested him with extreme rigour. Test him to the point of breaking him. I will not have him back in my home until you have. I will not see him again.'

She had gone. He smelled the milk in the mug on the chair beside his head. The bed hurt his back and hip but he would never complain of it to her. It would have been a similar bed on which his father, Jakob, had eked out the last days and nights of his life – hacking and coughing, a victim of pleurisy – in the criminal camp north of Perm; dead and gone when his son was four. It was on similar beds that he had slept during his conscription service. Others alongside had wept, but he had not . . . or from the beatings of the NCOs.

He had not heard her return, but the door opened. She looked down at him. 'You have not, Reuven, drunk your milk.'

'I'm waiting for it to cool. I will, of course, as I always do.'

She wore a thin dark wrap and it was tight round her tiny body. She was at the end of the bed, by the iron rail. 'Do you remember my story of trust?'

'Every word.'

He listened, as he had so many times, and saw the trees of the Forest of the Owls and the concrete supports of the central watchtower, and the path that was the Himmelstrasse of sixty-five years before – the Road to Heaven. He saw it today and saw it then, and heard her voice.

Three hundred Jewish girls – that was the figure we heard from the rumour – were brought from Wlodawa many months after I had come to the camp. It was February 1943, and I was surprised, when I heard of their arrival, that there were still Jews left in the town. They must have been among the last.

I did not see them. Had I, then there would have been girls I knew, those I had been to school with and more who had come with their fathers to my father's shop. They came in a larger transport – I do not know it for certain but the rumour said they arrived by train and were then separated. Old men and young, older women, who were mothers and grandmothers, and all the children were sent ahead of them into the Tube, or the Himmelstrasse as it was called. Three hundred Jewish girls were kept back.

It was said that they were put into storage, as meat would be put into a refrigerator. After the rest of the transport, their relations and friends, had gone down the Tube, the band had played, the fraudster in the white coat had led, the Ukrainian bastards had driven them on, the doors had closed and the engine had started . . . they were put aside.

We did not know then why three hundred young Jewesses remained in the Tube. We were not fools. If a man or woman lives as close to death as we did, then the sense that interprets events will rear. We did not know, but we had opinion. All the talk that evening in our barracks hut, among those who had only the intention to live another week or another month, was of the Jewish girls who were in the Tube, in the area that had been cleared of the suitcases and travel bags that were normally left there. I believe those girls would have trusted, thought there was truth in what they were told because the kitchens in our section were ordered to produce bread and soup for them. It was the first time that food had been taken to those who had entered the Road to Heaven. They would have slept with the comfort of trust.

The following day – it was 11 February: I cannot say how we registered the date of each day of the week, each month of the year – although we did not know, the opinions grew, flourished and fattened. We were taken off our usual work. The sorting of jewellery and money and clothing was stopped. The tailors and bootmakers were taken from their benches. The laundry was given more people to help and the best uniform of each German was brought for pressing and starching, their boots for polishing. I was among those women who were escorted to the SS quarters, the Swallow's Nest, and others went to Commandant Reichleitner's office, which they called the Merry Flea, and we had to clean and scrub the floors until they shone. The capos would not say what was expected but, of course, we realized a visitor of the highest importance was expected. The men used pine branches to brush the sand of the compound where the snow had been cleared. I remember that it was bright, sunny, and there had been a heavy frost, but we had not had snow for more than ten days. There was bitter cold, and ice hung from our huts, but in the Swallow's Nest a fire burned, so it was good to work there. I do not believe that any of us – I did not – considered the cold in the shed where the three hundred Jewish girls were kept.

And another night passed. We shivered in our bunks, we held each other for warmth, and another dawn came.

It was 12 February. I was with those who were taken again to the Swallow's Nest to do more cleaning, which was ridiculous because the rooms could not have been cleaner. I saw, through a window on the first floor high enough to have a view over the fence with the pine branches, that policemen on horses rode round the edge of the camp. All the Germans were excited, and nervous, and they shouted at us, and the capos hit us if we looked up from cleaning the floorboards.

We were being led back to our compound when the train came. The outer gate was open. It was possible to see through it, when he got out of the carriage. Then we were in our compound, and it was impossible to see more. The image of him was frozen in my mind. He wore a long open leather coat, spectacles without rims, and he was saluted with a forest of raised arms. An older woman knew, Miriam Bloch. She had survived because she was the finest seamstress in the camp. She had seen him. Miriam Bloch said he was Heinrich Himmler.

Because Miriam Bloch had identified him – Heinrich Himmler – we now knew why three hundred Jewish girls from Wlodawa had been kept back from the transport. They had been in the baggage shed for two days and nights. Did they still trust in the lies they had been told? Were they still calm? We were now at our normal duties, but we listened. That day I worked in the section that sorted clothing. There had been a Dutch transport a week before, and the clothes worn by Dutch Jews were superior in quality to those of Polish, Ukrainian and Belarussian Jews. The clothing of the Dutch would be shipped to Germany for issue to those who had lost their possessions in the bombing. The capos were fierce and had whips that day; we were told we might be inspected and might not, but if we were visited by Heinrich Himmler we should not look up, should not speak, should carry on with our work.

He did not come to us.

We listened.

There would have been time for coffee to be served to Himmler and his party in the Swallow's Nest, and time for him to walk along the path cleared of snow to reach the Himmelstrasse, and time for the procedure to be explained to him by the commandant. More time while the liar in his white coat gave his speech on the need for delousing Jews, then began to lead them – the three hundred Jewesses – down the Road to Heaven. Perhaps, even then, most believed him and trusted his words. More time while Heinrich Himmler watched as their hair was cut, as the three hundred Jewish girls stripped naked, as they shivered in the cold, then began to run after the trotting white coat, with the guns of the Ukrainians behind them, inside the narrow width of the Tube towards the doors of the chambers. I think they would have used three, and I think Heinrich Himmler would have strode forward quickly after them so that he saw the doors opened and the girls forced in, the doors slammed shut and the bolts pushed home.

We listened. Some, afterwards, said they had heard the singing of the girls, the prayer of despair. I did not. I was collecting silk blouses when I heard the engine of Gasmeister Bauer switched on, and I had started to cut off the labels from Amsterdam, Rotterdam and Eindhoven when the geese began to squawk, and then there was quiet.

Before leaving on his train, Heinrich Himmler stayed to dinner in the Swallow's Nest. We heard later that he had offered his congratulations to the officers, and that he had promoted Commandant Reichleitner to the rank of Hauptsturmführer and Deputy Commandant Niemann to Untersturmführer. And he left us. We lay on our bunks in the barracks and heard the train pull away. Had he smiled when he first saw the Jewish girls?

I did not cry myself to sleep that night, 12 February, in the knowledge that – for a demonstration of the efficiency of the process – three hundred Jewish girls from my own town, Wlodawa, many of whom I would have known, had been put to death with fumes from

Gasmeister Bauer's engine. I was alive. I would face another day. I could hate and loathe. I survived, and they did not, to see the light of dawn seep into our barracks' windows. And that day there came a new rumour. It said that the Germans had suffered a defeat in battle against the Russians, at the city of Stalingrad, and that they were in retreat ... But I had no trust and did not believe that another would save me – only myself. I was, as we all were, alone.

'Where is he?'

Adrian pointed down the length of the shadowed street.

Dennis said, 'Third doorway from the far end, this side.'

'I'll do this on my own.' Lawson left them and strode off down the pavement. He heard steps behind him – Davies and little Charlie, the cuckoo girl. He went fast and fancied they hurried to keep up. Once he flicked his fingers, irritably, behind his back as a gesture that he didn't want them close, but they ignored him and kept coming. He had been fast asleep, dreamless as usual, when the call had come, and he had pulled on clothes over his pyjamas.

He remembered Clipper Reade's story. Clipper had had a good story for a similar situation ... Dennis had said: *From the body language of him, we're about to lose him.* It was the same as Clipper had faced on the bench in the park below the old fortress at Gdansk. He'd listened well to the big American's story, told over two pots of Earl Grey, some thirty years before.

He came to him.

He looked down into the dark of the doorway. The man was curled up, foetal, his shoulders seemed to shake, his hands were clasped tight below his knees but still trembled, and his head was sunk. Well, small mercies, while half recovering from the confusion of that damn call coming in he had made one correct and important decision: to keep bloody Shrinks out of it.

He turned. Caught Davies and the cuckoo girl in his glance. 'You stay back. On no account do you interfere. You are not a part of this.'

He crouched. With a short jabbing movement, he slapped November's cheeks, right and left, little stinging blows – and the eyes in front of him opened wide.

'Do I have your attention?'

The eyes, glazed, stared back at him.

Lawson spoke briskly: 'I'm not getting into a debate about your state of mind. Neither will I tolerate some navel-gazing examination of what we're about and where we're going. I will, however, remind you of one thing. You were a volunteer.'

He saw his man stiffen and anger glowed in the eyes. Better.

'It's not acceptable, if you didn't know it, to be Volunteer Man on Monday, everyone gets to speed on Tuesday, and become Quit and Run Man on Wednesday. There is a team behind you, good men and women at the top of their game, but your response is to hunker down in a doorway and snivel. You happy with that?'

A fist clenched and the body, Lawson thought, was coiled with anger.

'Right now you're pathetic. You're a disappointment, at acute level, to those working with you. So the going's rough. Well, sonny boy, you volunteered. Get up off your backside, start walking, and walking fast – oh, and before that, tell me, words of one syllable, about dinner at Reuven Weissberg's, and when the move out is scheduled for.'

He had to strain to listen, but his man was now standing. Lawson leaned close, had an arm on the shoulder, felt the tightness of the muscles, and heard the story of the evening.

'Right, that'll do for a start. We're here, think on it, in your wake – and think also that you're one cog, just one, in a complex but dedicated machine. Not least yourself, you've let down many people this evening, this morning. It cannot happen again. When the pace quickens, you may have cause to cringe in a corner, but not now. Now we're barely started. On your way, young man.'

Lawson was shouldered off the step, and nearly fell. He had to grope for the wall, where there was a brass plate, to steady himself. He had felt the aggression as the shoulder had buffeted him aside. Aim achieved.

His man, November, shambled a few paces, then stopped. Lawson watched. He saw November kick out a leg, then almost march forward, as if a decision had been taken. Lawson breathed hard. Saw him reach the corner, shoulders thrown back, turn into the next street, and lost sight of him.

From behind, Davies hissed, 'That was pretty unnecessary, about as savage as anything I've ever seen, and—'

Lawson said evenly, 'Well, you're young, inexperienced, and have seen very little, so your comment is quite simply inappropriate.'

'—was brutal and vicious, and I feel dirty to be part of it. Have you made a career of walking over people and—'

265

'Keep your toys in the pram.' Suddenly so bloody tired. He started to go, slowly, back up the street towards where the surveillance men were. She skipped up to be alongside him. Little Charlie, the cuckoo girl, matched his step and her head bobbed by his elbow. Yes, so bloody tired.

Matter-of-fact, she said, 'I've been putting it together, Mr Lawson, the little bits and pieces that drop from your table, what you've said for us low-life to hear, and what's happened. If the people I work with knew what you'd done they'd be standing in a line to kick your head in. It's all very clever, Mr Lawson. I suppose that winning, to you, justifies everything.'

He did not say that losing was unacceptable. If he was right in his judgement, and a warhead was now travelling overland towards some damn place on some damn border from faraway Sarov, for purchase and collection, then – indeed – losing was not an acceptable option.

'How did it go, Mr Lawson?' Adrian asked him.

'He's fine.'

'Stiffen his spine, Mr Lawson?' Dennis asked him.

'Did what was necessary.'

He slid into the car's seat, was bloody near asleep as soon as he did so.

He kissed the cheeks of his wife gently so that she wouldn't wake. Then, in stockinged feet, the Crow went out into the corridor and along it. He pushed open the door to the children's bedroom, went to each bed and kissed the forehead of each child.

In the hall he put on his shoes, lifted his bag and hitched it on his shoulder. He left nothing behind him, no mobile phone or laptop computer from which evidence might later be taken. He unlocked the front door, and the first smear of dawn was coming from across the Gulf sea. In the middle distance, he could see the crane on the building site. A taxi waited for him. He did not know when, if, he would return home to his wife and children. He hoped to, but did not know if it would be possible.

The taxi drove away. If he never again saw his wife, whom he loved dearly, or his children, if he took delivery of the weapon and was successful in moving it on to the target zone, he believed the sacrifice of his family would be easy.

The taxi took the Crow to the airport.

His mind churned with the implications of what he was committed to, and Sak had not slept. In the narrow single bed, he lay on his back and the thoughts rampaged.

If, when he had embarked on his journey, he was suddenly aware of men round him with guns, would he run or would he stand and raise his hands? Would they give him the chance to raise his hands or would they shoot him down? He had seen himself, in the night, spreadeagled on a pavement with a pistol barrel crushed against his ear, or crumpled, with blood flowing from the bullet wounds and a crowd gathered at safe distance from him.

Also in his mind, intruding, were the images and voices of his visit to Summers, the chief security officer. *Your clearance to work here is, with effect today, withdrawn* and *security and the safety of the nation demand, in these difficult times, that we make hard decisions*; he doubted, now, that any at Aldermaston remembered him, that any recalled seeing him walk like a zombie from the headquarters building to the hostel, clear his room and pack his bags, and that any spoke of his going to the main gate, feeding his card into the machine, knowing it would not be returned, and going to the bus stop. He had fear, but had hate to counter it.

The house was quiet. He yearned to sleep but could not. The thought jolted him.

At his journey's end he would not be a lowly technician in a school physics laboratory. He would be a man of importance, substance and stature, integral to the plan of those who had recruited him. Could hold his head high, yes, because the examination he would make and the utilization of his expertise were not for money. He was not owned by greed, avarice, could tell himself that his acts were governed by principle.

Igor Molenkov did not sleep. Beside him, Yashkin slept after a fashion, but the rhythm of his breathing was punctuated by groans.

Every muscle in Molenkov's body ached, every joint had pain locked in it, and every time he moved, it got worse. The floor on which he sat was concrete hard, and the two blankets they had been given were too thin to offer decent protection against the cold. At least the noise had stopped and the mechanic's work was finished.

They had been – he did not know how many hours before, had lost count – on the final stage of the run into Bryansk. The countryside, flooded fields, flooded rivers and flooded forests, had been behind them. They had reached the lines of factories on the approach to the city and – of course – it had been raining when the engine had died, without a cough of warning. It was as if it had simply given up the ghost and gone happily, but inconveniently, to the arms of St Seraphim. It was twenty-four years since his beloved wife had passed on – twenty-four years, one month, two weeks and four days, never forgotten – and she had gone like that. She had been in the hospital bed, listening to his awkward talk, had turned to the window, where the rain lashed the glass, and had died, without warning. They had pushed the Polonez at least three-quarters of a kilometre, him at the back where the fucking useless heap was heaviest, and Yashkin at the side with his hand through the open window, manoeuvring the steering-wheel. Traffic had built behind them, horns had blasted, but no one had helped. They had pushed the Polonez half the length of Komsomolskaya Street, almost reached the city, when Yashkin had wrenched the wheel and they had been on the forecourt of a small garage.

Molenkov had sagged against the car's roof and gasped for breath.

Yashkin had negotiated. Of course, the men were about to finish their day. Cash had oiled the palm of the chief mechanic.

Molenkov had heard the man say that the Polonez would be repaired and ready for the road by morning – the description of the engine's death indicated an electrical malfunction, and the two old gentlemen should find lodging for the night.

And he had heard Yashkin say that they would sleep on the floor with their car. The chief mechanic had suggested that the Polonez be unloaded, the weight in the back taken out, before the car was pushed on to the ramp above the pit, and Yashkin had refused, with vehemence, then winked, as if he were an old thief moving stolen goods, or contraband. More money had been passed. More than a half of the cash they carried between them had slid into the back pocket of the chief mechanic, the fucking criminal.

They couldn't have gone together to find a café and food. Molenkov had lumbered off into the night in search of rolls, cheese and an apple each. They had eaten, then lain down on the floor, with the dirt and the sump oil.

An hour ago, Molenkov had heard the engine started, and the old girl had run, he'd admit it, sweetly. He had tried to wake Yashkin to tell him that the repair was effected, but he had been sworn at and Yashkin had rolled over on to his side, away from him.

He shifted again. The bones of his buttocks dug into flesh. No respite to be found on the concrete floor. A night light, dulled, had been left on. He saw it. Was not certain, at first, of what he saw, then had confirmation. A rat quartered the oil-covered floor around the edge of the pit.

He looked across and saw the tail of the car weighed down.

He thought of what the car carried – lost all hope of an hour's sleep in the last hour of the night – its weight, what *he* did, and what Yashkin did, and—
A convulsing cough broke next to him. Yashkin shook, his head jerked up, and his hands rubbed hard at his eyes.

Yashkin grinned. Then he punched Molenkov's shoulder and chuckled. The pain in his body was sheer and clear-running, and Yashkin chuckled.

Yashkin said, 'I wouldn't have believed it. In all this shit, on the floor, I slept like a baby. As good a night's sleep as I can remember. What's the matter? Didn't you sleep?'

Molenkov had been awake to think of guilt.

Yashkin's arm was round the shoulder where his punch had fallen. 'I can sleep anywhere. I feel refreshed. You know, Molenkov, it could have been worse.'

Molenkov stood up, went to the pit, reached up, lifted the tail door and removed his bag. He unzipped it and took out his razor, some soap and the shaving-brush. He went towards the back of the workshop where there was a stinking lavatory and a grimy basin.

Yashkin called after him, 'We should face the new day with confidence. What a team we make.'

He came out of the bathroom. Carrick had run the shower at full power as hot as he could bear it, and his skin tingled. He thought he had put some warmth back into his body. He had towelled himself with aggression, every word spat at him and every nuanced gesture from the night's actions and encounter alive in him. He stepped over the sodden suit, shirt and shoes that littered the carpet.

The alarm went. He had reached the hotel some fifteen minutes before, had shown his guest card to the night porter or would not have been admitted. In the room's mirror, he had seen himself half drowned, dishevelled, and had stripped. He had put on the TV. God alone knew why – maybe for company.

Carrick killed the alarm. He stood naked in the centre of the room, grimaced, and let his fingernails scrape into the skin of his palms, as if that would purge him of what he had done. He blanked out the insults spat quietly at him. The TV showed commercials. He took a plastic laundry sack from the wardrobe and dumped his clothes and shoes in it. He wrote his name and room number on it, as if his work still had a future ahead of it. He dressed. Had only the one change. A weather forecast played on the TV. He buttoned a shirt, knotted a tie, smoothed his hair, buffed his second shoes with a handkerchief, pocketed his wallet and the mobile phone, had everything, and was three minutes away from changeover time.

He left his laundry outside his door. Went the few paces down the corridor. Knocked. If the surveillance hadn't tracked him, if the bastard hadn't come to the step in the doorway on Fuggerstrasse, he wouldn't have been at the outer door of the anteroom now, and it would have been over. Damp passport in a damp hand, taken from a damp jacket, offered at Tempelhof, and a flight home, telling himself he didn't give a damn, a bus into London and a walk to a Pimlico street: 'Sorry and all that, George, but I wasn't up for it. Anything else on the horizon?' The door was opened and he saw Viktor.

Carrick thought the man studied him. He thought the eyes covered his hair, his face, his tie knot and the clean shirt, the well-pressed suit that had been hung long enough in the wardrobe to lose the bag's creases, the shoes.

Carrick was hit by it. Why did a man coming on guard duty at four in the morning, to lounge for four hours on an anteroom settee, shower and shave as if it was party time, put on a clean shirt and suit and change his shoes? Couldn't answer it, and didn't know whether Viktor asked. And didn't know whether the Russian, an hour or two back, had come out of the anteroom, gone to his door, rapped on it and not been answered. Viktor had on scuffed shoes with the laces undone, crumpled trousers, a shirt open halfway to his waist and no tie. No comb had been through his hair. When Viktor turned to fetch his jacket, Carrick saw the pistol in his belt.

'Is there anything I should know?' he asked.

He thought Viktor smiled but could not be certain of it, then shook his head.

'What's the programme for the morning?'

Now Carrick was sure Viktor smiled, and was gone.

Chapter 10: 13 April 2008

They drove out from the new centre of Berlin.

Carrick had come off duty in the anteroom. He had missed breakfast and had been on his bed for perhaps an hour. Then Viktor rapped hard on his door and told him to be dressed, ready to leave in ten minutes. He had sensed a different mood in the man; something smug, contented, as if a decision had been taken.

Viktor was at the wheel and Carrick was beside him, the Bossman on the back seat. No talk. Viktor concentrated on traffic, the tail end of the rush-hour, but they were going away from the commercial district of glass, steel and concrete towers, and went through old streets. Many of the signs there were in Turkish, and a street market, a long line of stalls that backed on to a canal, had appeared. The day was starting up. Clothing was being hung on rails, meat was being displayed, vegetables and fruit carefully heaped in pyramids. Music wailed from radios and speakers. Carrick did not know where he was because he had no knowledge of Berlin. Neither did he know where they were headed because he had not been told; it was not right for him to ask. He sat beside Viktor, eyed the pavements and acted the role of bodyguard.

He thought his Bossman was subdued and that, in contrast, Viktor had found confidence. He reckoned that the route and destination had been agreed by Josef Goldmann and the minder, but he was not inside the loop.

Carrick sensed growing danger, but could not identify it so could not respond. It was what they talked about endlessly in SCD10. The sensing of danger and the response to intuition were subjects they chewed at daily. It was an unwritten law, at SCD10, that the safety of the officer was paramount – but he'd thought the law had no writ over Golf, who had lectured and humiliated him in the office-block doorway. At SCD10, there was a laid-down tactical approach of specifics and generalities. The agent was not expected to hazard his security in pushing an investigation the extra mile. Where possible, meetings with targets should be in public places, restaurants, bars and hotel lobbies, so that the back-up could be close enough to intervene; and there were those dark times of uncertainty when an eyeball view of the agent was not available, and it was said that those times, for the handlers, were like the old space shots when the returning capsule was on re-entry and radio contact was lost, and they must wait for the call sign to be given, the sight again of their man. They also said, in the Pimlico office, over tea and coffee, that the first rule for an undercover was to hatch an idea of his exit route. Where was the door? Where did it lead to? Carrick didn't know, now, where there were firearms in close support – whether they even existed – and he had no idea of where his exit route should be, but his sense of danger cut the silence in the car.

They had gone past the street market.

The buildings around him were more dilapidated.

There was the greyness of neglect. Shadows fell further and deeper.

Women, kids, old men wearing caps, fags hanging from their mouths, stared at the big car crossing their territory.

Then they were beyond the blocks and the rain fell harder on the windscreen, the wipers working faster.

Into a cul-de-sac. There were steel security railings topped with spikes and rambling coils of razor wire. A gate was open. A man stood by it and waved Viktor inside. Carrick could not see the man's face because he had a scarf across his mouth and cheeks. In the mirror, the gate was closed after them. The first rule of the Pimlico office was to know the exit route: he did – it was that gate set in a spiked, wired fence. He thought that, behind him, Josef Goldmann's breath came faster and, beside him, that Viktor smirked. The car braked in front of an old brick-built warehouse. Some of the windows were open to the elements, the glass panes smashed, and some were boarded up. Water cascaded from two useless gutters, and grass grew from the space under the eaves. A small door was set in the brickwork where Viktor had stopped the car

They walked through, his Bossman first, then Carrick and Viktor . . . Guys came to SCD10 and lectured. A few were from the FBI but most were older men who had packed up doing undercover for a living. Some dealt with it – what was going through Carrick's mind and louder than the alarm beside his bed – and some spoke of it only when questioned. Yes, they all looked for exit routes. No, they had never used the cop-out and run. Yes, they had all felt the instinct of danger. No, they had never quit, thrown that bloody lamp through the window, or made an excuse, gone out through the door and turned their back on the business. The last FBI man to come to Pimlico had used the word 'iced' to describe an undercover pulled out because the danger was thought too great . . . No chance that the head honcho, Golf, would lift him out – no damn chance.

Their feet crunched on broken glass, and once his Bossman slipped on the corridor floor. Carrick thought he might have stepped in a dosser's shit, or a dog's.

They went through a door hanging crazily and on to the floor space that had once been a factory with machinery, all stripped out. More rain came down from the high roof's skylights, spattered and bounced. Must have been the noise they made, but when they were in the middle of the open space there was a shout that echoed in the emptiness. His Bossman turned towards it.

A partition of wood sections was in front of Carrick. The shout came again. His Bossman looked behind him, seemed to bite his lip, then headed towards it. At the end of the partition, Mikhail waited for them. He stood in front of Josef Goldmann, made him check his step then pointed to the side. The eyes glistened, were on Carrick, and he gestured behind him. A chair was in the centre of the space.

There was no exit route. The chair was screwed to the concrete floor and had thick, strong arms. It was like the one his grandfather had had in the dining room where the family had eaten only on Sundays after morning worship, but his grandfather's carver did not have leather straps with buckles nailed to the arms. There were dried stains at the feet of the chair that had not been scrubbed away. Mikhail gestured for Carrick to go to the chair. He saw a table with a cordless drill on it, and a small chain-saw half under it.

Reuven Weissberg sat close to the table and Josef Goldmann went to him. Carrick saw that the light, life and blood had gone from his Bossman's cheeks.

He stood in front of the chair, Mikhail before him. Carrick saw a wart on the right side of his nose, a scar on his cheek, and all the places where acne scabs had left craters. He smelled the man's breath and thought Mikhail had eaten strong salami not an hour before. His arms were yanked out, and Mikhail's foot went between his legs to kick them a little further apart. He was frisked. Thick muscular fingers were under his arms and at the small of his back, the waist of his trousers, fingering the stitching, and down to the crotch, pushing up into Carrick's groin. It was as good a search for a wire as would have been done by police. There was no wire, no microphone, no recorder or transmitter, no battery pack for him to find. Mikhail stepped back and motioned for Carrick to sit.

Carrick did not sit.

It had been what they called in SCD10 a 'dustdown'. The instructors preached that any undercover must expect to be searched for a wire, and they taught a response. The response was hammered at recruits.

There was a moment when surprise clouded Mikhail's face, and he tried to push Carrick into the chair. His fist brushed Carrick's chest.

No exit route. No way to call for back-up. Carrick took a half-step forward, fast and sudden.

Reuven Weissberg saw the blur of movement and the shock spreading on Mikhail's face. Saw it, and enjoyed it. Two fighting cocks put against each other, or two starved rats, and good sport – except that the matter was more important than play-acting.

Carrick yanked Mikhail's arms up, turned him, shoved him against the partition wall, then kicked his legs apart. Reuven understood. 'I permit it,' he called.

The man, Carrick, he had been told, was a former soldier. He thought the turning of Mikhail, his bodyguard, was done in the military fashion. He wondered when, last, Mikhail had been subjected to a body search, fingers into the groin and armpits. The weapon was taken, Mikhail's pistol, from the shoulder holster, checked, cleared, then thrown – as if casually – towards him. Reuven caught it.

He did not know about a dust-down as a response to suspicion.

It was brilliant, theatre. He put the Makharov pistol on the table. The man, Carrick, had searched Mikhail for a wire as if he, too, threatened as an infiltrator . . . Incredible. Carrick nodded as if satisfied, went to the chair and sat, but Reuven noticed that his knuckles whitened as his fingers gripped the chair's arms. Mikhail had demanded it, Viktor had supported Mikhail. Josef Goldmann, the launderer, had backed away from involvement. Should have had a fucking opinion. Josef Goldmann had brought the man.

Reuven turned to him now. 'Speak for him.'

He despised Josef Goldmann. Reuven thought he

provided a service but had never taken a strategic decision, was merely there, a lapdog at his heel. He ordered Goldmann to repeat the story.

He despised Josef Goldmann because he had admitted his debt but only vaguely stood in the corner for his man. He should have raged at the insult to his own judgement that his saviour was treated in this way, an object of suspicion. Reuven sat back. This was work for the men who had been with him since the early days of building roofs in Perm. Fifteen years before, he himself had led the one-time hard men recruited from State Security, and they had followed. For Reuven Weissberg, they went down into the gutter.

Questions came.

How had Carrick been approached?

What had Carrick done before the approach?

Why had he chosen to work for Josef Goldmann?

Tricks thrown into the game. Who did Carrick report to? How often did he report? Tricks mingled with questions . . . It was difficult for Reuven to understand the English-language questions posed by Mikhail, some with aggression and some soft-spoken, but he was less interested in the answers than in the face of the man who sat in the chair.

When had he left the military? How long between leaving the military and his first work as a bodyguard? How many employers? How much did the employers pay him? Viktor scribbled the answers. He would be on the telephone to Grigori, giving him details for checking. How often had he seen Simon Rawlings before the suggestion of work was made? How often had he met the contact? How much did he know of the business dealings of Josef Goldmann? He did not see a mistake made, or recognize evasion – but it was early.

Carrick was told to produce his mobile phone. He did so, and Mikhail passed it to Viktor. Questions, most of them repetitive, were asked as Viktor hit the keys and opened the memory. Answers, all repetitive, were offered. Reuven was interested that the man, Carrick, used statements of few words to explain himself. Did not ramble, did not say in four ways what could be said in one, offered minimal explanation. Viktor leaned towards him and whispered that no calls had been made on the mobile since Carrick had reached Berlin, and no calls had been received.

But it was early. A cordless drill lay on the table and a chain-saw underneath it.

'You are too convenient. You came too easily. You do not explain it.'

'I have explained it.'

'What to you is Josef Goldmann?'

'My employer.'

'To die for?'

'Do what I am paid to do.'

'And report to a senior officer? How many times?'

'You're talking shit. You know nothing.'

'How often did you meet your controller?'

'You were a policeman once?'

Reuven saw Mikhail flinch. 'I ask—'

'You were a crap policeman. We had interrogators in Iraq and you wouldn't even have made a junior.'

Mikhail spat, 'You are the angel when *someone* steps off the street and *supposedly* attacks Josef Goldmann, and you have the chance to shine . . . That was convenient. Yes?'

'Never been in a combat situation? No? Well, you wouldn't know, would you, how a man reacts? Too fucking ignorant.'

281

'The story, I tell you, is too good.'

'Ask Mr Goldmann. He was there and you were not.'

'And the angel – what we have to believe – is prepared to give his life for a man who is a stranger to him. Why? Why?'

Viktor had been close to Reuven. He moved now, edged away and stayed close to the partition wall, moved cat-quiet to be behind the chair, was poised to strike . . . and Josef Goldmann did not speak up for his man.

The answer was quiet. 'If you had been in combat you would know, but you haven't so you do not.'

Reuven thought the man, Carrick, had not made a mistake, but still it was early. It interested him that the man hit back, was not intimidated – should have been if the suspicion was justified.

Molenkov asked the question that had circled in his mind since they had driven from the garage. 'What's it for?

Beside him, Yashkin frowned. 'What's *what* for?'

'We take the thing, sell it, we—'

'You can speak the thing's name – it doesn't bite. A Zhukov, as you know, is a Small Atomic Demolition Munition. It has a serial number of RA-114. It is, for the moment, benign. You can talk about it.'

'You always interrupt me. I was thinking aloud. I—'

'You were rambling like an old fool. I repeat, "What's *what* for?" Tell me.'

The one-time political officer had been able to allow his thoughts to flow freely because the engine of the Polonez ran sweetly. Their wallets were half empty but he fancied the car had received a better and more thorough working-over than it had had for ten or fifteen years. Flat countryside slipped behind them, with little to engage him – less to compete with burdens that seemed to flourish like a virus in his mind – nagging and unwelcome.

He stumbled through what he had to say. 'We're paid, that's the deal – it was agreed. We get paid and—'

'We get paid a million American dollars. We divide a million American dollars into two equal parts. The story ends.'

'Security officials are always arrogant. They interrupt.'

'And a *zampolit*? Is a political officer not arrogant? The most unpopular and disliked individual in a camp is a *zampolit*. True or false? True.'

'I concede. I don't want to fight. There are *two* unpopular and disliked individuals in a camp. You were one and I was the other. Nobody loved us, and we didn't care. It's ridiculous for us to bicker . . . What's it for?'

It was, of course, long gone. He could think, sometimes, of who Colonel Igor Molenkov had been. If a call came for an official, a scientist or manager to attend at a specified hour the office of the *zampolit*, any man, however senior, sweated, fidgeted, lost sleep and went over in painstaking detail what he had said to whom in an unguarded moment, in an aside with sarcasm – and had that individual reported him? His only friend had been the security officer who had had the same power to destabilize a man's confidence: a quiet remark in a canteen about documents rated classified having been taken out of the secure zones could reduce anyone working at Arzamas-16 to a trembling wreck. But they had no power now.

'What's *what* for?'

'My friend, you don't make it easy for me.'

'Beat my ear, why don't you? And warn me of the right turning at Trubcevsk, and the road for Pogar. I'm listening.'

Molenkov breathed hard. 'A half-share of a million American dollars, what's it for?'

No answer.

Again, Molenkov tried. 'What will I do with a half-share of a million American dollars? Is it for a tin under the bed? Is it for an apartment in Cannes or Nice, or on the Black Sea? Is it for hoarding or spending?'

Yashkin kept to the centre of a straight and narrow road, lips pursed, forehead knotted, but did not respond.

'I am now sustained by anger,' Molenkov said, 'bred by what was done to me. Dismissal. My pension paid only erratically. My status taken. Cold to freezing in the winter because of the cost of fuel, hungry throughout the year because I have to scavenge in the street market for the cheapest food. All around me is corruption, an anarchy of criminality, the disease of Aids and the affliction of narcotics . . . and so, my friend, what will I do with a half-share of a million American dollars?'

Past sodden fields, and a river about to burst its banks, past dripping forestry, the horizon short, misted by low cloud.

'We talk about it, make jokes, and dream of the apartment in Sochi or above the Mediterranean, and the wealth that comes from the sale of *it* . . . My friend, would you leave Sarov? Your wife wants her remaining years to be spent close to the monastery, to be in the quiet company of St Seraphim. She'll want to sweep the floors there and bring flowers, meditate on the story of his sainthood, when the thieves beat and crippled him, when he argued before the court that mercy be shown them. She would wish to be in Sarov to celebrate the day of his birth and the anniversary of his canonization. Not important to you or me, my friend, but she won't go with you. Will you abandon her? Will you take the money, drive back to Sarov and put the money in a tin? Spend it slowly for fear of attention being attracted to new-found and unsubstantiated wealth? I ask you, what's it for?'

Yashkin said, 'I think we're close to the turning. The next village is Trubcevsk, and I think the road to Pogar will be off the main street.'

'Can't you answer me?' With growing desperation, Molenkov hurled the question at Yashkin. 'Or won't you?'

Yashkin said, in a flat monotone, 'It's important we don't miss the turning at Trubcevsk or we'll have to go many kilometres off our route.'

Molenkov said, 'Tell me, because I want to hear again, how you took the thing out.'

He was told. The detail never changed. A dozen times in the two months since Viktor, the friend of his dead son, had come to Sarov, Yashkin had told him the story. All bullshit, bluff and the authority of rank, the creaking cart, the grunts of conscripts and the salutes of the sentries. He had to laugh.

Molenkov said, 'Today, surely, it wouldn't be possible to get one out.'

Yashkin said, 'Then there was a window, and it was wide open. I assume now that it's closed. Then, as I did, you could walk through it.'

That day, at that hour, an American general of the Strategic Command was the guest of a Russian general of the 12th Directorate. His tour was of the storage zones and silos at the Federal Nuclear Centre outside Sarov in the Nizhny Novgorod *oblast*. The American regarded himself as a trusted friend of the Russian and had escorted his opposite number to missile installations in the Midwest of the United States. As military men of experience, they talked a similar language. A coffee break had been called, and an opportunity for a comfort stop. The American used the time to speak quietly into the portable Dictaphone he carried, the better to remember his thoughts when it came to writing up a report that would be studied by a congressional committee.

It was a whisper. 'I believe old suspicions and anxieties about security at Sarov are now groundless . . . I have seen, in an action exercise, Special Forces troops who are now deployed on the base perimeters, and they were working with gunship choppers. They are élite troops, well motivated and well paid . . . Old stories of scientific personnel taking to the streets in demonstrations and, in effect, striking on the grounds of non-payment of wages are surely a matter of the past. I have been shown sections of outer and inner fencing around the storage zones, which are fitted with high-technology security sensors donated by the US and identical to those in place at our Los Alamos installation, New Mex, and I am assured that minor thefts of equipment and material are now blocked. One silo for nuclear warheads in storage was opened for me. It was behind two steel-reinforced doors, which were sufficient to withstand any conventional or nuclear bomb blast. I am informed that the military of the 12th Directorate have a good handle on the personnel in sensitive positions, and they're thoroughly vetted. Conclusions on the visit here: Sarov is in the hands of serious, high-quality people. I do not believe leakage is possible, and it is denied with emphasis that any such leakage of warheads or materials took place in the past.'

'This is it. Go right. This is the Trubcevsk turning,' Molenkov said.

Yashkin thanked him. His friend had said the previous day that he promised to try not to talk of the thing, but might not honour his promise . . . and in the centre of that community, where no signpost stood, he swung the wheel and turned right.

Could the man not stop talking?

Molenkov asked, 'Where, friend, will it be hardest?'

Yashkin answered, 'At the border. We cross it tomorrow. Molenkov, do you talk to hear your own voice when you're frightened, or because of the profundity of your opinion? Tomorrow we face a challenging difficulty. Tomorrow we cross the border. Don't ask me what's at the border on our side or on the Belarus side because I don't know. I have no knowledge of the equipment there. If there's equipment for detection I don't know how sophisticated or sensitive it is. Please, my friend, can we just drive?'

'After the border we have five hundred more kilometres to go. How will you feel then?'

'Excellent. We're going to the river where we'll meet your Viktor's employer. I think him to be a man, at his trade, of ability.'

'He's criminal scum, no more or less. However,

he'll be carrying a million American dollars.'

'My knowledge of such people – obviously limited – tells me he'll be careful, and all the people with him. The border is the difficulty, not people who are careful with their security. Molenkov, please, give me some fucking quiet. Such people understand security in a way that I never – and I don't hesitate to admit it – did.'

Viktor had him by the throat, but that was Viktor's second movement.

Mikhail had given the signal, and Viktor's first movement had been to a wrist, then to the straps and his fingers had wrestled the buckle into place. Mikhail had fastened the other wrist to the chair arm. He had long missed Viktor, his old friend and fighting companion. It had been a bad day when Viktor was ordered to London.

He had the chain-saw started. Fumes in his nostrils. It had taken four pulls to wake the engine and he had revved it so that the chain raced on the cogs. Now the saw was near the Englishman's feet, but out of reach of his kicks. It idled and spluttered. Mostly the chain-saw was for show, and he didn't like using it because of the blood it threw into his face, but he had used it when he thought it necessary in Perm, Moscow and in Berlin.

Mikhail held the cordless drill, and worked his index finger on its trigger.

The drill made less mess.

With questioning, lowering over the man, sometimes shouting and sometimes hissing the questions, he had attempted to create fear – had failed. He sensed now that he had little time. In Perm, in the first months since he had gone to work for Reuven Weissberg – Viktor with him – it had been hammered into his mind that he must create fear. Without fear he was nowhere, no roofs sold, no customers coming and no rivals backing off. He was paid well to make fear. He had little time, knew that because Josef Goldmann was whimpering like a fucking kid, and Reuven Weissberg had shifted twice in his chair as if bored that the questioning had led to no admissions. Sweat streamed on the man's forehead. He had done interrogations, enough of them, in his work with State Security and had rarely felt the need to raise his voice. Now, because failure faced him, he screamed the questions as he held the drill, racing, close to the kneecap. Mikhail had never in his life gone to an Orthodox church, had never sunk to his knees, had never offered up a prayer, and he did not believe in angels. He did not believe this goddam man, but sensed the threat of him.

His screams rose, were incoherent. He mixed the English language with his own. 'Who controls you? Police or Intelligence? How are you to contact your control? *The attack on Goldmann was bogus, do you not admit that?* What is the briefing of your control? What do they want? *Is the target Goldmann or is it Reuven Weissberg? Do they know of the delivery?* Is it the washing of cash or the delivery?'

The response, repeated: 'I have answered that . . . have answered that . . .' Silence when the questions were in Russian.

His hand shook, and the drill tip wavered a few centimetres from the trouser over the kneecap. He couldn't make the fear. His arm stiffened. It was what Viktor had told him, and it had not before seemed important. Mikhail clutched at straws, was drowning.

'You left outside your room, for laundry, sodden

clothing. Why were you out in the night, in the rain? Did you meet your control in the night?'

He saw his man flinch. At last . . .

He hit again, and the drill tip spun not five centimetres from the kneecap. 'It rained. You were out. You met your control.'

There was a surge of breath. Mikhail held the drill steady, let it race. He waited for the confession, and the smile spilled at his mouth.

He heard, 'Reuven Weissberg, your employer – arsehole – has a bullet wound in the arm. I saw it. Where were you? Fucking a whore or with a hand down a kid's trousers? Where were you, arsehole, when Mr Weissberg was shot?'

He was about to drive the drill tip into the trouser covering the kneecap. The voice behind him was a murmur. 'Enough.'

He stopped. Mikhail let his finger slide off the trigger and the power died. He would never disobey an instruction from Reuven Weissberg. Weissberg was the only man he feared and he was at the point of success, but he would not disobey an order. He let the cordless drill slip from his fingers. It bounced on the concrete and splashed in a puddle of rainwater.

The voice behind him said, 'Free him.'

Beside Reuven Weissberg, shaking and sobbing, was Josef Goldmann.

As Mikhail bent to loose the man, their eyes met. He thought the man's eyes laughed at him.

He was in the minibus.

It should have been the time that Shrinks exuded authority and competence, was listened to. He sat hunched and stayed silent.

A full half-hour earlier he had slid back the

290

minibus door, gone to the car and said to Lawson that, in his considered opinion, their man was in extreme danger and, following the description given him of the night's events, was in no realistically fit state to defend his cover. Lawson had responded, 'When I want your contribution I'll ask for it, and right now I do not,' then pulled his door shut. The younger man, Davies, had rolled his eyes and shrugged, and Shrinks had returned to the minibus.

He had not worked with Lawson before. A little of a fearsome reputation had reached him, but he had dismissed that as jealousy – there was enough of that at VBX – but he had been on the team long enough to believe each last syllable of the drip of criticism addressed to Christopher Lawson. Small mercies, but at least the man was an interesting subject. 'Interesting', but not the centre of his attention.

His focus was on November. From the far end of the long approach to the warehouse yard gate he had seen the cars drive in. Then he had had Deadeye's binoculars passed abruptly to him, and there had been a flash sight of November's head, front passenger seat, blurred, then gone. Precious little to work from, and the features had been expressionless, but he'd seen wide-open eyes and the pallor that stress brought. He had gone to the car, to Lawson, to tell him that the agent was defenceless and critically vulnerable, and his cheeks had flushed at the blatant rejection. Where would his advice have led, had it been accepted? Obvious. To go in and get the man clear – he had heard, faint but clear above the cries of wheeling gulls, the sounds of a chain-saw. Lawson, that 'interesting subject', had shown no hesitation and not a modicum of doubt in dismissing him. God, if he ever had that man, with certainties by the bucketful, on a couch ... His own science, that of forensic psychology, was inexact and men who apparently harboured no doubts had always fascinated him.

Shrinks – he hated the name but it had stuck – worked two days a week at VBX and had been allocated a cubbyhole on the second floor in the Medical Section; the other three days he spent at University College Hospital in old Bloomsbury where he was attached to the Department of Psychiatry. Most of his colleagues at UCH treated varying degrees of mental illness, but he researched all aspects of human behaviour – and at VBX he sat in on selection of recruits panels, had influence in the planning of courses and monitored the progress of the younger officers. Normally he was listened to and what he said was used and seemed valued; this was the first time he had been ignored, then rejected, when he had stepped out to let his opinion be known.

The ambition of this big, shambling man – a couple of months short of his thirty-sixth birthday – was to be taken on at VBX full time. The secrecy and need-to-know culture appealed to him. The building burgeoned with excitement. He was, and had no problem admitting it, an enthusiast, and the two days a week when he jogged across the bridge and flashed his card at Security, then fed it into the machine at the entry barrier and went inside, gave him the greatest happiness he knew. Had to be careful in expressing that. He lived with Petra, a wood sculptor, in a housing-association one-bed-room flat in Islington. He could not blather on to her about his greatest happiness being at work ...

Petra, hacking away at wood with chisel and hammer in her council-sponsored studio, did not know where he was. The secrecy of the life, up to the time he sat cramped in the minibus and with the pain in his constricted knees, had thrilled him.

That ambition, he believed, was now threatened.

He wondered, even at that distance and through the crumbling brickwork of the building far ahead, if he would hear a scream of terror, of agony.

If he were to return to VBX having been an integral part of a team that had lost its most valuable asset, its agent on the ground, his ambition would crumble. He needed the operation to succeed. He had long hair that fell to his shirt collar and his fingers worked in it. The girl bit her fingernails, Bugsy stared fixedly ahead, and Deadeye hummed the same damn tune again and again. Then he saw the receiver light wink on Dennis's lap.

The minibus was in fast reverse, and when Shrinks looked out through the back window he had a view of the car turning the corner.

'Don't mind me,' Shrinks said, and the tension had reached him. 'What's happening?'

'Adrian's found a vantage-point where we may get an eyeball,' Dennis said.

He thought they would see a weighted bundle carried out of the building, two or three men taking the strain. He realized he knew so little of the trade of VBX. It was simple and straightforward to sit in on selection boards and have young men and young women recite their CVs and all the dubious reasons they had concocted for joining the Service. But this was different: he had seen, just a flash of it, the face of a man taken to the limits and knowing it.

There was much that Shrinks could have said, had he been asked ... Could have said that an agent working beyond the reach of back-up must possess supreme motivation, not that of a crusading knight fighting criminality, but have the self-induced need for success, and syringefuls of it. Could have said that a degree of stress was beneficial to the agent, that lack of stress was a road to complacency, but the stress levels the far side of the brick walls were beyond his experience as a psychologist. He liked to say, when a candidate had gone from the interview room and before the next was called forward, that he looked for 'an organized mind'.

They were at the door of a derelict three-storey building, ancient bullet holes on the rendering. There was a gap in the doorway, where a nailed barrier had been prised back. Shrinks thought he would get a grandstand bloody view of a body being removed for disposal.

No one helped him, nor would he have asked for help.

There was an aged staircase with one in two, or two in three, of the wood steps missing. Those that were in place creaked and protested at their weight. At the biggest gaps Lawson sank to his knees, crawled and straddled the spaces, but no one looked back to see if he was able to bloody compete. On the first floor of the building – once an apartment block – there was a doorway and a distant window, bird shit on the floorboards. Trouble was that the bird shit lay on the boards that remained, and there were not too many of those. He hesitated in the doorway. Adrian was at the window. Davies and the cuckoo girl, Charlie, were halfway across the room and walked on the beam that had once supported the boards, not much more, damn the thing, than a couple of inches across. Davies had gone first and had good balance, held his arm out behind him and her fingers rested on his. She matched his steps. The drop between the boards and the beams to the ground floor would have been twenty-five feet. As if they had tossed for it and the loser went first, Bugsy stepped on to the beam and Shrinks had an arm out, held tight to the shoulder in front of him and might have had his eyes half closed. They could not back off, he knew it, because he was behind them. He waited his turn. Perhaps squatters had been in the building. His turn had come. Water came down, heavy and continuous, missed the beam by less than half a foot, and went on down. He could hear its patter far below. The beam shook as Bugsy and Shrinks joined Adrian, Davies and the girl on the one board under the window. Lawson went across. They were not looking at him. At the final stride, no hand reached out. He controlled his breathing.

He inserted himself beside Adrian. There was a clear view out across a bombsite not yet developed, the roadway that went nowhere, the building of weathered brick and the small doorway set in it. He saw the cars parked there, and the man who watched the gate.

The rain had come on heavier.

Then Davies said, 'Well, Mr Lawson, here we all are with a Grand Circle view. What's going to be the show? Tragedy or a comedy with a bag of laughs? Me, I'm banking on tragedy. I think it's pretty well known that Russian organized crime gets about as vicious as any – unless it's the Albanians on a red-letter day. You could – damn you, Mr Lawson – have picked that poor bastard up out of the gutter last night, when he was down and beaten, and called time on all this, blown the whistle. Not your way, was it? Gave him a verbal kicking and sent him back into that snakepit. I suppose you followed the edicts, as handed down on bloody tablets, of the peerless Clipper Reade . . . Well, look where it's dumped our man.'

He remembered it well, Clipper's story of the meeting on a park bench at the south side of the city of Gdansk, underneath the ramparts of the fortress built by Napoleon. With Clipper had been the young Pole, just past his twenty-first birthday, who worked in the division of the railways that cleared the tracks for military traffic. The kid had been buckling, and was refusing to continue supplying information on the timetables and content of the traffic that rolled at dead of night. Clipper had lashed him with his Texan tongue. Had achieved two more dead-letter drops. The second had listed the passing through the Gdansk junction yard of twenty-four MAZ-543 launch vehicles, with Scud-B missiles mounted, all loaded on flat-bed stock. Scud-B had high explosive and chemical and nuclear warhead capability, and it was Clipper's biggest success story in 1978 that he had identified the shipment coming through the junction yard at Gdansk and on to Polish territory. After that dead-letter drop, no more. The kid had been correct in his assessments that time was running short for him. Arrested, tried *in camera*. An American diplomat expelled from Warsaw, and a tit-for-tat reaction in Washington. Clipper Reade long gone from the scene, selling tractor spare parts somewhere else, and the kid with the timetables had gone off the radar – maybe beaten to death, maybe hanged, maybe executed by pistol shot, but he had not coughed a description of the big American from the Agency. Clipper had said he'd quite liked the kid, that he was decent, honourable and probably a patriot, but that his life – 'Because we don't ever go squeamish, Christopher' – was fair exchange for knowing that Scud-Bs, with nuclear capability, had gone through the junction yard at Gdansk. The night the courier – a Canadian exchange student – had brought back that information, collected from the dead-letter drop, Clipper Reade and Lawson had killed two bottles of German sparkling wine with chasers of Earl Grey from the pot.

'What you did should lie on your conscience.' The hissed whisper was in Lawson's ear. 'You sent him back . . . Where he is, that's the sort of place those bastards take a man they suspect. It'll be their damn *abattoir*. Feel good about that, Mr Lawson, do you?'

He was nudged. Adrian passed him pocket binoculars. It took him a moment to get the focus right, and voices were in his ears.

Adrian's murmur: 'That is unbelievable. Incredible.'

'Never, never would I have reckoned it,' Davies mouthed.

Shrinks's voice, breathy: 'It's the Stockholm thing. It's that syndrome . . . but I couldn't have predicted it. Only you could, Mr Lawson.'

He had the sharpness of the image. Josef Goldmann seemed to run in front of the group as if he needed to be gone from the place and was scarred by it. The lenses raked over the two hoods, Viktor and Mikhail, who hung back. There was frustrated fury on their faces and their feet seemed to stamp as they walked; Lawson felt the chuckle in his throat. His man, November, lifted out of an office doorway in the night, came with a weak, loose step towards the car, and was supported by Reuven Weissberg, who had his arm round November's back and his fist gripping November's coat. He had the focus clear now. Reuven Weissberg reached up with his other hand and, as if they were friends, pinched November's cheek. November would have fallen if Reuven Weissberg's arm had not held him up. Lawson knew what Stockholm syndrome was, and had aimed to create it.

Adrian said, 'It's a triumph, Mr Lawson – and we need to move fast.'

They ran to the stairs and were going down, skipping over the gaps where the steps had been taken out. Bugsy and Shrinks helped each other. None of them looked back. Lawson started after them. Bloody well past sixty-one years, bloody near pensionable. Was wobbling on the beam. Should not look down. Heard the clatter of them on the steps. Felt himself going, but Lawson did not cry out, then seemed to see the face of Lavinia, his wife, and Harry, his son. They looked away . . . Had hooked his right leg over the damn beam and had a hold of it with his left hand. Was suspended. Could look down and see them all crossing the lobby, going quick, not looking up. Thought the left arm was about ready to come out of its socket. Then he'd fall. The angles of the beam were sharp enough to cut off his right leg at the knee, and then he'd fall. Took the strain. Pulled himself up. Was astride the beam, and panted. Crawled along it, and came to the doorway. His fingers clawed on the wall and he stood, went down the steps and crossed the hall. Funny that, first time since he'd reached Berlin that he'd thought of his wife and son.

The car was already gone, but the minibus waited for him. He climbed in.

He spoke, silent and without lip movement: 'Just as you said it would be, old boy . . . Pity me, Clipper, with all these damn Thomases for company.'

Stone-faced, Viktor drove.

Josef Goldmann had a hand on Carrick's shoulder, leaned forward and spoke in his ear: 'How did you know, Johnny?'

Play dumb and play ignorant. 'Know what, sir?'

'How did you know that Mikhail was with Reuven Weissberg at the shooting and did not react until the shot had been fired, and it was only Reuven's good fortune that the shot took the flesh of the arm and not the chest or skull? How did you know that?'

'I didn't know it, sir. I guessed it. I wouldn't have a kneecap if I hadn't guessed something.'

Laughter behind him, but hollow.

'Mikhail was not fucking a tart when Reuven was shot, and he was not masturbating a young boy. He was there, Johnny, but he was slow with his reaction. You were not slow when I was attacked. It was a good guess.'

'Yes, sir.'

Chapter 11: 13 April 2008

He was numbed and quiet. Carrick sat in the apartment's kitchen. The grandmother moved around him, but it was as if he weren't there. A coffee mug had been placed on the table near to his elbow, and he had nodded but was not acknowledged. The grandmother spent her time washing dishes and saucepans in the sink, then drying them and putting them in cupboards. Afterwards she prepared a meal, peeled vegetables and stripped cold meat off a bone. He believed her to be wary of him, but felt her suspicion was ingrained, not personal.

When she had made his coffee, she had taken a tray – four mugs and a steaming pot – out of the kitchen and had been gone two or three minutes. Carrick had not moved from his chair at the table. Reuven and Mikhail, his Bossman and Viktor were in another room. If a door was opened he could hear their faint voices, but the language used was beyond him. Mikhail had brought the tray back.

He had carried it into the kitchen and put it on the draining-board. Carrick would have expected some brief expression of thanks – obvious, whatever the language used – and then for Mikhail to go back to the meeting. He did not. Carrick watched him. Mikhail rinsed the coffee dregs from the mugs and sluiced the pot, then took a cloth and dried them, did it with care, and placed the mugs on a shelf in a cupboard. Carrick saw this as a slight but unmistakable sign of servitude.

What thoughts were in his mind revolved on the racing, spinning tip of the drill. Carrick could not have said how close he had been to confession – shouting, screaming, anything to get the hand holding the drill to move back and away from his kneecap. If he had made that confession he would have gained himself a minute, a few minutes, a half-hour, of life, but by now he would be dead. Too right. Dumped. A ditch, a shallow grave. So, the closeness of it had numbed him, left him quiet.

They taught in SCD10 that an undercover, when pressured by suspicion, should not try to twist his way out but should turn and confront. 'Change the direction,' one instructor had preached, 'throw it bloody back at them, deflect their attack, make them answer some bloody questions.'

'Be outraged at the very thought of their accusation being true,' another instructor had said.

Everyone worth listening to on the courses reckoned that an undercover, working with level-three criminality, would find his legend threatened and must hit back.

His kneecap would have been pierced, no doubt about it. Adrenaline had exploded in his mouth – the pure instinct of survival, not planned but made on the hoof – and then the soft response, in words he hadn't understood, of Reuven Weissberg.

He could still feel the grip of Reuven Weissberg's fist on his coat, and had known that he would have stumbled, might have fallen, crossing the wasteground from the warehouse to the car. Mikhail stood in front of him, and seemed to eye Carrick.

Carrick stared back. If the grandmother had not been there, Carrick reckoned Mikhail might have spat in his face. Wouldn't have dared to, not in her presence. On-the-hoof decisions were accepted by a cover officer and a control in SCD10. There was acceptance that no damn manual could legislate for the unexpected crisis, and a crisis was having a cordless drill with a hand on the trigger, the tip spinning a few inches from a kneecap. If he hadn't seen the puckered wound of a bullet's entry, when Reuven Weissberg had discarded his coat, *if* . . . But he had. The accusation had not been thought through, and it had saved him. Now, the adrenaline was long drained out, and the numbness had taken hold.

Carrick could recall the words, the sounds, that he had not understood, *Enough* and *Free him*, and he had seen Mikhail's eyes in that dance of disbelief, had heard Josef Goldmann's weeping, but it was Reuven Weissberg who had stood, come to the chair and waved Mikhail back. Then Viktor had loosed the straps and lifted him from it.

He thought Reuven Weissberg had saved him from the pain of the drill and then had saved his life. He sat in the chair at the table and gazed down at the dregs in the bottom of the mug. He would not have survived but for the intervention of Reuven Weissberg. He had felt the strength of the man through the leather jacket's sleeve, had seen the strength of the eyes, had heard the soft command of the voice – and owed his life to that man.

Mikhail said, 'I am to tell you that we move on in the evening.'

Carrick shrugged, acknowledged, but did not speak. Did not press for explanation – where, when, why? He thought Mikhail believed nothing of his denial, and that an enemy had been made. Carrick presumed that the outside of the block was watched. They had found him in the night, which meant that a surveillance team was in place, and he presumed, also, that they had been outside the warehouse. They had not intervened. He had been a second, two seconds, from having a drill pierce his kneecap. But for the quiet words spoken by Reuven Weissberg, he was meat, beaten and bloodless.

Carrick had lost count of how many times he had studied the last undissolved grains of coffee in the mug. He lifted his eyes and found the picture. He searched among the depths and darkness of the trees but could not find no meaning there. The only meaning he knew was that Reuven Weissberg, not those who had sent him, was his protector.

She packed his bag, always did. 'Do you want him as a trifle, a bauble, because he belongs to someone else?'

He stood beside the bed. She folded two shirts, underclothes, a pair of jeans, and already in his bag were the heavy socks he would wear with boots. Reuven said, 'When did I ever want anything as a toy?'

'Because he belongs to Josef Goldmann. Do you want him for that reason?'

'No.'

'He's not of your blood or your faith.'

'Blood isn't important to me and I have no faith.'

She sighed, long and slowly. 'You're ignorant of him.'

'I've seen enough of him to know him.'

'You don't need him. You have Mikhail.'

Reuven said, 'I have Mikhail, who didn't protect me. Josef has Viktor and Grigori and they didn't protect him.'

'Is protection so necessary now that you wish to bring a stranger to stand alongside you?'

'Because of where we go, what we buy and to whom we sell, I need a good man in front of me, behind me and alongside me. A good man . . .'

'A stranger.'

'A proven man.'

She zipped the bag shut. It was old, battered, scraped and scuffed. He thought of the bags he had seen, from across the street, carried by the porter into the hotel when Josef Goldmann had arrived. Three of them, and they had shone with quality. His own bag had come from the market in Perm, from the stall of the man who had been his first customer, who had bought the first roof that Reuven had sold there. Two rivals had been bludgeoned for trying to take back the customer's trade and impose their own roofs. The zip worked, the hand straps were still secure, it did not have breaks in it from which the contents could fall, and he had no need for a newer, more expensive bag. She washed his clothes by hand, and ironed them. No maid was allowed into the apartment. No luxury was permitted.

She asked, 'Are you wise, Reuven, to trust?'

'I can't watch my sides and back.'

'You have Mikhail.'

The bitterness was a quiet rasp in his voice. 'And he did not watch my front.'

'How long will you want him for, the stranger?'

He softened. He took her old fingers in his. 'You trusted, once.'

She would never weep. Since those days as a child, when his father was dead in the corrective labour colony from pleurisy, his mother was going to the East, as far as it was possible to go, to look for work as a bar singer, and he had been dumped with a plastic bag of clothing in the home of his grandmother, he had not seen her cry. He could see the eyes but not beyond their glaze . . . One thought was perpetually shut from his mind. What would he do when she died? His grandmother, Anna, was now in her eighty-fifth year. She was so frail . . . He wouldn't think of it.

He knew the story, every word.

It was 27 September. Autumn was coming quickly to the forest outside the fence, and there was a heavy damp in the air because the summer of 1943 had been poor. On that date a train came from the Minsk ghetto, and it transported more than one thousand seven hundred Jews to our camp. A few were POWs of the Red Army.

As the Russian prisoner soldiers were marched into our compound, we could see them from the barracks hut where we worked. Immediately it could be recognized that one man among them was different. He was tall, had cropped hair under his military cap, was sallow-skinned, and wore the uniform of a Soviet officer. They arrived early in the morning, and at the midday break we came out of the places where we worked and met them as they stood around, trying to focus on where they were now held. I think there were ten of them, chosen for their stature and because they were still capable of work. They stank of the cattle trucks in which they had spent four days and nights without food, water or a latrine.

That late September was a time of particular crisis for

those of us who clung to life in the camp, a time when despair edged closer. Rumour ran rife. Before the transport from Minsk arrived, no trains had come to the forest sidings for three weeks. Rumour said that the camp was to close. Then we would not survive. We lived because the camp lived. If the camp died, we died. All of us who had clung to life would be put to death when the camp had no purpose. Rumour said it was 'soon' that the camp would close.

It achieved little, but at the camp – among the workers servicing it – there was an escape committee. A few of the men who went into the forest for woodcutting, in the last months, had broken away and run into the trees. They had been advised by the committee on where to hide the first night, where they might find partisans and where they should avoid the murderous Polish farmers and foresters; each time there was an escape attempt the rest of the work party were shot. The head of the committee was Leon Feldhendler, who was from Lublin.

I did not hear it, but others did, and each word of the first conversation between the Russian officer and Feldhendler careered as free charging whispers among the prisoners. The name of the Russian Jew, the sole officer among them, was Sasha Pechersky, a lieutenant. Pechersky was a fighting soldier, not a cook or a lorry driver. Each exchange between him and Leon Feldhendler came to us by relay of mouths . . . It was a day of fine rain and the cloudbanks were low over the fences and the trees, but there was darkness that day over all of the camp except on the north side where the glow of fire turned the cloud orange. The darkness was from smoke. He asked, Pechersky, what was burning, but Feldhendler told him not to ask. He asked again, in innocence, and demanded an answer. Feldhendler told him, 'It is the burning of the bodies of those who came on the train with you.' And, Feldhendler told Sasha

Pechersky of the Road to Heaven, the sealed chambers, the engine of Gasmeister Bauer, the work parties who took the bodies from the chambers to the dug pits and the others who burned them. He explained why there was dark smoke against the cloud and the firelight. It was said by those who were closest that there were tears in Pechersky's eyes.

A young soldier was standing a step behind the Russian officer. I thought he was my age. A smooth face, no beard or moustache, and downy hair on his cheeks. Our eyes met. Pechersky had just been told why there was smoke and fire. The young soldier looked at me and I at him . . . He was beautiful. Quite slight, with fine, gentle hands, a clean white skull where his hair had been shaved, but he stood tall and not like a prisoner, as tall as Pechersky. He smiled at me. In all the months I had been at the camp, no man had smiled at me. He called his name to me – Samuel. I blushed and called my name back. I couldn't say why I let him have my name. In the compound of Camp 1, I had survived by trusting no one, man or woman, but I did it . . . Then guards came and an SS officer, and they were led away to start work.

The next day rumours spread of Pechersky.

The SS officer, Frenzel, took the work party into the forest to cut timber. When he brought them back to the camp, Frenzel demanded they sing, and said they could sing in Russian. Did they sing an anthem? A love song? A lament? Pechersky, the leader, told his men to sing 'If War Comes Tomorrow', a partisans' song. They marched back to the camp, and Frenzel did not understand, but the Ukrainians did and didn't tell him.

> *If war comes tomorrow*
> *Tomorrow we march.*
> *If evil forces strike,*
> *United as one,*

All the Russian people
For their free native land will arise . . .

It was defiance, and word spread.

On his third day there were more rumours of
Pechersky. He had been set a challenge by Frenzel to hack
apart a tree stump within five minutes. He would have
been whipped had he failed, but he had achieved it with
half a minute to spare. He had refused Frenzel's offer of
cigarettes as reward, and refused half of a fresh-baked roll
from a Ukrainian's lunch, saying that the rations at the
camp were adequate. I tell you, with honesty, there was
no defiance at the camp until that man came. To refuse
cigarettes and fresh bread was defiance on a scale not
seen before. Everyone, by the evening, knew of it.

Each time I saw Pechersky, I saw Samuel. He walked
a step behind Pechersky, always close to him. He looked
for me and I looked for him. I had been long enough in
the camp to have had burned from my soul any trace of
emotion. I have to say it – each time I saw Samuel I felt
as if sunshine fell on me. It was as if, for the first time, I
nurtured a trifling hope for the future. I hardly dared to
think of such a distant goal, but it had captured me.

A new rumour, like an infecting virus, ran in the
camp on the fourth day after Pechersky's arrival. It was
said that on 15 October the Germans would have completed their work at the camp. We would not survive
that. Before, the rumours had been vague as to the
timing. Now a date was talked of. Two moods gripped us.
Pechersky had created a changed atmosphere, almost one
of resistance. And there was despair with the talk that we
would all be forced at bayonet point down the
Himmelstrasse, thrown naked into the chambers and be
there, body against body, when Gasmeister Bauer started
the engine.

The capos were quiet that night. They patrolled with

their whips but did not use them, and did not shout.

It was the night, also, that Pechersky came to the women's barracks and met Feldhendler. I did not, of course, know it then but it was in our barracks hut, used for better security, that Feldhendler offered Pechersky total authority over any escape attempt he might consider. They were at the far end of our hut, huddled together, and spoke softly so they could not be overheard. Samuel had come with Pechersky, and we talked a little at the window. He held my hand – he had fingers as thin as those of a musician – and he told me he came from the city of Perm and had been captured when on a reconnaissance patrol west of the Moscow suburbs. I told him I was from Wlodawa, that my father had repaired clocks and wristwatches, and that all of my family were dead.

I asked him, 'Is it possible to hope?'

He answered, 'You have to believe in Sasha Pechersky. If anything is possible it will be because of Sasha Pechersky. It is what he carries on his shoulders, the hopes of us all.'

'What can he do?'

'I don't know.'

Hope has a small, frail flame. To make it burn, I gave it trust. I offered trust to the young man who held my hand beside the window. Then I felt weaker and cursed myself. We looked out of the window at the tops of the trees nearest to the wire. They seemed beyond reach, and between them and us there were fences and guard towers, water-filled ditches and a minefield. I remember I heard the owls call from the forest.

He edged closer to them. Tadeuz Komiski had long had the skill, practised over many years, of moving silently among the trees.

They planted pine trees.

His feet, in old boots, stepped on the mat of decayed leaves and fallen needles that had dropped from the canopy. The light was failing, the rain pattered around him, but he did not put his weight on any dead branches.

They brought pine trees that were already a metre high on three wheelbarrows. Some dug the holes, some lifted the pines and placed them with their rooting compost in the holes. Some stamped down the compost around the slender trunks and others watered the base of the trees with a rubber pipe that led to an oil drum. Some hoed the ground where the next holes would be dug. They were, Tadeuz Komiski thought, like a labour detail, but they had no guards and there were no guns, no whips . . . He could remember when there had been guards, SS Germans and the Ukrainians – not well but with a halting clarity, but then he had been a child.

Men and women were planting the trees and clearing the path, some his age but most were younger. They worked hard with enthusiasm, which was different from when there had been a labour detail in the forest. They had strong, cheerful voices, but there was no laughter. He went closer. They stopped, broke off from the work. Komiski, behind a tree, saw flasks opened – they ignored the rain falling on them – and sandwiches taken out of plastic boxes.

He had not eaten properly for three days at least. The scent of their food and their coffee wafted to him, and his feet moved silently forward but there were always tree trunks between him and them.

A voice hit him from behind.

'Hello, friend. Don't watch us eat – we'll share with you.'

He understood German, enough of it. He recoiled, felt trapped. He was between the big group and one man, and froze, but he yearned for food. He turned. The man was young, clean-shaven, and his features blazed warmth. He was zipping up his flies and then he fastened his belt. He held toilet paper and a short-handled spade was propped against his leg.

Komiski could not speak.

'Did I frighten you? I apologize sincerely. Come, join us – I'm Gustav.'

His arm was taken. They had taught him German at school but it was a full sixty-five years since he had heard it spoken in the forest. He was led to the group. The young man, Gustav, spoke fast to his colleagues, and a sandwich was offered him with a plastic beaker of coffee. Tadeuz Komiski wolfed it and gulped the coffee, spilling some from the side of his mouth. He thought the members of the group too polite to laugh at him, and bent to pick up a crust he had dropped. Another sandwich was given him.

He was told, 'We're from Kassel. We're an anti-fascist group. Only two of us are of Jewish origin, but ethnicity isn't important to us. We're making a memorial of the Road to Heaven. Those of us who are Jewish had relatives who died in the camp, but the rest of us are here because this is decent work. The Road to Heaven was the path used by the SS to drive victims of the extermination programme from the rail platform to the chambers where they were asphyxiated. We're lining the route with good pine trees we bought from the forestry authority. We won't finish this year, probably next.'

An apple was given him and the beaker was

filled again. The coffee scalded his mouth. He held tight to the apple.

'And we'll put stones under the trees on which will be carved the names of some who went this route to die. We believe that the trees we put here and the stones will last for many years. Then this place and what was done here won't be forgotten. We consider it would be a crime if the memory of the camp's evil was lost.'

He took a bite from the apple.

'I think, friend, you're quite old. Excuse me, because I don't wish to intrude, but you would have been a boy when the camp existed. I wonder, were you here when there was the break-out? Did you live in the forest with your parents? Do you remember when the camp revolted?'

Hands held out more sandwiches wrapped in cellophane, and a slice of fruit cake. His stomach growled. Tadeuz Komiski heard the sirens, rifle shots, and the rattle of machine-guns, which was clearest because they had been fired from the elevated watchtowers.

'Do you remember . . . *remember* . . . *remember*? Were you here . . . *here* . . . *here*?'

Remember? It was never out of his mind. Tadeuz Komiski was always in this place, among these trees. He dropped the beaker and the remnants of the coffee slopped on his trouser leg. He threw away the half-eaten apple, turned his back on the sandwiches and cake, and ran.

'Well, I suppose the best that can be said of it is that bloody Lawson didn't show up. Anyway, here's what's come through.'

In a basement of the embassy building, Deadeye was passed two packages by the station chief. Big and bulky, wrapped in the thick brown paper used to send heavy parcels through the post for kids' birthdays. But the packages weren't presents, the courts had ordered that Deadeye had no contact with the children of his three failed marriages, and they hadn't come through the post but by diplomatic courier.

The station chief said, 'Don't think of opening them here. I saw the inventory and didn't want to know that much. Another of Lawson's hare-brained games? Count me out. Just give me a signature.'

On the paper offered him – and it referred to the delivery and collection of 'unspecified items' – Deadeye scrawled an unrecognizable name. He picked up the packages, one under each arm. Under his right elbow, beneath the paper, was a canvas bag that held a Heckler & Koch machine pistol; under his left elbow, and beneath that wrapping, was a holdall with stun and smoke grenades, a Glock 9mm pistol, sufficient ammunition for the two weapons to fill five magazines, and a field medical kit.

'So that there are no misunderstandings – and please pass this to the esteemed *Mr* Lawson – should any of these "unspecified items" be used inside the borders of the new greater Germany then he, you and whatever ragtag army he has in tow will be pegged out to dry. Still living in the Good Old Days, is he? From me, please quote verbatim, the time when we could run round like an occupying power is gone. No offence, and nothing personal, but just fuck off out of here soonest.'

He was shown the door. Deadeye was led up a staircase, taken through the lobby, damn near slung out of the embassy entrance. 'Wanker,' he murmured. Rain dripped on to the paper wrapping. He walked down Wilhelmstrasse, past the German police guards – more wankers – and threaded through the chicane of concrete blocks in place there to prevent a suicide bomber in a vehicle achieving martyrdom. He used few words, wouldn't have wasted them on the station chief. Truth was, he rather liked *Mr* Lawson. That he did not walk easily, down Wilhelmstrasse, in the late afternoon when the pavements were crowded with the spill-out of ministry workers, had nothing to do with the weight he carried under each arm. In the bathroom, before breakfast, he had checked his testicles and the bruising was still there. After three days there were still technicolour shades round them, but Deadeye hadn't complained, was never a moan-merchant. In fact, he was pretty damn pleased that *Mr* Lawson still called him up.

His name, Deadeye, had been with him for twenty-six years: once he had been a young marine, cosy in the sanger on top of Londonderry's walls with his rifle and its mounted telescopic sight. The Provo guy had been eleven hundred yards away and had taken the M-1 carbine out of the boot of the car and been sniped. His company major had called it the 'finest exhibition of marksmanship I ever heard of', and his colonel had congratulated him on 'bloody fine shooting, real Deadeye Dick stuff'. It had stuck. He was Deadeye in the Special Boat Squadron when he was married to Leanne, Deadeye as an instructor at the Commando Training Centre, Lympstone, when he was married to Mavis, Deadeye in the first Iraq war as an increment with SIS, holed up with a big bloody radio and his rifle in a Kuwait City apartment block, when he was married to Adele . . . He was still Deadeye, but wasn't married to anyone.

He turned off Wilhelmstrasse and, in the far distance, saw the minibus. The rain had come on harder, but he reckoned the paper wrapping would hold till he reached shelter.

That he worked at all, that his loneliness in a one-bedroomed flat on the outskirts of Plymouth was ever broken, was due to Christopher Lawson. No one else called him. The bloody wives didn't, or the kids. He didn't do reunions, men getting pissed and polishing reputations. He had no friends. To kill the time he put together expensive models of men o' war from Nelson's time, with intricate rigging, and waited for the phone to ring. That loneliness, with the model kit for company and the phone not ringing, hurt deep.

He reached the minibus, dragged open the door, climbed in. They were all there, squashed in, except Dennis. Lawson was in the front, had the passenger seat, and Adrian was at the wheel. Their breath had misted the windows. Deadeye squeezed between Bugsy and Shrinks, then chucked the packages in their wet wrapping over his shoulders on to the laps of Davies and the girl. He didn't give a toss for his grunt and her squeal. Lawson looked at him, quizzed with a raised eyebrow, and Deadeye nodded.

'How was my colleague?'

Deadeye said, 'He badmouthed you, Mr Lawson.'

'Predictable . . . He won't for much longer, if I'm right. Yes, time for a bigger picture.'

Deadeye thought Mr Lawson always did the big picture well, and he settled back in his seat to listen. Well, it would help to see the big picture, help good.

* * *

'I told you, back in London, that my supposition was of a warhead being brought from Russian territory – to be precise, as I was then, from the former closed city of Arzamas-16 – for delivery and sale to a Russian ethnic criminal organization. I believe, after that sale, a second deal will be struck with a purchaser who will attempt to detonate that warhead in a city in western Europe, probably in the UK, or in the United States of America. The aim of Operation Haystack is to disrupt such a deal and to destroy such a sale. To that end I am endeavouring to insert our man, November, as far as I can into the bowels of that criminal organization. We have made progress.'

Lawson paused. He seldom rushed on explanations when they had to be given. He believed a stuttering drip-feed of information better held the attention of an audience. By stopping in his monologue, he had the chance to look around him, to study the faces and see where support rested, where antagonism built.

'Take the story of *Oliver Twist*. Forget about Oliver, but recall the character of Sykes. Sykes had a dog, a much whipped mongrel that harboured no malice and followed its vile master. After Sykes had, most brutally, murdered a pretty girl, he fled. There was a hue and cry. Diligent citizens pursued Sykes, anxious to apprehend him, see him tried, condemned and hanged – but they lost him. Sykes would have escaped but for the loyalty of the mongrel, which refused to be abandoned. The dog trailed him, found him. He could not throw it off. Allusions to this may be flawed but the conclusion is justified. The pursuers followed the dog. The dog handed them their man. We have a dog and we call him November. Understood?'

No questions, but Bugsy passed round a little box of breath-freshener pills. He looked into the faces of the girl and young Davies, saw outrage and enjoyed it.

'At every opportunity presented me, I have endeavoured to push our man, November, further from dependence on us. I have no interest in him believing that we hold his salvation in our hands. We are achieving this aim. We saw it today, November supported by Reuven Weissberg. Links are in place. Reuven Weissberg, and our mongrel has led us to him, is a considerable player in the ranks of organized crime, well capable of purchasing and selling on a device from Arzamas-16. He is—'

Shrill, a voice from the back: 'I don't think I'm hearing this . . . Are you just using Johnny Carrick – yes, he does have a bloody name, is not simply a codeword and a file number – like he's a half-dead fish hooked on to a treble and lobbed into a lake to catch a damn pike? He's owed more, a bloody sight more, than you're offering.'

'Charmingly put, my dear. As I was saying, our man is embedded in the world of Reuven Weissberg. If I'm correct, Reuven Weissberg will travel in the next few hours to the East and will have a prearranged rendezvous to take delivery of the device, the warhead, whatever. Our man has to lead us, show us where to be. Then we deal with the matter. Questions?'

He saw that the girl shivered. Saw also that young Davies had slipped an arm loosely round her shoulder, doing the comforter role. He thought questions, accusations, were blurring the girl's mind and her lips moved, but she didn't cough out her hatred of him.

Bugsy spoke. 'I'm not one to cringe. Don't get me wrong, Guv'nor. I'm up for this like we all are. How safe is this thing likely to be? I think it's only fair we should know.'

'Drop it on your foot, Bugsy, and there will not be a mushroom cloud but you will have a broken toe. In the heart of this weapon – the pit – if it's to be sold on, there will be plutonium or highly enriched uranium. Pack round that pit several kilos of commercial or military explosive, along with a detonator and a wire to a button switch or a remote, and you will have what we laughingly call a "dirty bomb". A dirty bomb, when triggered, will contaminate a city centre to the extent that it has to be abandoned. It is a dirty bomb that Reuven Weissberg will take delivery of and sell on, and Josef Goldmann is in place to make payment for it, then accept payment on sale. I hope, with your help – and November's – to stop him. Questions?'

He sensed it had welled up, but was controlled. Young Davies asked, 'Did you consider sharing your suspicions?'

'With whom?'

'Well, for a start, we're in Germany – sharing with the BfV. Allies, aren't they?'

'Unreliable, burdened with bureaucracy. Next question.'

'If the device is coming from Russia, and the Cold War's over, why not share with them?'

'For a decade the Russians have rebuffed insinuations that their nuclear arsenals are porous. It is not accepted that a weapon could be missing – it would be regarded as "provocation" to suggest it. The Cold War's over, is it?'

'So, just us and the agent stand between peace for the great unwashed and Armageddon. Too damn proud to share . . . Down to us and him?'

'About right,' Lawson said.

'That's ridiculous.'

'It's the way it will be.'

'And should we fail on the interception, should we lose *it*, or inconveniently lose *them*, what happens? Do I hear you say, Mr Lawson, "Let's go for a beer"? Do we stand at the bar, wait for the big bang and—'

'I think we're aware of your opinion and the prejudice it carries.'

'You'll be damned, Mr Lawson – oh, did Clipper Reade not share? – if you fail.'

'I do not intend to fail.' He was hurt. Wouldn't have shown it. The sneering reference to Clipper had wounded. Couldn't have explained his reverence and respect for the big Texan. The best damn years of his life had been with Clipper, and Lawson could well recall his desolation when the American had left Berlin and taken the flight down the corridor out of Tempelhof. He had known that Clipper, in a week, would be en route to the States and retirement. He had written once, now twenty-seven years ago, to the Agency's personnel department, just a chatty note in his own hand-writing, and it had been returned in a clean envelope with a slip inside stating *Addressee instructed no forwarded mail*. Had only the memories, the wisecracks and the wisdom to hold on to. He had shredded that chatty note, never written again, and had never asked Agency people what had happened to his mentor, but had kept the past alive . . . And a little wet-behind-the-ears bastard had sneered at that name. 'And with your help and cooperation I shall not fail.'

The silence hung inside the minibus, as if it was a burden.

He was anonymous, a stranger in the city. The Crow had not visited Damascus before. He was in a lodging-house, two streets back from the north end of Semiramis Square. He had bought food from a street stall and taken it back to his room.

He lay on the bed. An electric fan on the table ruffled his hair but its constant whine was insufficient to distract him. He reflected. Of course, the Crow felt no resentment at what he believed his future held. Alone in the aircraft that had brought him to Syria, and on the pavements of its capital city, he had considered his position, and the future. Some, faced with such a situation, cut off thoughts of those they had loved, found a new woman and a new life. He would not. He couldn't imagine being in the bed of another woman or holding other children in his arms. They knew nothing of what he did, what he planned. Those he had left behind were in complete ignorance of who he was. They would learn.

It would happen. It was inevitable. In the hour before dawn, in a week, a month or a year, the front door of his home would be bludgeoned open and men of the Interior Ministry's investigation unity, the *mabaheth*, would pour into the villa, with Americans of the Agency trailing behind them. While rooms were ripped apart, his wife and children would cower in a corner and questions would be screamed at them. It would happen. However close the security around an operation, traces were always left. So many of the leaders' names were known once the work of an operation was completed. The very attack opened the road for the investigators to follow. Now the Crow was unknown, but in the hours after an explosion and as computers pored over the minutiae of travel arrangements, his name and picture would materialize. He would be running, would be in hiding until the day he made a mistake or was betrayed . . . The love of his wife and children would be stretched to breaking-point as investigators rifled through their home.

He would have inflicted that pain on them. He couldn't apologize. He couldn't ask their forgiveness. He was a soldier, committed to war, and he believed he had the chance to attack and wound his enemy.

'Please, don't do that,' Sak said, emphasized it.

'What's the problem?' His mother stood in the kitchen doorway, hands on her hips, her head shaking in confusion.

'There is no problem.'

'I said, reasonably enough, if we need to reach you while you're away we'll get your accommodation address from the school.'

'Don't.'

'Why the mystery? You're on school business. They'll know where you are.'

'You shouldn't call the school. They wouldn't like it.'

His father, more confused than his mother, intervened from the sofa. 'But you said yourself that your mobile won't be on.'

'Don't call the school.' He flounced out, crossed the hall, stamped up the stairs, slammed the door of his room.

Sak fell on his bed.

He imagined them. His father would again be slumped in front of the television and his mother would be doing her final tidy of the kitchen before coming upstairs for the night, and he had perplexed them both. It had been an aside from his mother: 'You said you didn't know your hotel when you're away. Should we need to contact you, I don't know why, but – well, the school secretary will tell us . . . because you say your mobile won't be switched on.' All innocence. His mother, almost, had caught him in the lie of his doing reconnaissance for a school trip later in the year. He was a poor conspirator, recognized it.

He wouldn't have dared now to back out of the conspiracy.

There had been a moment when he had stood in front of a metal-faced gate to the garden of a villa on the outskirts of Quetta when he might have. But he had sucked in a big breath and pressed the bell. Inside, under a walnut tree, sitting on the dried earth, welcomed, propositioned, he couldn't have backed out – hadn't wished to, and had felt himself, at last, to be important. Couldn't have backed out when the car had pulled up beside him as he walked away from the school gate, and he was told what he should do, and when – not in the form of a request but as an instruction. He had been told to take holiday from work, to find an excuse for his absence from his family, and he had been ordered to leave his mobile phone behind, because, when switched on, a mobile phone left a footprint.

He lay on his bed, with his packed bag close to the door. A life of failure swam past him. Sak had no idea of the enormity of the conspiracy he had joined, or of the many who were part of it.

* * *

'I tell you, Yashkin—'

'What?'

'You always fucking interrupt . . . I tell you I feel better.'

'A pity we have no wine to celebrate.'

They were long past Pogar and had gone through Starodub, a miserable little place, Molenkov had thought, and were now on the main route, the M13. Not from choice, but there was no side road on which Molenkov could navigate them to Klincy, where they would sleep. He sensed that his friend's sour mood came from his directions that they must use the highway. Every car sped past them, and every van, every motorcycle, every lorry hooted in a cacophony because the plodding Polonez was an obstacle. Drivers held up behind them hit their horns and flashed headlights, and when they came level they pointed to the hard shoulder, as if that was where a slow old car should be.

'Are you sulking because I've omitted to ask *why* you feel better?'

Molenkov smiled. 'You could ask humbly and I could reply graciously with an explanation.'

'Fuck you. Why do you feel better?'

'At last I feel luck is with us. Do you understand me? In thirty-five minutes, my estimation, we'll be in Klincy and—'

'I know nothing of Klincy, its history, industry or layout. Where we will sleep, I don't know.'

'Can you not interrupt me, Yashkin? Then we'll be at the end of the fifth day, and will have achieved three-quarters – almost – of our journey. We've survived, haven't fought each other, have kept the wreck on the road. With each kilometre we travel we're each nearer to a half-share of one million American dollars. Those are achievements, and they tell me that luck is with us.'

'You believe in luck, my friend?'

'I do. What was it but luck that caused the sentry at the main gate not to search the cart and find the *thing*? More luck for you that I, the political officer, didn't see you dig the hole and bury it, because I would have reported you. More luck that Viktor came and you, my friend, confided in me. I believe in luck.'

'We'll need luck for two more days.'

Molenkov, now sombre, said, 'I think you have to earn it.'

They were dwarfed by lorries, most with swaying trailers, that streamed past them. The passenger in the cab of a lorry that hauled timber had his window wound down and hurled abuse at Yashkin, who gave him the finger. Molenkov turned in his seat, cursed the stiffness of his pelvis and reached back. He let his fingers fall on the rough canvas that covered the thing. He thought of his wife, dead, and his son, dead, and wondered with growing bitterness why they had not earned luck. A horn screamed at him.

The voice chirped in his ear. 'You want to know about luck, Molenkov?'

He turned his head, saw bright mischief in Yashkin's eyes.

'A story about luck?'

'Go on.'

'Have you heard of the luck of the scientists at Arzamas-16 who did the first test?'

'No.'

Yashkin said, 'It was the twenty-ninth of August, 1949, the test was to be called Operation First Lightning, and the bomb was on a tower in what has become the Semipalatinsk test site. Lavrenti

Beria, head of security for all of the Soviet Union, was overseeing the programme to build the bomb and he came to view the test. The device was fired. It worked. The bomb was the triumph of Igor Kurchatov. Beria then read, with the mushroom cloud in the sky, a letter of congratulation from Stalin, addressed to all the scientists who had made the firing successful. Kurchatov was lucky. He spoke afterwards to close colleagues of his luck and theirs. He said Beria had carried two documents from Stalin: the letter of congratulation and the warrant for the scientists' execution. Had they not been lucky, had the device not exploded, they would have been killed – Kurchatov said so. One document in the right pocket of Beria's jacket, and one in the left. You could say that Kurchatov earned his luck . . . There were nomads who lived in transient villages inside the zone of radioactive fall-out and they were not lucky. They were not moved before the test. As always, luck must be earned. You look miserable, Molenkov. I tell you, we'll earn our luck, and take what's owed us.'

They came off the M13 and drove into Klincy.

Lawson came to the car, panting. Davies followed, carrying the bags for both of them. The car was parked on the kerb behind the minibus, a hundred and fifty metres up the street from the hotel.

The girl pushed open the rear door for him, and said, 'Goldmann's wheels are at the front. All of that party is loaded up, their gear in the boot. They're moving out. We're ready to go.'

Lawson slipped into the rear seat and closed the door abruptly. Wasn't going to tolerate young Davies beside him. He had exchanged only banalities with him since the spat in the minibus. Not that he wanted more. He preferred quiet. Not ten minutes ago, he had been in his room. Throwing his clothes into his bag, he had seen the biro he had used beside the notepad on the bedside table, had bent to pick it up, and his hand had brushed the telephone. He had not called Lavinia since he had left London. He had not told her where he was headed. He could have lifted the phone, punched the numbers, muttered a couple of platitudes to the answerphone, or even spoken to her.

'Are we all fit?'

'Never been fitter.' There was still that bloody sneer in young Davies's voice.

'Ready to go,' the girl said.

Lawson remembered the telephone he hadn't lifted, the number he hadn't dialled, and a slow frown formed on his forehead. He had been away from home for two nights, and he couldn't have said with certainty that Lavinia would have noticed his absence.

'A little change of plan,' Lawson said. Like a bloody bright light that had come on – God, his mind was clouded, confused, and he'd not acted on an impulse. Should have done. They were staring at him from the front. 'Slipping, sorry. Luke . . . Apologies to both.'

He said what he wanted done.

He climbed out of the car, took his bag from the boot and started to walk to the minibus. Wasn't damn well losing it, was he? They'd be standing in a bloody great queue winding round the corridors of VBX for a chance to take a peek at him if word surfaced that Christopher Lawson had lost the plot. He reached the minibus, pulled open the side door. 'Coming with you, gentlemen, wherever we're headed. They'll be following tomorrow.'

* * *

Mikhail was at the wheel of the car that had stopped behind theirs. Reuven had come to the front passenger door of their car and opened it. Clear enough what was intended.

Josef Goldmann was out, quick as a rat up a drain. Reuven was talking fast, but quietly. Josef Goldmann gaped. Reuven's finger pointed to Carrick, who knew nothing. Showed no interest because that wouldn't have been expected of him. He thought Goldmann tried to argue, that he was brushed aside. Carrick saw his shoulders slump.

Goldmann came to Carrick's door. Beside Carrick was Viktor, who would have heard and understood but was impassive and stared straight ahead. Carrick opened his door.

'He wants you to go with him.'

'Sorry, sir?'

'Reuven wishes you to travel, Johnny, in his car.'

Carrick said, 'You are my employer, Mr Goldmann. I ride where *you* want me to ride.'

Carrick saw defeat cut Goldmann's face. 'Thank you, Johnny. *I* wish you to ride in his car.'

'As long as you're happy, Mr Goldmann.'

'I am happy, Johnny.'

He went, sat in the Audi. Mikhail's smile was as cold as bloody winter. Wondered then if, in fact, he had failed the test as the drill tip had neared his kneecap, wondered if he was dead. Recalled the support given him by Reuven Weissberg when they had walked from the warehouse. Knew nothing. Reuven Weissberg passed him a peppermint. Knew less than nothing.

Mikhail drove fast into the Berlin night, and headed east.

327

Chapter 12: 14 April 2008

They came into Warsaw at dawn. The horizon ahead, to the east, had no brightness, only degrees of grey. It was a landscape of greyness. Merging the land and the sky, a carpet of smog hung in the air. Carrick had not been told why he had been scalped from Josef Goldmann's car to Reuven Weissberg's.

He had not been questioned during the six hours on the road. Mikhail said nothing to him, spoke only – occasionally – to Reuven in Russian. Carrick found the silence unsettling. The radio was on softly, but only to catch road reports. The long quiet times were difficult for Carrick because the motion of the car and the warmth of its interior lulled him. He had decided he had been taken from his paymaster, Josef Goldmann, his Bossman, as a gesture of supremacy. Simple stuff. Someone else had something that was wanted, desirable and valued, and it was the mark of Reuven Weissberg that an alpha dog could take what it chose to.

Well past Poznan, with the signs showing for Warsaw, he had decided his assessment was flawed.

When he was stalking Jed and Baz, or Wayne, he had seen the greed that ruled them, the need for the pecking order to be displayed and worn, as uniformed officers hankered after their rank badges. Greed was the biggest factor in criminals' lives. Either side of Poznan and in the quiet of the car, he had been applying ill-founded stereotypes, had stuck labels on his image of Reuven Weissberg, which had drifted away as the kilometres were swallowed. More to this man . . . No sign of a mistress, but the grandmother who displayed authority over him was there. No indication of affluence in the apartment, just heavy old furniture that would have filled up the back of a junk store in London or Bristol. No top-of-the-range car, and the big Audi that Mikhail drove had gone past a hundred thousand kilometres on the clock. The clothes weren't Armani and the hair wasn't styled. Would have walked past him on the street and not noticed him.

Wrong. Carrick would have noticed him, had he looked into Reuven Weissberg's eyes.

Coming into the suburbs of Warsaw, Carrick's thoughts took new turns. Behind him, Weissberg had discarded the big leather jacket with the scuffed elbows and frayed cuffs and it lay on the spare seat beside him. He wore a clean, ironed shirt with short sleeves. The leather jacket had been shrugged off outside the Berlin hotel when it had been demanded that Carrick walk away from Josef Goldmann. Then Carrick had held open the car door, and as Reuven Weissberg had dropped into the seat, the right sleeve had worked up. Again, Carrick had seen the closed hole where a bullet had punctured the flesh.

Now, as Mikhail took the car up on to a main route flyover, Carrick believed he understood. When they had tested him, pushed him to the limit, and he had exploded with the yell of accusation about a gunshot and lack of protection, then – like a thunderclap – a mood had changed.

About protection . . . about the boasts of Josef Goldmann that he was protected by a guy who would risk his own life to earn his corn, about protection in a world of acute and extreme danger. It had been almost enough to make Carrick laugh out loud. But he did not . . . He could have laughed because a criminal feared for his own safety and had taken possession of his associate's bodyguard, as if that bodyguard was a flak jacket, proven against small-arms fire . . . All about protection. As a child, Carrick had been taken by his grandfather into the Cairngorm mountains to the south of the Spey's mouth when autumn turned the high slopes golden. They had gone, then, to lofty viewpoints, with binoculars and a telescope on a tripod, and his grandfather had searched the range for stags and hinds. The season of the rut, when the king stag mated with his hinds, fascinated his grandfather and bored the child Carrick near to death – unless there was combat.

Younger stags approached the king, and there was the bellowed defiance of the big old boy who controlled the herd. Some pretenders plucked courage and came to fight – horns locked, wounds made, blood seeping. Rare, but he had seen it, a pretender usurped the big old boy, sent him from the field where the hinds grazed. At the sight of the one-time king creeping away, injured and desolate, his grandfather always let rip squeals of excitement and thought his grandchild should ape him.

They said, on the courses he had done and in the office when time was idled, that the fear of every major criminal – at level three, into organized crime with international links – was that a young gun would topple him. They did not, of course, retire and slip away to the villa with the pool and the patio, milk the building-society account and allow an old world to drift away. They tried to stay the course and hang on to power, authority. They ended up, damn near the lot of them, in handcuffs because of the one 'final' big-shot deal, or dead in the gutter from a contract man's weapon, with blood coming off the pavement and heading for the drain. Carrick remembered the strength of Reuven Weissberg's grip on his sleeve and the way he had been held up when they had left the warehouse.

The car swung off the flyover and came down a slip road, then swerved across traffic lanes. They came to a hotel whose floors reached, almost, to the cloud base. Porters hurried forward but Mikhail waved them away. He did his own parking and they carried their own bags inside. Only Mikhail went to the desk to check in and collect the key cards. Carrick noted it. He did not have to give a signature. Neither did Reuven Weissberg, nor Mikhail. They waited a few minutes, not many, then Viktor came with Josef Goldmann.

Funny thing, but Johnny Carrick had never thought of Josef Goldmann – in the months he had been with him – as anything other than a target, and he sensed that Goldmann was small fry and insignificant in comparison with Weissberg. And he had never thought of Reuven Weissberg – in the two days since he had met him – as a true target.

He was told he should rest because it was the last day and the last night that there would be time to sleep. Difficult, standing in front of a lift, then entering it, feeling its surge up through forty-something floors, to remember that he was an undercover with SCD10, but on secondment, and that a matter of national security involved him . . . Too damn difficult to comprehend.

He stood at the plate-glass window as the rain ran on it and stared out. He said quietly, 'I wonder if, at the end of it, they'll have the balls?'

Viktor shrugged. 'It was their proposition. If they hadn't talked of it, how would I have known of it?'

Reuven grimaced. 'We have to believe they'll be there.'

'They made the approach.'

'Old men, both. Each kilometre takes them further from what they know.'

Viktor now smacked his fist into the palm of his hand. 'Me, *I* take responsibility.'

'You believe in them.'

'Yes.'

His room faced the Palace of Culture, the Stalin monument to domination, and his window was level with an aspect of its upper structure. For a moment, Reuven Weissberg's tongue wiped his lower lip, darting and hasty. 'Should we have agreed it?'

He saw puzzlement scud over Viktor's features. 'You can't hesitate now. I say that with respect, but you *cannot*. The deal is done. Not only us, and the old men. Others, too, are travelling. It's not possible to withdraw.'

Turning, the smile at his mouth and the brightness in his eyes, Reuven Weissberg said, 'If you say that the old men have the balls and will reach the place you agreed with them, I'll be there. And I'll honour the sale onwards. Do you understand the past?'

'Yes,' Viktor said.

'What was done in the past, you understand that?'

'Yes.'

'Because of the past, I buy and sell . . . Will we hear from the old men again?'

'We heard that they'd started out, and that's enough. There's something I wish to ask of you.'

Weissberg listened. He recalled what his grandmother had said, and heard the boasts of Josef Goldmann on the pedigree of a bodyguard. Reuven Weissberg accepted the advice offered him. Then he caught Viktor's arm, held it vice-tight and whispered that it would be the last time Johnny Carrick was tested.

She recognized quality, and she thought the guy was good. First up, he didn't mess with the puerile codenames, so she was no longer C for Charlie, and he was no longer D for Delta. All explained for her with a grin, and it had made her chuckle. G was not for Golf, the call sign, but was for the sour old fool's insistence on the 'Good Old Days', and D was for Disciple: the poor creature trailing around after the lunatic.

They were at the door. He rang the bell.

Dinner was at the café on Hardenbergerstrasse, and Luke Davies had imitated Lawson ordering dinner the previous evening, not showing the menu but insisting he do it himself, speaking German with the English accent that destroyed it, and selecting the wine as if he alone knew his way round the list. She'd sat where Lawson had. Same chair that the man had used perhaps twenty or thirty years before. Luke Davies, she thought, had been good company, and fun, and she was short enough of that.

He pressed the bell three times, long rings.

He had taken her back to the little *pension* in the side-street, had booked himself again into the room he'd vacated in the evening, and her into what had been Lawson's room. He'd ordered the nightcap in the bar downstairs, and talked of his work – not the classified stuff – and she'd warmed and told him about what little amusement came out of the Pimlico office. She'd sensed it was an age, if ever, since he'd talked of his work with an outsider to VBX: she'd known it was the first time she'd spoken as an insider of SCD10 to someone outside the loop. They'd gone up the stairs and paused by their doors. He'd smiled at her and she at him, he'd wished her a good night's sleep and they'd parted. Maybe it was because of the wish, but she'd slept well, right through till he'd banged on her door . . . What they hadn't talked about, because there'd have been no fun and no laughter, was N for November. Truth to tell, once he'd been called to the Audi and away from Target One, and Lawson had changed his bloody mind, given new instructions, she hadn't thought of Johnny Carrick, which might have been selling him short.

A sharp, reedy voice answered the bell, distorted by the connection to the grilled speaker.

Katie had confirmation of the quality of Luke Davies. Damn good German, and what she thought was bloody good Russian. Not rushing an old woman high in the building above them.

She knew what he'd said because he had rehearsed it with her.

He was a student, Jewish. She was a student, not Jewish. He was involved in Holocaust studies and

334

she was working on contemporary Russian history. Frau Weissberg had been recommended as a prime source for the era covered by the Second World War. How did they know the address? Because they had been given it by Esther Goldmann, wife of Josef. Had Josef Goldmann, who, his wife had said, was in Berlin, not told her of their visit? Esther Goldmann had said Frau Weissberg had a history of suffering, heroic courage. Students would be privileged to hear her speak of the past. A whistle of breath, then the click of the outer door unlocking.

When he had rehearsed it with her, Katie had said, 'How do you know she's affected by the Holocaust?'

'In a forest, in fatigues, holding a baby. Photograph in the kitchen. Partisans in the forest. That's "affected" . . . Next?'

'What about "suffering" and "heroic courage", are they guaranteed?'

'In the forest with a baby, with partisans, her hair white at twenty, twenty-one. They fit.'

'She calls Josef Goldmann, wherever he is, on a mobile. Checks you.'

'Doesn't. Knows mobiles are tracked. Basic security, mobile off.'

Katie had said, 'So, she calls Esther Goldmann for verification.'

'Then we blow out, but she won't have done. I'd bet on it.'

She'd pulled a face. 'On your head be it.'

He'd blinked. 'Wrong. On Carrick's head.'

And the lift rose smoothly and fast.

He said, 'Don't forget the old bathroom routine, and getting her to show you. Lead, and look harmless.'

She was undercover-trained. Had done the same courses as Johnny Carrick and heard the same lectures. Her major experience was as a girl trying to break into the gang doing a street opposite King's Cross station, and having to leg it each time the pimps, Ukrainian and Albanian, came after her. She brought them out and was the bait for them to break cover. The camera in the parked van did the identification, and she'd played the part of the girl-friend on three different operations. She knew what she had to do, but seemed not to mind being told.

It was always bullshit.

Bullshit opened doors.

Katie could do that smile, the one about melting butter, and do it well, and Luke Davies was good. She didn't know what he said in the shadowed gloom of the hall, as they were taken through to the kitchen. She was doing smiles and he was doing sincerity, and it was bluff and it was bullshit. A pot of tea was made, and poured before it had stood. It was thin and tasted stewed. Katie kept smiling, and Luke was nodding, as if what he was being told was a message from God. The old woman, Anna Weissberg, made short, staccato statements that were, Katie thought, bare of redundant explan-ation. Maybe it was five minutes before the tea was poured, and maybe five more before the mugs had been pushed towards them.

Katie understood. She saw the increasing agitation of the grandmother of Reuven Weissberg. Too right, my old girl, because it was a piss-poor decision to let in soft-talkers off the street, with an introduction that couldn't be checked. Fidgeting and fretting, answers drifting to brevity, then to one word. She was at the door, and holding it open for them. Katie did her stuff. The toilet, please. Could she use the toilet? Always worked . . . and couldn't find the switch for the light, and was shown it. She stood inside the toilet, heard the slippered feet shuffle away – wondered if Anna Weissberg had any clothes other than black or whether she mourned perpetually – counted to fifty, pulled the flush and came back into the hall.

In English, Luke said to her, 'I am afraid that Esther Goldmann was presumptuous in offering us this introduction. Anna Weissberg was in a camp, was freed from it and lived in the forests with partisans. Her grandson's father was born in the forests. It was a time of great strain that she doesn't feel happy talking about. It would have been better if we'd waited till her grandson was at home. That's what she's saying.'

'Please would you thank Mrs Weissberg for her kindness, Luke, and for the tea and for letting us into her home, and say we hope we haven't disturbed her and woken bad memories. For that, if we did, we apologize.'

It was translated.

The welcome had been outstayed. Katie recognized the discomfort they had visited on the woman. The brilliant bullshit had wormed them in but couldn't keep them there. She sensed a loneliness into which they had intruded, and an isolation that had been fractured, and thought the woman would regret, damn deep, permitting them to enter.

The door closed behind them. They heard a key turn in the lock and a bolt go across, but they had broken into a fortress and lies had done the Trojan Horse for them.

'What did we learn?'

'I'm not sure,' Luke Davies answered. 'Don't know. I mean, we've accessed a big player's home, but inside it's what I imagine a functionary's apartment would be in fifty Russian cities. There's nothing. No wealth, no opulence, extravagance. So, what's the motive for criminality, doing the big deal that Lawson blathers about? I suppose she's central, but I don't know why. All I can say is that she had white hair when she was in that forest, and she would have been about twenty.'

'Could a scarring emotional experience turn your hair white?'

'I suppose so, but I don't know.'

'And that's it?'

'That's it. We go and find them.'

Katie nodded. She did the mobile call, reached Lawson. Did he want a run-down? He did not. She didn't bother to express her opinion that Luke Davies had been bloody double-time brilliant in gaining entry, and that she had achieved the hoary old one of needing the toilet and had won him half a minute alone in the kitchen. She didn't think Lawson would have jumped for joy. They should drive to Warsaw.

She took the wheel, and he did the maps.

The sign said it was still two kilometres to the Customs point.

Right to the last, before accepting the inevitable and joining the crawl of the queue, they had debated whether a diversion north or south, and an attempt to use side-roads, was worthwhile. Had decided, with grim reluctance, that the M13 was the only possible route. Molenkov's finger traced the frontier line on the map across his knees, and he'd bent low over the unfolded sheets to see the detail better. He had muttered of an absence of roads, too many rivers that would not have bridges

338

and would be so swollen as to make ridiculous the thought of fording them, forests that were great blocks on the map.

Earlier there were two, three opportunities when they might have turned off the M13 and gone south, towards Klimovo, or to the north and on a side road to Svatsk, or tried for a larger loop and gone far north and west to Krasnaja Gora, but Molenkov had pulled a long, mock-despairing face when they had come close to the signs and Yashkin had driven on. They had reached the queues. At first they had progressed in little darted movements. Then it had been a crawl but continuous. Now they were halted.

Molenkov's cough was hacking. Yashkin checked the windows. They were, of course, closed tight against the rain but something of the foulness around the Polonez seeped in. The lorries belched fumes from their exhausts. Yashkin thought they were surrounded by a fog of polluting gases. The taste was in his mouth and dried his throat, seeming to scratch rather than tickle it.

Did the Belarus authorities have modern detection equipment to scan the vehicles crossing to their territory? Did they have the devices that would read radiation traces? He had not thought so, and Molenkov had not known. Because of rivers and forests it was decided, after the debate, that the chance must be taken: fucking Belarus, with an economy still back in medieval or at best Tsarist times, would *not* have the equipment to recognize the signature of a plutonium pit in the heart of a Zhukov weapon.

Another anxiety, now more pressing, intruded on the mind of Yashkin. It would not have reared itself if they had driven fast and directly to the twin

Customs points. What he would have called, all those years before when he had worked, the 'human factor'. The pompous official, the man who revelled in the power given him, the arsehole consumed by self-esteem, the bastard who sauntered to a vehicle, peered through its windows, examined passports and driving licence, then demanded a search of the interior. That worry had been a pimple head, a mosquito's bite, but the irritation was now scratched and had become an open sore.

He drove the car forward, braked again, saw tail-lights in the queues ahead, watched the drift of the fumes across the windscreen. He told Molenkov that the anxiety for the equipment should have been secondary to the worry over the human factor of an official demanding to search the Polonez.

'I mean, it's hardly hidden, only covered. Well, tell me – you'd know, my friend, because you could act the part of a *zampolit* and be pompous, an arsehole and arrogant. You were the small bureaucrat official with no status beyond that given you by the uniform.'

His friend was grinning. Between the violence of the coughing, Molenkov gave a black chuckle. 'Can't you see yourself, Yashkin? Weren't you such an official?'

Hands raised, Yashkin accepted his point. 'What do we do?'

A little frown from Molenkov, an index finger tapping his chin as he thought. The pursing of lips because a decision was reached. 'It's the uniform.'

'No riddles. Speak clearly.'

'You said it yourself, idiot, the uniform is his status. The official withers to insignificance when he doesn't wear a uniform.'

'But when he sees us he's in the uniform. Russian Customs or Belarus Customs, they have a uniform. We can't expect him to be naked when we reach him.'

Molenkov said, 'We brought our uniforms. We didn't know for what purpose. We use medals *and* uniforms. I talk and you're silent. We both wear uniforms.'

They went forward again, stopped again.

Yashkin eased his foot off the brake pedal. 'Full uniform?'

'Full uniform and medals, the medals over the ribbons.'

'Good.' Yashkin chuckled, then switched off the engine. It guttered. 'I was stupid not to realize that a minor bureaucrat, a political officer, would understand the limited mentality of a Customs arsehole.'

They climbed out, stood and stretched. The fumes made Molenkov's coughing worse. The side door was opened, and each took out his uniform, then searched his bag for his medals. They carried the uniforms and medals to the verge and climbed a couple of metres up a shallow bank. They stood in the rain among the dead grass of winter and stripped. They gave a show, heard shouts of mock-abuse and derisory whistles. Engines roared and noxious fumes spurted from the exhaust pipes. Molenkov was convulsed with coughing. Horns bellowed. The vehicles edged forward but those behind the Polonez couldn't move.

'Do I look the part?' Molenkov demanded of his friend.

'Yes,' Yashkin responded. 'You're the perfect example of a minor official.'

Molenkov punched him. He was grinning, but

341

the blow made Yashkin gasp. The shouts, yells, whistles and the noise from the horns burgeoned. They picked up their clothing, took time to fold the items roughly, then skipped through the moving lorries and went back to the Polonez. Yashkin started up and cruised the space left empty in front of them. When he reached down to change gear he could hear, satisfyingly, the tinkle of the medals. The fit of his tunic disappointed him. It hung on his chest now as a loose cloak would, and it was the same with Molenkov's but he wouldn't tell his friend.

Molenkov said, 'Do you remember the power of that uniform?'

Yashkin paused, but only briefly. 'The year before I was dismissed an NCO was brought to me. He had been caught at the wire of Zone Twelve and was about to carry three typewriters through a hole he'd made in the wire. Not radioactive material, not the blueprint of the layout of a warhead, but three fucking typewriters. He was so frightened of me – of my uniform – that he messed his trousers. I told him to take the typewriters back to Zone Twelve, after he had changed his trousers, and gave him extra night duties on the north perimeter where it was always coldest. He thanked me for my clemency and was blubbering his gratitude, weeping like a kid. He would have been on his knees had it not been for the escort holding him up. That was the power of my uniform.'

Molenkov said, 'An engineer in explosives was reported to me for saying at a party that our warheads were technically a decade behind those of the Americans at Los Alamos, and that we didn't service them often enough because we lacked the financial resources to do the work, and many would fail to detonate if fired. He was brought to me. I berated him for "negativity" and "defeatism" and for "spreading lies" and "disloyalty to the state". He cringed in front of me. I could barely hear his response because he squealed in fear. I think he believed he was headed for the gulag. I had been twice to his apartment as a guest. My wife was the friend of his wife. To have pursued him would have meant more trouble than it was worth – reports to be written and sent to Moscow, investigations, inquests as to the effectiveness of my work. When I told him to go home, and not to be such an imbecile again, he fainted. I shan't tell you his name, but he was one of the brightest stars of Arzamas-16 and to have lost him would have created a void hard to fill. He was carried out of my office. That was the uniform.'

Yashkin braked, waited, then nudged forward again. 'Did you ever see him again after you'd been dismissed, and no longer wore the uniform?'

Molenkov said, 'I was passing the museum. It was three years ago. I'm older than when he knew me, and my clothes were those of a vagrant but he would have known me. A face doesn't alter whatever circumstances affect the body. He walked right past me and looked through me. He would have thought himself as of the élite and me as a functionary. I wasn't wearing the uniform.'

'I saw that NCO, and definitely he saw me. He was with his children, parking his car outside the cinema. I wore that old coat – the one from the street market with the moths – but he knew me. How do I know he knew me?'

'How *do* you know he knew you?'

'Because he spat at my feet because I wasn't wearing the uniform.'

Without thinking, Yashkin chopped the heel of his hand hard on to the steering-wheel. The shock went from his wrist to his elbow and then his shoulder joint. But he felt no pain. Yashkin said, 'We owe them nothing, *nothing*. Be certain of it.'

Nodding fierce agreement, Molenkov began to pick fluff from the material of the tunic above where his medals were pinned.

In their finery of former days, they stayed locked in the queue and, metre by metre, were taken forward, at snail's pace, to the Customs point where they might be confronted by a vehicle search. Silence fell, as if talking were no longer valuable. They were alone and sealed in the car, their attention directed at what lay immediately ahead, not a wider world.

She was one of those who was rarely remembered. If she was remembered, she was easily forgotten. Not recognized as skills by her line managers, her characteristics had helped to create a rather dogged individual, with the trait of persistence.

The problem gnawed in the mind of the liaison officer, Alison. It had been with her for close to two days and nights. It was the matter of Haystack, the name of Johnny Carrick and the sense of responsibility she felt that had distracted her. She could have taken a blank sheet of paper, drawn a vertical line down it from top to bottom. She could have written on the left side: '*Imminent danger? . . . Where are we on a scale of one to ten, Mr Lawson?*' And written underneath it: '*A scale of one to ten? Probably between twelve and thirteen.*' If the gaunt, brusque Christopher Lawson was to be believed, and national catastrophe loomed, she had been morally and operationally correct in divulging the name of

344

Johnny Carrick, an undercover of SCD10. It was the sort of difficulty she had not faced before, but she had no inclination to head off towards her line manager's office and unburden herself while still existing in such ignorance. It had come to her, what she should do, at around four o'clock that morning, and about damn time too.

The power of the computer she was linked to from her work-station was immense. From it she could enter bank records, credit-card transactions, driving-licence details, telephone-usage printouts, pension schemes, electoral registers, marriage and birth certificates. She could open a man or woman's life, split it wide and examine it.

She might, later, have to justify such an intrusion, but that was a minor concern. Information spewed on to her screen. Him, a wife, a son, an address . . . and she felt the chance to shift a minimum of that burden from her shoulders.

She had driven without stopping. The big car with the big engine had eaten the miles between the eastern outskirts of Berlin and the western approach flyover into Warsaw.

For Katie Jennings, the long drive was like fulfilment. She was in her thirty-second year, had been brought up in a Worcestershire village under the bleak spine of the Malvern Hills. Her father had been a Water Board engineer and her mother had taught at junior level; they were now adrift, had packed in their jobs before retirement age and spent half of the year scraping the hull and painting the interior of the *Summer Queen*, the other half navigating the canals of southern and western England; they had achieved a sort of freedom, and she hadn't.

She had thought, once, that joining the Metropolitan Police, aged nineteen, would provide the independence and drive she yearned for – which she recognized her parents now had – and had grown disillusioned. The first flushes of excitement had faded. And then she had thought, four years before, that the transfer into SCD10 would give her the adrenaline surge – and it had at first. She had done King's Cross where the 'toms' paraded and had known that back-up was reassuringly close. She had done the trips to the Spanish island, where her job was to sit with the big players' women and pick up the little morsels they offered in their asinine conversations, and then she had been pulled inside the Pimlico office. There, she did the filing, made the tea and kept the diaries for Rob and George. Katie Jennings did not know whether she was relegated to office duties because of a personal failure or, a simpler explanation, because she was convenient and it was comfortable to have her in the building. She knew the way the system worked and, most probably, Rob and George dreaded the day she moved on and they'd have to find the next sucker who understood the work, made good tea and coffee, and knew what fillings they liked in their sandwiches. She had become professional in the quality of her moans, not that she showed them.

It was late afternoon when she brought them into the city.

Part of the stereotype of the 'little woman' was that she should have a fling with Johnny Carrick. The star, the guy who was trusted and worked at the edge, had no attachments. If she slept with him she wasn't a marriage-wrecker. That, too, had seemed a route to excitement, but no longer. He didn't do it well any more, was too tired, too frazzled or too stressed, and the sessions on the bunk bed in the *Summer Queen* had been of consistently poorer value to her. Bloody hell. It was what she thought about as she drove through the Warsaw suburbs below the flyover. She had seen Carrick come out of the warehouse, leaning for support on and half carried by Reuven Weissberg, their top target. What it added up to: the trusted stellar guy, Johnny Carrick, had lost his lustre. Was that pretty bloody cruel?

Luke Davies, beside her, had not talked much, had not dug for her life story, had not done the superior bit and had not been clever with her.

She'd thought – on the stretch beyond Poznan and hammering past the magnificence of the domed churches and the hideous concrete towers of apartments – hard, of a childhood image back in the village under the long range of hills. It was not part of her job description that she should shag Johnny Carrick, in the hope of keeping him on the road for undercover work.

And another thing she liked about Luke Davies was that he didn't flinch when she went through the gears and stamped on the accelerator. Twice, she'd shivered as she'd come past a truck's cab, then had to swerve hard because the big bastard coming at her wasn't about to give way. More than twice she'd felt the rush of blood as she'd done the overtaking on a bend and across the brow of a hill. She was trained and categorized as an advanced-level driver, she had been on roads at home to speeds in excess of a hundred and forty miles per hour. He hadn't gasped, gulped. He hadn't reached for the dashboard to steady himself. It was as if, she thought, he reckoned her dependable, not just the bloody token in a man's world – SCD10 was that, male territory. There was quite a lot about him that she liked.

He took her off the flyover, did navigation, dumped the maps and used his palm job for the final run-in. He didn't have to call them. He took her right up to and alongside the minibus, which was in a car park beside a church and had a view of the front area of the glass and concrete edifice of the hotel.

He said quietly, 'Great ride, thanks.'

She pulled a face. He had attractive hands, thin, sensitive fingers. His accent appealed. Not smart and not trying to be what he was not. She'd enjoyed it, the drive, and she'd seen his quality at the apartment of Reuven Weissberg when he'd talked them in.

He went to the minibus and the side door was dragged open. From behind him, she saw Christopher Lawson on the back seat. Heard Lawson, 'Well, what did you learn?'

And heard Luke Davies, 'Not enough to tell it all over the mobile.'

'Wouldn't have expected you to.'

'I gained access.'

'Did you, now?'

'I spoke with Anna Weissberg. She was in a camp, freed from it. She had a child in the forest, and was already white-haired. She's a powerhouse, not physically but there's an extraordinary strength about her, difficult to describe it. I saw the photograph of her, and the painting.'

'Describe the painting.'

Katie heard Luke Davies stutter in his answer. 'Not easy . . . It's dark, like the light doesn't get there . . . pines and birches. Has depth, like infinity.

348

I don't know, a place of hate, a frightening place. She didn't tell me where it was.'

'Where else? Sobibor.'

Lawson threw back his head and his eyes were closed, but his lips moved as if he repeated the word, *Sobibor*, again and again.

Luke Davies said he was going to find a sandwich, and Katie Jennings said she was going to find a toilet, and the side door of the minibus was pulled shut on them. Was it like, in her mind, she'd kicked Johnny Carrick when he was down? Didn't know, and wasn't going to agonize over it.

Carrick sensed the new atmosphere grow in intensity. He was at the heart of it, knew it, but was not included.

Another anteroom, another deep, comfortable easy chair, another bedroom beyond a closed door. Josef Goldmann had come to the anteroom but had avoided Carrick's glance and gone inside. There had been a murmur of voices from the bedroom, his Bossman's and Reuven Weissberg's, but they had talked Russian and he had not understood. On coming out, Goldmann had walked past him, then stolen a quick, secretive look at Carrick; it told Carrick that Josef Goldmann had made another concession . . . It was the look he had given, but with more sadness tingeing it, before they had gone to the warehouse, and before Carrick had been ordered to Reuven Weissberg's car. Their eyes had met and Carrick had tried to hold his glance steady, but Josef Goldmann had scuttled out of the anteroom.

Without knocking, as if Carrick's territory had no more importance than a damned corridor, Viktor had come in. Carrick had been on his feet. It was his bloody job to be on his feet as soon as there were footsteps outside the main door of the suite and as soon as the handle moved. He had stood and half blocked the way across the anteroom. Viktor had skirted him, all the time seeming to mock him with the sneer at his mouth, and gone through the inner door.

Carrick could not judge the extent of the crisis. Then Mikhail came, no warning. For a big man he moved well, without sound. First that Carrick knew of him was the door handle turning sharply. Carrick was half up, hands on the chair arms, pushing himself to his feet, and Mikhail had paused in front of him, then pushed him back down. Not a sneer but pure malevolence. The fist that pushed him held a street map of the city.

The new atmosphere corroded Carrick's confidence. Where to put faith? There was no Transit round the corner with a half-dozen uniforms and the familiar Heckler & Koch machine pistols, magazine on and one in the breech. Once, voices were raised, could have been Mikhail's and Viktor's but he didn't think the argument was between them. Sensed they attacked Reuven Weissberg.

Where to put faith? He thought his faith should lie with Reuven Weissberg. The inner door of the bedroom opened.

In Mikhail's hand was a black box, the size of a fat paperback book. It had a dial on it, and a short, stubbed aerial protruded. Mikhail did not speak but went round the anteroom and aimed the aerial at every floor plug, held it close to them, and the telephone plug, then ran it across the television screen. He paused under the smoke detector set in the ceiling, reached up and held the thing there.

There was a constant hum from the machine but no bleep. He walked close to Carrick, stood in front of him, then leaned forward with it. The machine was inches from Carrick's chest and stomach. He knew what was expected of him, what he had to do. His fists unlocked and his fingers snaked forward. Maybe it was surprise he achieved. He snatched the machine, felt the blood rush, then thrust it right up against Mikhail's jacket and over his crotch. He looked into Mikhail's face and his gaze never meandered from Mikhail's eyes. He gave him back the bug detector.

Now Carrick looked away, the gesture made. He should have been Mikhail's friend or at least tolerated by him, but he had reinforced the enmity.

Reuven Weissberg was at the inner door and Viktor hovered at his shoulder. Carrick thought a grin was on Weissberg's lips, as if the spectacle of rats fighting was better if the vermin were half starved.

'Tonight we move out, go on.' Then, as if it was an afterthought, 'Do you know Warsaw, Johnny?'

'I've never been to Warsaw before, sir.'

'Then I will show it to you. Later we will go to the Stare Miasto, the Old City, and I will be your guide.'

'I'll enjoy that, sir. Thank you.'

Why? He didn't know. Carrick couldn't comprehend why the major player – level three in organized crime – wished to walk him round the streets of a city and do tourist junk with him. Why? Had no idea.

Chapter 13: 14 April 2008

Carrick came out of the hotel. He carried his bag from the swing doors, and there was a siren in the air – might have been fire, ambulance or police answering an emergency, might have been for a politician's convoy. He looked up. Had there not been that distant sound of a siren and had he not done that everyday thing of trying to identify where it came from and where it went, he wouldn't have seen her.

She was sitting on a low wall. It ran along the front of a schoolyard, which was beside an ornate church façade, and kids were screaming and chasing behind her. She had a magazine on her lap but had glanced up from it. She was, perhaps, a hundred yards from him and they had visual contact but it was as though she looked right through him and focused on nothing. Two days ago, or three, it would have given him a lift to see Katie, would have raised his morale, spirits, motivation, whatever he ran on. But Johnny Carrick was a changed man, accepted that.

He saw Golf with her, and the young man who called himself Delta. There might have been others with Golf, Katie and the young man, but he was not certain if the group included others who lounged nearer the school gate.

The eye contact should have given him exhilaration . . . He went down into the depths of his professionalism. The instructors spoke of that: a guy could feel himself isolated, could think he was abandoned trash, but could survive if he clung to the creed of professionalism. Behind him, Viktor supervised the moving of Josef Goldmann's quality luggage on to a porter's trolley. Carrick went to Goldmann's car, and a man was there, working on the bonnet paint. In front of that car was Reuven Weissberg's. The man polished the paintwork with a soft duster, but not with enthusiasm; he made short savage movements, halted, then resumed, as if it was unimportant what the goddam car looked like. He wore the obligatory dress of faded jeans and a heavyweight leather jacket. His skull was covered with close-cropped hair and a snake tattoo was wrapped round his neck. He didn't look at Carrick. Carrick dropped his bag, turned to Viktor, seemed to ask the question with his eyes, eyebrows: which vehicle was he to travel in when they moved on? As if in answer, Viktor zapped Josef Goldmann's car doors. Couldn't bloody Viktor speak? Silences, the lack of communication, should not have crushed Carrick as they did. He threw his bag into the boot.

So, he was going walking, would do the tourism bit, and he didn't know why.

The siren was long gone. Carrick stared over the burnished roof, and the car park, through the wire fencing and across a street, and watched her as she sat on the low wall of the schoolyard.

It could still rule him, professionalism.

He stood aside from the boot, and Viktor

353

supervised the stowing of Josef Goldmann's bags.
Carrick said, 'I'm going to get some mints.'

Viktor didn't answer.

Carrick said, 'Going to get some mints from a
kiosk.'

A small frown formed on Viktor's forehead.

'I'm not buying them in there.' Carrick gestured
towards the hotel's swing doors. He was breaking
a law of the trade he practised, was failing on due
care, diligence. Needed to create the opportunity
of a meeting but shouldn't have started up on
explanations: least said, best. Broke it. 'Not paying
the prices they want in there.'

A shrug, distaste. He didn't know how much
Viktor was paid for being the hood in Josef
Goldmann's shadow – might have been two
hundred and fifty thousand euro a year, might
have been more. Himself, he had been promised a
new settlement, new terms of employment – not as
part of the conspiracy of laundering – and the
upgraded role of personal bodyguard: maybe a
hundred thousand euro a year. Why would an
employee of Josef Goldmann quibble over paying
two euro for a tube of mints from a shop in a hotel
lobby, and instead need to go down the street to a
kiosk, or a small bar, and pay one euro for the same
item? Convenience cost an extra euro, was that
important? Explanations split open a legend. An
instructor would have shuddered.

Tried to make a joke of it. 'I suppose it's sort of in
the blood, not wasting money. Have to get the best
deal . . .'

He walked away from the car, and from Viktor.

At the street corner, beyond the car park, he
paused and waited for lights to change. It was an
excuse for him to check both ways. He saw, coming

up the pavement and with a good stride, that the big man – the bastard Golf who had ripped into him in the doorway, had humiliated him – closed on him . . . a bloody window of opportunity was presented. Didn't see Katie with him, and was undecided if that mattered to him. He couldn't look behind him, didn't know what Viktor did, whether he was followed.

The lights changed.

Carrick crossed the street.

He was in a flow of people, anonymous. He passed the door to the library of the British Council and saw in the hallway a poster advertising the chance of rail travel from London to the Lake District. There was a shop ahead with a rack of newspapers outside it.

Mikhail came to the cars. 'Where is he? Didn't he come down?'

'Gone to buy mints.' Viktor's response.

'Why?'

'Because the mints in the hotel are too expensive.'

'You're joking.'

'No.'

'Where's he gone?'

'Round the corner to a shop or a kiosk.'

'How much will he save?'

'I can't say. His bag's in my car.'

The grimace played at Mikhail's mouth, and his hand rested on Viktor's sleeve. 'If I'm correct, he won't be needing a place in your car or mine. He'll be in the fucking river without a boat.'

He pulled the street map from his pocket. He talked, jabbed with his finger at the creased paper, and Viktor listened, and did not interrupt but nodded approval of Mikhail's planning. They had entered State Security the same year, they had worked in the city of Perm and in the same section of investigations into corporate fraud, and they had been together when recruited by Reuven Weissberg. They had done protection together and had killed together. They had been together, day in and day out, till the day Reuven Weissberg had moved to Berlin and Josef Goldmann had gone to London. The separation had not divided them. They were like brothers, and wounded by the intrusion of a stranger.

Viktor said, 'If it's there, we'll find it.'

'I believe it is.'

'Find it, watch him go into the river – and see him sink.'

British Homing World boasted that it was 'The World's Premier Pigeon Racing Weekly', and on an operation Bugsy was never without it – or, more likely, without a minimum of three copies. On any trip of more than a week, the magazines were read, reread, and his invaluable companion. Their worth to Bugsy was that they lessened the frustration brought on by failure.

For hours now, all day, he had watched the two cars but the opportunity he waited for wasn't offered.

In the pocket of Bugsy's anorak was the tag, but the chance to clamp it had not come.

He had been through the stock lines of birds for sale, and their price, and in his mind had checked the cost of 'Quality farm cleaned: Tic Beans, Maple Peas, Oil Seed Rape and Whole Maize . . .' Without the magazines, he would have raged.

But it was clear to him, and this conclusion could

not be avoided, the chance of getting a tag into Reuven Weissberg's car had not offered itself. The goon had been there all the hours that Bugsy had watched. The guy with the lump-hammer head and the tattoo round his throat hadn't even gone for a piss. The car shone. Would have made the job a hell of a sight easier if the goon had gone walkabout – hadn't . . . Maybe the job of putting a tag into the car wouldn't happen and maybe it would mean risking a wire on the undercover. Needed to happen, something did, because they had driven as if the Furies chased them to get to Warsaw, hold the contact and the visuals, and the bloody old minibus had been a croaking wreck after what had been asked of it.

Bugsy had listened closely to the guv'nor's briefing. He'd been on big operations, enough of them, but he'd sensed this to be on a scale of threat greater than he'd known before. The guv'nor had authorized him to try to place a tag, but it just wasn't possible. He saw, from his vantage-point, the bags loaded into the cars, and that just lifted the weight of the failure.

So, again, they'd be careering on the seat of their pants, and it would be down to the driving skills of Adrian and Dennis – and they'd bitched like fuck at what had been asked of them, Berlin to Warsaw.

'I don't know how long we have. Spill it.' Lawson was at his shoulder.

'You've taken your bloody time.'

His man spun. Carrick had been pointing to a tube of mints in a cardboard box on a shelf behind the shop woman's head. Didn't finish. Lawson thought him like the familiar old rabbit in the headlights and reckoned the degeneration faster than he'd anticipated. 'I'm here, we're here. What's new?' Did the calm and quiet bit, that of the man in charge.

'Well, for a start, I damn near had my knee taken off with a drill.' A rising voice, at the edge of hysteria. 'Try that for starters.'

'But you didn't have it taken off so can we get to something of relevance?'

'First, in that bloody place I'm quizzed, and the hoods aren't believing me – how close were you?'

Not the time to make assessments as to whether a man was a potential coward or a potential hero. Clipper had always maintained that the true hero was frightened fit to piss his pants, and that the true coward would concoct an excuse and slip away to the shadows. He thought the man was brave enough for what was asked of him, and he said what might just encourage the bravery he needed from him. 'Close enough, always close enough, and with firearms. You could say it's just a matter of sliding a safety and you're back with us – but then we'd have lost the big game. Don't mind me, but can we hustle?'

Two kids had come into the shop, had pushed past Luke Davies, who stood just inside the door. The woman at the counter, arms folded, had been waiting for their discussion – in a language she hadn't a word of – to be resolved. Lawson didn't do ceremony, pushed his man aside and let the kids through.

'I think – yes, I'm sure – the time is about right for me to know what the "big game" is.'

'Dream on, starshine . . . You don't get big pictures. You have a target, Reuven Weissberg, and you stay up adjacent to him. Consider pilchards in a tin. That near.'

'What do you think I am? Some sort of fucking robot?'

The kids had their sweets, and pushed back out, and again the woman waited on them.

'What did you come here for? What was the excuse used?'

'To buy a tube of mints.'

'Well, buy them, young man.' Lawson turned to Luke Davies. 'Go on, buy a pocketful for him. You're moving on, what's the destination?'

'Don't know, haven't been told,' his man said. 'Look, what we have to do is simple enough, we—'

'Whose confidence do you have, and whose enmity?'

'Reuven believes in me – not Viktor and not Mikhail. But if you were close enough to intervene when my kneecap was on the line, you'd have known that, wouldn't you?'

He saw the flush in the cheeks and the blaze in the eyes of short-fuse temper. 'We were close enough . . .' He had oiled. Didn't believe in splashing it liberally, thought the brusque tone better, like that was a short-cut to a slap on the cheeks. 'Now, are we doing inquests or are we looking forward? Cop on, and get a grip. Should you have a wire on you?'

'A sweep's just been done on the room, and on me.'

'Understood.'

'What we have to do is this. We need a system of meeting, or connecting, having communication every few hours. And I have to know what I'm expected to learn about. It's that simple.'

'No, young man.' Lawson stood his full height – he hadn't the bulk and weight that had made

Clipper Reade formidable – and jabbed his finger repeatedly into the agent's chest, as if it was an emphasis tool. 'What is simple is that *I* make decisions and *I* exercise authority at all times. As I said, your one job – only job – is to be up against Reuven Weissberg. Later, when you've got to where he's taking you, I may – might – consider a wire on you. Not possible today, but an option for the future. Only a beacon wire. Do the job that's given you, and only that job. And – it's exercising me – why is Reuven Weissberg demanding you at his side?'

'He was shot, had a flesh wound. That was in Moscow. When that creep came after Josef Goldmann, and I – well, Goldmann boasts about it. I'm the bloody angel.'

'Is that so? Very fortunate for us . . .' His little moment of wry irony was lost on the man. Time pressed, wasn't there for wasting. 'And you don't know where the end of the road is?'

'Do you not listen? No, I do not. Short term is what I know.'

'I doubt we've all afternoon to converse. What's short term?'

'He's showing me the Old City, don't know why. We're going to leave from there. Him and me are walking, then the hoods pick us up, and I don't know where we go then . . . Are you really close to me?'

'You couldn't get a cigarette paper through the gap, believe me.'

'It's not fucking easy, you know.' The head hung and the voice muttered.

Lawson took the seven tubes of mints that Luke Davies had bought, thrust them into his man's hand. Did the smile, the confident one. 'Nobody said it was.'

'I'm isolated.'

'Just keep cuddled up with Weissberg.'

'If I lose his patronage, I'm dead.'

'But you won't, will you?' He pushed him out. Took his collar, led him to the door, had Davies open it, and did the push, sent him out on to the pavement, saw him half stumble, then regain his balance and walk away. And Lawson saw the bright paper wrapping of the mint tubes in his hand. He counted to ten. 'I'd have liked to give it longer. Can't.'

He went outside, and Davies closed the shop door after them. Their man turned the corner, seemed bowed, and was gone.

'Well, what's your gripe?'

Luke Davies said, 'He's all but done for. He's screwed up. There's not much more left in him.'

Lawson sniffed. Seemed to him that an entire nation had smoked on that street, and he took the air into his lungs of a thousand smoked cigarettes, smoked cigars and smoked pipes and felt better for it. 'He'll do. He'll last.'

'For how long?'

'Long enough, because it's near the end. More to the point, young man, will we last the course?'

'I don't understand.'

'You will. It's us that the pressure's on now, believe me.'

They walked back down the pavement, past Katie Jennings, and went towards where the others waited. In front of the hotel, on the far side of the street, he slowed, sauntered and tossed his head back so that he could admire the height and majesty of a modern hotel. In so doing he took the opportunity to see his man stop beside one of the two cars and stand apart from the hoods. Could he have guaranteed it? Not with confidence. Would his man last the course? No alternative existed. The man stood alone, and his shoulders were hunched, and there seemed about him, to Lawson, despair.

High up and with a crow's view, Reuven Weissberg had his face pressed hard against the window.

He saw Carrick join Mikhail and Viktor, saw also the man who watched the cars, saw Mikhail look down sharply at his watch, then Viktor, and saw the slump in Carrick's back.

He wanted to believe in the man's loyalty. He craved the loyalty that had been the possession of Josef Goldmann. He had himself ordered the killing of men protected by bodyguards, and had made the equation that – in the crisis moment – the bodyguards hesitated and looked first for their own safety, then for the survival of the paymaster. Each time he had ordered the killing of protected men, in Perm, Moscow and Berlin, the bodyguards had lived. The blood on the street had not been theirs. And he could well remember the moment, the few seconds, when he had faced the pistol barrel as he came down the bank's steps, and Mikhail had not thrust forward to stand in the way of the aim. They said, the bodyguards, that they were not 'bullet-catchers'. Could remember the hammer blow in his upper arm, the pain, losing the ability to stand, and then, only then, Mikhail had reacted. The memory was clear. Mikhail had fired, killed, had had the look of pride, satisfaction, triumph, had picked up the spent cartridge cases from his weapon, *then* had gone to the man who paid him, knelt and examined the wound. Josef Goldmann told a different story.

He wanted to believe in Johnny Carrick's loyalty,

but had agreed to one last hurdle being put in the man's path.

Reuven Weissberg checked his room a last time, then the anteroom, closed the outer door after him and went down the corridor to the lift. He craved to be able to place trust in a man's loyalty. He had been to the funerals of many men who had put their safety in the hands of bodyguards; men who had ordered before death three-metre-high grave-stones of malachite or serpentine, dead men on whose corpses vodka would be poured and banknotes scattered to see them comfortable in the 'afterlife', decaying men whose waxen cheeks had been kissed by living rivals. He didn't know of an *avoritet*, alive or dead, who could swear on the loyalty of a bodyguard.

His grandmother had schooled him in suspicion, but he knew her story of the one man in whom she had laid trust, knew it well.

It bloomed. It had no right to be there but it was. In the grimness of that place, in its awfulness, it grew.

How could it have been nurtured there, love? I mean love, not the coupling of dogs when a bitch has her season. I mean tenderness, gentleness, shyness. We thought it was love.

I didn't know how long love could last. My father and mother had loved and would have believed it would endure until death took them in old age; they wouldn't have believed that they would be separated and pushed naked down the Himmelstrasse by men who didn't acknowledge love. Myself, I didn't believe in the possibility of love until chance threw me close to Samuel. For us, love was stolen moments. Moments in the food queues that were kept apart by the Ukrainian guards when our eyes met. It might have been when I worked in the sewing room at a bench beside the window and he was taken out on a work party that went by our hut. He would look at the window, and his face would light. It might be when we stood near to each other in the exercise yard before we were sent to our barracks for the night and we would simply look at each other and have nothing to say. It might have been when we touched hands, his fingers rough and calloused from the forest work and mine bruised black from using needles at the sewing bench.

Once he brought me a flower. He said that it was an orchid and grew wild in the forest. It was small, delicate, with violet petals. He had carried it from the forest inside the front of his tunic. When he gave it me in the evening it was already without life, but I could imagine it when it grew and flourished. I could have killed him if I had kissed his cheek in gratitude for the orchid. Physical contact between prisoners, male and female, was forbidden. Had I kissed him and been seen from the central watchtower or by the Ukrainians at the gate of Camp 1, he might have been shot, and I might have been . . . I took the flower into our barracks hut and laid it between the planks of my bunk and the straw palliasse that was my mattress.

We lived beside death, we walked with death. Our love might survive that day, or next week, we didn't know. It was clear to us that the old role of the camp was ending, and the transports of those destined for extermination were rarer. None of us believed that we would survive the camp's closure. It might have been at any hour of any day of any week that we would be taken from our huts, whipped to the Himmelstrasse, terrified, screaming, stripping, then be running down the last stretch of the path to where the doors were open and waiting for us; at the last we would sing, us women, the anthem and demand of God why He had forsaken us.

364

Because of my love for Samuel, I was not given more strength. Now I had another to care about, which weakened me.

I gave trust. By doing so I lost a little precious strength. I hated to do it, give trust. It was dragged from me.

It was 13 October. I walked one way in the compound and Samuel walked the other. I had seen men slip away from one of the male barracks huts, and among them had been Pechersky, the Russian officer, and Leon Feldhendler . . . and he told me what I should do the next day. He walked north to south and east to west, and I did circuits that were south to north and west to east, and when we passed he told me a little more.

I should try to find thick, warm clothes and wear them the next day, 14 October.

The next day was the first day of Succos, which follows Yom Kippur, the time of Atonement. I was not good in my faith, but in the camp it didn't matter to me.

I should beg or steal the heaviest, strongest boots I could find and wear them the next afternoon.

The holy days of Succos celebrate God's protection of the Jews who had escaped from captivity in Egypt and wandered for forty days in the desert before coming to the land of Israel.

The next day, in the afternoon, I should watch for him. I should try to stay close to him. I should follow where he led. Whatever happened, whatever, I should stay near him.

He broke away. He had done three circuits. I realized the enormity of what he had done, had given me complete trust.

I made one more circuit. I seemed crushed by the weight of the lights above the fence. It had begun to rain. The drops bounced and glistened in the power of the lights, and some of the drips came from the barbs on the wire at the top of the fence. There was a fence I could see, beyond it was a ditch – which I had not seen – and past the ditch a minefield. Beyond the minefield was the forest. He had sensed that I returned his love, and had trusted me as I had him. He did not know for certain that I wouldn't go to a capo, one of those who thought collaboration with the barbarian would extend a lifespan, to a Ukrainian or to one of the SS officers. Some would have.

I was prepared to trust him, him alone.

To wear extra clothing for warmth, and stronger boots, to watch for him and follow him on the first day of the festival of Succos meant an attempt to escape. I wasn't an idiot. Idiots didn't survive at the camp. Was it possible that we – starved and exhausted – could defeat the power of the 'master race'?

I didn't sleep that night. Who would have? I alone in the women's barracks knew, and I alone had the broken, faded beauty of a flattened and lifeless orchid under my palliasse. The next day, in the afternoon, I would learn what was possible and what was not – and would learn where trust took me.

The two cars had gone in convoy. Carrick was with Reuven Weissberg, and the man who had polished the bodywork had driven. They had been dropped by a shallow mound of dead winter grass, and the signs said they were on the junction of Ul. Mila and Ul. Zamenhofa.

The cars pulled away fast, but Carrick had seen the look, keen and hating, of Mikhail, and that of Josef Goldmann, which was expressionless, as if in denial. He couldn't answer the question bouncing in his mind: why had he been taken into the city to walk with Reuven Weissberg?

Not for him to talk. For a full minute Reuven

Weissberg stood by the mound in silence. Carrick searched for the explanation, but it didn't come.

Then Weissberg turned to him. 'You are not a Jew, Johnny?'

'No, sir.'

'Do you have a prejudice against Jews, Johnny?'

'I don't think so, sir. I hope not.'

'Do you know Jews?'

'No, sir. Before being employed by Mr Goldmann, I didn't know any.'

'Do you know what happened to the Jews of this country, in this city, here?'

'We did a bit of it at school, sir. That's all I know.'

'There was a ghetto here for Jews, Johnny.' Reuven Weissberg spoke quietly, almost with reverence, and Carrick thought it was humility. 'Jews from all over Warsaw and the near towns were brought here. Nearly half a million Jews were in the ghetto behind walls. They were taken from here to the death camps, those who were not already dead from starvation and epidemics. In April 1943, the Germans decided to clear the ghetto and send the last survivors to the camps. Weapons had been smuggled in, enough to start a resistance, and more were captured . . . As you are not a Jew, Johnny, you may not be interested, and I will keep the story of this place short. It was called the "ghetto uprising" and it lasted a few days short of a month. Below this place was the last bunker of the resistance – it was known as ZOB, which, loosely, is Jewish Combat Organization – and the leaders committed suicide rather than be taken. The name of the Jewish commander was Mordechai Anieliewicz, but if you are not a Jew you would not have learned of him. Then the ghetto was finished and all the Jews who lived were murdered ... but this is where the bunker was, where they fought.'

'Thank you, sir.'

'Why do you thank me?'

'For teaching me, sir, what I didn't know.'

They walked back up the street. By the edge of a park where the old leaves of the long-gone autumn were still not swept up, there was a monument of big granite blocks. Set into it was a carved grey façade in stone of near-naked bodies, the women stripped to the waist, the men with bared chests, and some held weapons.

'There are many monuments in this city, Johnny, but they do not bring back the dead.'

'No, sir.'

'Would you despise a man, Johnny, who looks to the past – to what was done?'

Carrick said, 'If I was a Jew, sir, and if those things were done to my people, my blood, then I'd not think it right they were forgotten.'

For a moment, Reuven Weissberg let his hand rest on Carrick's sleeve. They crossed the street.

Carrick looked back at the gaunt power of the monument. 'Sir, did they have no help? Didn't the Christian Poles help them?'

'The Christians came. They stood behind the perimeter made by the German Army. They wore their Sunday best clothes and they watched the destruction of the ghetto. They lined the street when it was finished to see the Jews, their country-men, marched away to the trains to go to their deaths. There was no help.'

Carrick couldn't read him. There was no ex-pression in his words, their passion withheld. On the skyline were the spires and domes of churches, and he thought it was there that the Old City would be.

'Where are you going?'

Molenkov spoke: 'We go, retired officers, to a military reunion to be held in Minsk.'

Two of the Customs officials were by the open window. One was bent low to hear Molenkov and the other examined their passports.

'What arm of the military did you serve with?'

'State Security, in the field of national defence. We were both privileged to serve in areas of exceptional importance.' Molenkov had smiled, then tapped his medals, and the official chuckled.

'And may I assume, esteemed Colonel and esteemed Major, that an unpleasant duty at a reunion such as you will attend might be the taking of drink?'

Molenkov turned to his friend Yashkin . . . Behind him, close to the back of the seat was the fucking great lump under the tarpaulin that was worth a life sentence in gaol, and a half-share of a million American dollars, and had in its pit the warmth of a four-kilo perfect sphere of plutonium, Pu-239. He made a face of the utmost gravity. 'Major Yashkin, will there be occasion in Minsk when we are among colleagues for the consumption of alcohol?'

'Never.'

'Never.' He beamed at the official, shed the gravity.

Yashkin chipped in: 'We would *never* consume alcohol before breakfast, never. But, believe me, we take breakfast early.'

Laughter pealed around them. Their passports were handed back. Sweat ran on Molenkov's body. He heard one official mutter to the other, as they were waved forward, 'Old farts, they'll be drunk as rats by each mid-morning. Sad bastards.' Beside him, Yashkin started the Polonez.

A kilometre ahead was the Belarus Customs shed. Over it the flag hung limp in the rain. Beyond was the horizon, cloud and treetops. Molenkov couldn't stop his hands shaking and the sweat was now on his forehead, forming silky drips from his nose. He took out his handkerchief and wiped his face, then his neck. He clutched it in his fist, screwed it up, then laid his other hand on the fist but the trembling continued. They were over a white line that was hard to see because many thousands of tyres each day went over it and the paint was nearly obliterated. They went up a slight hill and tucked into a lane as far from the centre of operations as possible.

'What do you know of this fucking shit-heap, Yashkin?'

'Not much. Two American balloonists in an international race were blown off-course into Belarus airspace. Their balloon was shot down by a gunship helicopter, and they were killed. Also, they had troops weld up the gates of the residences of the American and European Union ambassadors, which made life intolerable for them so they left. They assassinate their journalists, they imprison their opposition politicians. They are in a verbal and diplomatic war with Moscow and Washington. It's a state the ghost of Josef Stalin still stalks. Today there's a personality-cult dictatorship and total economic stagnation. Outside, nobody loves Belarus. Inside, nobody in Belarus cares.'

'Are they right for more of the same?'

'More of the old shit, heroic veterans meeting heroic comrades in Minsk.'

The light for them to go into the check bay

should have been green but was still red. The barrier that should have been raised automatically to permit entry to the bay stayed down until an official heaved it up, then waved them forward.

'You see it, Molenkov? A fucked-up place where nothing works. Do they have radioactive-material detectors? Do pigs fly? Do your stuff.'

An official came forward, greeted them, and Molenkov came awkwardly off his seat and out of the Polonez. His medals jangled as he stretched and straightened, and another official had started a slow walk round the car and was behind the tail, peering through the murk of the rear window. Molenkov handed over the passports. They were studied.

Before he had launched into the matter of the veterans' reunion, alcohol and fraternal friendship between two fine peoples, a question was asked: Did they have anything to declare? Were they carrying any banned items?

Sweat pumped from Molenkov's pores.

She had done the bit about the neat prettiness of the garden, and the taste displayed by the new wallpaper. Had done also the quiet remark on the aptness of Mrs Lavinia Lawson's hairstyle. She was in the kitchen, sitting at the table, had been given tea and had remarked, without an over-fulsome gush, on the mug's nice floral design. She had utilized the tactics laid down by the course instructors at the Service for skewering a way into a house and home.

She must have won something or she wouldn't have been admitted past the front doorstep, but that victory was trifling.

The liaison officer, Alison, said, 'I'm grateful to you for seeing me.'

Christopher Lawson's wife washed up.

'Very grateful. I have to say my visit to you is highly irregular.'

The head with the aptly styled hair was turned to her. The neat, pretty garden was behind her, seen through a picture window, quite a big garden for an Edwardian terrace in the south-west suburbs.

'I'm not authorized by my line manager to be here. Probably he'd blow a gasket if he knew. I'm about to explain why I came, having looked you and your husband up in the computer system, which is at best an *irregular* action. There are three courses open to you, Mrs Lawson. You can ask me to leave, and I will. You can ring Thames House or report my having been here to your husband's office, and I will face dismissal pretty damn fast. Or you can talk to me and I'll listen. It's about a problem I have.'

Plates and bowls, a pan and a solitary wine glass were dried. Cupboards were opened and the items put away, but most often the eyes of Mrs Lavinia Lawson were locked on her.

'I'm not very important. I do the work that's pretty dreggy, and right now it's liaison between our place and your husband's. I had to send him some information on something – you won't want me to be specific – and it was all a bit eccentric as we met in the rain and outside on the Embankment. I needn't have done, but I gave him the name of an undercover police officer who was on a criminal investigation and close up with the principal target. I thought that would help your husband. Mr Lawson said to me that national security was threatened – was at risk big-time – and I felt giving him the name was the right thing to do. Now, back at Thames House, I hear nothing but badmouthing of your husband. I can put that down, perhaps, to the juvenile rivalries that men have. Then I was at a meeting on their ground, Mr Lawson's, and it was the same refrain. Your husband was condemned as selfish, arrogant and a user of men. Mrs Lawson, I put a man into your husband's hands, and I'm doubting now whether I should have. You are not, of course, under any obligation to tell me anything, you can show me the door and dump my career, or you can talk to me.'

She had a carefully fostered urchin's look. Dark hair cut short on her scalp, no cosmetics, no jewellery, not even stud earrings. The appearance that the liaison officer, Alison, cultivated was one of earnest simplicity. It usually did the business for her.

She was asked, 'Do you know what I do?'

Honesty always did the business. 'I looked you up before coming. It's victim support, yes?'

'There's a crime epidemic on our streets.'

'Yes.'

'And money's short for services, resources are slashed and customer numbers are rising.'

'I realize that.'

She was offered more coffee, and accepted. Lawson's wife tossed aside the tea-towel, let it lie on the draining-board, came and sat opposite her, and pushed aside an unopened copy of the day's newspaper.

'Well, my dear, I could throw you out and dump your career, or I can help you with your problem. You were never here, were you?'

'I was never here.'

She listened. Alison was a good listener and could use the innocence of her eyes to nudge a narrative forward.

She was told, 'To keep my desk minimally clear, and to stop the line of my customers stretching round the corner of the street, I leave here, five mornings a week, at seven, and I'm back here at seven in the evening. You were lucky to find me, but I've the start of a cold and got away a little early. At the weekends I do paperwork, expenses and reports. You see, my dear, we don't actually live together. Under the same roof, in the same bed, meals at the same table, but I'm too damn tired to talk. He does his own breakfast, I do the supper and the crossword, and he's at the word teasers, and we read our books in bed – maybe ten minutes – and we're asleep. We go for the same train in the morning, so we're walking beside each other and usually hurrying, and he's never home before me. Are you getting an idea of our life? We're adjacent to each other, certainly no closer.

'Our son might have bound us once. Not any more. He's in Vietnam, does aid work in the Highlands there, tries to help communities around Pleiku start up cottage industries that can be marketed in Europe. He hasn't been home in two years and when he was last here he hadn't anything to say to his father. Put bluntly, I don't either. We don't share hobbies because I haven't time for them. We used to do holidays, but not any longer – there isn't a common area. Now I go on those all-inclusive trips where you get painting or sketching instruction in France or Italy. He, for his annual leave, which they force him to take, goes to the West Country and scours the villages for churches, fourteenth or fifteenth century, and the bed and breakfast he's staying at will find him someone who'd like their dog walked in the lanes and along the bridleways. He lives for his work.

'He's a driven man. Nothing else matters to him. I think, but he doesn't confide now and never has, that he came from one of those army families where showing affection was forbidden, then boarding-school and university. Quite a good degree from Oxford, where we met, and he was recruited on the old-boy recommendation, which was the routine. I don't think he ever believed that a job which might be completed that day, or evening, should be left for tomorrow. Went against his nature. Exacting standards were set, still are, and those who fail such examinations are rated failures and set aside. And one day, of course, it will end. There'll be a leaving party, and I'm damn sure I won't be there, and he'll be home. This place will go on the market and we'll buy something small and easy in Kingswear or across the river in Dartmouth, and I suppose we'll rattle around, and maybe we'll find each other.

'We used to be a pretty normal couple, with the baby. He was posted to Berlin, three years, and married accompanied. We were out at the Olympic stadium. I did a dinner party every week and had a circuit of some of the most devastatingly boring men and their wives to entertain. Then one Saturday night he invited an American. I bitched about it when he told me whom he'd asked because it was going to get the numbers wrong and I had to scrape up a secretary from the field station to match the table up. He had a ridiculous name, Clipper A. Reade Junior. He lit his first cigar when I served salmon and salad – I promise you, my dear, it was a meal I haven't forgotten – and smoked it right through the next course, beef, and kept it going when I gave the guests fruit salad and meringue, stubbed it out and spread ash across my tablecloth, then lit another when I did the cheeseboard. He talked the whole time, barely ate, didn't drink the wine and I had to dive into the kitchen repeatedly for little pots of tea for him. At first, at that meal, as the American hogged the conversation, others tried to ignore him and talk among themselves, but he steamrollered them. By the end of the meal, they were hanging on what he had to say on the craft-work of agent-running. He did anecdotes so well: near misses with the Stasi, the KGB and the others, triumphs that were fascinating and not boastful, techniques and tactics of brush contacts and dead-letter drops. But the silence when you could have heard that lousy cliché fulfilled, *could have heard a pin drop*, was about the loss of an agent – shot and drowned – in the Spree river, by the Ober-baumbrücke. Nobody spoke as that story was told. No emotion to it, and no passion, could have been the description of the death of a pet rabbit, and it sort of killed the evening. I remember, all our other guests left pretty early. Christopher never admitted it, but good old female intuition did the job. My husband was present when the agent was lost, but he gave no sign of it and let the story unfold. I hazard it for you, my dear, but Christopher was under the spell of that American, was – by then – a changed man with his personality altered and soft in that man's hands. Needless to say, Clipper Reade was never invited to dinner with us again.

'Where is my husband now? His life is his work. I don't know. Wherever. Why is he there? I'm not included. He'll come back, wash his own clothes and probably iron them, and he'll tell me nothing. He's not a crusader, doesn't wear patriotism or ideology on his sleeve, but I don't believe it's acceptable to him to fail. Those stupid little word puzzles, the teasers in the paper, if he can't do them he's coldly furious but he doesn't come to me for help. To fail is not on his agenda, and it was certainly not on the agenda of Clipper Reade – I curse him – and he doesn't believe anyone else should contemplate failure. For that he lost the love of his son, and stretched me near to snapping-point. He wouldn't recognize the cost of the agenda.

'Heavens, the time. I've kept you. I've not talked about Christopher like that to anybody before. Should you have given that name, put that police-man into my husband's clutches? I can't say. Have I been of any use to you? I can't see how I have been. I don't know where he is, or what danger he faces. My dear, he won't back off, or allow those with him to back off. Do you recognize what I've said of Christopher? Did you like him?'

The liaison officer, Alison, stood. 'You've been very helpful, and I apologize for the intrusion. No, I'm not with the big battalions – I liked him very much. Whatever is happening is close, I think, and for all involved these are desperate times. I'm grateful to you.'

The Crow, that afternoon, had taken the bus from the airport into the city.

At the terminus he had been met. The contact had been good. He had been barely aware of the man coming up fast behind him but he had felt the slip of paper wedged into his palm and snapped his fist shut on it. He could not recall the man's face.

He stood on a pavement in a narrow street of shops, apartments and a hotel. The wealth with which he was familiar in the Gulf was not here. Drab grey concrete walls pierced by drab windows of sparse goods for sale seemed to close around him. The paper had been the section of a map that covered this street. There was a drab light over the desk inside the hotel lobby. He gave a name, false, filled in his passport details, false, in the register, and paid cash for one night in advance. He was handed a room key, then a sealed envelope with the number of the room written on it in pencil. The Crow tore open a corner of the envelope, enough for him to see that it held the onward flight ticket he would use the following day.

Did he want anything? An explanation: did he want a woman for the evening? The Crow shook his head, smiled at the drab face behind the reception desk of a back-street Belgrade hotel. He didn't want a woman, not then and not ever.

On the platform at Wolverhampton, Sak waited for the train to Birmingham New Street. For the schedule he must keep, he could have gone an hour later, even two. The atmosphere in his home had suffocated him, and each time he'd emerged from his room there had been more questions. When would he be back? Was he certain there was no contact number should they need to reach him in an emergency? Had he enough money – cash and cards? So he had gone early.

At New Street station, it had been decided for him that he should change, then take a later train directly to London. He would cross London and reach the Eurostar terminus. He would travel by night, would be at his destination by dawn.

He felt excitement and believed himself valued.

He had been shown monuments and plaques.

Carrick had stood in front of a montage of

double-life-size figures, sculpted in bronze, who wore uniforms and army helmets, carried rifles, machine-guns and hand grenades and seemed to run from one point of cover to the next. Reuven Weissberg had told him it was the commemoration tableau for the rising by the Catholic Christian Poles against the Germans, and it had happened a year after the fall of that bunker, and that it was done by men who had not lifted a weapon to help the Jews. He had seen, against an old wall of red brick, a statue of a child who carried an automatic weapon and whose helmet dwarfed a little head. A wreath of flowers was tucked under the statue's arm, and Reuven Weissberg had said that the Catholic Christian Poles helped themselves but had not supported the Jews. Plaques had been pointed to and Carrick had not the language but realized they marked the streets where captured men had been shot by firing squad, and where units had made their command posts, but it had been a year after the Jews in the bunker had killed themselves rather than surrender. His feet had been on old manhole covers and below had been the sewers through which the uprising had been resupplied and, at the end, a few had escaped. He must not show feelings – he was a bodyguard, a cipher, a servant – but the relentless criticism of those who had died fighting for themselves, and had not risen in defence of the city's Jews, disturbed him. The bitterness confused him. Here, there was defeat, and the bitterness could flourish. Images seemed to bounce towards him that he had not known before – the scale of a slaughter beyond his comprehension.

'You want to know how many died in the uprising, Johnny? They say twenty thousand of the

379

Christian Poles who were fighters died – and two hundred and twenty-five thousand of the Christian Poles who were not fighters died . . . but more Jews died, Johnny.'

The light was failing as Reuven Weissberg led Carrick across a wide square, past shops that were closing for the evening. He heard the scrape of steel shutters falling. There were horses between the shafts of the open carriages, but the tourists and visitors had gone, the rain dripped and they were idle. Ahead of them was the Old City, and he followed Reuven Weissberg, and did not know the purpose of it.

Chapter 14: 14 April 2008

Now Carrick understood. He knew what was done, and why.

Reuven Weissberg had brought him to the main square of the Stare Miasto. They had passed the Royal Castle and the cathedral and had cut down a street where shop staff were removing trays of amber jewellery from the windows. The square was long, broad, and in front of them was a black statue, in bronze, of a rampant woman, naked, protected by a circular shield and holding up a short-bladed battle sword, and all around him were the old town houses, four storeys high, and faced in plaster that was painted in ochre shades, pink and dull yellows. It didn't matter what colour the buildings were because now he understood.

It was an exercise in counter-surveillance, and he remembered a long-ago pub evening off the long main drag in Colchester. Carrick and other recruits to Bravo Company, 2nd Battalion, had listened in hanging silence to a veteran sergeant whose star turn was to tell the stories of the Province postings he had survived, and had a Distinguished Conduct Medal to prove his knowledge of what he talked about. He thought of himself, part of an exercise in counter-surveillance and not able to influence its outcome, as bait. The sergeant had been big on bait. He, Carrick, was bait and it was difficult for bait to survive.

They crossed the square. Waiters were lowering the big parasols over the outside tables and chairs of the restaurants, and dusk was falling. He had no option but to follow Reuven Weissberg – freedom to help himself did not exist.

Carrick imagined that out of his sight and hearing, there had been one last dispute between Reuven Weissberg and the hoods – it would not have involved Josef Goldmann. Of course he would be followed. He did not know how many of them trailed him. They had been at the Glienicker bridge, and on the street at night in the rain, and had led Lawson to the kiosk round the corner from the hotel. They would be tracking him.

What did his life depend on? On how damn good they were.

They stopped in front of windows and Reuven Weissberg professed to study the last trays of amber items, watches, pendants, necklaces and bracelets, and in front of restaurants where the menu boards were going inside, and by a church door through which a few of the faithful – men, women and children – scurried to catch a late Mass.

Were they good, were they expert, those who followed him? Were they the best, or just those who had been available and dragged out of the duty pool? They were on a wide terrace and the rain had slackened, but the wind still blew in thumping gusts against the brick walls topped by the walkway platform. In the half-light, a young man flew a kite. Reuven Weissberg paused and

382

studied him, then looked for the kite, high in the growing dark of the clouds, and he found it. Carrick's sleeve was tugged and it was pointed out to him. He had to strain his eyes to see it. The kite was a scarlet speck, and the young man gave it more line. Carrick estimated, loose and without a vestige of proof, that the line might have stretched a quarter of a mile or more. The kite speck was over the river . . . the goddam river.

He assumed that, at the end of the game, Reuven Weissberg would lead him towards the river – where better? – and by then the darkness would have gathered tighter on them. Mikhail and Viktor would sidle from the shadows and whisper in the big player's ear. Carrick would not know what they said. Would not know whether he had won or lost. He could see, from the elevation of the platform on the old walls, big branches going down the river and the swans, small and bright in the closing dusk, kept to the gentler eddies in bays at the far bank. Shadows lengthened on the near grassed areas, their side of the Vistula river. Maybe he would be in a cone of shadow, and unable to sprint, run, get up on to his damn toes and flee because he wouldn't know what was said.

Who could save him?

Carrick bit his lip. He had lost sight of the scarlet speck. Again, he followed. Would Reuven Weissberg save him? If the tail was seen, showed out, if the whisper in the ear was of a tail confirmed, would Reuven Weissberg help him? No damn chance. He could look into Weissberg's face, study the eyes and their depth, the expression at the mouth, and learn nothing.

Had to believe in Reuven Weissberg. They had turned away from the kite-flier and the view of the river, and walked back into the Stare Miasto and were among narrow alleyways. In front of them was a low arch. Without warning, Reuven Weissberg stopped and Carrick cannoned into him. He wondered if Weissberg sought to remember which way he should go, right or left or under the arch, which route should he be led on.

It was rare for Carrick to speak without reason but he was badly stressed. He said, and tried hard to lose the quaver, 'It's very beautiful, sir. It's a fascinating piece of history.'

Reuven Weissberg, almost startled, looked at Carrick, took a fold of Carrick's cheek in his fingers and squeezed the flesh. 'It is not old, not from history. It is a fraud. All of it was destroyed in the war, every building that was here, the year after the ghetto uprising. It was rebuilt, stone for stone and brick for brick. It is a sham. Nothing is as it seems.'

For Adrian and Dennis, there had been confusion. It had not lasted.

Dennis was ahead, and Adrian trailed his colleague. From Adrian's view there was a shallow arch across the road. The earpiece he wore had been moulded for him and fitted exactly. The days of cables trailing under his collar were long gone. The earpiece had the double function of receiver and transmitter, but he – and Dennis – preferred the wrist microphone attached to the cuff of the anorak and the discipline of raising the hand across the mouth to mask the movement of the lips when talking. He wasn't a bloody ventriloquist and needed to move his lips when speaking for clarity. They were encrypted.

'To A One. Are you reckoning this is a choke-point? D One, out.'

The answer came back into his ear, soft and murmured: 'To D One. I'm reckoning it's a choke-point. Can't see any other reason for this bloody caper. You got one? A One, out.'

'To A One. You still have an eyeball? D One, out.'

'To D One. Target Two going under the arch with November – yes, still have an eyeball. A One, out.'

Adrian lit a cigarette, which brought his hands over his mouth, and a tourist couple, might have been Germans, smiled warmly at him. A cigarette was the best reason to have a hand in front of the mouth when he transmitted.

'To A One. Assuming it's a choke-point routine, don't have another answer. Think you should leap-frog? D One, out.'

'To D One. Going for a leap-frog. Yes, I'll buy it as a choke-point. A One out.'

He didn't throw away his cigarette. Adrian hated them, had a printed sticker on the front door at home that said, 'No Smoking', but he kept it in his hand. To have thrown it down on to the clean-swept cobbles would have attracted attention, the great sin of his trade. He had ground to cover, to catch up on, and that made a difficulty in itself. Nobody noticed a man who sauntered and had time. Everybody remembered a man who hurried. He was able to dump the cigarette in a litter bin and felt better for getting shot of the damn thing. He went after the target and into what was reckoned a choke-point.

In Adrian's world of surveillance there were three stages that were common practice. They had seen the men get into the two cars, with attention focused on the target's, and that was the 'lift'. A journey had started. When it reached its end, that had the name 'housing'. Mid-journey, between start and end, was known to him, and the guys and girls he worked with, as the 'control'. But was not, quite, *control*. Was not 'control' because, right now, Adrian was going – fast – up to do a leap-frog, and pass Dennis to take over the eyeball of the target. In doing so he would have to funnel himself through a choke-point. 'Choke-point' was when a target led the way through a narrow entrance, or across a bridge, or into a subway, and the surveillance had to follow or lose out on the eyeball, and the entrance, bridge or subway was under close observation. Not likely that he or Adrian would show out at the first choke-point, but there would be a second and third.

But they had to follow where they were led. Couldn't pack it in, just call it quits, because then the target was lost.

He was coming up close behind Dennis and passed him in the shadow of the arch. Fag in the mouth, hand up with the lighter, he strode past Dennis, saw his colleague's little gesture, so slight, of a hand over the hip pocket and one extended finger pointing right. He did as he was directed, swung to the right, and the alleyway was darker. He didn't look left. If this was a choke-point it was most likely where the guys were, the Russians. Had become passably familiar with the Russians these last few days, since the bridge and the Wannsee lakes in Berlin, but he didn't look for them . . . He kept on going and then he saw the shoulders of the target and November.

He lit his cigarette again. It had been burning well enough, but he needed his fist up again and over his lips. Adrian said, 'To D One. OK, I have the eyeball. It's not right to have a chit-chat, but we've a problem. A One, out.'

'To A One. Only *one* problem? Spill it. D One, out.'

'To D One. Bloody funny, yeah, yeah. Problem is, we're doing caravan and trailer, and we should be doing the box. A One, out.'

'To A One. Hear you. Leave it with me. D One, out.'

Saw a bin, and dumped his cigarette. Caravans and trailers were towed along. 'Caravans and trailers' was the old way of doing foot surveillance when resources were short and the perceived wisdom was to follow a joker along the street, keep back, have a newspaper ready and a packet of fags, let the joker lead. That technique of surveillance was now considered flawed because of what he had just been obliged to do, shift himself and hurry to do the leap-frog past Dennis. How many times, he liked to demand of recruits, was a guy ever seen running down a street or up a pavement? Wasn't that guy always remembered if he was seen? New thinking, modern practice – which he and Dennis taught on the courses – was to use the box for-mation, and that slotted, in the exercises they laid on for the rookies, for the 'control' stage. When the box was formed there was no need for an eyeball; the target walked on a street and the box was far ahead and far behind him, in the next street to the right and the next to the left. The box was brilliant, but Adrian didn't have it.

He swore.

It had to be a second choke-point.

The target had stopped at the top of a steep flight of steps. Adrian had that good peripheral vision, was using it, and didn't see a way right or left. The steps dropped a level, went down to a little closed-in park. What he saw, what he noticed most, were the fine street-lamps – could have been the Warsaw equivalent of Victoriana, like they had in Holmes films for Baker Street – and they must just have been switched on as the gloom grew. Decision time.

In his lectures to rookies, Adrian liked to speak of the 'heat stakes'. It was one of his favourite patter lines, and always drew grim smiles from his class. The heat stakes went from one to ten, and ten was when the surveillance officer was busted, like he went to gaol. They were going down the steps, the target guy and November. Put crudely, simply, Adrian and Dennis were expensive pieces of kit. It was not a lightly taken decision to deploy them. They hit the street, as increments of VBX, when matters were serious, and nothing that Adrian had worked on before had seemed more serious than the briefing on a 'dirty bomb'. He would tell the rookies, the recruits, with an old man's confidence and experience, 'If the next stage is to show out, we pull out.' Easy enough said at a training session. He knew the consequences, potential, of losing his target, and it sort of hammered in his mind like a bad nightmare that he would have to call in on the encrypted net and report. Would have to live with it. He went back to some old basic ones – bent and untied his shoelace, then knotted it again, and they were at the bottom of the steps. He saw them veer left at the bottom, under the furthest light. He turned his back to the steps, lit another cigarette.

'To D One. I'm sure it's a choke-point. Don't feel I can follow. Leg it, pick them up – good luck. That's two of them, but there'll be a third. A One, out.'

'To A One. Getting there. D One, out.'

Then there was the crackle in Adrian's ear, and silence. He walked back up the alley and looked into the darkened window of a little gallery, old prints in faded frames, counted to fifty and it seemed an age, then drifted back to the head of the steps. He went down slowly. He thought, and it came to him like the blow of a pickaxe handle, that he had never before handled a matter of this importance. Couldn't remember, not on anything he'd experienced, feeling frightened at the enormity of it.

He let it wait, knew his colleague would be suffering, until he had the eyeball. They came towards him.

It was 'dry-cleaning' in reverse. Dennis had done that often enough. Dry-cleaning was when they did choke-points to ascertain whether an agent had a tail. The agent used a prearranged route and specific locations were watched, but the tables had been turned. He hadn't seen the Russians. Knew them well enough from the last several days, and would have recognized them if they'd been obvious. Because he hadn't seen them it didn't mean to Dennis that they didn't employ choke-points. He was a man with few delusions.

It would have been a delusion to believe that former KGB-trained officers were in any degree inferior to himself in the trade of surveillance. He thought he'd done well to pick them up, Reuven Weissberg and the agent, but he was not a man to let complacency intrude on his concentration. He could sense the strain on the agent, and the stress that had built in him. There was no talk between them. The level-three *mafiya* man was a half-pace ahead of the agent, November, and seemed to have no conversation, just drifted along the street and didn't look into the closed shops and restaurant fronts where the last of the day's customers were drifting away. To safeguard the agent, best thing would have been to back off, but backing off lost the trail and the trail led – Mr Lawson had said – to a dirty bomb. He had the agent's survival in his hand, could only protect him with professionalism. Bloody hell – and a hell of a number of people's survival.

He had a handkerchief up to his nose, blew, and spoke. 'To Control. I need the girl, whatever we're calling her, sorry and that. I need her. Have to have her. Me and him, it isn't enough. D One, out.'

In his ear, 'To D One. Will happen. She is C for Charlie, C One. Where to? Control, out.'

They went past him. He was doing a window bit, using reflections. It was why Dennis – and his colleague, Adrian – liked to work with Lawson, the guv'nor. Old ways used, tried and tested ways. He stayed very still, kept all his muscles tight, locked his gaze on the window. First the *mafiya* target, then the agent. Would have liked, no messing, to spin, reach out a hand, grip the poor sod's arm and whisper a sweet-nothing of comfort in his ear . . . and they were gone. The reflection gave him the route they took at the end of that street. He had his handkerchief up.

'To Control. Get C One to the old wall, the Barbakan end. It's where they're headed. Just hammer at her that it's about choke-points. D One, out.'

'To D One. Will do.' The pause lingered. 'Up and running, C One is getting there. Control, out.'

He couldn't say whether that narrow street was the third choke-point, or whether it would be up by the walls and the barbican gate. He glanced, as any visitor would have, at his little street map. Yes,

Dennis respected men trained to KGB standards. Had done a trip to Moscow two years before. The rage now was for the use of the electronic dead-letter box, the EDLB in jargon-speak. It was thought of as a star performer. An EDLB was built into a 'rock' of shaped reinforced plastic and left in a park, with leaves and earth, even dog turds, to half cover it, and the idea was for the turned guy, the man recruited by VBX, to drive up and park within twenty metres of it, and squirt from his little handheld piece of gear. Maybe he did that every Wednesday. Maybe the embassy man, from VBX, drove by every Friday, and used his laptop, hidden on his knee, to suck in what was transmitted to the 'rock'.

Dennis had been sent two years back to do the old-fashioned clearance check and give the all-clear that the 'rock' wasn't compromised. It had taken him two weeks to come up with an answer, two weeks of frozen bollocks on a Wednesday and a Friday – and not a decent meal on any evening or wine to wash it down on the expenses VBX would meet – and four random tails on the agent going to work in the ministry and coming away. His answer was clear, given in person to the station chief at the embassy. What had he seen? Three times he had seen a man in a car use the same lighter, one of those metal Zippo jobs, and twice he had seen a woman who was once blonde and the next time a brunette but she'd had on the same damn boots with the little metal buckle for decoration.

He told what he had seen to the station chief, and was listened to, and gave his opinion that the FSB, successor to the KGB, had the bodies identified and the 'rock' under surveillance, and he'd known that he was only the bloody messenger who brought unwelcome news: all he could offer, of course, was his opinion, and he'd flown home. About a month later, could have been five weeks, it was in his paper stretched out over the breakfast table. A Russian was in custody, faced a charge of treason, and the station chief's deputy and one of the staffer kids was identified and accused of espionage while under diplomatic cover. Mr Lawson, the guv'nor, would have believed him.

Yes, Dennis had a high regard for the quality of KGB-trained operatives. Hadn't seen them, which didn't mean they weren't there on the ground.

He walked slowly. The guv'nor would have believed him, but might have said the stakes were too high to call off the operation. Never could tell with the guv'nor, but at least Dennis would have been believed.

Dennis went the far way round the alleys and across the square, then doubled back and tried to estimate where the *mafiya* man and the agent would be, and whether a minimal part of a box was in place, but held out few hopes for it. A box – if it was in London, run by Thames House and the target was a bloody jihadist – would have involved two cars and a motorcycle, a dozen on the ground sealing the target inside the box. His pace quickened, didn't want to go faster but couldn't help himself, and his stride lengthened. It was his hatred of a situation when he didn't have an eyeball and neither did Adrian.

He passed a wedding party, in their best gear, men in suits and the girls in smart frocks. They had taken over a little square and there was a raised flowerbed in which the ground was covered with wood chips, the pruned rosebushes were not yet in bud, but the party had brought bouquets and laid them on the chips. With the flowers were brightly wrapped packages. New lives starting, hope and optimism, bloody good news.

The squawk came into his ear. 'To Control. I have an eyeball, on the wall, west from the barbican. C One, out.'

He gasped. Felt his knees weaken, turn to jelly. He thought it a good voice in his ear, authoritative and without bullshit. Should have been enjoying it – adrenaline and the chase, that crap – and was not. Just felt raw relief that they had, again, an eyeball. But couldn't say for how long the game would be played out.

The dog alerted him. It came from its place by the lit stove and bounded to the closed door. It lifted its head, hackles erect, and its bark deafened him. Then its paws, claws out, raked the door. The barking died and was replaced by a soft, menacing growl that came from deep in its throat.

He listened.

When he heard the car, which the dog had heard a half-minute before, Tadeuz Komiski started up from his chair. He had not eaten that day, or the one before. He swayed on his feet and had to lean on the table to steady himself. The dusk had come early that evening, brought on by the raincloud over the forest, and he had no light on in his home. Nor had he drunk any coffee or tea, only water. A car approached. He sensed it made slow progress and was driven carefully because the ruts in the track were deep and rain-filled. It would have tried to find a route at the track's sides.

Lights hit the window beside the bolted and locked door, and the dog renewed its frantic barking.

He groped forward, keeping to the shadows beyond the throw of the car's headlights, and reached the window. The car edged forward, swerving. The lights dipped and bucked. He made his way back across the room to the table and lifted his broken shotgun. He checked and, from the lights spearing inside, could see that both barrels were loaded. He snapped the gun shut. He held it loosely and went forward to take his position against the wall beside the window.

The car braked. The lights were steady, then switched off. Darkness plunged around him.

A door groaned open, then slammed, and he heard the squelch of a footfall on the sodden ground as someone came to the door of his home. His finger was on the guard of the trigger. The dog had gone quiet but he could feel its bulk against his leg and hear the wheeze of its breathing. He sensed it was coiled, ready to spring, if the door should be forced. He had known that one night, under cover of darkness, they would come. The curse afflicting him had demanded they would come because of what he had done.

The door was rapped. Not hard, not with aggression. He felt a lessening of the fear that had been with him since a man had seemed to search for a grave, then sat against a tree and watched his home. The knock was repeated. He stayed quiet, and the dog hissed in defiance but did not bark.

Then the voice he knew: 'Tadeuz . . . Are you there, Tadeuz?'

He didn't answer but lowered the gun's barrels until they pointed at the floor.

He thought the voice sounded nervous. 'Tadeuz . . . I think you're inside. It's me, Tadeuz, Father Jerzy. Please, Tadeuz, answer if you're there.'

394

Outside, beyond the door, the priest would have heard the dog growl. He went to the table, broke the shotgun and placed it, angled and ugly, on the old newspapers there.

'I think you're there, Tadeuz. Let me in.'

Tadeuz Komiski unbolted and unlocked the door, then murmured into the ear of his dog, which slunk, belly low, to the place beside the stove. He opened the door. He saw only the silhouetted outline of the priest's shoulders and head. A match was struck, held up by the priest, and in his other hand a plastic bag hung heavily with the weight of its contents.

'Are you not well, Tadeuz? Why no light? Are you ill?'

He scurried back. He put a paper strip into the stove, and moved it sharply until it found embers and caught, then used it to light the oil lamp. Now he saw the priest look around and grimace in horror, shock, disgust. His nose twitched and his lip curled.

'This is no way to live, Tadeuz, with this smell, in the dark. It's wrong to live like this, and not necessary.'

Father Jerzy peered at the sink. In it were the dishes that Tadeuz had not washed, and he had not eaten for the whole of that day or the previous one.

'Do you have any food in your house, Tadeuz?'

He shook his head, and felt that the lamplight caught his shame.

'Can you make coffee, Tadeuz?'

He gestured with his hands, helpless, that he had none.

The priest wiped the seat of a chair and sat on it. He reached across the table, pushed the shotgun carefully aside, so that its barrel was aimed at the window, then laid the plastic bag by the stock. He had a cheerful face, weathered, and his cheeks shone with scrubbed cleanliness. He took a small paper bag from his coat pocket and lifted out two biscuits, then held out his hand flat with the biscuits on the palm. The dog came to him and wolfed them, then laid its head on his lap.

'You didn't come, Tadeuz. You didn't bring us the wood you usually bring. To be frank, we have little wood at the church house, and next Sunday we'll have used the last in the boiler. There's an old saying, Tadeuz: "If the mountain will not come to Mahomet, Mahomet must go to the mountain." I say that in jest because you're not a mountain and I'm most certainly not Mahomet. I thought you were not well, that you hadn't the strength to cut, haul and split wood, so I came to find out.'

He didn't know what to say, so he said nothing, but hung his head. The priest's hand fondled the dog's neck.

'I had Magda ask in the shop. I didn't think you would have gone there and not brought us the wood. Magda confirmed that you hadn't been in. That's why I believed you were ill, and that you'd have no food. Magda did this for you.'

The plastic bag was opened. A pie was shown to him, and gravy had run down its tinfoil tray. To show his gratitude, Tadeuz Komiski dropped his head.

'But you're not ill, not in body . . . Tadeuz, I expected to find you had suffered an injury or an accident, or had pneumonia. I look at you, the darkness you keep and the weapon close to you, and what confronts me is a great sadness about you. Tadeuz, I'm a priest and you have no obligation to answer me, but have you done wrong? Why are you hiding from the world?'

He gazed with longing at the pie made for him by Magda, housekeeper to Father Jerzy, and saw the strong hands gentle at the dog's neck. Another biscuit was placed in the slobbering mouth.

'Have you committed some crime? Hurt somebody or taken something from someone? Confession cleanses. Is there something you wish to tell me?'

He felt his chin slacken, and his lips were dry. His tongue whipped over them, and an owl called from the trees beyond the door. He did not answer.

'I made enquiries before setting out to come here, and I requested the same of Magda. People in the village, Tadeuz, think you're *strange*. They believe you to be *different*, but none has told me or Magda that you'd do anything deceitful or violent, yet the gun is readied and you're frightened. I ask myself: why does an old man who lives in the house where he was born need to arm himself and be protected by a dog? Tadeuz, I'm young, only seven years out of the seminary at Krakow, and I know little of men's minds. What I do know is that confession purges guilt. You show the signs of guilt.'

Tadeuz felt tears well in his eyes and put his hand across his face.

The priest said quietly, 'I ask, why does an individual who is not a criminal fear guilt? I believe, Tadeuz, that you were born in this house – the house where you now cower with a dog and a lethal weapon for company – in 1937. I think of you as a man who has done no criminal wrong, but you were a child and you were here. As a child your home was among these trees, in this forest, close to *that* place. In my last year as a student at the seminary, a rabbi came to visit us from Germany. It was a very special visit and we listened to him with close attention. He spoke of the Holocaust, and the next day he was to visit Auschwitz-Birkenau, an hour by train from Krakow. He said, and I have never forgotten it, that survivors had told him, "For Jews, the Germans were evil but the Christian Poles were worse." Was it when you were a child? You don't have to answer me – but the only palliative for guilt is confession. All I can say, Tadeuz, is that if ever the chance is given you – it is unlikely – to right a wrong, then seize it. Please, and soon, bring me more wood. They were difficult days.'

The priest, Father Jerzy, left.

The two of them, Tadeuz Komiski and his dog, ate the meat pie, shared it in equal parts. It rang in his ears, *to right a wrong*. He took the last crumbs of the pie and picked off the table what had fallen, then let the dog lick the tinfoil plate clean.

He was jolted, alert and aware. Carrick gaped but Reuven Weissberg had not seen them.

They walked on the wall's platform and below them, to their right, was the moat that had, in history, surrounded the Stare Miasto. To their left, below the platform, was a street of impatient pedestrians, surging to be gone now that their shops, cafés and workplaces had closed for the evening. The couple were like a stone on a beach and the incoming tide flowed round them. It was as if they were lovers. His arms round her shoulders, and hers round his waist. He couldn't see the face of the young man, buried in her hair, but she looked up as if in exaltation of the moment, and saw Carrick, as he saw her, Katie.

And he was gone, moving on, the moment lost.

It was like a wound, his girl from the bed in the

narrowboat in the arms of another man. He trailed after Reuven Weissberg, and felt the sting of imagined betrayal.

'To Control. Have an eyeball. On the wall, going west. C One, out.'

Katie Jennings broke clear of Luke Davies, but he took her hand as they started to walk. She realized that was the right thing to do, because she didn't know how closely they were observed. She'd done it before, hugged a man, held him, and felt nothing for him. It was a part of a surveillance routine, and she knew it from the days when she had been the token girl in SCD10. He held her hand tightly and she allowed him to entwine his fingers in hers.

A cigarette was lit, a hand masked a face.

'To C One. That was good, thank you for doing guiding. Suggest you return to Control and leave D One and me for the rest. Well done. A One, out.'

Smoke filtered in the evening air from a cigarette.

It defeated Yashkin. He could see no reason why his friend should sweat.

He did not have the heater on in the Polonez, but he reached across Molenkov and wound down the passenger window.

It was not just sweat, there was pain in his face, and apprehension.

The one-time security officer would have been the first to admit that the one-time political officer had turned in a bravura performance at the Customs point. Yes, there had been sweat then on Molenkov's face and hands, but insufficient to be noticed – not like the wetness that dripped from him now. It had been an exercise in command, authority and control: out of the car, ignoring the question of whether there were items for declaration, steering the official to the front bumper and away from the tail door behind which *it* was hidden under the tarpaulin. Molenkov had assumed the role of interrogator. Did the officer believe the tyres of the Polonez, front near side and front open side, would get them to Minsk? They would, but new tyres were needed. Did the officer have the knowledge to check the oil in the engine? The bonnet had been lifted, it had been done, and Yashkin had marvelled at the skill shown, and the oil amount was satisfactory.

The questions had kept coming: take the M20 or the M1 for Minsk, or take the Bobrujsk route? Did the officer have relatives who had served in the armed forces? Was the forecast for rain and . . . ?

Yashkin had sat in the car and heard the rattle of the medals on Molenkov's chest, the murmur of their voices, and had seen the passports returned, the shaking of hands, heard the expression of thanks for courtesy and the wishes for a safe journey. Molenkov and the officer had parted as bosom friends, and then they had driven away. They had stopped at the first café kiosk beyond, and out of sight, of the Customs point, and used the toilets that were spotlessly clean, and would not have been so in Sarov, to change back into their civilian clothes. The medals had gone into the bags, and they had bought a fresh loaf of bread, cheese, a small jar of pickle and they had eaten. He had thought it the reaction to the tension of the Customs point that had caused Molenkov to gobble his food and stuff hunks of the cheese, anointed with pickle, into his mouth.

His friend's hands came up and seemed to grasp

his chest. The sweating was more acute. Molenkov groaned. Yashkin drove on.

The groan was a sigh, almost a sob, and the mouth contorted. The fingers held tighter to his shirt. A croak. 'Yashkin . . .'

'Yes?'

'I'm ill, seriously.'

'Are you?'

'I have a heart attack.'

'Have you?'

'Should you stop?'

'Why?'

'No, go on to Gomel. It's agony . . . There'll be a hospital in Gomel.'

'Perhaps, perhaps not.'

'Yashkin, my chest. The pain . . . will kill me.'

He drove on, neither faster nor slower, and was looking for the turning to Dobrus where he would leave the M13.

'For fuck's sake, Yashkin . . . it's a heart attack. In a few minutes I'll be dead – do something, please, my friend, anything, something . . .'

Yashkin pulled on to the hard shoulder. He said briskly, 'Get out.'

Molenkov staggered out of the car. Yashkin didn't follow him. Molenkov was doubled up and tottering.

Yashkin leaned across the passenger seat, spoke through the open door. 'First, Molenkov, unfasten your belt. Go on, do it . . . That's better, good. Now undo the top buttons of your trousers. That's right. No one who drives past will care if they see you with your trousers at your knees. You should use both hands to massage your stomach hard – get on with it. Now fart. Get the gas out. Breathe deep. Take it down. Do you still have a heart attack, Molenkov?'

401

He heard the escape of the wind, and smelled it – like poison gas out of a sewer. The colour was seeping back into his friend's face. Yashkin said, 'You'd eaten too much too fast. Then you sat. Your belt was too tight and constricted the passage of the food. The pain was from the build of acid inside your oesophagus. Can we move on now?'

Shamefaced, Molenkov sat in the car and pulled the door shut. Yashkin eased away from the hard shoulder and nudged into place among the lorries and trucks.

Molenkov asked him, 'How did you know it wasn't a heart attack?'

'Your hands were in the wrong place.'

'My hands were over my heart.'

'No – the heart is higher and to the side. Your hands were not on your heart. You were suffering, Molenkov, from gastric indigestion made acute by eating bread and cheese like a pig swallows acorns.'

More wind filled the car, and Molenkov's belt hung loose. Then he belched. 'I feel better but I thought I was dead.'

'Look for the turning, please.'

'What would you have done if it had been a heart attack? We have a schedule.' Molenkov pointed. 'There, the sign for Dobrus and Vetka.'

Yashkin knew what he would have done, and was glad to have the excuse not to answer the question.

The young man wanted a fight. Well, he would have it. Lawson thought Luke Davies was a young colt out in a field, pawing the grass with a hoof.

They were all at the minibus except Adrian and Dennis. Deadeye was Control and had the street map on his knee in the back; Lawson liked Deadeye, respecting the man's quiet. He only spoke when necessary. Bugsy had said again that they needed to get a harness beacon on their man; agreed and no further discussion required. Lawson respected Bugsy too. Shrinks had been near the cathedral when the agent and the target had gone by, a full two hundred metres away, and would have had a view of them for no more than fifteen seconds but with the magnification of pocket binoculars; probably had had nothing to add that had not already been said. And Charlie, the girl, had done well when she'd been called forward, and most likely hadn't needed Davies with her but he'd horned in. Lawson thought her adequate, not a passenger. Luke Davies was the one who would confront him, and maybe it was time for a clearing of the air.

He'd get it over with. Lawson stepped out of the minibus, and knew Davies would follow him. He walked a few paces towards the walls of the Royal Palace – quite well restored – and heard another door shoved open, then slammed.

'Have you a minute, Mr Lawson?'

'Always have time for anything of importance.'

Davies came round in front of him, blocked his walk and his view of the palace, home once of King Stanislaw August, and he was near to the fine statue of a rampant King Sigismund III. He had been here with Clipper Reade.

'I want, Mr Lawson, to lodge my protest at the way this business is being conducted.'

'Do you now? How fascinating.'

He and Clipper Reade, the tractor spare-parts salesman, had been in this square on a July evening thirty-something years before, lost in a great crowd that gazed up at the clock face in the Sigismund tower.

The complaint exploded out at him: 'I saw him: he walked right by me. He looked pathetic. He's crushed and bowed. God knows what level, should he survive this, of post-traumatic stress he'll be subject to. He's down there on the floor.'

'Is that right?'

The clock in the Sigismund tower had been stopped at the exact moment that the first bomb from a Luftwaffe Stuka, in response to the uprising of 1944, had hit the tower and wrecked the clock's workings. The crowd had gathered to hear it start to click again, and see the hands move . . . He'd been in a good mood that evening, as Clipper Reade had, because they had come from a clandestine meeting, the initial contact, with an engineer of the central telephone exchange who had taken the Queen's shilling and the President's silver dollar, and had accepted recruitment.

'You've hung him out to dry. What you've done to that man is shameful, disgraceful. I suppose you wouldn't recognize that. Some sort of sacrificial lamb and you playing God with his welfare, his life. You just don't care, do you?'

'I've come to expect the dull and mediocre from you, Davies, and expectations are seldom unfulfilled.'

'And the way this business is being conducted is just so unprofessional. We're barging around, bumbling and stumbling, without local co-operation. I suppose, in your warped world, the Polish intelligence community are unreconstructed Communists, the same people as in the blissful Good Old Days. I know that when I've been in Lithuania, our station chief has said—'

'You were irksome when you started. Now you are merely tedious.'

'You don't care, do you? You're devoid of decency and humanity.'

In his mind, Lawson had been back in '84, after Clipper Reade had left Europe, and he'd done a tour of the palace, had seen King Stanislaw August's apartments, and the Canaletto Room, and the chapel that held the urn where the heart of Kosciuszko, the leader of an eighteenth-century revolt, was laid. And seen the Study Room where Napoleon, on his way to Moscow, had slept, and the Ballroom where the nation's finest ladies were on display for him that he might more quickly choose a mistress.

Davies's voice spat. His features were contorted. 'You won't survive this. Believe me, you will not. I'll make it my business to see that you're hauled before an ethics committee, trampled on and shown the door. Not only are you old-fashioned, a dinosaur, you're also, *Mr* Lawson, an individual of quite extraordinary self-regard. You play God with people and think it acceptable. You don't care.'

The weariness was back in him, and his view of the palace blurred. Lawson said, and kept his voice even, 'You know nothing. You're a wet-behind-the-ears boy – probably should've found a niche at Work and Pensions. Go away, lose yourself.'

'I'll see you damned because you have no care for an agent's welfare. Lose an agent through negligence and bad practice and say, "Let's go get a beer." Your callousness has no place in a modern world.'

His name was called softly. Lawson turned, looked back, and Deadeye was half out of the minibus, pointing towards the steps leading down from the square to the Vistula river. Didn't know,

405

did he, whether a trap was sprung or whether an agent walked free? Would find out soon, and age crawled through Lawson's body as he walked to the low wall above the long flight of steps.

He stood in shadow, where he had been led to. Beside Carrick was Viktor. There were street-lamps that glowed dimly but they were far separated. Their light didn't enter the shadow, but a little of their power reached the dark flow of the river. Mikhail whispered in Reuven Weissberg's ear.

He had no table-lamp to throw through a window. He didn't know, now, how far away back-up was. Right and left, the walkway was empty, and the rain had come on heavier. Carrick saw the motion of the water, and its strength, seemed to feel its cold. He stood stock still, and knew his life depended on what Reuven Weissberg was told and how he reacted. All others were beyond reach. They might throw him in alive, might stab a knife into his back, then heave him on to the low parapet. Mikhail backed away, and there was not enough light for Carrick to read his face.

Reuven Weissberg came towards him, took the back of Carrick's head tight in his fingers. He kissed him, first on the left cheek, then on the right. Carrick heard, guttural and accented, 'I do not apologize to you.'

He did the dumb act. 'I don't know that there's anything for which you should apologize, sir.'

'It was necessary to take that time and walk through the Old Town.'

'If you say so, sir.'

'It was necessary for Mikhail and Viktor. I have to listen to them because they have been with me since I was no more than a kid. They wanted it.

406

If you had not been what you say you are – I believed you but they were not certain – *if* you had been an agent of the police or an intelligence agency that targeted me, you would have been followed, to see where I took you, to keep track of me and of you. They are very expert, Viktor and Mikhail, and they did not find a tail on you . . . but I do not apologize.'

Carrick said quietly, 'There would not have been a tail because I am not an agent.'

He was hugged. Now exhaustion caught him, and he wobbled on his feet. He was led towards the cars. Josef Goldmann and the polisher waited in one, but Mikhail opened the door of the other – for Carrick.

Carrick thought it the right time for him to stand tall, and said, 'My man was not shot, sir. You were.'

In the car, in the front passenger seat, with Mikhail driving, they went across the wide, high bridge that spanned the Vistula river, going east. Mikhail leaned across him and tapped the glove compartment in front of Carrick. He dropped the flap and saw what had been placed there for him. He lifted out a Makharov pistol and with it two magazines of ammunition. Further back he found a pancake holster.

They went fast, and new confusions burdened him.

Chapter 15: 15 April 2008

'A teacher said I was old before my time, had the body of a child and the mind of a man – do you understand that, Johnny?'

He wasn't expected to reply, and did not. Carrick sat beside Mikhail in the front, and Reuven Weissberg's voice was soft behind him, but clear.

'My father was dead and my mother had gone to do strip-tease in the East at the oil-exploration sites, so I do not think it was remarkable that my mind was old, and I lived with my grandmother. There was no place in my life to be a child, to have such a luxury. My grandmother had fought and she taught me what was necessary. You fight to survive. It was what she told me. She knew . . . And I was a Jew. I doubt you could understand what it was, *is*, to be a Jew in yesterday's or today's Russia.'

Carrick stared ahead into the night, and the headlights showed the road in front of him. Villages, little towns, fields and forests slipped by and were gone.

'We had nothing. No saved money, no possessions of value. My grandmother was a cleaner in a ministry building in Perm. She was a Jew and they would not give her regular work, and she had the worst jobs – lavatories and waiting areas for the public where filth came in off the street – and at the end of each month she did not know whether she would work for the next four weeks or not work. I looked at her and saw what it was to be a Jew. She said to me, and it was repeated every morning and every evening, that I must fight to live. It was like I was in the Kama river that flows in Perm and was sinking and the water was in my nostrils and I must struggle and kick and thrash if I am not to sink. That is what it was to be a Jew in Perm. I fought and I survived, and I was a Jew. I could only do *business*. Business was survival.'

He thought of them as people who meet in a hotel bar, who talk for an evening then separate and go to their rooms and will be gone their different ways by the early morning and will not meet again – but they talk. He remembered himself as a kid, at school and bored, probably messing about, and a teacher had read a poem that had caught his mind. Afterwards he had found the anthology and learned it. The American writer Henry Longfellow:

> *Ships that pass in the night, and speak each other*
> *in passing;*
> *Only a signal shown and a distant voice in the*
> *darkness;*
> *So on the ocean of life we pass and speak one*
> *another,*
> *Only a look and a voice; then darkness again and*
> *a silence.*

Little from classroom days had stayed with him, but those few lines had.

'I did *business* at school. I am twelve or thirteen

years old, I am condemned as a "disruptive influence" and as a "malcontent", and several times I am beaten by teachers, but more often I am sent home. Each time I was sent home my grandmother returned me to school. She lectured me on how to survive, and I did, and I played at *business*. To survive is to fight. To fight you must look into the eyes of an opponent and show him you have no comprehension of defeat, no fear of pain, supreme determination. The enemy may be bigger, more muscles, have more friends, but you must find and exploit his weakness – she told me. I did. If a teacher punished me, I went to his house. In the night I broke the teacher's windows and built a fire at his door, and I would hear his wife scream and his children cry, and in the morning he would smile at me and be polite. If the leader of a gang of kids objected that I tried to take money from those he protected, I fought him. Boots, fists, teeth, nails, I used them. Always I won. When I won – I standing and the other not – his allies, his kids came to me. I grew. I did roofs in the school, and was paid. Children brought me money – stole it from their parents – and for the money they had my protection. I made money and the only other Jew I knew of was Josef Goldmann, and he cared for my money.'

In the darkness, with the motion of the car lulling him, Carrick thought himself exposed to a great truth. He lived a lie, and he believed Reuven Weissberg lived a lie – but a greater one.

'If you are in *business*, Johnny, you must always expand, grow bigger. You cannot stand still. I had an empire in Perm, in the district where my grandmother lived, and it was a battlefield while I built my roofs, and took traders from under other roofs.

She would treat me when I had fought and was hurt, would bandage me, clean the cuts, and could stitch slashes because she had those skills. I never had to come back to her and tell her of failure. She would have despised me if I had not fought and won. Then I was conscripted. There, I was thrashed, beaten, and I was far from my grandmother, but I never cried out. I did good *business* in the army, buying and selling, and each week I posted the money back to Josef Goldmann, who was excused the military because his feet had fallen arches. There were great warehouse stores of equipment for selling, and narcotics for buying and trading. That was *business*, and it prospered. I did well. Even senior officers came to me because I could get for them anything they wanted. I had control of a market. I came back to Perm. You find it interesting, Johnny, my story?'

The lie they shared was about loneliness, isolation and an absence of trust. He could have asked where they were going, and what *business* took them at hammering pace on the road to the East, but Carrick did not. For himself, he understood what it was to feel the pang of loneliness, the pain of being isolated and the desolation of living without the possibility of having a friend in whom trust was placed.

'From the army, coming home, I had to re-establish authority in Perm. It was a fight, but I succeeded. Everything I did to regain my *business* position I talked of first with my grandmother. I had the control of the open market in Perm, which was remarkable for a Jew, and Mikhail and Viktor had joined me. Then the city of Perm had no more for me. One day I was there, and one day I was gone, and my grandmother came with me, and

411

Josef Goldmann, Mikhail and Viktor. It was the same in Moscow. There were powerful *business* groups in the capital city. I did what I had done before, fought. Then, the rivals in *business* came and offered accommodation, compromise, because they had no stomach for war. I told you, Johnny, in *business* you cannot stand still, lean against a wall and let the world pass. You must run – run faster, run a greater distance. Moscow to Berlin. Roofs and deals, more roofs and more deals. Running and never stopping. Do you understand what I say to you, Johnny?'

What he understood was his growing fondness for the man sitting in the car behind him, talking in the quiet voice – showing his own loneliness and isolation, and starting to give that precious thing, trust. And, in his blurred mind, he valued the man's confidences.

The city prided itself on the title 'Gateway to the World'. It boasted the most advanced container port ever built. Hamburg, in northern Germany, was sited on the Elbe river, sixty-five land miles from the estuary spilling into the North Sea. From its docks flotillas of cargo vessels sail on journeys to all points of the globe.

The Crow had flown from Belgrade to Munich, then taken a taxi to the railway station there, paid cash for a ticket to Cologne and taken the night train to Hamburg. Dawn was breaking. A low mist slowed the morning light, and the rain spotted his shoulders, but he walked well, not furtively. Instructions and directions had been given to him, and a schedule, and he followed them exactly. They took him away from the Hauptbahnhof, and across an empty square where the first flower-sellers and traders in fresh fruit and vegetables were setting up their stalls and erecting canopies to catch the rain. He went on to Steinstrasse, then took the left turning as instructed.

There was little traffic that early and he was able to hear the call to prayer, the first of the day. He saw the minaret of the mosque, topping chimneys and the roofs of office blocks. The tower was a beacon for him. He thought for a moment of those who had been in that mosque, had worshipped there, and flown the aircraft into the Twin Towers and into the Pentagon building, of their commitment to their faith and their cause. He was humbled by them, but dismissed it. The world had moved on, and a new war had developed. Many had died and many more had been taken to gaols and torture rooms. He followed a route given him. His focus was on the memorized instructions and directions. He came to a door.

The Crow pressed the third from the top of seven buttons.

He heard a guttural cough, then the request that a stranger identify himself.

The Crow gave the word he had been told to use, in Arabic, spoke it to the microphone hidden by the grille.

He heard the lock click open.

The Crow climbed three flights of stairs.

He stood on a landing and waited until a door was opened and he was admitted.

The Crow was asked, hesitantly, by an older man, if he had had a good journey.

He said it had been satisfactory and ducked his head in appreciation at the courtesy of the question.

The Crow was told of the arrangements in place, confirmed by this *hawaldar*, for the transfer of a bond valued at one million American dollars to a bank in Leipzig, and the coded number that would release it for transfer to accounts in Greek Cyprus specified by Oleg Yashkin and Igor Molenkov, both Russian citizens. Then it was confirmed to him that a further sum of ten million American dollars was now available for payment to the Russian citizen Reuven Weissberg, and it was understood that such payment would be overseen by another Russian citizen, Josef Goldmann.

He confirmed, of course, that payment for purchase and sale depended on safe delivery and verification of the capabilities of the item under negotiation.

The Crow added that such necessary verification would be carried out by a qualified expert.

They shook hands, then hugged, kissed briefly, and he was on his way out into the morning mist that rose from the Binnenalster lake, the Oberhafen canal and the Elbe waterway.

He was exhausted, had not slept. With a swaying, shambling step, Sak walked from the Haupt-bahnhof. The British passport in the inside pocket, against his chest – it had been shown on the Brussels-to-Cologne leg of the journey – was in the name of Steven Arthur King. The previous evening, he had left the St Pancras terminus on a Eurostar connection to Brussels and had used a Pakistan-issued passport giving his identity as Siddique Ahmed Khatab. He saw stalls of bright flowers, fine fruit and the best vegetables, and the rain dripped from the striped awnings protecting them.

He could have caught a direct flight from Birmingham International to Hamburg-Ohlsdorf, but that had been forbidden by those who had planned his journey. Sak had taken the last train of the evening from London, then sat alone and fearful in the Brussels station to wait for the night connection to Hamburg. The great station had been darkened while the hours had eased past. Under the one pool of lights was a cluster of seats and he and other nightbird travellers had waited there. He didn't understand fully why he had not been permitted to fly. The lit area seemed to him an oasis of safety. He had joined a few students and a few grandparents and had sat up through the rest of the night in a carriage with dimmed lights and hard seats.

In the dawn, with rain running ribbons down the window, the night train had brought him to Hamburg.

The worst part of the whole journey, he would have said if asked, was the walk from the train door along the platform, up the long flight of steps, and the length of the bridge over the tracks towards the dull light of morning, the stalls and the taxi rank. What caused the fear was the halting memory of boasts made. The boasts had been of his importance in the structure of the Atomic Weapons Establishment at Aldermaston in the Thames Valley, and had tripped easily off his tongue in the garden of a villa on the outskirts of Quetta. He had been listened to with respect in that garden, and the enormity of the betrayal he had suffered had seemed irresistible in the telling. Walking the last few strides towards the light and the traffic roar, seeing the spread of the square in front of him, Sak realized his liberty was now in the hands of others: those he had met in Quetta, those who had spoken his name in communications, those who had put forward his name, those who had staked out the pavement between the school and his home, the young woman – not robed but in hipster jeans, a T-shirt and a Puffa anorak, with lipstick on her mouth and highlights in her hair – who had given him the tickets, had accosted him by the machine that measured blood pressure, and those he had not yet met. So many knew his name and had decided on his journey.

The fear made him shiver until he was out of the railway station and into the heart of the square, but he was not felled from behind and there was no gun barrel against his neck and no handcuffs on his wrists. He began, then, to control the trembling.

As he had been told to, Sak took a bus to the west of the city, up the Elbe estuary, and in his mind was the address of the car-rental company he must get to. With the shivering not eradicated but lessened, self-esteem returning slowly, the old arrogance and bitterness coming back to roost within him, he could not imagine how an operation of such sophistication, of such extraordinarily detailed planning, could be obstructed or by whom.

Mikhail came off the highway, did the half-circle on the roundabout, then braked abruptly. A lorry slewed away from behind them, and there was a fanfare of a horn's protest. Mikhail, as if it were his privilege on a roundabout to change his mind, swung the wheel and went round again.

Carrick play-acted the game, used the passenger side mirror and the central mirror.

It was the old and familiar one of checking for a tail – as old and familiar as doing shop-window reflections. Nothing crossed Carrick's face, no sardonic amusement at the manoeuvre. He wore

416

the Makharov in the pancake on his belt. It was loaded now and he had checked the mechanism. The safety was depressed and the weapon could not be fired without that lever being moved . . . but he carried an illegal firearm and it was loaded with illegal ammunition. He seemed not to care over what line he had strayed.

That line was well whitened or double-yellowed. It would not have been tolerated for a police under-cover, for any SCD10 man or woman, to step so far out of legality. He had not carried a firearm since his army days, and the anniversary was coming up soon – next month – the fifth, since the improvised explosive device, the bastard IED, had been det-onated alongside his wheels. But Johnny Carrick was crossing many lines, all the colours of the rain-bow: he liked the man.

'Maybe he will buy you, Johnny.' It was said with a hint of humour, but that was bogus.

'I didn't know I'd been put up for sale, Mr Goldmann.'

Now sadness in the voice, as if something precious had been lost. 'He can buy what he wants, Johnny, anything.'

'Yes, Mr Goldmann.'

'You know what is worst about being with him, Johnny?'

'I don't I'm afraid, Mr Goldmann.'

'What is worst is that you get to sleep too often in motor-cars. I cannot abide to sleep in a car. Because of him I have to. A bed is nothing to him. Johnny, do I smell?'

He sniffed loudly. 'Can't smell anything, Mr Goldmann.'

There was a snort, disbelief. They had pulled off the main road, before the city of Lublin, and had gone on to the concrete track that led to a farm. That was the place for sleeping, and the car seats made the beds. The smell of three bodies, Reuven Weissberg's, Mikhail's and Carrick's, had been foul, and his throat had been raw and . . . He had thought that if they were avoiding a hotel reception desk then the *business* must be close. They were parked in a side-street off the town's main square. It sloped away, was newly cobbled, a picture-postcard view of the town of Chelm. The square had a sign up that announced a European cash grant for modernization and reconstruction, and boutique-type shops lined its sides. When Reuven Weissberg had walked out into the centre of the square, Carrick had gone to follow but there had been a sharp whistle from Mikhail. When he had turned he had been waved back. So, Reuven Weissberg who did *business*, who fought for his survival, who was the target of an operation mounted by the Secret Intelligence Service, had space and was alone.

Carrick stood with Josef Goldmann.

'Do you know why we are here, Johnny, in this shit-hole of a town?'

'I don't, Mr Goldmann . . . but I don't need to be told.'

'This is Chelm. It is where his grandmother would have come as a girl, as a child. This square was here then. The Jews were one in three of the population. The town had their culture stamped over it. His grandmother, Anna, would have been brought by her parents to Chelm for special days, like a birthday. He tries to live his grandmother's life, Johnny. Do you understand that, why he does it?'

He could have answered, 'Because of the

418

loneliness.' He shook his head. In front of him, Reuven Weissberg walked towards a little wood-built shed, in which a hatch was open. Inside, past a woman's shoulder, he could see shelves of sweets, chocolates, gum. The shed was on a wide plinth of neatly set cobbles.

'There was a similar kiosk shop there when his grandmother was a child. When she was brought to Chelm, on any day of celebration, and wearing her best clothes, her father would have bought a news-paper there, printed in Yiddish or Polish, I don't know, and some sweets for his children. There is little now that remains of the Jewish past in Chelm . . . this kiosk, a cemetery – the cemetery has been cleaned, but now it is a place for addicts. He had two fears, Johnny, and I do not know which is the greater. One fear is that he should die, be killed, gunned down on a street, and that his grandmother is left to live her last years, or months, solitary, for-gotten and without a carer. The other fear is for the day when she passes on, now she is in her eighty-fifth year, and who then is left for him to love and talk with? There are great fears in his life.'

Carrick watched the man's back, thought of the old woman marooned in the apartment in Berlin, high above the pulse of the streets, and he saw Reuven Weissberg go on across the square, leaving the kiosk behind him, then pause at the top of a side-street that ran down a steep hill. The man whose fears were now identified to Carrick gazed at a building. Carrick followed the eyeline and saw a big sign on it: McKenzee Saloon. It had once been, he thought, a fine building.

'His grandmother would have been there on those celebration days, when she was a child. It was the synagogue, the holy place, the place of

worship, learning and culture. She was there ...
For many years it was a bank. Now it is a bar. She
is the past. Everything about him is controlled by
the past, his grandmother's. Be careful of him,
Johnny. As his grandmother controls him, so he
controls men. I tell you, be careful of him. I think,
Johnny, you are too honest a person and would not
welcome the contamination of poison. He has
poison fed to him by his grandmother. Believe in
me.'

Reuven Weissberg was still at the top of the
narrow street. A window cleaner now worked at
the first-floor windows of the McKenzee Saloon.
Carrick had the picture in his mind, the woman
who was young and held the baby, a weapon slung
loosely on her shoulder, and had brilliant white
hair.

'Has he told you about fighting, Johnny, fighting
against the world? He will. He can recite stories of
suffering, agonies and fighting. He knows them, is
perfect in each word of them. They were taught
him by his grandmother, from the time he sat on
her knee to today. She has fashioned him. He is her
creature. He likes best the story of when she fought.
Stay with him and you will hear it.'

*I did not know where he was. All through the day I
looked for Samuel, but I could not see him.*

*I had done what I had been told to. I had dressed as
warmly as was possible in the clothes I owned. I had no
shame, no guilt, but I took a jersey from a woman in our
barracks who was sick. I stole it. I didn't think she would
need it because she wasn't strong enough to go out of the
camp. Later, as the days became shorter and the nights
colder, she would have needed it, but I thought only of
that day and the coming night. I was able to 'borrow' a*

pair of boots. I told another woman, who worked in the section that converted the clothes of the dead into clothes that could be sent to Germany for those put out in the streets by the bombing, that I wanted her boots for the day and would return them in the morning. They were good boots with strong soles, and I told her I would do a shift for her in return for what she 'loaned' me. At first light I was ready. I wore the jersey and the boots. At breakfast, I begged for a third slice of black bread and was given it.

All through the day I was ready, but I didn't see Samuel.

The morning passed so slowly. Because I knew, had been trusted, I sensed an atmosphere. I wouldn't have recognized the changed mood among a few of the men. Where was Samuel? I never saw him through all the hours of the morning, or when the detail came back from working in the forest. It doesn't matter where he was, but it was agony to me that I hadn't seen him. I didn't know how it would happen, or when.

It rained that day.

The darkness came early.

The lights were on above the fences and the rain made jewels of the barbs in the wire. Above the fences and lights were the watchtowers. On each of the watchtowers, with the Ukrainians, were machine-guns. I saw everything . . . I saw the height of the fences, the brightness of the lights and the size of the machine-guns, I saw the guards and the swagger of the Germans. I couldn't imagine how it was possible that we – starved, exhausted, weak – could defeat them. I think I was losing faith . . . Then I saw Samuel.

He came out of a hut, the one beside the kitchen where the bread was made. He looked past me, then through me, as if determined not to attract attention to me or to himself. He tried to walk by me, but I held in my palm the

421

flattened orchid he had given me and opened my hand to show him. He reached out and I saw that fresh blood was on his hands, and he was wide-eyed – as if in shock. I knew it. It had begun. I could not know how it would end.

I did not have to be told. I followed him.

I went into a hut, the one where we ate. There were, perhaps, thirty men inside and I recognized Feldhendler and a few who had been in the camp as workers all the time I had been there, and all the Russians. The speaker was Pechersky. He was on a table and spoke with the intensity of a fighter. I caught the end of what he said: 'Our day has come . . . Most of the Germans are dead . . . Let us die with honour. Remember, if any of us survives, he must tell the world what has happened here.'

There was no applause. I looked at the faces, grim, haggard, but determination lit them. On many hands there was blood, and I saw guns in the hands of a few, and knives or axes, which were stained and wet.

Samuel whispered to me, 'The first was Wolf. He was killed in the tailors' shop. Then it was Beckmann in his office and with each stab on him there was shouted in his ear the name of a relative of Chaim who had died here. Chaim killed him. Unterscharführer Ryba we killed in the garage. Stay with me, trust me.'

We went out into the dusk. I think it was five o'clock. The whistle went. Prisoners lined up, were in their formation and ranks. The roll was called. I could see the fences and the gates. I didn't know how it could be done. The women were in a group apart from the men but I kept my eyes always on Samuel. He stood in the rank behind Pechersky. In a moment of silence there was a shout. Very clear. We all heard it. A guard cried: 'Ein Deutsch kaput'. The shooting started.

Some ran for the gate.

Some stayed in the ranks.

Some ran for the wire.

Insufficient Germans had been killed. Frenzel organized Germans and Ukrainians at the main gate.

Samuel ran to me, took my arm. There was shooting at the gate, incessant, and the screams of those hit. Samuel took me to the wire. It was laced with pine branches and easy to climb. We were between two towers. We reached the top of the wire, were together, and the barbs caught in my clothing, ripped it. He jumped down, crouched and called me. Men came down from the wire all around us. I think the few who had guns were shooting at the Ukrainians in the towers. I looked back. I remember my shock at what I saw. Many had stayed behind, like statues in their ranks.

Did they believe, those who stayed, that the Germans would look kindly on them? Did it take more courage to run at the wire than to remain in the lines for roll-call? I think half stayed, and half ran.

I came down from the wire, fell. Samuel broke the impact. Then I was beside him.

In front of us was open ground, and beyond it the forest. He held me. He gripped my arm, and I couldn't have broken away. Others came off the wire, tumbled, regained their feet, ran.

The explosions deafened us. If Samuel had shouted in my ear I wouldn't have heard his words. The machine-guns traversed the top of the wire, and some screamed, some cried out and some swung from the barbs. Samuel and I were the only ones who stayed at the base of the wire. The ground lifted, flew. The noise of the mines detonating was awesome, terrifying, but many still ran, driven like cattle in headlong flight, and I saw legs taken off and thrown clear, stomachs slashed open, the head of a man sliced off cleanly. That was what awaited us.

He pulled me up. He loosed my arm and took my hand. He pointed to his feet, then to mine. There was chaos around us, terror. The machine-guns were constant, the mine explosions frequent, scattering shrapnel. It was hell, at the base of the wire. He stood but was bent at the waist. Without warning, he jerked me forward. How desperate must you be to run into a mine-field? So desperate. There was no turning back.

I saw some, a few, reach the trees. I saw some, many, felled in the minefield. I copied Samuel, was on the toes of those boots I had 'borrowed'.

It was the first time in so many months that I had seen the trees of the forest, their darkened depth, and I sucked breath into my lungs. I knew what I had to do ... Samuel ran. He wove, skipped and danced – and I saw then that Pechersky was ahead of him. I understood that his feet landed always where others had gone before, had detonated the mines. We went past those who were down, who had lost limbs, who held their intestines in their hands, whose faces had been taken off by the shrapnel. Where the open ground was cratered, he put his feet. I followed, dragged forward, and my boots went on to the loosened ground where his treadmarks were. He had waited, as had the other Russians, for those in panic to clear a path. We took advantage of others' death and mutilation. We went through the minefield.

More were cut down between the minefield and the tree line.

Samuel, now, did not swerve. He ran straight, fast, bent low. I tripped once, fell, was on my knees. He did not stop or hesitate. With all of his strength he pulled me up. He held my hand so tightly.

We hit the trees.

We had fought them. The gunfire, their death camp, their world, their evil was behind us. We ran till it was muffled and distant. Rain dripped from the trees. We ran till the breath would not go down into our lungs, till we staggered. There were so many in the forest, blundering

424

and crying. I could go no further. I said it to myself,
again and again, that we had fought them. They were
behind us, with their guns, fences, the Himmelstrasse
and the chambers for gassing with carbon-monoxide
fumes.

And I was trembling and gasping. 'What do we do
now, Samuel? What should we do?' It would have
wheezed from my throat,

'We have to find Pechersky. We depend on him.
Pechersky will save us.'

He said it with faith. He trusted. I believed him.

'I really have to speak, Mr Lawson.'

'If you have something to say, say it.'

The target had walked back from the summit of
a side-street, had crossed the square and gone close
to a slatted wooden shed that served as a shop, had
come back to the agent and had seemed to whisper
something in his ear, then had slapped the agent's
shoulder. The target's arm had stayed loose across
the agent's shoulder as they had gone right and out
of sight. Adrian came by them in the car and
cruised to get locked into the tracking position
behind the target's vehicle.

What Lawson could recognize, what seemed
a priority factor to him, was the increasing
exhaustion of his team, Adrian and Dennis at the
top of the pecking order for rest, but no opportunity had yet shown up for handing the beacon
harness to the agent.

'It's the body language, Mr Lawson.' Shrinks had
paused.

Lawson said, 'If you have something to com-
municate, spill it. Don't wait for my prompt. God
Almighty . . .'

'Yes, Mr Lawson. What I wanted to contribute is

about the body language of the agent. He demonstrates the characteristics of pure Stockholm syndrome.'

'Get to the point.'

'Of course, Mr Lawson. We talk about a universal strategy for victims of personal abuse. Could be hostages, battered women, incest victims or pro-cured prostitutes. In all cases, the victims ingratiate themselves with their abuser. The victim believes absolutely in an actual or perceived threat to his or her personal safety – that's what we call a "precursor" to the syndrome. A second precursor is the relief if a gesture of kindness, mercy, is made by the abuser to the victim – could be as little as a smile or a gentle word. The third common precursor involves the circumstance in which the victim exists – in isolation from any normal, familiar environment, cut off from contact with the outside world. Our last precursor is the victim's belief that he or she cannot walk away, escape. All of those factors now exist for November. We have threat, we have humanity and isolation, and we have the inability to turn his back, walk off down the street towards sunlit uplands. Put bluntly, Mr Lawson, your man regards Reuven Weissberg as a more important figure in his life than you.'

The girl, Katie Jennings, drove the minibus off the square. Lawson liked what he was told, but wouldn't show it.

'He is, of course, Mr Lawson, a highly trained and motivated officer. I venture to suggest that nothing in the agent's training would have pre-pared him for this situation. Stress factors for him will be high. Motivation will have been weakened by the factor of his being outside a net of regular contact with us. We should—'

'Summarize – without waffle.'

'I'll try, Mr Lawson. Your agent has colluded with his abuser, and that is a classic symptom of the syndrome. I would suggest that his perspective on events ahead of him is not that of a serving police officer. His perspective is that of his abuser. The victim becomes, we've found, hyper-vigilant to the abuser's needs.'

'And you're getting all that from the body language, with your viewpoint ranged from a hundred yards plus away?' Lawson snorted sarcasm.

'I am. The agent cannot now divorce himself from the target – a battered wife remains with a violent husband. The agent's greatest fear is of losing the only positive relationship left him. He's in denial of reality. It's that simple.'

Lawson reckoned Shrinks was frightened of him. Looking into the minibus front mirror, he could see that the girl wore an expression of suppressed anger, and that young Davies, beside her, fought to hold his silence. Probably both detested him. He had the back seat to himself, and the jump seats behind him were taken by Bugsy, Deadeye, Shrinks and their luggage. He stretched his legs. They were out of the square, plunging down the hill and away from the modernized prettiness of the old town into the more recent concrete shapes of Chelm.

Lawson said, 'Yes, very helpful. Do you want a mention in dispatches?'

'Just trying to do my job, Mr Lawson. Getting nearer, isn't it, whatever the conclusion will be? And that's piling the stress on him. Difficult thing to handle in his circumstances, acute stress.'

'Everyone, Shrinks, will be feeling the stress in the coming hours,' Lawson said cheerfully. 'I guarantee

427

that stress, like piano wires pulled to break-point, will play a part in the actions of everyone involved.'

He licked his lips. Molenkov couldn't help himself. 'Yashkin, where we are now, is it inside the Chernobyl area?'

'You know as much as I do.'

Their leg for the day was from Gomel to Pinsk. It would be one of the longest. On the map, Molenkov had reckoned, it was around three hundred and sixty-five kilometres. They had not rejoined the M13, and Molenkov had guided Yashkin to the side roads going south. They were on a single-carriageway road, and had crossed a long, narrow bridge over the Pripat river, were among a wilderness of uncultivated fields, sparse forestry and stagnant lakes. Where there had been villages there were only slight indications of habitation. The meltdown at the nuclear reactor on the outskirts of Chernobyl had occurred two years after the death of his wife and a year before the death of his son.

'I know little of Chernobyl, only that the country to the north was contaminated, that there is a considerable exclusion zone, that the poison will stay for many hundreds of years and—'

Yashkin snapped, 'And the level of radiation at Chernobyl, which is due south of us, is on average measured at 1.21 milliroentgens, and that's a hundred times more than the natural level of radiation.'

'Then you know something.'

'I know that thyroid cancer is up for those who lived inside the zone by more than two thousand per cent, congenital birth deformities are up by two hundred and fifty per cent, and leukaemia has doubled. There was fall-out here. It came down in rain. I talked once with a "colleague", an oaf from Belarus, at a conference I attended. He said that Russian territory was not affected because our air force seeded rain clouds that would have blown over Russia, used chemicals to induce premature rainfall, and prevented the radionuclides from coming down on our territory but instead on Belarus. Is that enough?'

Molenkov pursed his lips and a frown slashed his forehead. Thoughts cavorted in his mind. He could see little from the side window because the rain was beating on the Polonez's roof, coming from the south, then flowed in rivers down the glass. The wipers on the windscreen hummed on full power. He watched the slow flight of a stork, the big wings flapping lethargically, as it traversed the road and stayed low.

Molenkov asked, 'It reached this far, yes?'

'What reached this far?'

'Don't mock me, Yashkin. Did the poison reach this far?'

'It did.'

'And will it last for ever, for all the horizons of time that you and I can think of?'

'Watch the map.'

Molenkov breathed in hard. He thought of what he wished to say, how to express it. His friend of many years, his neighbour, his confidant, his partner in the enterprise, kept his eyes on the road, didn't look at him and wouldn't help him.

He said, 'We worked at the place where weapons were made. The weapons, if ever used, would have spread the same poison, left the same disease in the air, in the ground. Am I correct?'

'Wrong. We had mutually assured destruction.

With MAD there was no question of the weapons being used. The safeguard against nuclear war was that *they* had them and *we* had them. It couldn't have happened. It would have been national suicide for us and them.'

It had formed in his mind, what he would say and the action he would take. Molenkov could not have said why he had lingered so long. He took another surging, gulping breath. In his mind, pictured there, was the device in the back of the car, covered by the tarpaulin. He could have reached back, twisted, ignored the pain in his pelvis and touched it. If his hand had been able to go under the tarpaulin and under the webbing cover of the *thing*, and if he'd had a screwdriver and had unfastened the casing, he could have touched it and felt its living, breathing, hideous warmth. He did not reach behind him, but he pictured it. 'What we carry, what we intend to sell, will do the same.'

'You're talking shit, Molenkov.'

'It'll make the poison.'

'What do you want, Molenkov?'

'I want no part of it.'

'See if I care.'

'Do you want a part of it?'

'You're too late to ask that.'

'Stop the car, Yashkin.'

A hand didn't come off the wheel, didn't go to the gear lever and change down. The Polonez did not slow. The brake pedal was not pressed. Yashkin kept the car at his steady speed, fifty kilometres per hour.

It welled in his throat, and Molenkov shouted, 'Stop the car! Turn it round! We should go back.'

Yashkin said, without anger, 'If you want to go back, then do so. I go on. Without you, Molenkov, I go on.'

'You couldn't. You haven't the strength, not on your own.'

'I go on, with or without you.'

'Think of your wife. Come back with me.'

Now the hand moved fast. From the wheel to the gear lever. The Polonez lurched and slowed. Molenkov saw the foot stamp on the pedal. Yashkin reached across him, opened the passenger door, thrust it wide, then jerked round, caught a strap of Molenkov's bag and dumped it in his lap. He reached for the uniform on the hanger and threw that, too, on to Molenkov's knees.

Molenkov climbed out. His feet went down into a water-filled pothole. He felt the damp settle in his shoes and saturate his socks. Rain hit his face, and within the first few seconds his uniform was spattered. He looked right and saw only trees on the near side and a lake on the other. He looked left and saw a wood-plank home, but no smoke came from the chimney and no washing was out.

The door was slammed after him. The car started slowly to pull away.

He had no food. He had little money in his wallet. He told himself then that he was a man of principle, not a criminal. Told himself, also, that Yashkin would go a hundred metres, find the entrance to a field, turn and come back for him. Told himself as well that he and Yashkin were joined at the fucking hip. The car had disappeared round a bend. He thought of the cold that would now have settled on his small home, and the damp because a fire had not been lit, and he thought of going back to the bed and the musty sheets, and of setting off for the street market of Sarov, spending a day searching for scrag meat and old vegetables that he could afford, and the previous day's milk, which would be sold off cheap. He thought of the great gate and the sentries, and of the men behind it who despised him because he was a *zampolit* and a former political officer of the old regime. He had no other friend.

He started to walk. He didn't go in the direction of Sarov, twelve hundred kilometres back. He followed the road the Polonez had taken.

The Polonez was, of course, round the first corner, parked at the side of the road. When he reached the car, the door was opened for him.

He threw his bag and uniform into the back, on to the tarpaulin, and dropped down into the seat. 'Fuck you, Yashkin.'

'And fuck you, Molenkov.'

They hugged . . . All around was the desolate land of the marshes and swamps where the poison of Chernobyl had fallen, but Molenkov no longer thought of it.

Adrian called, reported he had lost the target. Dennis spoke on the net, said they had lost the target and the agent, code November. Adrian then made the confession: they were both so damn tired. Dennis added that exhaustion was killing them.

Katie Jennings grimaced at Luke Davies. He grinned.

She said, with a hint of smugness, that in the minibus they had an eyeball, and Davies touched her arm, as if the success over the professionals – however sleep-deprived they might be – was cause for congratulation. Lawson said nothing, but Bugsy contributed that it was well past the time that the agent, November, should be wearing a beacon harness. Deadeye said that when the circumstances were right he'd go forward and hand over the gear.

Shrinks said that exhaustion was a killer and could wreck them.

From a distance, they sat in the minibus and watched, kept the eyeball. Katie Jennings heard a rasped snore, turned sharply. Lawson was behind her, flopped back on the seat. His mouth was wide and the snore a growl. She leaned her shoulder hard against Luke Davies, then buried her face in his coat to stifle her giggles.

Davies did not acknowledge it, had the binoculars up, saw them.

They stood in the rain, back and by the gate.

Mikhail said, 'He's like a kid who's been given a new toy.'

Viktor said, 'I see him as an old man with a young whore sitting on his knee.'

Josef Goldmann said nothing but he watched Reuven Weissberg move among the stones and with him was Johnny Carrick, whom he had thought special, loyal, and now did not know him.

'And all other toys, us, are dumped.'

'The young whore will turn the old man away from his family, us, who have cared for him.'

Josef Goldmann hated the world, everything about it. He was forbidden to make a mobile call to his wife for fear it could be tracked. His stomach for the trading, as he stood in the tipping rain under trees without leaves at the gate, ebbed.

'We have looked after him, helped him, worked with him, are rejected.'

'And the Jew woman, his grandmother, the witch who has never laughed. We looked after him and her, but are ignored.'

Josef Goldmann, watching them, felt his influence slipping.

Mikhail said, 'I don't need to work as a servant for a kid with a new toy and that woman. I have enough. I haven't been there but I hear Cyprus is good.'

Josef Goldmann thought of what he craved beyond all else. He thought of a life without deception, without fraud, a career of legitimacy. He was in the rain under a bare-branched tree beside a rusted gate that hung askew. He thought of the parents he met at school evenings, their legitimacy, and he thought of meetings in the City to which his deceit gave him access. He thought of staring down at the street from the first-floor window of his salon, and seeing it filled with police cars.

'We're all trapped men. You are, I am. Whether Johnny Carrick is the new toy or the young whore, he's trapped too. So, I hear you both. Now answer me. Will you go to him, Mikhail, and say you wish to leave and go to Cyprus? Will you do it, Viktor? Will I? Does it only rain in this fucking country?'

They shuffled, fidgeted, smoked, and they waited as they had been told to, and the two men moved among the stones, tortoise fast, in front of them.

Carrick was led. He sensed that, long ago, all of the stones in the Jews' cemetery at Chelm had been toppled and that some were replacements for those broken an age ago. A month after the invasion of Iraq and a few weeks before the roadside bomb had exploded, he had been to another cemetery, on the outskirts of Basra. He had held his rifle warily and had walked with others in the patrol among flattened headstones and fractured ones, had trampled in the weeds that grew there and had paused several times to read the faint, wind-scoured, sun-bleached words carved, and he had learned of young men who had died far from home and had served in regiments that had been disbanded after the Great War of which they were casualties: *We shall remember them* . . . Yes, an effort had been made here to right an old wrong and to give a trifle of dignity to the graves of the Jews of Chelm. No, the cemetery outside Basra would not have been repaired and the dead there would not be honoured.

Their feet squashed down layers of wet leaves.

They did a circuit of the graveyard.

Turning, facing the gate where Josef Goldmann, Mikhail and Viktor waited, Reuven Weissberg said, 'You ask little, Johnny.'

'If I talk I don't concentrate, sir. If I don't concentrate I can't do my job.'

'And you don't ask about what I involve you in.'

'In its own good time, sir.'

'As yet I have shown you nothing, Johnny. But I will. I will show you what governs me.'

'Yes, sir.'

They reached the gate. Carrick ignored the hatred shown him in the eyes of Viktor and Mikhail, did not need to note it because he had his own, supreme, protector.

Chapter 16: 15 April 2008

Another town. Another fine church for Catholics and another magnificence for the Orthodox, the one with elegant towers and the other with a great onion dome. Another memorial to the bravery of the Red Army soldiers who had liberated the town, and it was eroded as if the stonework had been eaten by termites. Another neat little square with the clean paving that showed a minimal amount of European grant money had reached the town, and the square had been the priority for renovation. Another street market, where the thinness of clothing and the cheapness of footwear demonstrated that the economy of this forgotten corner of the Union was wrecked. Another corner where a bank had opened, but had more staff than customers, and another pavement where kids lounged with hoods over their heads.

Wlodawa was sited on the Bug river, a triple-junction point where Polish territory met Belarus and Ukraine, and he assumed – from the map he had looked at in the car – that the frontier was in midstream.

Again, he followed, a half-pace behind Reuven Weissberg, and he had the pressure of a pancake holster, filled, on the right side of his belt. He sensed it to be a well-worn trail. He saw nothing that threatened and his right hand hung loose and relaxed against the coat pocket that hid the pancake and the Makharov. They turned off a main road. There was open ground, worn, mud-smeared, with the tracks of cars and bikes, and with split-open rubbish bags on it, and there were concrete apartment blocks.

His man stood, hands on hips. At every other moment, his man had stature and magnetic authority, but here, staring at open ground and blocks of raggedly crumbling apartments, he seemed to shrink, his shoulders to sag. Carrick saw it, and thought he recognized humility.

The rain had eased but sufficient fell on the sloped roofs of the blocks, and he saw the waterfall from two places on the nearest where the guttering was broken or blocked. But, Carrick thought, in his man's eyes this was a shrine, and his man was a pilgrim.

Carrick did not ask for an explanation as to why they were there, why the *mafiya* criminal stood in front of a mess of apartment blocks, his shoulders rounded as if defiance was gone. He looked behind him, as a bodyguard on duty would, and saw the two parked cars but only Mikhail was out of the lead car, lounging against a lamp-post and smoking. It was a shrine. His man was a pilgrim.

Reuven Weissberg said, 'It was where they lived. "They" were the parents, sister and brothers of my grandmother. And where her cousins lived, her uncles and her aunts. It was the place for Jews in Wlodawa. There were small streets, with mud, not tarmacadam, and small houses. Most were built of wood, and there were shops here in kiosks. In other streets there were Polish Christians, the neighbours of my grandmother's family. He, the father of my grandmother, was an expert repairer of watches and clocks and many came to him, Jews and Christians. His skills gave him a reputation. Then there was the war. The Jews were moved, taken to the synagogue and kept there in filth. They were treated no better than cattle. No, I am wrong, it was worse than cattle. Do I bore you, Johnny?'

'No, sir.'

'After many months they were moved again. I believe the father of my grandmother would have kept a few of his tools, what he could carry, when they went to the synagogue. He would have had them with him when they were moved the last time. Did you see the synagogue, Johnny?'

'No, sir.'

'I did not identify it for you. I did not think you would be interested in every place in this town that is important to me, that is in my blood. The street where my grandmother's family had lived was flattened, but there were other streets where Jews and Christians had lived beside each other and they were not destroyed. Christian Poles now lived where Jews had lived, had stolen the homes. Neighbours of the Jews and the customers of my father, whose watches and clocks he had laboured over, abused the column of Jews, threw mud and stones at them. It was done here, where now there is concrete and open ground. And they were marched by Germans and Ukrainians across that bridge. Do you see it?'

'Yes, sir.' Carrick could see an old bridge of steel girders, had a view of it between the blocks.

'Across that bridge. You will see today, later, where they were marched to.'

'Yes, sir.'

'I told you, Johnny, it is in my blood. What happened here and in the forest is in the veins that carry my blood. Can you understand that?'

'I am trying to, sir.'

Carrick thought his man, Reuven Weissberg, a prisoner of a past that had been shaped long before his birth. He seemed to see that column of humanity, men, women and children, young and old, tramping under guard past abusers and their missiles, and seemed to recognize a man who carried, perhaps in an old leather bag, the tools of his trade. Seemed, too, to see a young woman from a photograph, but her hair was as dark as the ravens over the Spey's mouth, not pure and brilliant white.

'I want you to know, sir, that I think I can imagine your grandmother and her family being marched here at gunpoint, and I can hear the abuse given them by those who had lived beside them, and I can feel the blows of rocks hurled at them. I can, sir.'

It was the truth.

Reuven Weissberg reached out, took the hair at the back of Carrick's head and ran his fingers through it. Carrick had not seen him do that to Mikhail or Josef Goldmann.

He did not believe himself to be a wasp or a fly, trapped in a gossamer web, unable to break out. They walked back to the cars.

There was a long embankment, newly built, the Customs buildings, then a modern bridge that spanned the Bug. Flags hung desolate from poles and the wind could not stir them.

Davies had demanded they come here. 'Stands to

reason, doesn't it, that a road crossing of the frontier will be here?' Davies had said. 'They went to Chelm, and this is the road over the border, so it's where it will be. What do you think, Mr Lawson?'

He had won only a slow, sardonic smile; pretty damn typical of the old bastard. Then Lawson murmured about going in search of a toilet, and headed for the café.

It was the Dorohusk Customs point. It straddled the main road from Chelm, Route 12, that crossed the Bug and went on into Ukraine. The only other road links were fifty kilometres to the south, at Ustyluh, where the Bug curved to the east, or ninety kilometres to the north at Brest-Terespol. It had to be here, at Dorohusk, that the weapon – if it was more than a figment of bloody Lawson's imagination, if it *was* a warhead – would be brought over the Bug. They'd be here to meet it, of course. Luke Davies stood beside the minibus door and looked at the creeping flow, the pace of wet mud on a slope, of lorries and trucks, vans and cars that went both ways along the embankment road. If it existed – there would be due warning because the targets would have parked up and the undercover would be with them – it would be on a vehicle such as those in the slow, edging motion towards the bureaucracy of the Customs checks. Their intervention might not be necessary, and that amused Luke Davies. British guys from Revenue and Customs had been on attachment in Poland to drag the locals up to speed, and the Germans had shipped in good detection equipment.

Davies had found something to focus on. A car went forward, a dozen yards at a time, a tiny four-door saloon. It might have been a Fiat, and was heading for Ukraine and it had three – yes, *three* – fridge-size cardboard crates perched on and bound to its roof. He thought this to be the most miserable, God-forsaken corner of the world. The town behind them had been rain-saturated,with an old tank mounted on a plinth in its centre, had oozed failure and decay. There had been life in Sarajevo, sunshine and crisp snow, mountains to get up in summer, and the start-up of wine bars and cafés; even the fought-over villages and small towns of Bosnia-Herzegovina had tried to pull themselves up after the ceasefire. Poverty ruled here, and deprivation, sheer damn drabness and rain.

Lawson had returned, chewing chocolate, and didn't offer him a piece. Shrinks and Bugsy were in the minibus.

'What, in your wisdom, have you decided?'

Damned if he was going to lie down. He wasn't a bloody mongrel with a stomach for scratching. 'This is where it will happen, if anything happens.'

'That's your considered opinion?'

'It is. I don't have, Mr Lawson, the rank or the authority to countermand you – if I did, I would – so I have to plan on the basis that we don't have the help of the Polish agencies. Personally, I would think it could only be beneficial to be alongside the Agencja Bezpieczenstwa Wewnetrznego in this situation.'

It rather pleased Luke Davies that he could reel off the name of the Polish counter-intelligence set-up, not have to rely on the initials, but Lawson gave him no encouragement, was impassive.

'Yes, the ABW would give us additional sur-veillance capacity, and firepower, and would enable the area to be sanitized. The way you're doing it, Mr Lawson, we could be in place, we could have an eyeball, and a hundred and one

441

unforeseens could create a foul-up and we've lost it, whatever it is. Don't, please, have any misplaced ideas of me thrusting myself forward and taking flak when it's your responsibility. Then you'll be on your own and I'll be cheering from the sidelines. Don't say I haven't fronted up with you, Mr Lawson.'

'Put it all in your report at the end, young man, and I'm sure it'll receive due attention.'

He saw Lawson walk away and the fist crumpled the chocolate wrapper. The paper was taken to an overflowing bin and laid on top of the rubbish. Lawson had walked through what was almost a dense carpet of cigarette packets, dog ends, empty crisps bags and other junk. Davies thought it the gesture of pomposity. His temper was rising, and his inability to rouse reaction hurt him.

'And another thing. I heard what Shrinks said. He talked about the syndrome. I spoke to him about it. A victim of the syndrome will need aftercare, maybe hospitalization and certainly counselling. He will be traumatized and potentially scarred. It's down to you, Mr Lawson. You've thrown our man, November, into the arms of a psychopathic criminal. That, too, will be in my report.'

'It'll be a weighty volume.'

He could have hit the man. Luke Davies could have clenched his fist, swung it back and punched his full weight quite happily and he was breathing hard, towards hyperventilation. No, no, damned if he'd lose his career for this priggish, vain old man.

He heard Lawson say to Bugsy, at the driver's window of the minibus, 'I think young Davies has concluded his comprehensive reconnaissance, so it'll be safe to leave this place. It's totally irrelevant as a location, but he's been humoured.'

The engine started. Lawson had taken his place on the wide back seat. A door was left open for Davies. He stamped to it. He didn't understand where, if not here, a contraband package of the size of a warhead – if it existed – could be brought across.

Mikhail had a GPS wedged between his legs. It bucked when his feet moved on the pedals. With gum, he had stuck a scrap of paper on to the dashboard at the base of the wheel, but the characters scrawled on it were in Cyrillic. Carrick couldn't read them. They were off the main road.

The track was deep-rutted, sandy soil. Trees pressed close to it, broken only occasionally by small fields in which the grass had no goodness. Carrick thought the snow had thawed only days earlier. Small houses were in the trees or at the fields' edges, and there was a cross of white-painted stone with its arms broken off. The wide nests of storks were on high poles.

He had seen lakes on the left side, wide and rippled by the wind. Reuven Weissberg had not spoken. Neither had Mikhail.

Carrick could see a wide expanse of water through ranks of birch trees that sloped down to it. Mikhail passed the GPS back over his shoulder, then the paper with the numbers. Carrick understood. The numbers were longitude and latitude co-ordinates, and now they matched the GPS reading. An oath was spat behind him. Doors snapped open.

They tripped down the slope, swerving between the trees, and reached the water's edge. Carrick was not called and hung back. Josef Goldmann and Viktor came to him. Carrick swung to face them

443

and saw Josef Goldmann shake his head slowly and sadly, as if it was a moment of defeat, and Viktor grimaced as if to indicate that the problem was not his, or the solving of it. The water stretched away, and Carrick saw the tops of fence posts jutting up, and on the far side of the water a dense tree line and in it a place of bright colour. He squinted to see the source better. There was a red post. He understood more.

He understood about rain, about floodwater rising over fields, about frontier markers, about co-ordinates given for a meeting-place.

Carrick would go to Reuven Weissberg when he was called, not otherwise. Understood that they had not taken cognizance of the floodwaters rising in Ukraine and filling the Bug river far beyond its capacity. He heard Reuven Weissberg's howl. The volleys of his swearing seemed to bounce away over the water as if flat stones were thrown and skipped. Beside Carrick, in his good coat, Josef Goldmann sat on wet sand and leaves, and held his head in his hands.

Carrick walked away, stepped carefully over the loose, sodden ground, and took a place among the trees. He'd thought that the banks were steeper less than a quarter of a mile from where he was, and that where the banks were steeper the river was deeper, faster and better confined.

Storks came upstream, flew prettily with a slow wingbeat, but they veered off when confronted with the oaths, blasphemies, obscenities of Reuven Weissberg.

He had a large-scale map of the place. The Crow had driven his hire car south-east from Hamburg and he was out in the depths of the Lüneburger

Heide. The instructions given him had guided him to a point north of the town of Münster and west of Ebstorf. He turned into a car park.

There were the skeleton frames of swings and kids' slides ahead of him, and near the entrance to the car park was a wooden-faced toilet block. Just beyond the gravel-stopping area a rail prevented vehicles going further. One car was there, its interior light on, engine running, fumes billowing from its exhaust, but the toilets were padlocked and the play area was deserted.

His headlights moved on the swings and slides, the toilet block, flitted over the expanse of gorse and bracken and caught the bare branches of birches at the end of their reach. Then they came to rest on the other car. The Crow's lights had no power because the late afternoon was not yet evening, and he had only a marginal glimpse of the man in the driving seat. He thought he was young, clean-shaven, with neatly cut hair, but it was only an impression. He came to a stop about twenty-five metres from the other car but on the same side of the parking area, and switched off his engine.

The quiet fell on him.

He knew little of quiet. The greater part of the Crow's life was lived among the deafening action of major construction sites. To be heard above the roar of dumper trucks, excavators, bulldozers, pile hammers driving down foundation columns, it was usual for him to shout and for that harsh voice to resonate; his voice was heard throughout the big building developments of the Gulf. When he went to Pakistan, to the crowded towns and cities of the North-West Frontier, it was his habit to hold his meetings and exchange information in the noisiest, most crowded bazaars. He was at home in noise, bustle and confusion. He moved on the car seat to ease a slight stiffness, and the squeak of the springs rang in the interior. So quiet . . . He wound down the window. More quiet flooded round him.

He had no photograph and no name. The Crow knew only that the man was from the subcontinent, had no facial hair and was in his early thirties. He had been given a sentence to start, and the contact would complete it.

He strained to hear, but there was only the low purr of the car's engine along that side of the parking area. They could be in the gorse, or the bracken, or in the dunes where the birches grew, or behind the toilet shed. They might have weapons, high-velocity sniper rifles and low-velocity machine pistols, trained on the two cars. He approached, and knew a moment of maximum danger. He knew of no operative – as experienced as himself, or as inexperienced as he expected the contact to be – who did not dread the 'cold' meeting with a stranger. Then the chance of compromise was greatest, and of ambush, arrest and the nightmare of interrogation. It must be done. His heart pounded. The Crow was a survivor, long term with the Organization, had adapted from the disciplines of the old central authority of the sheikh and his inner circle and taken on the broken cellular system with cut-outs and fire-walls. But he felt the hammering tension in his chest as he opened the car door.

Cold wind hit him. Rain specked his cheeks. He shivered. He wondered if they watched him and if they had guns aimed on him.

He walked towards the other car, and the light around him was fast fading.

The window was lowered.

The Crow spoke in Arabic: 'Where was the cave in which Gabriel appeared to the Prophet . . . ?'

He said what he had been told to say, said it exactly in the Arabic that was so foreign to him. 'The cave in which Gabriel appeared to the Prophet was in the mountain of Hira that is near to the holy city of Mecca.'

Sak hoped he had pronounced it correctly. He had rehearsed it endlessly while he sat in the car in the parking area on the heath.

He saw a man with lined skin, thin lips and scars on his face. The hands extended to him were rough, calloused. Sak had thought that the man he would meet, who held seniority, would have the appearance of a scholar, an intellectual, a thinker and a hero. His fingers were crushed briefly in the fists of a labourer – and the voice was frightening. The words had been croaked at him.

He had waited for three hours, had agonized at the isolation of the heathland. No children had come to play here, no hikers or dog-walkers, and the fears in his mind had multiplied like bad dreams. They had stacked up, one after another. His fingers were loosed. Three hours . . . The man turned away. Three hours, and the contact moment, already, was broken.

'Please, what should happen?'

'We rest, we wait.' The man spoke over his shoulder. 'We wait until they come.'

'When will that be?'

'They make their collection in the morning before dawn. They should be here at the end of tomorrow, but perhaps before.'

It was said like a dismissal, but Sak pressed: 'For

447

the night, do I come to your car? Do you come to mine?'

The man had not turned. 'And you see my face better, you hear my voice better, I see your face and hear your voice? No . . . And we have no names, no life histories. We work and we part.'

Sak felt as if he had been kicked. The man went to his car, reached on to the back seat and lifted clear a big plastic bag, well weighted. When he returned to Sak he had adjusted his headscarf so that his cheeks and mouth were obscured. The bag was dropped through the window on to Sak's lap.

He was abandoned. Often he would look across the empty space at the other car, but he never saw movement in it before the dusk thickened. He sat in the car, trembled and thought that, at last, the war he had been recruited to was real, touchable. He held the package close but didn't open it.

They were out on their feet, Deadeye had reckoned, but they'd done well. Now Adrian and Dennis would be in the car, one sprawled out across the back seat, the other wedged against the wheel, the handbrake and the gear lever, and they'd have crashed. They'd brought Deadeye to within a half-mile of the river. Beside the car he had slipped on his camouflage coat, then threaded sprigs and branches into the cloth slots. He wore a woven mask over his face. Deadeye had checked his appearance in the side mirror of the car and been happy. He'd gone forward.

He'd recognized that limping walk.

He'd seen the agent sidle away from the cars and the Russians, had recalled the little bastard he'd jumped on the step of a City of London office block, and had watched him move upstream, then settle and take a position against the base of a tree trunk. Deadeye had seen a kingfisher flash past, low over the water, a spark of colour in the gloom.

Time to do the business.

He did a long loop behind the agent. He would approach from the far side, away from the Russians and the main man, the target, who was still at the bank, but whose cursing was now sporadic, not on automatic. Far back in the trees, Deadeye walked quiet and easy on the balls of his feet. Coming closer, losing the dense cover and the darkness, he was bent double, minimizing the shape and silhouette of his head and torso. He tested each footfall and had the sensitivity in his toes, through his boots, to find dead branches that a sprinkling of old leaves might have covered. Shape and silhouette were important, but sound was as big on Deadeye's check-list.

When he was within fifty yards of the agent, Deadeye went down on his hands and knees. It would have been best to use the good old leopard crawl, but that would have disturbed too much of the detritus on the forest floor, and he'd have made a noise like a damn pig rooting. He still had the suppleness in his elbows, shoulders, pelvis and knees, good at his age, to match a crab's advance, and his stomach was held at a constant couple of inches above the leaves and twigs beneath him. He couldn't see the agent's face, only the top of his arm and his kneecap.

He had learned to survive off cold meals-ready-to-eat, to wrap his faeces in tinfoil, to defeat the interest of sheep, cattle and farmers' dogs, to be a hidden creature on the move.

He reached the agent, was behind him.

'Don't make a fracas, mate,' Deadeye whispered.

The head twisted, eyes raked him.

'Don't jump, shout. Keep still.' He pulled the mask netting off his face. 'That's right, mate, nothing sudden and nothing loud . . . like nothing's happening.'

The package, light, narrow cloth straps and the box, which was the size of one for safety matches, had been snug in his pocket. He lifted it out.

'Now, mate, without a fuss, swing yourself round a bit, body this side of the tree.'

The agent did. Well, that was a shock for Deadeye. He'd seen the man at a distance – in Berlin, in Warsaw, in Chelm that morning and in Wlodawa that afternoon – but it was the first time he'd been up close to him since the pavement in the City. God, he'd bloody aged. 'That's good, mate. Now your coat off, easy movements, nothing sharp.'

The agent had that haunted look in his eyes, a pallor on his skin, and the lines at his mouth were deeper set. Then the light was in the eyes, and they blazed.

'Look, mate, I don't have time to mess. Just get the coat off.'

The straps and the box, the tracker beacon were in Deadeye's hand. The eyes were on him, recognition knotting the forehead, but the fingers fumbled for the jacket fastenings.

'You were, I saw you – you . . .' A stammering voice.

'I was, mate – doesn't matter. That's right, coat off and shirt open.'

'In London, you were . . . The gun. You tried to—'

'Nothing's what it seems, mate. I didn't try much. It was you did the action. Now, arms out.'

He reached inside the shirt and started to thread

450

the straps of the harness across the agent's spine and over his shoulder.

'You fired twice, you tried to kill . . .'

'Easy. You gave me a bloody great kick in the goolies. Not black still, but bloody yellow.'

'You fired twice. It was to murder—'

'You know nothing, mate.'

'Two bloody shots. I know about that.'

Deadeye grinned. God, the agent was an innocent. He shifted him, worked the straps round the spine, then tightened them for the Velcro to grip. And when the agent shifted, Deadeye saw the pancake in the belt, and the butt of a handgun. God, the agent was an innocent and had gone native. Didn't think Mr Lawson would like hearing that November had packed a weapon provided by the bad guys, wouldn't like that at all.

'That's it, nice and steady, just fastening it up. You've led the surveillance a fair old dance. They can't keep it up, have to kip, so we need the tag on you. Very nice, good fit.'

He eased his hands back. Didn't like the handgun, and Mr Lawson wouldn't . . . The harness was close to the agent's vest, and he smelled – and Deadeye smelled. Probably they both smelled equal to well-hung ducks, or like the badgers' carcasses that were tossed into the ditches alongside roads. He saw anger build in the eyes.

Wasn't for Deadeye to button up the shirt and refasten the jacket. 'So, mate, that's it. Oh, so's you know, we're all with you. It's a good job you're doing. Keep at it, mate.'

The hiss in the voice. 'You tried to kill my boss. You fired twice. He was dead if I hadn't intervened. I could have taken a bullet. I was unarmed, my boss was – I reckoned it rivals, hoods, *mafiya*, not my people. Two men, defenceless . . . That makes you a right bloody coward.'

'Dead? Ooh, yes. Coward? Right you are, mate. Great imagination.' Those who knew him, had worked with him, didn't regard Deadeye as chatty, thought of him as a man of few words, usually necessary ones. Not just Adrian and Dennis who were tired. Deadeye was too. Hadn't slept properly in four nights, hadn't slept at all in the last forty-something hours, and was pretty much at the end of his tether.

'Imagination? The weapon discharged twice.'

Deadeye had the agent's shoulder in his fist. 'That was blanks. Didn't you know that? Thought you were a paratrooper. There was nothing real. Only thing real was the kick in my goolies, and the bruises. The worst the blanks could have done was singe you. It was to push you, give you the shove into their arms. It worked, just as the guv'nor said it would. Don't call me a coward.'

The agent stared at him and it was like the light died in those eyes, and the anger.

Deadeye had the receiver box in his hand and a green light flashed. Had he tweaked the volume he would have had a constant bleep. Good signal, strong.

He was gone.

On hands and knees for the first fifty yards, bent low for the next hundred, fast on his toes and the balls of his feet till he reached the car. They were both snoring gently. Deadeye put the receiver on to the grille on the dashboard, beside the satnav. He crawled into the back, eased a bit of space for himself from Dennis but didn't wake him. He closed his eyes and let his head drop. The bleep was good, comforting.

* * *

Yashkin had set himself a target, a challenging one.

The target of Major (Ret'd) Oleg Yashkin was to find, that evening, entertainment in the Belarus city of Pinsk that would change the mood, ease the melancholy, of Colonel (Ret'd) Igor Molenkov.

The light had dropped and the rain had not lifted when Yashkin drove the Polonez into the inner streets of the city. His first impression: Pinsk was a pit. He said, with bogus cheerfulness, 'I reckon it looks a fine place.'

'You must be blind,' Molenkov growled. 'It's a shit-hole.'

'A fine place, and one where we'll find a meal, a bar, somewhere to sleep for three, four hours before we move on.'

'You think, here, we'll find a good meal without cockroaches in the kitchens, a good bar where the glasses have been decently washed that's not for whores to work in? You're optimistic. What do we know of Pinsk?'

'A definition of optimism: "Whatever is, is right." I was told that by Poliakoff, the academician in theoretical physics in my time. It was how he coped with the regime, pressures, then the scaling down in resources. The quotation is from the German philosopher, Leibniz.'

'It's shit. I repeat, what do we know of Pinsk?'

Yashkin could have told him what he'd read in the guidebook when he'd planned the legs of the journey. Pinsk was on the confluence of the Pina and Pripat rivers, had been a Slavic centre in the eleventh century, sacked by Cossack marauders and the captured wounded buried alive. A canal linking the city to the Vistula river and the Baltic Sea was in disrepair, but it had the church of St

Barbara and the Franciscan monastery . . . but he didn't know where they could eat and drink.

'I know nothing, except that we must eat something, then sleep a little and move on.'

'Yes, yes,' Molenkov said heavily. 'And after that we must make our delivery.'

Yashkin found a parking place at the edge of the old town. It was dark, poorly lit. In front of him was the start of what he presumed would be a network of narrow streets. He saw few cars – and those that were there sped past – and fewer pedestrians, who were hurrying as if anxious to be elsewhere. He looked for neon signs advertising food and drink, and a hotel that would have secure lock-up garaging, and saw only shadows. The schedule, to be kept to, allowed for a meal, a drink or three, a short sleep, then the last section of the drive west. The rendezvous point from the code message was now – Yashkin estimated – a mere hundred and thirty-five kilometres ahead. He stepped out of the car, went to the back and unlocked the tail hatch.

He gazed at the bulk of the tarpaulin. He reached inside, past their bags, wriggled his hand under it and let it lie on the canvas coating of the Zhukov. He was smiling to himself. Had he expected to feel its warmth? Of course not. Was he certain he hadn't expected to register on his fingertips the evidence that it lived? Well . . . no, not certain. He understood and was tolerant of the doubts, hesitations, confusions that battled in Molenkov's mind. Molenkov had not lived with the beast for the past fifteen years – it had not been in his garden, under lettuces and carrots, cabbages and potatoes in summer and under the winter snow, it had never been on a cart pushed by conscripts under

Molenkov's control, going through the security of the main gate at Arzamas-16. He took his hand from the roughness of the canvas, strewed sheets of newspaper over the uniforms to hide them, then slammed the hatch. He locked the Polonez, walked round the car and tested each door, satisfied himself that the vehicle was secure and offered no target of opportunity to thieves.

Molenkov was up the street and called, 'Yashkin, up here, on the left. I think there may be a place.'

Yashkin wondered if they could eat fish there, or whether Pinsk was too near to the zone of Chernobyl and that part of the Pripat river. He would like some fish – carp or bream, but a pike would be best, with herbs . . . A dream. Yashkin would eat anything, and wash away the taste with beer – was there a local brew? Food occupied him, and drink. He felt the acute stiffness in his hips and lower back from that long leg, and the legs he had driven in the previous days. He did not look around, was not alert, had no suspicions. The street was empty except for Molenkov and a distant light in garish red and green. He did not ask himself why it was empty and what district of Pinsk he had come to.

He remembered. Now Yashkin remembered what the book had said in the library reading room in Sarov. Beer was indeed brewed in Belarus – three beers. Now he could recall the names of only two: Lidskoe and Krynitsa. He struggled to remember the third, and he was ten paces from Molenkov.

'Age, my friend, the ravage of age. I can't name all the Belarus-brewed beers, only two of three. One escapes.'

He would have expected Molenkov to give him a finger of derision, to laugh at him or curse the irrelevance of his memory difficulty, but he saw, instead, Molenkov sag to a crouch, his mouth wide open as if to shout, his fists raised. The blow, from behind, felled Yashkin.

He was clubbed. The impact point was between the back of his neck and the centre of his left shoulder-blade. The breath sang from his throat. He gasped, but had no voice. His legs were kicked from under him. He collapsed, sprawled on the darkened pavement. Two men came past him.

He could barely distinguish them. They closed on Molenkov. Yashkin had no strength and less will to fight. Didn't think, had he wanted to, that he could have struggled to his feet and gone to his friend's aid.

Molenkov fought them.

His eyes welled, but he was able to blink hard enough to keep back tears, but the pain was a cruel ache that spread down his arm, up his neck and along his back. Maybe in Molenkov there were faint stirrings of the memory of an unarmed combat course in his early days as an officer recruit in State Security. Maybe, before going to the arsehole spying role of political officer, Molenkov had been on a gymnasium mat and shown how to throw men around, near break their arms, legs, whatever. Yashkin could only watch, couldn't intervene.

They laughed. The two bastards laughed.

They stood away from Molenkov for a moment, and their laughter – more a fucking giggle – rang out on the street. Molenkov confronted them, dared them to advance on him, but the crouch posture made it seem he was about to crap and his hands were raised, like they did in bad movies. They laughed one last time, then went in on Molenkov. Punches broke through his guard, and the short cosh swung down. Molenkov slumped, and the boots went in. Still he fought them. They were over him, fucking hyenas, and his legs thrashed at them. He must have bitten one because there was a stifled scream, then an obscenity, then a shower of blows. Yashkin thought it brave of Molenkov, and didn't know whether he would have dared to do the same. They were bent over his friend, and Yashkin saw the wallet held up. Then one broke away, came to him and knelt over him.

Now Yashkin knew he would not resist, not imitate his friend. He was curled up, and his head was hidden by his hands but he could see through his fingers. Hands came into his coat, searched, pried, and found the fold-over wallet his wife, 'Mother', had given him as a May Day present thirty-one years earlier. It was taken, and the man stood. The smell of his breath, beer and nicotine, faded, but he saw a guy with a leather jacket, black, a tattoo on the neck, and a shaven head that the rain danced on.

He realized, and it came hard, that they were not any more a colonel and a major of State Security. They were two old men who did not have the wit to protect themselves in a strange city – fucking Pinsk. Their wallets were opened, the cash was taken out with the credit cards – not that they would be of any use in Pinsk – and the bastards took the time, had the arrogance, to count the money. Even divided it.

Their emptied wallets were dropped on the pavement.

The bastards did not run to get clear; they walked. They did not look back, as if they had left behind them nothing that might threaten.

He did what he was capable of. He crawled to his

friend. He took Molenkov's head in his hands and listened to the moan of breath sucked between swollen, bloodied lips.

Molenkov slurred, 'What did you say "optimism" was?'

Yashkin said, 'I said, quoting Leibniz, "Whatever is, is right."'

Molenkov staggered to his feet, and Yashkin supported him. The one-time *zampolit* said, 'I have a few coins in my pocket, enough for the toilet cleaner, but all my banknotes were in my wallet.'

'I have some coins in my pocket, and my wallet is empty.'

'What else is near to empty, my friend, if not quite?'

'I don't know.'

Each now held the other upright, breathing hard, seeking to control pain. What was worse than pain – Yashkin's view – was the humiliation of what had happened.

Molenkov tried to crack a smile, which hurt and his teeth ground together. He mumbled, 'It will be hard to be optimistic – "Whatever is, is right" – but we need money to fill the fuel tank, and we're against the red, very near to it. We have no money to buy fuel. Maybe enough for bread, but not for fuel.'

He sagged. Molenkov would have gone down again, on to the pavement, had Yashkin not held him. Yashkin took him back up the street and, near to one of the old churches, found a bench. He could see the car from there. Molenkov slept first, snored through his weeping, thickened lips, and Yashkin knew he would follow him.

He remembered it . . . He rejoiced. Yashkin remembered that the third brand of beer brewed in

Belarus had the Alevaria label but Molenkov slept and snored and he didn't wake him.

He heard a whistle, then his name was called.

Carrick did not know how long he had sat in darkness with his back against the tree, but the stiffness was locked in his hips and knees, and his balance almost betrayed him as he stood. He had to grasp the tree trunk to stop himself sliding down and away.

The whistle, then the call, had come faintly, but both were foreign sounds, recognizable against the constant rumbling murmur of the river. The clouds had broken. A moon flitted in the gaps and then there was light on the water. The rain came in spasmodic bursts and he was drenched from sitting against the tree above the Bug. He thought that if he lost his footing and went into it – if he went under – he would be lost. He might panic, open his mouth and swallow a stomach and lungful of water, might have his head hit by a submerged branch and be stunned, might be so disoriented that he swam for the centre of the river where the currents were fiercest and not for the bank where he might catch a root or a rock in his fist. If he went in, chances were that he was gone.

He started out along the bank, headed for where the whistle had come from. Deep in thought, Carrick had whiled away time. The harness was tight on his skin and the vest under his shirt, sweater and coat, while the box pinched the flesh at the small of his back when he moved.

In the darkness, he groped back towards Reuven Weissberg. Almost careered into him. Was a yard from him when the moon's light hit his shoulders and lit his face.

'What do I do, Johnny?'

'Tell me, sir.'

'They come to the far side.'

'You meet them on the far side, sir?'

'Meet them, then take back what they bring. Lift it across the river . . . I had not thought of the flood. I was going to use a rope between trees on their side and our side. I had not considered the flood. What do I do?'

Alone against the tree, while dusk had gone to evening and dullness to black, he had thought of the command in the warehouse that Mikhail back off, of the kiss on the cheeks beside the Vistula under the walls of the Stare Miasto, of the trust given him and the weapon handed to him . . . had thought of the friendship.

For a moment Carrick pondered. He filled his lungs, and didn't realize that the scales tipped further. There had been a week on the Brecon mountains in a tent bivouac, way up north from Merthyr, and there had been one of those shite courses for leadership evaluation. Carrick's platoon had been tasked to do the humping for the officer candidates, and a river was in spate. The winning team had had an officer – not the usual Rupert idiot – who had called the best solution, the only time he had spoken. Carrick remembered.

'How big is what they're bringing, sir?'

'Perhaps fifty kilos. The size would be nearly a metre high and nearly a half-metre across. Then I assume it has extra protection round it.'

'Can it get wet?'

'I don't think so. That cannot be risked.'

'Can the men who are bringing it take responsibility for getting it to this side?'

'No. They are old.'

Carrick remembered how the officer had planned the crossing of a river in spate in the Brecon mountains. He asked, 'Could you, sir, find a small boat?'

'I think I have seen one.'

'It's a small boat we need, sir, for you and me.'

And Johnny Carrick, beside the Bug river, which was huge and flooded with the rain falling on central Ukraine, did not see that his loyalties had blurred and slipped.

Chapter 17: 16 April 2008

They were beside a lake. To reach it, Carrick reckoned they had walked three miles.

He had thought it remarkable that Reuven Weissberg, the Russian who had lived variously in Perm, Moscow and Berlin, could follow trails and tracks through the forest, could move there with the latent confidence of an animal whose place it was. He had followed as exactly as possible under the trees. His target had stayed as the centre of Reuven Weissberg's back, and when he lost it, the penalty was to blunder into tree trunks or have his face whipped by low branches.

Carrick had been alerted that they approached the lake by the splashes and call of water fowl. Near to it, they had moved along a track wide enough for a tractor and trailer, and he had fallen into one of the deeper ruts left by a tyre. He had been pitched forward, his momentum catching Reuven Weissberg's haunches. For a moment, then, a hand had been at Carrick's throat, tight, hard and squeezing. He had choked once, then heard laughter. He had been on his knees and the hand had left his throat and lifted him ... Strange laughter, and not from a world Carrick knew. The same hand had gone to his shoulders and gripped them; then they had gone the last yards and the lake had been in front of them. Remarkable – no map, no compass and the GPS not used. Carrick thought that Reuven Weissberg knew the forest and the routes through it as a native would, or as a boar or a deer.

The tree line ran right to the water's edge.

He was told, 'I was here once. A man had been fishing. I did not speak to him and he would not have known that I watched him. He brought a boat to this place and tied it, then left it.'

He was not told why Reuven Weissberg had been in the forest, moving with the secrecy of a hunter or a beast.

The moon found a cloud gap. The water shimmered and there were ripples to match the squeal of the birds. They went to the very edge. He thought of those few seconds when his throat had been gripped, then freed, and when the fist had taken hold of his coat and the strength of the man had lifted him, of the ferocity of the first seconds and the kindness that had followed. The boat was there. Old abilities had returned. His vision in the darkness, augmented by the moon's glow, was more complete than it had been when they had begun the trek through the forest. Light reflected up from the water.

There was a small inlet in the bank, a little gouge, and there was a tree with submerged roots at its mouth that would have given shelter to the place. Across the inlet was the angled black shape. He could only admire the faith Reuven Weissberg had shown in his judgement and memory. That faith had bred certainty. He followed.

He murmured, 'I'll do the business, sir. I will.'

Carrick eased past. He held on to the splayed sprigs of branches as he went down and into the water. His hands groped the length of the boat – well, not so much a boat, more a small punt. It was the sort of craft that some towed behind a narrowboat while navigating the Thames or the Grand Union Canal. There were times when it was easier to moor on an open bank, perhaps where cattle were, and then a punt was needed to paddle across the river or the waterway to get to a pub or a minimarket. He thought of a failed loving on a narrowboat during the night that he'd been recruited, volunteered, and of her in the arms of the young man who had come with the old bully. His fingers found the punt's dimensions, narrow and squared off at front and back, and there was a single board across its centre where a man could sit, paddle or fish from. He reckoned that the sides of the punt were some nine inches, less than a foot, above the water line. He knew little of boats. They had no place on the Spey near its mouth. The water was too fast, there were too many submerged and lethal rocks, and the anglers going after salmon used chest waders to get to the head of a prime pool. Paratroopers did not do water and boats, left them to what they called the 'cabbage hats' – paratroops called anybody not wearing a red beret by that title, emphasized it for marines with their green headgear – and reckoned small craft were show-ponies' toys. There was a rope at the front of the boat and it was hooked to a ring, then looped up to a thick branch. It came away easily.

He took it and pulled the boat round, then laid the rope on his shoulder and heaved. It came up more easily than he'd have thought likely. It slithered out of the inlet, then up the shallow bank. The mud helped it.

He tipped it over and rainwater dribbled out. Carrick said, his voice a whisper, 'That's good, sir. It was holding water – it means it's sound. Know what I mean, sir? It doesn't leak.'

But he had nothing to boast of. The river in the Brecon mountains had been a fifth the width, maximum, of the Bug, and the flow had seemed strong when the officer candidates had crossed it but that strength was little compared to the rush of the Bug when he had sat above it. The plan was his. He, Carrick, had suggested it, had not kept his mouth shut. The punt, on the bank and at his feet, seemed so small, fragile, for the job.

'With this boat, Johnny, it will happen? We can cross?'

'Yes, sir.'

He saw, in that faint light from the moon scudding in the cloud base, that Reuven Weissberg had gone to the front of the punt and lifted it. Carrick asked for a minute's delay, moved off and went into the trees a few yards down the lake's bank. It didn't seem a big action to him, or a matter of great importance. He took off his coat, dropped it, and was satisfied that his actions couldn't be seen. Then he unbuttoned his shirt from neck to waist, and tugged at the Velcro on the straps. Not big and not great.

When he was back, that minute used up, he took a grip on the punt, and the weight was shared. They started to go back the way they had come.

On the little screen, Bugsy had the co-ordinates. With the numbers there was a green light that was constant, not flashing, and the numbers hadn't changed. Also on Bugsy's lap was the map, and he used a pencil torch with a small, narrow beam to check the co-ordinates against a location. He dozed and drifted into sleep, then out of it. If the co-ordinate numbers changed and the bug moved – as it had earlier – the light switched to red. He had its position.

In the minibus, Adrian and Dennis had taken the front seats. Every few minutes one of them would wake and Bugsy would put a hand on the shoulder, lean forward and murmur in the ear of whichever had woken to get back to bloody sleep. The poor sods needed it. Fantastic, they'd been, with their foot surveillance and vehicle tailing, and they needed the rest. His bug worked a treat.

Bugsy was beside Mr Lawson, the guv'nor, squashed up against the door while Mr Lawson had a full two-thirds of the seat. He'd tried a couple of times to shift him further back across the seat, once with the gentle prodding of his elbow and once with the sharp use of his toecap, but had failed to achieve more space for himself. In the back, behind him and wedged in with the bags and the gear, the jump seats folded away, were Deadeye and Shrinks. Shrinks slept, but not Deadeye. Bugsy thought that if they were going to repeat this caper and sleep in the vehicles again, they'd need to get to a ditch or a stream and get some *dhobi* done. He'd have smelled pretty grim on his own, but there were six in the minibus and the accumulation of them, their socks and underwear stank it out. Socks and underwear needed washing. Well, no one had known how long they'd be gone.

The light stayed constant and the figures on the screen did not alter.

Bugsy would not have thought envy a sin,

merely something that disturbed the equilibrium of colleagues thrown together on an operation. Mr Lawson, as was right for the guv'nor, was in the minibus, in a position to react at speed to information thrown up by the screen. The car was free. The two vehicles were off the main road now and had found a safe, out-of-sight parking place in a camping area about halfway between the river and where the bug beacon now was. Well, the car had been free ... The girl had gone to it ... The lanky lad, the guv'nor's sidekick, had headed there too. Maybe one was in the front and the other was in the back. Maybe they were in the back together. He didn't know, but he felt that little surge of envy at the thought of them – nice girl, and good at what she had to do. His wife said the only females he fancied were the ones in his lofts, those that could fly fast.

The figures on the screen did not change. Neither did the green light go to red.

Dawn came, and they gathered. With the first low rays of sunshine, they came back to the central point that equated with the longitude and latitude numbers given in the coded message.

The formation along the bank had seen Mikhail and Viktor take the two furthest reaches of the Bug river, and two hundred metres from each of them had been Reuven, their *avoritet*, and the Englishman they mistrusted. At the centre point, overlooking the river and the Belarus frontier marker, was Josef Goldmann ... The instructions had been quite clear. The men from Sarov should only approach the far riverbank, in darkness, and should signal their arrival by torchlight. No flashes, no signal had been given.

For the last three hours, an eternity, they had been spread out over eight hundred metres of the Bug's western bank. Had he been a Catholic or an Orthodox believer, Josef Goldmann would have said he had 'lapsed', or become 'agnostic'. The Jewish faith for him had never existed, not as a child and not in adult life but – almost – he had prayed to see a light wink on the far side, or to hear a shrill whistle from Viktor or Mikhail. There had been no signal, and he was at the meeting point to which they returned, and hidden behind him, under dead branches, was the boat, ridiculously small, that Reuven and Johnny had brought, and with it the length of coiled rope. What had been not a prayer but a fervent wish and a hope had not been answered. Josef Goldmann could not remember when, if ever, he had been so cold, so miserable and so near to despair. The hours had slipped away, darkness and moonlight had become a grey smear, then the lowest beams from the sun had pierced the trees on the far side. Dearly, he wanted to take his mobile from his pocket, dial the numbers and hear Esther's voice, but he dared not disobey the order given him.

They came coughing and spitting, stretching and grunting, cursing the new day, all except Johnny. The Englishman, his own man and saviour, was quiet, withdrawn. Josef Goldmann noticed that Johnny's jacket was unfastened and his shirt unbuttoned, and thought it extraordinary on a night when rain had laced down on them between the isolated moments when it had stopped and the moon had been visible and had lit the river.

He sensed the exhaustion in Reuven and Johnny. Before they had taken their spread positions, Reuven had spoken briefly of bringing the small boat from a lake by the village of Okuninka, carrying it through an expanse of forest so that its keel did not scrape a track, dragging it on the road and hiding at the side if cars came, manhandling it through the forest and past the old campsite where the killings had been done, and bringing it to the Bug bank. He had thought it incredible, a feat of strength . . . but the boat was so small and the river so wide, its flow so awesome.

Josef Goldmann, teeth chattering, said to any who might listen to him, 'Perhaps they will not come.'

Viktor, surly, answered, 'They will come. I arranged the detail. They will come.'

'Perhaps they can't come – an accident, a delay. A change of heart and—'

Viktor said, 'If they don't come, I'll go to them and break every bone in their bodies. They'll come.'

'A change of heart and the realization of what they're doing. Why do those men want a "million American dollars"?' He realized he was babbling and that his words, Russian and English, were jumbled. 'How can they spend a million American dollars? I don't think they'll come.'

He had seen, as he had spoken of money – the scale of it – in English, that Johnny Carrick's eyebrows rose a fraction, and then he had looked away fast. Maybe, too, Viktor had seen it. Of course, Johnny Carrick didn't know what would come across the river, if *they* reached it, didn't know what was worth one million American dollars.

Reuven said, detached, 'It's very simple. We watch again this evening.'

'So, we wait. What shall we do for twelve hours till the evening? What?'

He thought then that Viktor eyed him with

contempt, that Mikhail sneered, and Reuven didn't bother to answer him, and he thought that this purchase and sale had broken them, split apart the bonds of their group. It would never be the same again. Together they had climbed so high and so fast in Perm and Moscow, and Reuven had climbed higher in Berlin, while Goldmann had soared in the City of London.

He heard Reuven say to Johnny Carrick, 'Come with me, walk with me.'

'Yes, sir.'

They were gone, lost among the trees.

Now Josef Goldmann scoured the far bank of the Bug until the sun's intensity burned his eyes, and knew they should never have travelled to this place, but could not say why he felt a gathering fear for what they did and its consequences.

The journey that was Reuven Weissberg's life was a thread of cotton unrolled from a spool.

Carrick stood at the edge of the trees, with the forest behind him, and listened. He heard a story told without emotion.

The cotton's thread had been anchored here, and it had made a great loop but had come back and now the spool was empty. In front of him was an old rail head. From the junction one track continued into the forest he had walked through, trailing after Reuven Weissberg, but near to him now was a spur in the track, a siding that came to an end in the winter-yellowed grass and beyond the last sleeper was a buffer, a crude steel frame to which a heavy plank was fastened. He believed that everything governing the life of Reuven Weissberg had started and would end here.

He was told of the camp, two kilometres from the

village of Sobibor, that had been built on this site. A place for the living and a terminal for the walking dead had been built here under the terms of Operation Reinhard on virgin ground and beyond the sight of witnesses. When completed it was a killing ground. It had no role for forced labour, only for extermination. Those to be murdered were Jews.

He saw two wooden homes, one brightly painted in soft green, and learned that they had been called the Swallow's Nest and the Merry Flea by the German officers of the SS units at the Sobibor camp: they were now the homes of men working in the forestry industry. He saw a raised platform beyond the spur track's buffer. Great piles of stacked pit props lay on it, and open freight wagons were already loaded high. Jews had been brought to that platform from Holland, France, the Polish ghettoes, German cities, towns in Belarus and Ukraine and invited to step down from their transports. On that platform, where sunshine now fell, the Jews had descended and started the walk to their deaths.

As he listened, Carrick waited for Reuven Weissberg's voice to break, but it did not. He was told the story in a monotone. He wondered if passion, at this place, would have been disrespectful to those who had been herded off that platform.

He was not a Jew, and Carrick struggled to understand the enormity of the deaths of a quarter of a million people. They went down a path of raked sand, walked between new-planted pine trees, and it had been named the 'Road to Heaven'. The system of killing worked, the quiet voice in his ear told him, because the victims in the last minutes of their lives had been 'docile' and had gone 'like sheep' where he now

471

trod. There were stones laid between the new pines on to which had been bolted inscriptions: 'In memory of my mother [a name], my father [a name], my grandmother [a name], my grandfather [a name], my grandmother [a name], my grand-father [a name]. May your souls be bound up in the bound of life.' They came to a clearing, had come past a block of harsh stone, square and dominating, and a statue on a plinth of a twice-man-sized figure that held a child against a hip. It was ravaged by weather, and the sharpness of the sculptor's chisel was blunted. In the clear-ing a huge circular shape, a mound, was covered with fine white chippings. The shape was where the ashes of a quarter of a million souls had been gathered, heaped.

Birds sang. The wind rippled the tops of the pines and rustled the birch leaves on the forest floor.

There were no fences, no barracks huts. The killing was described to him, but the chambers into which the gas had been powered were gone and no sign of them remained. He closed his eyes as the story was told of the deaths, of the engine's rumble, of the geese squawking, of the final gasped notes of the anthem sung behind the sealed doors. After the silence and the switching off of the engine, he saw the doors of the chambers opened by emaciated worker ants who served to live another day, and the carrying away of the rigid bodies. And saw, also, a line of women at benches sorting the dis-carded clothes and suitcases of those who had come in ignorance or in terrified submission on the trains to Sobibor.

Carrick vomited. There was little food in his stomach but he retched bile and the cough scraped his throat. He saw the woman at the bench, Reuven Weissberg's grandmother, and she handled clothes still warm from their contact with those now dead. The bile gleamed at his feet. When he was finished, when there was nothing left in his stomach to bring back, he felt ashamed of his weakness, and kicked dead leaves over the mess.

Here – at this camp alone, at Sobibor – there had been a revolt and a break-out. At no other camp, he was told, had that happened. Trees grew where the fences had been, where the mines had been spread and where the compound for the work-prisoners was sited. The watchtowers had long been taken down. He listened to the soft murmur of the wind in the trees, and heard the cheerfulness of the song-birds. He heard the name of Pechersky, the Russian officer, the Jew who was a leader, and in Carrick's ears was the hammer of machine-guns, the rippling blast of detonated mines, the panic and screaming of those who ran towards the trees. Above every-thing, in his closed eyes and deafened ears, was the slowly summoned sight and sound of abject cruelty.

He thought that in his life nothing had prepared him for this place, and for the quiet telling of the story of those who had charged the wire. And climbed it. And gone through the mines to reach the trees. He thought he walked in a place of history. Words jumbled in his mind. They were *courage* and *desperation* and *fear* and *hunger* and *exhaustion*. It was made a place of history because here people had fought back against impossible odds. He was told then of more deceit, betrayal and a greater deception.

They were in the trees and the monuments of the camp, what scraps remained of it, were behind them. Carrick thought they followed a cotton thread laid long before as Reuven Weissberg recited without hesitation, as if it had often been told him.

We had spent the night in the forest. Always Samuel held my hand. He gripped it. I would have wanted, in that darkness, to lie down. I craved sleep. I had no strength, we had no food – I only realized when night came that what little food I had had from the morning had been in my coat pocket, which had ripped when we went over the wire. I had lost the food.

He would not permit me to lie down, to sleep. He kept moving, tugging me along. He was searching for Pechersky, for the Russian group of which he was a part. It could have been four or five hours that we had walked, stumbled, among the trees in the darkness and then we saw, both of us, that we had circled the camp and were back, almost, where we had started from. I could have wept, but he did not, so I stopped the tears. All of that strength had been wasted, but we began again.

I had told Samuel that I came from the town of Wlodawa, to the north, a few kilometres, but also confessed to him that I had never before been in this forest and had no knowledge of it. I could not help or guide him.

Sometimes we heard shots in the night, and then we would veer away. Twice we heard the voices of Germans and Ukrainians. We found people who were wounded; they had injuries from the mines or the machine-guns in the watchtowers. They had crawled on their stomachs into the trees. We came upon a man who had no leg, and another who was blinded by shrapnel. Both begged that we stop and help them – but we moved on. They cursed us. We heard their curses, growing fainter, as we left them. We were the living, and were whole, and it did not seem necessary to stay with them and help. What help could we have given them? The camp had taught us to help only ourselves.

Dawn came. Rain fell in the forest that early morning. Now we saw more who had achieved the break-out. Now, also, we saw through the upper branches of the trees that a small aircraft circled the forest and it was low enough for us to read the markings on the wings. Now shots came more often. The dawn light, of course, was from the east. To the east was the Bug river. It seemed right, the solution, to go east in the trees if we were to find Pechersky and Samuel's friends. Each group we came upon – three or thirteen, and one of thirty persons – recognized Samuel and his Russian uniform, begged him to lead them, and each time he held my hand firmer and broke clear. He said to me that the bigger the group, the greater the danger of the Germans finding us. I didn't argue. There were some we met in the forest whom I had known for weeks, even months – they had shown kindness to me, had shared with me, had comforted me, but I didn't return, then, the kindness, the comfort. We were animals. We loved only our own lives.

I think we must have been near to the river, perhaps a kilometre from it, when we found the group led by Pechersky. With him and his Russians there were forty others, mostly Jews from Poland. Pechersky was the leader, it was obvious. There was a confusion of voices until he spoke. Then there was silence as he was listened to.

The word from Pechersky was that all the bridges over the Bug were guarded by detachments of Field Police, that more Germans were now sweeping through the forest, that units on horseback had arrived to make the search more efficient.

Most of the day we stayed in that place. More fugitives had come. At the sight of Pechersky their faces, every one, lost the lines of fear and were lit again with hope. Pechersky was the saviour. During the day, the group would have grown to about seventy. All of us knew we owed our lives to him.

Many said there was no chance of survival if they were not close to Pechersky.

In the late afternoon, Samuel was waved forward.

He had released my hand. I think the feeling had gone from it, leaving it numb, because he had held it so tight and so long.

I watched him go into the inner core of the group. He stepped round and through the Polish Jews, who huddled near to the Russians. He was taken right in, near to Pechersky. It was not Pechersky who spoke to him, but others among the Russians. It was where the leadership was and the weapons, and they were the men who had not been inside Sobibor long enough to be exhausted and starved. There was talking, but so quiet that the Jews in the outer ring did not hear. Twice I saw Samuel shake his head very violently. For a few seconds he looked away from them and towards me, but I couldn't see what he thought. The Russians he had been speaking to shrugged, as if a matter had been discussed and an answer had not been found. Then he came back to me.

I didn't ask Samuel what had been said, why he had shaken his head as if refusing something. I had to rest. My weight was against his shoulder and his arm was round me. I think I slept, and I don't know for how long.

I slept pure sleep. I forgot about hunger and tiredness. I had no dream. When I woke, it was the afternoon. It might have been rain on my face, dripping from a tree, that had woken me. They were going in a short column. The Russians were going. I didn't see Pechersky and I assumed he was at the front. I started up. I knew we should follow them, but Samuel didn't move. When I tried to stand he pulled me down roughly. It was the first roughness I had seen from him.

I asked why we didn't stay with them, go where they went.

I could hear then the aircraft away to the west, more shooting. The last of them went. They disappeared into the trees. I lost sight of them.

I asked Samuel why we were not with them. He told me they had gone to find food, and he said it in a clear voice, quite loud. He said that the Russians, led by Pechersky, were the fittest and strongest and would be more likely to find food. In ten minutes – it is difficult to have any real understanding of time, but it wasn't long – Samuel helped me to my feet. For a moment we were at the edge of the group, and then we were gone from them. We slipped away. He led me by the hand and had that same secure, tight grip on me. We did not, either of us, look back. We left that clearing where the group was gathered.

Why?

The direction he took me was towards the fall of the light, towards the west. The Bug river was to the east, and the Russian army was in the east, but he took me west and deeper into the forest, almost, I reckoned, in the direction of the camp. We saw, on a wide track, four Germans on big horses – fine, well-fed and -groomed horses – and the Germans had rifle butts rested on their thighs. We watched, and were frozen against a wide pine's trunk. A fugitive broke clear, came on to the track, saw them and started to run. I heard the shots and the laughter, but I didn't see the death.

Why?

Samuel told me that Pechersky had not gone to get food. He had said he was going to get food, and to make his statement more believable he had collected money from the group and told them it would be used to buy food from farmers and woodsmen. Samuel told me that Pechersky did not believe so large a group had a chance

477

of crossing the Bug, that he had achieved what he had hoped, had led the successful break-out. He had responsibility now only for his Russian comrades. Pechersky had abandoned the group with one rifle.

I asked Samuel why he had not gone with Pechersky.

He almost stuttered the answer. I promise, then, that blood ran in his cheeks. He could have gone. They would, of course, have taken him – but not me. It had been said to him that if one non-Russian was taken, because of a friendship, a hundred should be taken because of friendships. Only those who were Russians would go with Pechersky.

I asked Samuel again why he had not gone with Pechersky and taken the best chance of living.

The blush made his cheeks scarlet. 'I refused to leave you. I told them I was with you and would remain with you. It was why they shrugged . . . but they wouldn't change their decision and let us accompany them.'

I had found love, and the ultimate moment of deceit. I believe I would have done it, told the lie and gained a better opportunity of survival. Samuel did not.

That was love. We went far into the forest. We were together, only us two. The aircraft overhead seemed further from us, the gunfire more distant. We moved on.

Carrick stood. Reuven Weissberg had hold of his arm, and there was venom in his voice. 'I owe nobody anything. I have no responsibility, no obligation, to anyone. There was one love, but around it were the layers of betrayal. They rot in hell and they don't matter to me, those of the past and those of today. For what was done here, for the lies spoken, I owe nobody anything.'

'I think I understand, sir.'

Shafts of sunlight pierced the canopy and made gold pools on the leaves of the last autumn. He seemed to see them walking, the boy and the girl, and maybe – in that false brightness – they laid the trail of cotton thread. He was captivated by the place and the images of it given to him, as he was captivated by the presence, personality and almost manic intensity of the man who had brought him there. Always they were in front of him, the boy and the girl.

It rang in his head. *I owe nobody anything.* He thought the birds sang prettily, but then, abruptly, their calls were overwhelmed by the distant whine of a chain-saw. He had crossed lines – demarcation strips of ethics and morality – had not seen them, would not have recognized them. He followed Reuven Weissberg.

Lawson had an eye half open.

He heard Deadeye quiz Bugsy, 'That thing still working?'

'Mind your manners. Of course it is. Good signal, clear and strong.'

'What's he doing, the subject?'

'Not doing anything.'

'Come again?'

Bugsy said, 'He's not doing anything because he hasn't moved. The location is at the side of a lake south-west-south of Okuninka, about a klick out of the place, and he hasn't shifted. A ten-metre move'll register, but nothing has. Must be sleeping.'

'Funny place to sleep.' Deadeye shrugged.

'Well, he hasn't moved, that's for certain.' Bugsy was defiant, always would be if his gear's capability was in question.

Lawson intervened. He had arched his back, stretched out his legs and coughed a little. He said, 'Chuck the item out of the car, Deadeye. Put yourself in it with Bugsy – please, my friend, if you don't mind – and drive into the metropolis of Wlodawa. I doubt there are croissants on sale, but some rolls and cheese, perhaps a bag of apples, coffee if you can find it – yes, and toilet rolls, some pairs of socks, if there's a shop. I would suggest the Okuninka road into Wlodawa. Well, don't hang about, Deadeye.'

He watched Deadeye go, and Bugsy follow him. They did, indeed, chuck the item out of the car, Davies from the front and the girl from the back, which was hardly red-blooded of either, and the car was driven away from the camping area. He could always rely on Deadeye, and he valued that man's abilities above the rest of his team – and needed the abilities. A phrase that had come from Clipper Reade, was trotted out in moments when crisis seemed to loom: an agent not showing, a covert observation post identified overlooking a dead-drop, a tail in place and seen. Clipper Reade would say, 'I think we have, Christopher, an IAP moment, don't you?' Clipper Reade was rarely vulgar. Lawson thought he now faced an Intensifying Ass Pucker moment, and felt that tightening of those muscles.

He kept it to himself, didn't show his increasing anxiety to the rest of them. And he thought time was ebbing, went fast through his fingers . . . and it would happen, yes, and very soon, but his control was slipping.

The Crow stared ahead, and had no wish to talk.

'Shouldn't they have been here by now?' The man had come to his car, opened the door and slid into the vacant passenger seat. He had looked with growing frequency at his wristwatch, and it was the third time he had asked that question. The first time the Crow had shrugged, as if that should have been enough of an answer. The second time, he had gestured with his hands, outstretched above the steering-wheel.

Now, the Crow said, 'There will have been a delay.'

'What sort of delay?' There was a squeak in the voice, apprehension and nagging worry. 'How can there be a delay?'

The Crow carried many burdens. He thought then that, chief among them, dealing with novices, those with necessary expertise but without experience, was the most taxing. Kids who had not been on the front line of the struggle stretched his patience and calm exterior almost to a break-point. They wanted chatter, demanded to belong, had no sense of being a mere valve in a great engine, needed to talk.

'There might have been a delay in the collection or in its transshipment. There are many reasons for a delay.'

'How long do we sit here? I've never slept in a car. I haven't eaten. How long?'

But they couldn't be ignored, slapped down, insulted to silence and left to sulk. So often an amateur from outside the inner tested circle of activists was needed – an engine didn't function without a 'mere valve'. A mighty sum of money, ten million American dollars, was to be paid over *if* this gabbling, fearful little idiot gave the assurance that the device indeed contained a core in spherical shape – the size of a moderate orange – of weapons-grade plutonium. He, the Crow, could not give such an assurance. Neither could the men who had planned his journey, nor those at the

481

container port in Hamburg's harbour who would move the device on, nor those who would take it from another dockside and carry it to the target area, nor those who would bring it the final metres of its journey and detonate it. None could give the assurance that the damage created would be worth the expenditure of ten million American dollars. When he had fought in Afghanistan, where he had been wounded in the throat and his voice changed by the Soviet artillery shrapnel, there had been similar kids who had talked too much, had wanted comradeship, and their bones were whitened by the ravages of the winter gales on the mountains. They had died because they had lacked the strength to endure silence; it was the hard, quiet men who survived, that war and this struggle. He did not show his exasperation, or his contempt.

'We wait through this day and into the evening. If they are delayed and are coming, I will be called and we will stay here until they reach us. If they do not call we will know it has failed. Later, I will get some food. You are a stranger to me but I regard you as my friend. And you should know that there are those senior to me who know your name, the sacrifices you make and the dedication you show. They have very considerable respect for you.'

He could lie, in his hoarse, rasping voice, with ease. The Crow excused himself, left the car and walked off into the bracken and gorse. He searched for a hidden place where he could defecate, and be free of the idiot's interrogation.

Molenkov still had that foulness in his mouth. It burned and his gums were raw.

They came to Kobrin, a small town. Molenkov knew that, because Yashkin had informed him that the population at the last census was fifty-one thousand. It was a mercy to Molenkov, as he nursed the poison in his mouth, and almost in his throat, that Yashkin knew little of the place, only its population and a brief history: in the eleventh century it had formed part of the Volhynian Vladimir, in the fourteenth it had been annexed into the Grand Duchy of Lithuania, then had been part of Imperial Russia, then a part of Poland, then had been a battlefield fought over by the Polish Army and the XIXth Panzer Corps of General Heinz Guderian, occupied by the Germans until liberation by the Soviets, a part of Belarus since 1991 and . . . It was a great mercy to Molenkov that Yashkin had not dug up more information from the library in Sarov. It appeared to him a dismal town, and without virtue. He coughed, spluttered and spat out of his open window, but couldn't free himself from the awfulness of the taste in his mouth. He watched, when not coughing and spitting, the needle of the fuel gauge, which did not leave the red zone, was trapped there.

'How much further?' The same repetitive question.

'Through Kobrin, then eight or nine kilometres.'

They crossed a canal bridge. The waterway was weeded up, its use as a navigation route destroyed by disrepair. Yashkin said it was a section of the waterway linking the Dnieper river to the Bug.

'I don't fucking care. I care about the fuel, what's in the tank and what's in my throat.'

It was early morning in Kobrin. The first stalls in an open market beyond the bridge were being set up, clothes hung out and vegetables stacked. The sun was shining, low, milky, unmistakable, and shadows were thrown from the stalls and reflected back from the mirrors that were the puddles. In the night, they had tried to get fuel in Pinsk.

Pinsk, then, had been a sleeping town, battened down for the darkness, the streets deserted. They had rested on that bench beside one of the old churches, and no police had come to question them, no bastard skinheads had made footballs of them or punchbags. They had driven away, then started to search. Had had to search because Yashkin, the clever one who knew every moment of history on this great route from Sarov, fifteen hundred kilo-metres of it, had not thought to include a length of rubber piping in the back. In a suburb of Pinsk, out-side the old town, there had been a house with a tap attached to the front wall, and a hosepipe coiled round it. On the short driveway, near to the tap and the hosepipe, was a gleaming Mercedes, apparently washed the previous afternoon. Molenkov had eased his old penknife from his pocket, climbed over the wire fence beside the gate, scurried to the tap and had been sawing at the hosepipe when the house security lights had come on. He had fled with the length of pipe back to the car and Yashkin had driven off.

'Are you an idiot, Molenkov?' Yashkin had asked him. Through his broken mouth and split lips, he had denied it. Yashkin had said, 'Did you not look at the type of Mercedes it was? You did not? It was a diesel.'

Four roads away, they had found a car parked at a kerb, and the house beyond the garden was in darkness. It was an old car, a Moskva, petrol-driven. Molenkov had said that he didn't think such an old car as a Moskva would be alarmed. Yashkin had stayed at the wheel, had pulled up close to the Moskva, had switched off the Polonez's

484

engine. Molenkov had gone, a thief in the night, to the back of the Polonez and had unscrewed the fuel cap. He had placed it on the roof, then had gone to the parked car and unscrewed the Moskva's cap after breaking its feeble lock with his penknife. He had inserted one end of the hosepipe into the hole, had gone to the Polonez, had stood at the back and put the other end of the hosepipe into his mouth and sucked . . . His mouth had filled – and the Rottweiler had thrown itself at the gate of the house. Fucking great animal, fucking great teeth. Gaped and gasped, and swallowed before he had spat. His mouth filled with petrol. Then lights were going on upstairs in the house, the Rottweiler was scrabbling with its front paws at the top of the gate, and he'd had a sight of the brute's teeth.

They had driven away.

It was now four hours since the petrol had swamped Molenkov's mouth, and the taste had not lessened. More had gone into the cuts in his lips and the abrasions on his chin.

Yashkin said, 'I hope we have enough. This town is—'

'Not another fucking history lesson.'

Yashkin grimaced. 'Kobrin is a frontier town. The frontier zone of a pitiful country, such as Belarus is, will be heavily policed. There will be State Security men as close to each other as the mosquitoes around the Pripet marshes on a summer evening. We cannot "borrow" fuel here, and we have no money to buy it. If we beg we draw attention to ourselves. We can only hope we have enough.'

'Suppose we get to the Bug and deliver. How do we move on to wherever?'

'You *are* an idiot, Molenkov.'

'Tell me.'

Yashkin laughed. 'We buy the fuel station. We have a million American dollars. We can buy—'

'Do we have sufficient to get to the Bug?' Molenkov refused to laugh.

He saw the smile stripped from Yashkin's face. The lips pursed, and the frown cut deeper. 'I don't know. Could we fail for a shortage of one litre of fuel? How far into the last litre are we? The gauge won't tell us.'

They drove on slowly, to conserve what fuel remained, and Molenkov did not look at the road ahead but at the needle that was steady at the bottom of the red area.

On the map, ahead of them, only the village of Malorita was marked, then the open space of forest, wilderness and marshland, the blue line of the Bug river.

Molenkov asked, 'Will you allow an idiot one more question? We're late. We lost the schedule searching for fuel in Pinsk. Will they wait for us?'

'Yes, they will. You worry too much, Molenkov.'

Molenkov heard the reassurance, the confidence, and didn't know whether his friend lied. He thought of them, together, on the bank of the Bug, flashing their torches in the evening dusk – being where they should have been in the last hour before dawn – and not seeing a light on the far side. It might be that his friend lied, and that no one would be there because they had lost time.

The call came.

Lawson fumbled through his pockets, found the damned thing. Only a handful of people had that number – Lucy, of course, and an assistant director, Lavinia, who had been given it years before but had probably lost it by now or shredded the paper it was jotted on, an engineer in the speciality work-shops that did the gizmos, a couple more who were scattered in that building by the Thames, and the director general. It had been Clipper's joke, the ringing tones were of the anthem *'Deutschland Über Alles'*, but there was much of Clipper Reade's that Lawson had made his own.

The chimes rang through the forest. He saw the astonishment spreading as he came clear of the minibus and the call tune continued. Must have woken the surveillance people, and Shrinks had the look of one who thought that this was a man around whom a serious case study could be built, but his young man, Luke Davies, eyed him as if the gesture of the anthem was not amusing but pathetic. Did it matter to Christopher Lawson? It did not. Did it matter that a bug had not moved in hours, not even by a few metres, and that the sun was climbing above the forest? It did. He pressed the 'connect' button.

'Yes.'

'Christopher?'

'Yes.'

'It's Francis – are we on "secure"?'

'Yes.'

His tone was brusque. Even a contact from the director general was treated as an intrusion. The voice was distant, tinny when filtered through the encryption and scrambler chip built into the phone. Of course they were on secure speech. He listened. 'I've been off base for the last twenty-four hours, but I understand you haven't called through. Where do we stand?'

'Our position is satisfactory. Where do we stand? Specifically, we are in a forest area, quite close to the Bug river. We are south of Wlodawa and—'

He heard the impatience. No one else he knew would have employed pedantry with the director general. 'Do we have a close surveillance aspect on our targets? What I mean is – damn it, Christopher, in words of one syllable – have we control? Are they, the targets, buttoned down?'

'Yes.' Lawson had not hesitated. He spoke firmly.

'Do you still believe the situation on which you briefed me?'

'Yes.'

'You have the crossing-point under surveillance, and the manpower to take action?'

'To both, yes.'

'Is it soon?'

'Within the next several hours is my estimate.'

'Should you have more bodies, additional back-up?'

'No.'

'Christopher, I'm saying this once, not again, and believe me, the image of failure runs in my mind – it's an apocalypse. Failure is not acceptable. I'm asking whether you should have the cavalry with you, Christopher.'

'Nice offer – no, thank you.'

'I can lift a telephone. I can get a battalion of Polish troops there, wherever it is, within an hour, two at the most. I can get that area made so secure that a rabbit—'

'We're well placed, Francis, and the cavalry is not required – for reasons we discussed, and agreed, in your office. I have the resources I need.'

'To put my mind at rest, you confirm that you have control?'

'Tight control, Francis. It was all predictable and there are no surprises.'

'And the agent? How is he performing?'

He told his director general, very frankly, of his assessment of the agent. He was staring across the camping area and could see up the track and almost to the road, and he looked for the car that would bring back Bugsy and Deadeye, and thought he knew what they would bring and what they would report. 'I really should be getting on with things, Francis, so if you'll excuse me . . .'

He ended the call.

The previous evening, Tadeuz Komiski had convinced himself – without effort – that the persistence of the rain excused him from going and looking for wood for the priest to burn in his home. Wet wood, however well seasoned, would merely smoke out the man's living room. But that morning the sun was out and his excuse was no longer valid.

Because of the expense of refilling it, he would not waste what fuel he had in his tractor's tank. He would go early into the forest and check where there were branches brought down by the weight of the rain and the strength of the wind, those that had already died, and he would look for the heaps where the forestry men had stacked timbers that were too thin, too split or too knotted to serve as good pit props. When, if, he found sufficient wood he would walk back to his home and collect his tractor. Komiski told himself that it was only because Father Jerzy had asked for wood that he would look for it, he would have done it for no one else.

He did not take the dog, or the shotgun, but he had hitched on his shoulder the short bow-saw with its razor teeth.

He did not use the tracks that were rutted from the woodsmen's vehicles, but he went as a wraith among the trees. Maybe it was the tiredness, maybe it was because he had not eaten – neither had his dog – since the priest had left the pie, maybe it was from the sense of freedom after closing the door of the house behind him, but he had not worked out with any precision what route he would take on his way to look for wood that was not too sodden to be burned.

The priest had asked, *Was it when you were a child and living in this house that the guilt was born?* Now, Tadeuz Komiski realized he was close, within a hundred metres, of where that guilt had been conceived – and there were voices.

Voices carried in the quiet of the forest. He crouched, then sank to his knees. He saw two men. He recognized one, saw the close-cut scalp, the power of the shoulders and the heavy leather coat that fell to the man's hips. He had not seen the second before, and thought him younger. His hair not cut short, he seemed to have a less threatening body and there was a limp to his stride. They were within a few steps of where the first grave had been, a few metres from where the later storm and the rains had uncovered the bones. Tadeuz Komiski had moved those bones, had carried them as far as he was able in an awkward, dangling bundle, then had retraced his steps to retrieve an arm bone and a whole skeletal foot that had fallen away from the main frame of the long-dead corpse. Then he had made the second grave and had buried the man whose death had bred the curse.

The sun dappled down through the trees. Flies danced in its light. The birds, warmed by the sun, flitted above where the grave had been. Had they known where to look they would have walked a dozen paces to the right. The excavated pit was a metre and a half in length, a half-metre in width and a metre in depth. Tadeuz Komiski came here often, was drawn to the place, which was the torment of the curse. Now, all these years later, the grave was a slight indent in the ground. It lay between two pines, one of which had a double trunk. There were enough markers for him to know exactly where the grave had been – and where *they* had been, the young man and the girl. Now the grave was filled with leaves and needles from the pines, and a branch had come down on it two winters back, obscuring most of it. The priest had said: *You do not have to answer me – but the only palliative for guilt is confession.*

They moved on.

He could not have said why he followed them. His back now was to the great mound of ashes, the grave for a quarter of a million persons, but it was the first grave of one man that had brought down the curse on him. The sun climbed, and he moved between trees, used cover and did not feel the aches in his old joints. Tadeuz Komiski had the skills gained from a lifetime spent – where ghosts were – in the forest. He told himself he would be satisfied to find out their destination. Then he would turn and look again for dried wood.

Their pace had quickened, and they passed – and did not know it – the place where he had reburied the bones.

Reuven Weissberg said, 'They were betrayed. My grandmother was betrayed and my grandfather. From her being taken to the ghetto in Wlodawa, from him being captured by the Nazi Army, they faced total and continuous betrayal. They were betrayed by individuals, and by systems and by

491

nationalities . . . and I am of their blood. Did individuals, systems or nations care about them? None did. They were not important, not valued. They had only one chance, and it was from themselves. Destiny was in their own hands – from every other quarter, every point around them, there was treachery. I have been taught it and I believe it. In me, what happened here – in that camp – is still alive. Do you understand, Johnny?'

The eyes, gleaming, dangerous and bright, overwhelmed Carrick.

They were near to the river where it narrowed, and upstream from where the floodwater had spread over fields. Trees sprouted on the steep banks of either side, and the force of the flow was intimidating. They had reached the small boat and were near to the gathering, dismal, bowed shoulders and dropped heads, of the Russians and Josef Goldmann. Little columns of cigarette smoke eddied up from them. He no longer fought. He had seen the site of the Sobibor camp, and had heard the story, and in his mind was the frail, emaciated woman in black, with the pure white hair, the survivor who had fashioned a grandson. He understood. Almost, he was part of this place. What he had done in the night, beside a lake, before taking his share of the weight of the boat was forgotten.

'Yes, sir,' Carrick said.

Chapter 18: 16 April 2008

Carrick stayed close to Reuven Weissberg.

Hours were there to be killed, the sun had started to drop from its full height and the shadows of the trees were thrust on to the river. Mostly Carrick just looked at the power and drive of its flow. Reuven Weissberg had talked to him about building a church in a village outside Perm, paying for its construction, and had said it was what many did who were in *business* and who wanted to put something as a legacy into the community. Carrick had nodded and let him talk, had no interest in a church built by a Jew in a place he couldn't picture. He thought the idea tacky and sentimental, but he didn't say so and made a pretence of listening.

He watched the far side of the river.

Behind him, hidden, was the boat and the length of rope. The greater preoccupation in Carrick's mind was getting a rope across the river, then using it as a line to cling to and heave on while they were in the boat. Pretty bloody incredible that the height of the river had not been predicted, or its strength, but he hadn't criticized.

When he watched the far bank of the Bug it was

without enthusiasm. Between where he sat, near to Reuven Weissberg, sharing the same patch of damp sand, leaning against the same wet tree trunk, and that far bank, the river careered by. He watched the far bank, the mess of sprig bushes and taller trees where the base and the roots were submerged, the coloured border marker, and tried to keep his head and his eyeline up. If he did not, he saw the river's pace and drive, the dislodged trees it carried. If he didn't watch that far bank, well lit by the sun, he saw the water and the debris running fast in it, and he would think of the boat, and darkness.

He was far from anything that was familiar. Back-up seemed beyond reach.

Carrick – tired, cold, wet, hungry – believed that only Reuven Weissberg cared for him.

He could make out a slight path that came out of the far trees, then dropped down to reach the water's edge. Maybe deer used it, or pigs, or foxes. The longer he stared at the path, the better he saw it. There would be a torch flashed along that bank, and the answering light would be the signal from Reuven Weissberg that they should move along and get opposite to where they now sat.

What was being brought that would bring the big boss to the God-forsaken side of a river on Poland's frontier? What was of such value? Not drugs – they came in bulk in container lorries. Not girls – they could be brought, he assumed, by the busload from Ukraine. Not forged passports and not bogus Rolex watches. Not computer chips and not cartons of contraband cigarettes. Didn't leave much that could take priority on Reuven Weissberg's shopping list.

He thought of weapons. Looking at the little path

across the river, he had gone back over the weaponry he knew from days in Iraq. The improvised explosive device, which had damn near shredded his leg, could have been put together by an engineer – or a car mechanic or an electrician – in the Basra equivalent of a lock-up garage. Rocket-propelled grenades and their launchers were washing about all over Europe after the Balkans fighting. The market was saturated. Ground-to-air missiles would be harder, if they were required to bring down an airliner on approach to or take-off from Charles de Gaulle, Fiumicino, Schiphol or Heathrow, but three or four would be big bulk in their protective casings, and as much as the boat could carry, and there would have to be an easier way to do a border than in darkness and across the Bug in flood.

He doubted ground-to-air missiles were enough to bring Reuven Weissberg here, certainly not Josef Goldmann. A former paratrooper with a hole in his leg from scrapping with jihadists was hardly the man for deployment on attachment to the anti-terror people, infiltration into a Muslim community and its mosque. Not even to be considered. Didn't matter. The Pimlico office of SCD10 had been cleared out one Tuesday morning in March two years back, had gone up to the Yard in best bib and tucker, had sat in a curtained-off area at the back of a lecture theatre with a few anonymous others and had listened to a lecture on the big three. They were microbiological weapons, chemical weapons and nuclear weapons. The lecturer had been a spook, and his name had not been given. He had not used the word *if*, but had talked of *when*. It had not made a deal of sense then, and Carrick had gone back to Pimlico and got on with reading up on the background biographies of Jed and Baz, club owners . . .

He thought of Josef Goldmann. Thought of Goldmann's pretty wife, decent children, swank house, respect in the City and the social scene of smart galleries and top-grade parties – thought that only weapons of mass destruction would bring him out to this wet bloody riverbank with a forest that had been a killing ground behind him, the river and the bloody Belarus border in front. The spook lecturer, from Box 500 on the Embankment, had talked of an explosion that scattered lethal germs, and an explosion that scattered an aerosol effect of nerve-gas droplets, and an explosion that spread radiation from a dirty bomb.

Carrick could not cope with the thought of it. Did not try to. Blanked it and blocked it. Felt the warmth and strength of Reuven Weissberg alongside him.

They brought the food in two brown-paper bags. They had bought rolls, fruit and cans of Coke. It was long past midday, and it should have been the team's breakfast.

Lawson understood.

It would have been Deadeye who had made the decision not to blurt out the bad news on a mobile-telephone link. Bad news always came better face to face, eye to eye. They had driven into the camping area, had closed the doors quietly behind them, had wandered – as if strolling in Sunday-afternoon sunshine – towards the minibus. Lawson had climbed out. Adrian and Dennis had followed him. Young Davies and the girl had come from a picnic table.

The food had been given to the girl.

Now, meeting Lawson's gaze full on, Deadeye twisted his head and nodded to Bugsy. Bugsy had that perplexed look, which said he'd gone into uncharted territory and didn't have a mental map for it. His fist went into his anorak pocket and emerged with the loose lengths of strapping, tangled with the Velcro, and the box hung down from them.

Deadeye said, 'He'd dumped it.'

Bugsy said, 'Well, someone dumped it. Might have been him, might have been one of the others. I'm not there, I can't say whether it was voluntary or under duress, and I can't say whether or not who he was with was aware of him doing it. It was hung from a tree. Might not have been done openly, because the last time the damn thing moved was in the night. That's where we are.'

Deadeye said, in the flat voice that didn't change whether it ranged across triumph or something worse than disaster, 'There are two sets of footprints there, only two. I would assume, Mr Lawson, that it was the agent with the main target. It's by a place where a boat was kept but a few yards from it. It's only what I'm thinking, the agent stripped it off and left it but not where our target would have seen him lose it.'

Bugsy said, like it was a slur on his capabilities, 'It was working well, had a very decent signal. It was going to do the job for us.'

Deadeye said, 'He gave no indication, not at all, that he wasn't prepared to wear it. What he's done, it's come out of a clear blue sky.'

Lawson pondered on it, kept his counsel and gave no indication – not a trifle – of the stampeding emotions in his mind.

Bugsy said, 'Well, that was me out of it.'

Deadeye said, 'The marks were of two sets of feet, clear enough in the mud. Then there was a scrape, like a flat-bottomed boat but with a keel had been hauled up from the water. It had been dragged along a path from the lake to the road. That was easy enough to follow and no effort had been made to disguise the track that was left. Then there was a road. It's the main drag, Wlodawa to Chelm. They'd gone along it. Of course, no traces. No scrapes, at the side, no footprints. I have to guess but it can't be a big boat. What took us so long, we went a mile up the road and looked for a trace, and a mile down the road, and we can't find it, Mr Lawson. Before you ask me, I don't reckon there was a vehicle involved. I'm almost certain of that. If a car had been pulled off the road and waiting there would have been fresh tyre marks, and if a car, or a pick-up or a truck, had been called up and arrived just for the loading, there would have been the stamped-down places where the boat had been and their feet while they waited. I'm thinking, Mr Lawson, that the boat was carried along the road and then they went back into the forest and towards the river. Stands to reason, they want the boat for the river. We searched for that point where they came off the road, and we couldn't find it. I'm not happy, but that's the way it is.'

'Why would he do that, Mr Lawson, ditch the gear? I mean, where's he coming from?'

First, Lawson searched his mind: there had been bad moments when he had been with Clipper Reade, the intensifying-ass-pucker moments, but nothing as desperate as the moment now confronting him. What would Clipper have done? What would have been the response of the big

Texan from the Agency? Well, for a start he would have lit a cheroot and – for a finish – he would have displayed no panic. Not a vestige. He asked how they were.

Bugsy said, 'I'm flat, on my heels – No, I'm fine.'

Deadeye shrugged. 'What do you need us to do, Mr Lawson?'

About as bad it could get was the loss of eyeball and contact in the last hours before an operation went critical.

He acknowledged the thoroughness of what they had done, thanked them for it, and suggested – not as an instruction – that they head for the river, that flooded area where Reuven Weissberg, his cohorts and the agent had been the last afternoon. He felt hammered by what they had told him, weak and old.

Lawson smiled broadly, displayed supreme confidence. 'Yes, head on down there and get an eyeball again. It's where they'll be, with their boat, at the river. On you go.'

They had left. He had watched them drive away. Now Shrinks broke ranks. 'I need to contribute, Mr Lawson.'

'Best that you contribute when you're asked to.'

'Mr Lawson, the last time I ventured an opinion, I suggested that the agent had stress piled on him – in fact, "acute stress". I seem to detect a marked lack of interest in what has been, and is being, inflicted on the poor wretch.'

'If your "expertise". . .' Lawson's tongue rolled contemptuously on the word '. . . is unwanted it could be because of its irrelevance.'

'You've already asked too much of him.'

'Have I?'

'The effect on him of what you've done may last with him for years, psychiatric disorder brought on by the trauma of stress.'

'Is that so?'

'Damn it, you pushed him there.' Shrinks's voice rose. Never had before. Couldn't have recognized himself. 'You are responsible, only you, for driving him into a condition of the syndrome from which he may not recover. Even with the best supportive intervention and the best counselling this could be a long and potentially unpredictable business. But I see no indicators of you losing sleep over the inflicting of long-term damage on this man. And now he's screwed you. What bloody irony. You pushed him that far, into the arms of those brutal creatures, and he has rewarded you by turning his back on you. Try this one. "Sow the wind and reap the whirlwind." That's about the limit of your achievement, Mr Lawson. You've played God with a man's mind, his decencies and loyalties, and I doubt you've noticed.'

There was a hoarseness in his throat, a dryness. What upset Shrinks most was that Lawson seemed not to have been jolted by his outburst. No grandiose threats of 'never working with us again, chummy' had been made; no conciliatory waffle about 'Let's sit down, get this off our chests and look for what's best.' Nothing. Lawson looked through him as if he did not exist, and as if his tirade had gone unheard.

He looked to the others for support, but they wouldn't meet his eyes. Then Luke Davies took Katie Jennings's hand and spun her. Shrinks saw that, and thought Luke Davies didn't care a fig what he saw.

* * *

500

Luke held the hand firm. He said, 'Can you think of anything useful you can do right now?'

'Can't.'

'Can you think of somewhere, other than here, you'd rather be?'

'Anywhere.'

'It's where we're going.'

'Why?'

'It has the failure smell about it. A bad smell.'

She said, 'I know about smells. It's what constables experience. The old biddy hasn't been seen for a month, and nobody's thought to report it until there's the stink, and we break the door down and go in first. Rats may have beaten us to it, and the maggots are hatching. That sort of smell.'

'Come on.' He tugged at her arm.

For a moment her heels stuck, dug in. 'Is that a good enough reason?'

He hesitated, then blurted. 'Absenting myself from failure is a part of it. Another part is being away from here and with you.'

He saw her eyes open wide, and then there was a mocking grin. He liked that mouth, no makeup, and the myriad little veins in her lips. She didn't answer, but let him lead. He ran his other hand through the shock of bloody ginger hair that stood him out in any crowd. He wasn't good with girls, women, never had been . . . The American in Sarajevo, Frederika, had been something of a convenience to him and he to her. There were girls, women, in VBX and there might be a meal after a film, but nothing had stuck. He took his mobile out of his pocket and held it up so that Adrian or Dennis or Shrinks would see it, stepped out and she didn't pull back.

They walked on a forest track, and a tractor's wheels had gouged it.

They headed for 'anywhere' and had no idea of where the track would lead. Far in front of them they heard the harsh whine of a chain-saw. She hadn't spoken, but her fingers were in his.

The sun came through low, dropped, the birds had quietened, and their footfall was silent on the carpet of the forest floor. He saw the lines of trees, birch and pine, and sometimes they were bright lit by the sun shafts and sometimes they were dark and held secrets. It was where that woman had been. He remembered the painting in the kitchen, the photograph of her and her whitened hair, the child in her arms. Almost, Luke Davies would have been frightened to be among the trees – beyond sight and reach – on his own. He was not alone, had Katie Jennings with him. She hadn't spoken, but she had that smile, not the grin, and a sort of recklessness went with the smile.

'Tell me.'

'I'm thinking beyond my station. I'm thinking of Lawson.'

'He's a bastard. He's a—'

'Let me bloody finish. Now, I've never been into your place. Nearest I've been is when we were all on the pavement outside. But I'm seeing him going in through the front door, and everybody who works there is looking at him and they know about his failure. I promise you, Luke, I'm not vindictive, but the thought of it is making me laugh. How's he going to cope with that?'

'Every piece of advice given him has been ignored. Now it's gone belly-up.'

'I suppose he'll try and bluster it out.'

'Not with me beside him,' Davies said. 'I'm not going down with him.'

She frowned and the smile was gone, and the laughter. She said, 'Nothing's for ever, Luke, is it?'

He read her. 'You can move on. It's not a ball and chain. You pack the bag, go to the station and leave.'

'Yes.'

'And maybe you finish up somewhere you hadn't planned on. It's what happens . . . and you can't feel bad . . . and "somewhere" you meet someone else.'

Her hand tightened on his.

They walked on.

Neither his mobile nor hers rang.

They were near to a railway track.

Luke Davies sensed death, with him and around him as close as the darkening trees, but she had his hand. The sun slipped, shadows lengthened.

'Should we turn back?' he asked.

'I wouldn't have thought so.'

There was a knock and the door opened before she had time to respond.

She looked up. She tried to remember when last the director general had called in on Christopher Lawson's office in Non-Proliferation – might have been a couple of months back, might have been three.

'Hello, Director.'

'Lucy, isn't it? Yes, hello.'

'I don't have to tell you, Director, I'm sure, that Mr Lawson is away and—'

'You don't, no.'

So why had he come to her outer office? Her desk was placed as a strategic barrier and it blocked the entrance to the inner office. A visitor in search of Christopher Lawson could not slip by covertly and bounce her man. She was his gatekeeper and had been for more than twenty years.

'How can I help, Director?'

He wandered across to the window. Her man, Mr Lawson, might be detested the length, breadth and on every floor of VBX, but he possessed impressive clout. The inner and outer offices allocated him, and her, and the open-plan where juniors worked, had a fine view out on to the river and across it to Millbank. He was at the window and his eye traversed the river, then came to rest on the edifices of Parliament. He turned and faced her. 'I spoke to him this morning.'

'Did you, Director?'

'Talked to him on a secure line.'

'Well, you're ahead of me, Director, as I haven't talked with him since he left – five days now. Wouldn't expect to. Would you like a coffee?'

'I would, thank you.'

She was up from her desk, and slipped to the electric kettle behind her. She'd use Mr Lawson's personal mug, the one with the spaniels on it. It wouldn't be out of order for the director general.

'You see, he didn't say very much.'

'Did he not?'

'I expected something more ... Some detail. Crisp is what I had, crisp, brisk answers.'

She spooned Nescafé into the mug, and took the milk from the small fridge.

'I offered him the cavalry. You understand? He was out on the banks of the Bug, a forest behind him and Belarus in front. With him is that tiny little team of increments. I asked when he thought it might happen, a collection by his targets of what he believes is being brought to the river. He said, quote, "Within the next several hours is my estimate". So I asked if he wanted the cavalry.'

The kettle boiled. She poured water on to the coffee grains. She held up the milk carton and he nodded. She stirred vigorously. The director general had the reputation of coming unannounced to offices, then wandering the floor space, rambling and musing, not wanting interruption. She believed it was a habit he employed to clear chaff from his mind. She passed the mug, and he ducked his head with old-world courtesy in thanks.

'Where was I? Yes . . . vI offered him the cavalry. You see, we go back a long way. When he was young he had an American as his mentor, and when my turn came as a rookie, Christopher was my mentor. He taught me a mass of detail, also the value of a good nose and its use in sniffing, the value of instinct. I learned to trust him and his instincts. Excellent coffee . . .'

He was pacing now, quartering the carpet. She watched and stayed silent. He seemed not to be talking to her but to the walls, the door and the window. With Mr Lawson away, Lucy had been busying herself with his paperwork and had tidied recent papers into the filing systems – he still used documents and the computer memory was for back-up – and the director general couldn't be accused of keeping her from something that was necessity. She thought him troubled.

'He's a difficult man to read, Christopher is. Anyway, I'm giving him the offer of cavalry support. We could get to him, within a couple of hours, the best of the Polish agencies, a unit of their military, perhaps American Special Forces based in-country. Certainly the whole team from our

Warsaw station could be there mob-handed. If he's right, if his assessment of danger is correct, then – and I told him – "Failure is not acceptable." Did he want the cavalry? A rather brusque answer: "Nice offer – no, thank you." I ask myself, why is Christopher not prepared to share the load of responsibility?'

He finished the coffee, put the empty mug down on her desk.

'It was a blunt refusal. Why would he have declined help and the chance of boosting his role as an interceptor? My difficulty is that I can see only one reason . . . I'm going back a few days to when he came to see me. He told me of his suspicions, hunches, and laid it out. More circumstantial than evidence. Very frankly, if it hadn't been Christopher, I would have rejected the propositions I agreed to. That one reason, refusal of the cavalry, has a simplistic answer that is increasingly nagging at me, irritating me. Does he believe it himself, this threat? Does he believe wholeheartedly in this conspiracy?'

Her chin dropped, her mouth gaped. She found control. 'I really wouldn't know, Director.'

'Is it just a figment of his imagination? Did I not examine it with due rigour? Does he not want support because the arrival of fresh teams would lead to a lorryload of witnesses to his fantasies? Well, I suppose we'll know soon enough. He'll be a laughing stock if he's failed, if it were never about to happen, and I doubt that a seasoned friendship would be sufficient cause to save him. So kind of you, Lucy, to make me coffee. I have to say that where I'm going is towards blaming myself for indulging him.'

He was gone. The door closed after him.

Herself, she had never doubted Christopher Lawson. She pushed herself up in her chair, gained a few extra inches of height and could see over the window-ledge to the river. It flowed dark, brown and steady, and she wondered what the river Bug was like, whether it was fiercer or calmer. It had been Lucy's intention to ignore a message that had reached her that morning, offering a chance to meet at a particular place and time. Now she checked it again. She would be late, at least a quarter of an hour. She stood, tidied her desk, looked through the glass door at the gloom of Mr Lawson's empty inner office, and her jaw was set in defiance. She locked the outer door after her, went down the corridor and past the open-plan area of Non-Proliferation towards the lift. She passed staffers but none acknowledged her. She had no friends at VBX, could not have done. She worked for Christopher Lawson.

Alison, the liaison officer, said why she had asked for the meeting, and thanked the older woman for coming. She had been about to leave the café, had finished two espressos, had gutted her newspaper, front to back.

The woman grimaced. 'You'll get no tales out of school from me, or anything classified. I came because I admire and respect Christopher Lawson and have felt privileged to work for him for more than two decades. I came because he spoke well of you, because he is about to be ridiculed and his superiors have lost faith in him.'

She hadn't intended it, but a wan smile crossed Alison's face. She thought she recognized that degree of loyalty, the same as that of the small dog her parents kept.

'You identified an undercover whom Mr Lawson took over. The undercover is leading him, and Mr Lawson is following in his wake with his team, and you had doubts: if you had kept your mouth shut, we might not have identified the undercover, so you may have put that man – and he's only a face in a file to you – into circumstances of extreme danger. You are agonizing . . . Should you have involved him? Is Mr Lawson a fit individual to run the undercover?'

She nodded, couldn't disagree with the précis of her concerns. It was a Greek-owned café. At other tables there were mechanics, bus drivers and some mail people just off duty. It wasn't a place where VBX officers and support workers came, and she reckoned that the location gave her credibility, that the personal assistant would talk here, not spend the minutes looking over her shoulder.

'He is obstinate, aloof, dismissive, sometimes cruel, and he is the most effective intelligence officer in that wretched building. That is who the undercover is working for. He is honourable, he has *honour*, and that is not a word often echoing through the corridors of our building. I don't know why I came . . .'

There were, she thought, tears welling in the woman's eyes, little glistening marks of wet, and redness. Alison reached her hand out and laid it on the other's.

'I came, I suppose, to stand in his corner. Easier to speak to a stranger. The high and the mighty, the brightest and the best have concluded that the mission is flawed. Wishful thinking on Mr Lawson's part. He's unwilling to call for more back-up and their conclusion is, therefore, that his confidence in his judgement has gone, and further back-up would merely expose it. He was never more certain, when he left here, of the shipment coming through – never more sure of the critical importance of the agent. For him, it's all about trust. He would not have trusted the integrity of the back-up offered. It's his courage that makes him take responsibility – that is, responsibility for the undercover you gave him.'

Alison offered, now, to go to the counter, get a coffee and a cake or a roll. It was declined. Instead, she learned about Christopher Lawson's refusal to take a post with one of the new beefed stations in the Middle East, or a position on one of the augmented desks tracking the Islamists and their martyr teams through Europe. She learned about a bomb, and unbridled havoc.

'It didn't happen, did it? I wasn't here.'

'Thank you for coming, Lucy. Neither of us was.'

Alison stood, picked up her handbag from the adjacent chair. A man beside her ate a cholesterol mountain of breakfast and it was late in the afternoon. She eased back the table and nudged the pram a young mother guarded as she smoked and talked with her friend.

She said, 'Please, one more question. Is it real, the threat they've gone after?'

The answer was given her when they were out on the pavement and the dusk thickened round them. 'Others may not, but I believe it's real. If it wasn't, Mr Lawson wouldn't have gone there and wouldn't have recruited that undercover.'

They split, went their separate ways. Everything the liaison officer, Alison, had done was in the name of a young man she had never met, but into whose life she had inserted.

* * *

A kingfisher had gone downriver, but had not returned. For a long time, Carrick had looked for it. Storks had flown up the river, but not the kingfisher. There was nothing else to distract him, and he thought of what he wanted to do.

It played repeatedly in his mind. It was as if, he believed, he required a target on which to vent the pent-up pressure-cooker grievances. It was what he wanted to do to Mikhail. He saw it in images: walking up to the man and having no fear of him, calling him forward, seeing his surprise at the curtness of the command and seeing him obey, lunging at him, taking on a street-fighter with the tactics of his own gutter.

And he did not care, not now, what would be the consequences of doing what he wanted – had no more thought of consequences than of helping Reuven Weissberg bring a package across the swollen river. He was a new man, changed, and did not expect the recognition of those who had known him before. He sought respect, satisfaction, and to be treated as an alpha player, and he wore a criminal's weapon in a pancake holster on his belt.

The last shafts of the sunlight, and the final warmth from it, were on his shoulders and neck. He heard Mikhail cough again. Maybe something from those thoughts passed over his lips, came from his throat, but Reuven Weissberg looked sharply at him, was puzzled, then glanced at his watch before resuming his study of the river.

Carrick dropped his hands into the mud beside his hips and heaved himself upright. His back was to Reuven Weissberg and he faced Josef Goldmann, Viktor and Mikhail. He let his right hand drift behind his buttocks and flexed his fist, tightened and squeezed it. He had never had a street-fight, but he had seen them and knew that surprise, commitment and speed were key factors. He felt good, and it was what he wanted to do.

He took his eyeline on Mikhail and walked towards him. The man smoked, sat hunched and seemed unaware of him. He saw that Josef Goldmann shivered, could not stop trembling, that Viktor had let his head fall back against the bank, where it was steep, eyes closed and might have slept.

Carrick said, in his mind, 'Something I want to show you, Mikhail. Over here, now.'

He repeated it. In a moment he would say it out aloud.

He did, said it, what he had rehearsed in his mind.

Mikhail looked up, languid, disinterested.

He said it again and hoped his voice had hardness.

Mikhail stood. Josef Goldmann watched, as if curious, but Viktor slept on.

Mikhail came towards him, seemed relaxed, not wary, but the shadow was on the face and Carrick wasn't certain of it. Two more steps, then Mikhail would be close enough for the first strike with the fist.

He sucked in air. His wrist was held. He had not heard the movement. His wrist, at his back, was held tight, then twisted up high against his spine. He realized he was helpless. He was edged back, the sharp, stabbing pain in his shoulder and elbow, and could not resist. He was taken to the place beside the river where he had sat, his wrist was freed, and the water swirled past. He saw Mikhail slump again beside Josef Goldmann.

Reuven Weissberg said, in his ear, 'He would

have broken your neck, Johnny. With a broken neck you are useless to me.'

'Where does it go?'

'Where does what go?'

'Life . . .' Luke Davies said. 'Us.'

'Does it have to go somewhere?' She faced him.

A great log had been left by foresters. Among the pines and birches it had been a rare oak, uprooted by a winter gale years back. The upper sections had been cut off and carted away, but where the trunk joined the splayed roots it had been left for the weather to destroy. Luke Davies leaned against it and Katie Jennings sat astride it. He held her hand, or she held his, and neither loosened the grip.

'It would be nice,' he said.

Her eyes rolled. 'That's a big word to use to a girl, *nice*, makes her feel pretty special.'

'I think it would be good,' he said, slowly and with care, as if taking steps on ground where cluster bomblets had rained down. 'Yes, pretty good, if things sort of moved on, went somewhere.'

'Are we talking *futures*?' Mouth open, eyes wide, mocking but not cruel. 'Is that where we're going?'

'I think it's where I'd like to go.'

'For a proposal of cohabitation it's a little off the obvious. Nothing agreed, right. Nothing accepted, understood. Just conversation. Where do you live? What's there?'

He said, 'It's a room in a house, Camden Town. A grotty road and a nasty house. I have a room, single-occupancy tenancy, and the rest is full of nonentities. I can't afford anything better. Shall I do my CV, what and where I am? I live there because what I'm paid doesn't let me get higher up the bloody property ladder. I don't have a car, and I save on the transport fares by cycling to work and back. I eat in our canteen because it's cheap and subsidized, and I'm working late most evenings. I'm twenty-eight, I have first-class honours in East European and Slavonic studies, I've been with the Service for five years, and I think what I do is important and—'

'And you're paid a subsistence wage, probably less than me.'

'—and most of the guys round me, and the girls, have had a lift up, financially, from parents. I haven't – my dad cleans office windows and my mum's a dinner lady. I have this bloody accent, can't lose it unless I do speech training, and that typecasts me at VBX. What I'm saying is that I work hard, I don't have any link left with home, and I'm not on everybody's invitation list in the section. I suppose I'm pretty lonely, and I don't like it.'

She grinned. 'You and your tragic life.'

'Sorry, I didn't mean, you know . . .'

'God. I have a one-bedroom place, with a living room, a kitchenette and a bathroom not much bigger than you'd need to swing a cat in. It's down in south-west London, where I did beat work. I'm well paid, I do all right. I like going to work each day. Remember the narrowboat?'

'I do.'

'It's my dad's. I have the run of it any time I want. Wake up in the morning, nothing but cows on the bank, and the odd rat, and quiet, and—'

'I remember it because he was there.'

'What did I say?'

'You said, "Nothing's for ever."'

Katie Jennings's leg was hard against his shoulder. He felt her warmth, the heat in her hand.

Her eyes danced. 'I decide who goes there. Me. No one else has ownership.'

'Do you think they need us?'

'If they need us they'll call.'

He kissed her. More exactly, she kissed him.

Tadeuz Komiski saw them, their bodies locked together. The search for Father Jerzy's wood had taken him longer, and he had gone further, than he had expected.

He stopped. Where they were, the curse had taken hold of him. He stayed. They were at the place where guilt had been born. He was among the trees, unseen by them, and a child's memories were stirred.

Lawson listened.

Bugsy hung back but Deadeye spilled it. 'We've been to the river, where they were yesterday. They'd left footmarks and fag ends but – and sorry about it, Mr Lawson – they're not there today, haven't been, and there's no trace of the boat. Stands to reason it was where they did the reconnaissance and where they expected to find their people on the opposite side. Not there. We backtracked up- and downstream, tried to find them that way. Didn't. We cut back into the forest and looked for the cars. By then, have to say it, we'd little chance because the light'd gone. Mr Lawson, we don't know where they are, don't know where to look. We've lost them. Somewhere they'll be hunkered down and waiting for their pick-up, but I don't know where to start looking for it.'

Lawson said briskly, 'What we need now, Deadeye, is a smidgen of luck.'

He thought he'd spoken with confidence and

authority. Where did luck come from? They stood in a half-circle but away from him. He thought they had such faith, deep reservoirs of trust. He smiled at each in turn, at Shrinks, Deadeye and Bugsy, at Adrian and Dennis, and they waited on him for an answer handed down as to where luck could be gained. He realized then how long young Davies and the girl had been gone, but they were not a solution. Two more bodies would make no difference.

He turned away from them. They should not see the deep worry lines that cut his face.

His one certainty stood firm. It would be here, close to the site of the Sobibor camp, that collection would be made and delivery taken. That much he knew.

'I give it an hour. We'll move then. Just let the light settle a little,' Lawson said. Anxiety squirmed in his stomach, but he summoned up the medley of confidence and authority. 'They won't come until it's decently dark, I'd bet on it.'

Two kilometres back, they had worked for two hours, Molenkov doing better than Yashkin, and had shifted a tree's lower trunk – three metres long and a half-metre in diameter – that blocked a trail into the forest. They had left an apology for a road, the only route going south from the village of Malorita. They had – together – sweated, cursed, grunted, sworn, gasped, but had moved it, and had been left with feeble strength after the log that had been embedded in winter mud was slid aside sufficiently for Yashkin to wriggle the Polonez past it. Then they had had to reverse the process. Molenkov had insisted on it. The log must be returned to its old place. It had sunk back into the

515

mud groove it had lain in before its disturbance. They had done it, and they had fallen on each other and hugged. Neither had known who supported the other. Then they had kicked out the rigid lines of the Polonez's tyres and used dead branches to smear the mess they had made in the mud. Yashkin had driven into the forest and Molenkov had the map on his knee. Each metre the car took them, with its petrol-gauge needle stationary at the bottom of the red section, seemed important and an unlikely bonus.

A kilometre back, the Polonez had sunk into mud on the trail. The engine had died after Yashkin had tried to accelerate out of the pit they'd gone into, then reverse out, and had failed in both. They had been there an hour. The solution, Molenkov had announced, was to make a secure base on which the tyres could find a grip. They had gathered up every branch and pine frond, every limb that the winter snow's weight had broken off. They had brought the wood in armfuls to the trail, had slapped it down into the mud, heaved the pieces against the tyres and insinuated them under all four wheels. Then more had gone in front and been stamped down. Yashkin had started the engine, Molenkov had pushed and mud had flown. He had thought he had used the last energy he possessed, had sworn oaths at the great mound in the Polonez underneath the tarpaulin and . . . the wheels had gripped. The Polonez had surged forward. Molenkov had been left, a filthy, grunting, muddy wretch, on his hands and knees.

They had come off the trail and Yashkin had woven between the trees, the lower branches scraping the car's sides.

Molenkov had his arms up as if he expected,

with each lurch of the wheels, to be thrown against the dashboard or the lower part of the windscreen, and he had tried to read the map. The light was failing, and his eyes could make out only the blur of a deeper shade of green and the line of the Bug. Among the trees, off the track, the ground was firmer than it was on the trail, and they made progress – slow but steady, Molenkov thought. Almost, he had relaxed. Almost, he had forgotten.

And then there was a cough, like a fucking death rattle. It was the way his wife had gone, a cough deep in the throat that persisted for three, four seconds and then quiet. When the quiet had come, his wife was dead. The Polonez, too, was dead, engine expired.

Yashkin could be an idiot, could be precise and disciplined. He was in the middle of a forest with a car that was going nowhere and had a dry fuel tank. His response was to set the gear in neutral and apply the handbrake.

They climbed out of the car. They met at the back, and each took hold of a corner of the tarpaulin. Together, they dragged it clear. It was not done with words but from some instinctive agreement. Each reached forward and laid a hand on the covering, where the writing was stencilled and the serial number posted. It did not breathe, did not hiccup. It showed no sign of life. Again, without consultation or debate, they took the side straps and heaved, lugged, dragged the fucking thing off the tail. Yashkin locked the car.

They took their positions on either side of it.

They lifted, felt its weight.

Yashkin asked, 'How far?'

Molenkov answered, 'More than three kilometres. My friend . . .'

517

'Yes?'

'Why are we doing this?'

Yashkin stuck his chin forward. 'To show that we can, and because we said we would.'

They went forward, towards the fall of the sun.

Carrick stared at the water, and saw only the dull flecks where the flow held debris in a swirling eddy. He waited for the moon to rise, and for a light to flash. Reuven Weissberg's hand still rested on his coat, and they were together. The others, behind them, were apart.

Chapter 19: 16 April 2008

Carrick felt the cold around him. He scanned the bank for a light.

With the darkness, Reuven Weissberg had been decisive: the boat had been dragged from cover and was beside them with the coil of rope. The instructions had been given for Viktor, Mikhail and Josef Goldmann to spread themselves out, take the positions at hundred-metre intervals, but that evening they were ordered to be downstream of himself. Carrick was told that Reuven Weissberg and he were at the best place for a crossing, where the flow was fastest but the river narrowest. He sensed certainty in the man beside him that the delivery would be made.

Carrick would have sat in the quiet that was threatened only by the rumble of the river, owls' cries and the motion of the high branches behind him. He did not need to talk. He was numbed by tiredness and hunger. Reuven Weissberg talked to him, and, if he had wished to, he could not have escaped the purr and persistence of the voice alongside him.

He wanted it over, done with, wanted to see the light, make the crossing and bring back what was bought.

The voice dripped in his ear.

Reuven Weissberg said, 'I could have arranged, Johnny, for it to be carried up north to the Finnish border, or taken into the Kaliningrad *oblast*, into Latvia or Estonia, because there all the frontiers leak. It could have gone into Ukraine far to the south or to a Black Sea port. I have the connections to have collected it at any of those places . . . but it had to be here, Johnny.'

Only blackness and lines of deep charcoal grey were in front of Carrick. He couldn't see the water, only hear it.

'From the time I was a child, Johnny, I have known of this place. She did not, but she could have taken a knife and used its tip to carve its name on my chest or my forehead. When I was a child, in Perm, when I lived first with my grandmother, I knew this place, the paths and huts inside the fences and the tracks in the forest better than I knew the route to the block where we lived and the streets around it. I could have walked from the hut where the clothes of the dead were sorted and the hut where the cut hair of the dead was graded and the hut where the valuables were parcelled, and I could have gone to the Happy Flea or the Swallow's Nest or walked on the Road to Heaven. If I was late for school, I ran. I was a child and was late for the bell at school, but I did not think of punishment from a teacher. I was always running from the fence through the minefield, then through the open ground and the machine-guns fired, and I was running through the trees in the forest. If I fought in the yard at school, it was not against an older child who tried to keep me from his customers over whom he had made a roof, but I was one of those who waited in hiding for the German officers to visit a place that it was routine for them to come to, and I imagined I hacked with an axe and stabbed with a knife. Everything about me was the creation of my grandmother. It was from this place.'

He waited and watched and did not see a light, and constant with the voice was the river's unbroken surge.

'I am shaped by it, Johnny. When I was a child she told me of it, and I sat at her knee. When I was a man, she came into my room before I slept. She would bring me a drink. She would not sit on the bed but would stand in the darkness of the room, not moving, and she would tell me of what happened here to her. You cannot free yourself from it. Man and child, after the door had closed behind her and whether or not I switched a light back on, I could not be free of it. No part of the story is better than another. It is a slide towards despair. The man does not exist to whom I am in debt. She was out of the camp, was with Samuel, was in the forest where dragnets closed on them. One enemy? A German enemy only, with a Ukrainian ally? No, Johnny, many enemies. Vultures circling to find food. My blood carries no debt to any man.'

We had made love that morning. For him it was the first time, and for me, the first time that it had been meaningful. It was after the dawn. We had slept on the forest floor and the rain had fallen on us, but we had slept and had held each other for warmth through the night. I think we were too tired to have done it in the dark and it was better, then, to sleep. The morning had come.

In the night the forest had been quiet except for owls, the bark of a fox and the fall of the rain. The wind had thrashed the trees. We had some shelter against a big pine. I wanted him to do it . . . Germans came near to us, and had dogs, but the rain had killed the scent we had left and the wind would have covered what tracks we had made. I think we were now five or six kilometres from the camp. They were in a line, and their officers could not ride their horses because of the denseness of the trees so they led them. The end of the cordon line they made would have been less than fifty metres from where we hid, and we held each other close. Samuel had whispered to me that if we were seen we would run together. It would be better for us to be shot than taken and herded back to the camp. And they were gone . . .

So we lived. To celebrate, two rats that the dogs had not found, we made love. He knew what to do, he said, because it had been talked of endlessly in the unit he had been with. Always they had talked of it. He was gentle with me. I wanted to do it, but was frightened . . . I was in a forest, I was hunted, I had lived more than a year in the shadow of death, and it was ridiculous to be frightened of love. He opened the clothing on my chest and touched me, and as he touched me I felt the wetness coming. It did not matter to me that the rain dripped hard on us. He had lowered his trousers to his knees, and I had lifted my skirt, and he had taken my hand and had guided me to hold him. It did not hurt when he came into me. I had thought it would, but it did not. The only sensation I felt was love, no writhing pleasure. It was love. I buried him in me, squeezed my muscles, held him, and did not want him to leave me. It did not last long, but I told myself I would remember each moment of it. He was spent. He was more tired than I after it. I held him close to me, and I could see his white buttocks and they had the marks on them where my fingers had been. His head was against my chest. It could have lasted for ever . . . Those minutes, gripping him and holding him, were the only ones in more than a year that I had lived. In those minutes the shadow of death was gone. They did not last.

Minutes of love were snatched. Death took them.

Men came. They were not Germans, not Ukrainians. They were of the Armia Krajowa. The first to see us shouted that he had found 'Christ killers' from the camp. Others came running. We could not run. Samuel could not because his trousers were at his knees and my old knickers were at my ankles. We were trying to cover ourselves. I was a Pole, Samuel was a Russian from the army attempting to liberate Poland, and they were Poles. To them – partisans in the forest who were from defeated units of the Polish Home Army – we were Jews and as much of an enemy as the Germans. They would have shot us, then and there, but did not – I believe – for fear of the noise of a gunshot. There were perhaps a half-dozen of them, and the leader was a bear of a man with a great beard. He stood over us, his legs apart, took the bayonet from his belt and fastened it – I heard the click, metal on metal, of the action. Then Samuel tried to save me. He fell across me. We were fighting each other for the right to protect the other, but Samuel had more strength than I. He was across me, covering me, and I felt the blows to his body as he was stabbed. Then there was a whistle, a signal. Again there was the shout of 'Christ killers', and they were gone. Perhaps they thought the Germans were close. They were around us. Then there was the emptiness of the forest.

I examined him.

He was conscious.

He was bleeding in many places, his back and sides. If the whistle had not blown the man would have had time to kill him, but the whistle had blown. He was in huge pain. Any movement hurt him. He said then that it would have been better if we had died on the fence or in the minefield. He thought himself too severely hurt to move, and tried to urge me to leave him and go on, further into the forest, alone. And the rain fell on his back and the water was reddened. I didn't know what to do. I was against the tree and he was across me. I had my shirt, my blouse, against the wounds. My chest was bare but I didn't feel the rain or the cold, only his pain. I wasn't strong enough to move him – if I had been able to move him I didn't know of anywhere I could take him.

I saw the child.

A child, a boy of five or six, stood among the trees and watched us. He had clothes on that were little better than rags. I thought him to be the child of a peasant family. He stood with his hands behind his back, and the look on his face was curiosity. I called to him to come closer so that I could speak to him, but he wouldn't move. He was among the trees. I didn't know whether the child was an idiot from birth, was simple, but there was no fear on his face, or excitement, and no charity. I was pleading with him to find me help, and he stared back at me. I lied to him. I offered him money: I had no money. I pointed to the wounds on Samuel – as if it were necessary to point. I showed him my hands, which were washed in Samuel's blood. I screamed for him to help me. And he ran. I shouted after him that he must bring help.

I was alone again with Samuel.

I don't know for how long. His strength was going. Too much blood had been lost. I couldn't save him. All I hoped for was that he would be comfortable and – in his own time – slip away. I talked to him and didn't know if he heard me. I said to him that I was privileged to have known his love and that I would survive to carry the memory of him . . . and I heard the voice of a child.

We, who were in the camp for a week or a month or a year, had forgotten how to weep or show joy. I could have cried, in my desperation, for joy when I saw that child and the man who followed him. The child led him, skipped ahead. He was a man of young middle age, rough-dressed and rough-faced, and he carried a woodsman's axe, a long-handled one, and a dog was with them. I heard the child's voice, then the dog barking, and I thought help had come.

The child's father had not come to help.

I saw greed in his face, and hatred.

He crouched over Samuel, who had wriggled across my body. At first he didn't speak but started to search through what pockets he could reach in Samuel's trousers, Samuel's coat. I crawled, writhed, was no longer under Samuel and turned on his attackers. I tried to stop him. Samuel screamed at the pain made by my movements and by the father's. The man shouted at me that all Jews had money, all Jews had jewellery. I struggled with him. He slashed at me with his axe but I was moving and it didn't hit me. The blade hit the top of Samuel's head. He came again: where was the money, the jewellery? I fought him. He had kicked Samuel with old boots, and that was his anger at his failure to find money and jewellery. I scraped my nails across his cheeks, hard enough to draw blood. He swung a fist at me, I caught and bit it, felt the bones of his fingers – and he backed away. He yelled now at me that I was worth a two-kilo bag of sugar at least. His voice had risen and his hand was bloodied. More blood was in his beard, and he told me he would bring Germans and the reward for identifying Jews in the forest would be paid him in sugar. He had the same hatred for me as the men of the Armia Karjowa had shown. He circled me. I faced him. I stood over Samuel and defended his body. I heard Samuel's labouring breathing and knew his death was close. The *forester did not dare to come closer to me. He said he would bring the Germans and spat at me.*

He went with the child. He hurried. He went to earn his two-kilo bag of sugar.

Death had come.

His last moments, those last struggles of his life, were frantic and brave, and he had attempted to stand that he might protect me. There was no dignity in his death . . . but neither was there dignity for those going to the chambers at the end of the Road to Heaven, or for those on the wire and in the minefield. There was no mercy there, in the camp or in the forest. Only betrayal .

I took Samuel's weight, had my hands in his armpits. I dragged him as far as I could. I cannot say where I found that strength.

I buried him.

With my fingernails, my hands and a length of dead wood, I made a pit for him. I worked him into it. I was exhausted to the point of collapse. I had to use my boots to push him in. I filled it, handful by handful, with earth and then I kicked leaves over it.

I was alone. I went on into the forest. I no longer knew the direction I took or what I hoped to find. So many had betrayed me, and at the end a child with an innocent face had joined the others. I vowed then never to love, never to trust, never to care about the deaths of others. I walked until the darkness closed on me, and kept walking, hit trees, fell into ditches – but felt no pain, only hatred.

'Do you understand, Johnny?'

'Yes, sir.'

'The story makes me the man I am.'

'I understand, sir.'

He thought the hatred, as expressed in the great mass of the forest behind him by a young woman, still lived with the same snake's venom as in the days its culture had been bred. Carrick thought of the hatred as something that could not be turned away from. Reuven Weissberg's world was his world.

'You will stand with me, Johnny?'

'Yes, sir.'

The punch hit his shoulder, rocked him. Johnny Carrick, too, was a part of the madness at the Sobibor camp. He seemed to see the young woman blundering among the trees in the darkness that hugged him, and he wondered if by then, in those minutes and hours, the lustre of her hair had changed to white.

The director general, Francis Pettigrew – without a knighthood yet, but it would come – tapped into the console and the lock clicked open. He went into Operations (Current) Control. The room was in the heart of the building, on a second floor down in the basement. He had not had the sword tap his shoulder, but possessed the necessary stature. He glided into the room, made a presence. He saw Banham hunched at a desk with a wall of screens in front of him, telephones, a flask, a half-eaten sandwich and . . . Of course, if the director general had believed without equivocation in the judgement of Christopher Lawson, it would not have been only Giles Banham here: the full team would have been out – Lambert, Amin and Carthew would have been competing for desk space.

The room was where operations of sensitivity were monitored in the hours up to the predicted climax of crisis, the time when it screwed up or the corks popped.

'Heard from them over there, have you?'

'No, Director, nothing. Left a couple of texts for

Lawson – had an FO response to each. At least to the point. I suppose he's getting a bit frantic. Don't mind me saying it, Director, but isn't this all a tad Ice Age?'

'It's the way it is, where we are, what we have.' The director general had known Banham since he was knee high, and his parents three decades. There were not many from whom he would have permitted that slight curled lip when Christopher Lawson was discussed. Not that he could pass blame to Banham. It was he, Francis Pettigrew, who had nominated minimal manning for the room. 'If something materializes across that bloody river, give me a shout.'

'You'll be, Director . . . ?'

'At the club.'

'I'll call you.'

He realized then what he had done. Banham, who would remain alone in the room and had already started to consume the remainder of his sandwich, was justified in his visible lack of excitement in a mission called Haystack. Had he merely humoured Christopher Lawson or had he sold him short? Pettigrew didn't know.

He slipped out. On that night of the week they did a rather good casserole at the club. Perhaps he had allowed his one-time mentor to bully him – shouldn't have done. He walked off down the corridor that led to the lift. Should have asked for greater provenance before signing off on Haystack and committing those resources . . . Well, he'd be charitable and decent when Lawson came on the phone: 'No show, Francis, may have been overegged. Worth a try . . .'

'Absolutely, Christopher, well worth a try.'

He didn't have a picture in his mind of where

Lawson and his increments were and what it would be like for them.

He took a lift up. His protection intercepted him, the reception people stood. Security opened the swing doors so that he did not have to swipe his way out. It was the departure of the king-emperor of VBX. His car waited.

And much else lay on his mind. The door was opened. Damn it, more was on his mind than the comfort of Christopher Lawson, who had taken squatter's rights on the banks of the Bug river.

They slipped away.

Adrian, Dennis and Deadeye headed for the river as they had been told to. Adrian had only a vague sense of history, and thought Deadeye got none of the romance and tragedy of it, but Dennis had a keen interest in the past and with it a love of all things French. Not merely the cooking and wine production, but France's military history. Dennis thought of their dispatch back to the river as the nearest thing to the final throw, the sending forward of the Imperial Guard – 18 June 1815 – on the field of Waterloo. If they – himself, Adrian and Deadeye – did not turn the day and locate their targets on the riverbank, it was lost. They were the last chance. It was reassuring, in a gallows sort of way, that Deadeye had retrieved a weapon from his baggage, loaded it and was carrying it.

They had left the guv'nor, the boss, with Shrinks, pacing, deep in his thoughts and murmuring to himself. If Lawson had felt a mounting panic, he had not shown it . . . Impressive, that. They went off and away, through the trees and towards the Bug, moving carefully because that was their skill, but he seemed to hear the tramp of those marching feet and the squelching mud of the Imperial Guard's advance. The last throw.

Yes, if they were coming – with their filthy, contaminated cargo – they would be near. That, at least, he could be certain of.

'Would you choose this fucking place to take a fucking holiday?'

'I would not, Molenkov. Nor would I talk. It takes breath to talk, and breath takes energy.'

'You're so pompous, always were and always will be. I talk about holidays. Where shall I go on holiday? Not here, so where?'

'Shut up, Molenkov. Use your energy to pull.'

'I have no energy left. I need to think of the beach, the sunshine, the beer, not mud. How far?'

He didn't answer. Yashkin heard the drip of Molenkov's voice and the moan of the wind in the trees. He heard his own gasps and Molenkov's wheezing hisses. How far? He didn't answer because he had no idea how far it was to the river, but he used the moon's climb behind him – between the trees – as a guide. It had risen high enough to show where paths and tracks had been fashioned through the dense planting of the pines. But every pit in their way was an obstacle filled with water, and sometimes they saw them in advance and could skirt them and sometimes they couldn't. The deepest pit took the water above their knees and doused the beast they dragged. Every rut, where the tracks were wider and long-ago forestry tractors had been, was filled with flooding pools and had cloying, clinging mud at the bottom. Yashkin did not know but he *hoped* the river was now within a kilometre of where they struggled, and he *hoped*, also, that his calculations on direction were exact. Each had hold of one of the side straps of the weapon, codenamed RA-114. Clear from a resting-place in the back of the Polonez, and without its tarpaulin shroud, it had the shape of a small oil drum and was encased in a canvas jacket. The straps were stout. The weight was in excess, Yashkin believed, of sixty kilos. Heavy enough when he had been fifteen years younger and had manoeuvred it from the porch at his home, down the side of his house and into the hole he had dug in his vegetable patch. Fifteen years of existing on the Sarov scrap heap had wasted his strength. The week of driving west had sapped what he had left, as had lack of sleep and food, the beating at Pinsk, the high-octane stress of the frontier crossing into Belarus . . . and for two hours or more they had slipped, slithered and dragged the thing through the forest. Little strength remained, and he thought Molenkov weaker. The weight and awkwardness of it seemed to grow with each metre covered.

'Yashkin . . .'

He heard the bleat of his name. 'Yes?'

'If we ever take the holiday – you, me and Mother – and we're somewhere that has a beach, sun and many cans of beer . . .'

'What?'

'Would they come after us?'

For a moment he gagged, then whispered, 'I don't know.'

'Would they try to poison us? Would they pay for a contract hit with a pistol? Would they explode a bomb under the car? You don't know, but what do you *think*? Tell me.'

'I don't know, and I don't think. Will you take your share of the weight, my esteemed friend? Do I have to do everything?' Yashkin swore. The pit in the track was deeper than the others. The mud at the bottom was stickier than it had been in others. Yashkin was in the pit, with the water almost at his crotch, and Molenkov had missed it, and was a half-metre above him, and the weight of the beast seemed to pitch towards him, and it was pushing him lower into the water. He realized what he had lost. Molenkov was pulling at him.

'Oaf – you're so clumsy. Get up, get out.'

'I've lost . . . fuck . . .'

'What have you lost?'

'My shoe.'

'What do you mean?' Then a chuckle. 'Lost it? Look at your foot, try there.'

He thrashed in the water. He came up the side of the pit. He was very close to hitting Molenkov with a clenched fist. He looked back. His left foot was already a frozen, unfeeling mass. He could see the water, silver in the moonlight, and the great ripples flowing on its surface. He didn't know where he had been in the hole when the mud had caught his shoe, clamped on it and torn it from his foot when he had struggled to free himself. He could have wept. The pit he had gone into was, perhaps, two metres long, a metre wide and more than a metre deep. He swore again. To grope in the mud and search for his shoe would require him to immerse his whole body in the water, maybe even his fucking head.

Yashkin said, 'I've lost my shoe in the mud and I doubt I can find it.'

He hopped at first and was reluctant to set his stockinged foot down on the ground. But the track was of soft compost, matted pine needles and old leaves, and had give in it. With each step he was prepared to test more weight on the forest floor.

They dragged it between them. They went down into more ruts and more pits. They kept going.

Molenkov had started again to talk about holidays, another beach, endless sun, beer without limit, but Yashkin didn't hear him. Above the wheezing and the gasps, the whine of the wind in the branches, was a far-away murmur that grew in intensity with each faltering step they took. He knew what he heard. There was no break in the murmur. He felt pride surge in him and the loss of the shoe seemed irrelevant. He made Molenkov move faster.

Yashkin said, 'I can hear, at last, the voice of a great river. My friend, we've done it, survived it. Soon you will have, maybe in an hour, a half-share of one million American dollars in your pocket, and you can take a holiday anywhere you want. We're very close to the river, to the Bug.'

Viktor saw them.

They had come through an open space – where a storm might have brought down a cluster of trees – and the moon's light had caught them. Two were together and one was a few metres apart from them, nearer to the riverbank.

Viktor was end marker. Upstream from him was Mikhail, Goldmann, then Weissberg and the bastard who was a stranger among them.

They were fifty metres short of him, he estimated. He rated the one nearer the water as being the more competent, moving quieter and not coming into the silver filtered light. He reckoned the pair were short on the art of crossing rough ground. Thoughts came very fast to Viktor's mind, and images to his memory. In the Stare Miasto they would have been on familiar territory; on the cobbled streets and the pavement slabs they would have been apart and expert in the environment. He could not recognize in that faint light what clothes they wore or their build, but he had no doubt of it: had the sun been high, had the forest been lit, he would have recognized them from the Old City of Warsaw. He would have seen the same men coming through the choke-points.

Viktor knew the art of surveillance and knew what gave professional esteem.

They had not seen him. Most of his body was sheltered by a birch clump. Beside it on the river's side, there was a similar open space to the one the two men had just come through, and the same degree of moonlight shone into it. Viktor stepped out. He exposed himself, stood tall in the middle of the space, let the light come down and catch his forehead. Maybe it would glint in his eyes. He could recall what instructors had done when he was a recruit officer in State Security and the course was on the finer art of surveillance; it had been done to a friend, not to him, but that recall was sharp, as was the humiliation of his friend. They had frozen, the two men. He couldn't see the third because his eyeline was directly ahead, locked on the two. Viktor had no doubt now that the surveillance had been on them from the time they had driven down the fast road to Heathrow. Vengeance would come later. It was not to be rushed – was like a good fuck or a good meal, best done at convenience and after consideration. They stared back. They were in their pool of light and he was in his.

It was his supreme moment.

He felt a slow smile break on his face. One thing alone irked Viktor. He did not have sufficient light to see their faces. He missed not having a big

534

flashlight to shine at them and catch the moment. He did it like that instructor had at the counter-intelligence school at Novosibirsk, when he had served in the 3rd Directorate. He could imagine what would be on their faces, ·the dumb shock, the astonishment and the shame.

Viktor waved to the two men. Not big, not flamboyant, just a raised hand and a short wave.

He was gone.

Adrian trembled, had never before felt that shockwave in his gut, his limbs and his mind – as if he had lost control.

In the craft talk of his trade, the top men preached a mantra: *If the next stage is to show out, you pull out.* He and Dennis had gone through that stage and not known it. They had shown out.

Casual, the target had waved.

And the conventional wisdom said: *We call it the heat stakes – one to ten. Ten is when you're busted, have shown out. Go to gaol.* They were busted. The dial needle had hit 'ten' and they had failed.

From the height of the target, Adrian had realized it was Viktor. Viktor was KGB-trained. The wave had been enough to show his contempt for them.

When they talked about 'sterile areas', 'control' and 'housing', the best men – and Adrian and Dennis would have reckoned themselves top of the tree – always exuded supreme levels of confidence. But a lecture session never finished without the final message: *The desperate moment for any surveillance officer, far and away the worst, is when the target looks you in the eye and waves to you.* Viktor had.

He thought himself a serious man, and Dennis,

535

was unused to the taint of failure. He had to clasp his hands across his stomach, but it was inadequate – however tight he squeezed his fingers – to kill the shake.

Adrian whispered the question, 'Did you see it?'

Dennis murmured in his ear, 'I saw it. We screwed up.'

Stuttered: 'Big-time.'

'Doesn't get any bigger. What to do?'

Adrian said, 'We can't go forward, not after that. I can't get my head round it. Never happened to me before. Twenty years of this, more, and it's the first time. I'd bollock a rookie who showed out as bad as that. He was laughing at us.'

'Me too, first time – I feel a prat. They could be anywhere along the bank, and they're alerted. You got a better definition, Adrian, of disaster?'

'Could be anywhere, could be a quarter of a mile upstream, more. What to do? That's the guv'nor's shout. Have to tell him, come clean. He makes the decision. Say it up front. We don't know where they are.'

'And lose what they're bringing across?'

'Got better ideas?'

In front of them, where the target had been and where he had waved, gentle and mocking, was a solid wall of darkness. They did not know whether he had backed off by ten yards or a hundred. Right to assume that he carried a weapon, Mikhail too, and that Reuven Weissberg – top target – was armed. They had heard Shrinks talk his syndrome stuff on the agent and knew he, too, was tooled up. They heard only the river's rush and the wind high above. They would back off, leave decision-taking to Mr Lawson, the guv'nor. Couldn't blunder on. They left Deadeye down by the water and suggested he didn't move . . . Adrian thought the wound was well shared, that Dennis would feel as bad as himself because a target had faced up to them and had waved.

Their professionalism demanded they said it, four square, to the guv'nor's face. Neither would hide the catastrophe of a show-out and a failure to locate the prime target.

'Come on,' she said.

She led. Katie Jennings had pushed up her sweater, undone her blouse buttons, hitched up her bra and put his hands on her breasts. He didn't do much for himself.

'It's all right, I don't bite.'

She was astride him. He was against a fallen tree, had his back to it. She heaved up her hips, lowered her trousers and pushed her knickers down her thighs. Hadn't done it like this since she was a kid, a couple of weeks before her sixteenth birthday. What was the bloody order of battle? She blinked, remembered what the guy had done all those years before because he'd known what he was at. She felt the cold air on her stomach and back, and on her thighs.

'Don't go all scared on me. You haven't a worry, I'm up to date with taking them.'

It was a sort of madness. She was, in reality, a mature young woman. Katie Jennings did not make a habit of shagging around. Those who knew her well, in the Pimlico office, her neighbours, and especially her parents, would have been shocked to observe her baring her buttocks to the evening darkness, then heaving at the clothing covering Luke Davies's body. It was the way the guy had done it when she was short of her sixteenth birthday; had worked then, didn't seem wrong now. She had his coat open and his fleece unzipped, his shirt open and his vest up. Then she went to work on the belt and his trousers. She accepted it, the madness. She could put it down to stress, strain, trauma, had the excuses stacked high – but didn't need them. She was tugging at his trousers. Rare excitement now gripped her. She could not have stopped herself and had no wish to.

'Just enjoy it, like it's a chauffeur ride.'

Under her the whiteness of his skin was made silver by the moonlight. Who cared about madness? Not Katie Jennings. A woman in a man's world, she had been subject enough times to what was called harassment, or gender abuse, but she had never complained of being rated the token female. She thought his body quite thin, spare, rather pretty. He was supine . . . No, he wasn't going to help her so she'd have to do the damn job herself. Hadn't a word to say for himself but his eyes were big and longing and his breath came faster – came a bloody sight faster when she eased back, reached down and took him. The eyes were big, popping, and he was staring over her shoulder. Then he was pushing her back. For a moment, she tried to fight him, then gave up – quit.

She looked over his shoulder, followed his line of sight.

'Fuck me,' Katie Jennings mouthed.

It had been, for Tadeuz Komiski, the incredible moment.

He was the child.

He was in his seventh year. He was in the forest two days after the shooting at the camp, the explosions and the howl of the sirens.

538

He remembered what he had seen as if it had happened an hour before.

A young man down and propped against a fallen tree. A woman crouched over him. The young man's skin white and exposed.

Two Christ killers on the ground among the trees. Filthy old clothes on both of them.

They were watching him, gazing up at him, and words spat from their mouths.

He had run to call his father. His father had spoken of a reward of two kilos of sugar for identifying where fugitives hid. He had come with the axe.

The curse had been made.

Much floated in his mind. They stared at him as they had then. Now he was a man and old, but once he had been a child. Visions came to him of his father's swinging axe and of the young woman fighting back . . . He remembered the painful death of his father from the cancers, the long, sad silences of his mother before she had gone to her rest, the birth of a dead baby and the slipping away of his weakened wife. He remembered the loneliness of his life and the nightmare dreams . . . the life of the curse.

Remembered, also, that men had been in the forest, had seemed to search for him and watch him. He had followed them that day and when the dusk had come they were by the river.

The man covered his skin. The woman wriggled. They shouted at him.

He saw the priest. The priest had brought him a meat pie, had asked him to bring wood to the church house in the village. He heard the priest's soft words: *Was it when you were a child and living in this house that the guilt was born? You don't have to*

answer me – but the only palliative for guilt is con-
fession. All I can say, Tadeuz, is that if ever the chance is
given you – it is unlikely – to right a wrong then take it,
seize it. Each word of what the priest had said was
clear in his mind.

Soldiers had hunted through the forest, and had
offered the reward of a two-kilo bag of sugar for
help in the capture of fleeing Jews, and again men
hunted and were down at the Bug banks. He had
betrayed a boy and a girl. It was to right a wrong
that he went forward.

They cringed away from him.

When he was closer, they stood. He saw now that
they took defensive postures, that their arms were
out and their fists clenched. He showed them his
own hands, empty.

He said, 'There are hunters in the forest. I can
take you to them. It will right a wrong. You can hurt
them and make vengeance.'

The girl hissed at the boy, 'What is he? Some
goddam pervert?' He did not understand her
language.

He said, 'I will show you them, and lift the
curse.'

He reached out his hand, and the girl was shrill:
'What you reckon? Going to watch us and jerk off?'

He took the boy's arm. He said, 'The curse is my
burden, help me . . . The hunters are here, I will
lead you to them and you will destroy them. I beg
you, come with me.'

He had hold of the boy's sleeve. '*A deranged
lunatic, what else? Sorry and all that. I was up for it.
Just get rid of him and let's get the hell out.*' He tugged
at the coat.

The boy spoke in German. 'Where are they?'

'Beside the river.'

'Can you show me where they are?'

'I will. It is to be free of the curse.' The boy allowed him to pull at the coat and didn't try to break away from him.

'You're not bloody going with him . . .'

'He knows where they are. I am.'

The great weight, the burden of Tadeuz Komiski, seemed shed. He led them. He knew what he would do when the curse was cast off, and felt happy. He took them through the forest, away from where the old fences had been, the huts and the watchtowers, the burning pits and the chambers joined by the rubber piping to the truck's engine, away from where the geese had been chased so they would scream louder. He glided among the trees, as he had when he was a child.

He had spoken to Mikhail. With Mikhail, he had found Josef Goldmann.

Together they talked. Where was the nearest international airport? Was there any indication of a cordon or roadblocks? Which passports were available to them? Which of the cars should they take? Would they tell Reuven Weissberg that they were fleeing into the night?

When Goldmann had wavered, Mikhail had gripped his shoulders. 'We do not have a meeting, we do not set up a committee, we do not debate and discuss. We go. You've seen him when the fury's alive. That anger burns. Would you tell him? I won't. Viktor is clear. Viktor reports on men tracking along the river. Who, in darkness, comes covertly along the banks of the Bug? A farmer? A forester? A tourist? Surveillance officers from an intelligence agency? I think so. I think also that we have very little time.'

541

Viktor could not have faulted Mikhail.

He pushed Josef Goldmann, a violent shove. The man half fell but Mikhail caught him, then threw him on. Mikhail would not have told Reuven Weissberg that he was abandoned, nor would Viktor. He imagined, a brief thought, a tonguetied and terrified Josef Goldmann stammering out a message of treachery and the voice would have died before it had been blurted. They went.

They held Josef Goldmann between them, as if he was their prisoner. They hustled him away from the river. They took him because he was the banker. He had made the investments, he knew in which banks' strong boxes the deeds of ownership were held, he had the account numbers in his head. Josef Goldmann had control of the millions of dollars, sterling and euros, hidden under layers of nominee names and code numbers, that would offer a comfortable future to Viktor and Mikhail. Without him they would be paupers. Paupers would have no protection, and paupers could not buy a roof.

They dragged Goldmann behind them, his feet scraping the forest floor. Viktor had no sense of wrongdoing, or of betrayal: he did not recognize such feelings. He had a sense, though, of anger. It had been Reuven Weissberg who had demanded the outsider walk alongside him, who had treated the outsider as a favoured toy, an indulged pet: he would have liked to hurt the toy, heard the pet squeal. He could not take out that frustrated anger on Josef Goldmann because the flabby, pasty-faced Jew knew the codes, the numbers and the banks.

Bugsy said, 'It's gone down the tube, Mr Lawson. Normally I'd not speak out, but I'm going to. It's down the tube, Mr Lawson, because of you. There's going to be shit in the fan, but I'm not prepared to take the rap for it, and I don't reckon any of us is, or should. They were your decisions, Mr Lawson, and you'll have to stand by them. They were the wrong decisions.'

Adrian and Dennis were at the edge of the group, had said their piece alternating the delivery of news that was awful, then inched back. In his career, Christopher Lawson had not experienced what was, almost, a moment of mutiny.

Shrinks said, 'If you'd treated your agent with a modicum of sensitivity, Mr Lawson, this fiasco wouldn't have been bred. You contaminated the man's loyalties. In effect, to drive him deeper into their arms, you lost him. The result is plain as a pikestaff. We have only a vague idea of where this hideous weapon may be brought to. Your leadership, or lack of it, has engulfed us in abject failure. When we get back, when there's the inquest, don't expect me to respond to your usual bully-boy tactic. I'll put the knife in and twist it.'

He could see their faces. They despised him. It was as if they had torn off badges and insignia, had thrown them into the mud and sought flight – sought, above all, to preserve reputations. What to do? It exercised him. Didn't know. What option was available to him? To move along the bank of the Bug, only the moonlight to guide them, and *hope* for a visual sighting.

Dennis's torchbeam caught them.

Well, it didn't take an intelligence officer of Christopher Lawson's experience to read the runes. Her coat was open, and in the V-neck of her pullover it was clear that the blouse buttons were fastened out of kilter. Davies's fly was unzipped. He had little fight left in him.

The girl did the talking for them both. 'Everyone here, except Deadeye. Does that mean you've no eyeball?'

He didn't bluster. Didn't refer with cutting sarcasm to the state of her dress or Davies's. He nodded.

'We've had an eyeball on the riverbank,' she said, calm and no triumphalism. 'It's why we've been so damn long. It goes on for ever, the explanation . . . Enough for now, a deranged idiot, babbling, Luke says, about hunters and vengeance, took us down to the river edge. Sod his code-call, Johnny's there and Target Two, Reuven Weissberg. We saw them and beetled back.'

He thought, but couldn't have been certain in that frail light, that she grinned. He thanked her.

'Well, is that what you've been waiting for? Our idiot buggered off but we can lead you.'

Did he allow relief to flicker on his face? He did not.

'Right. Let's be on the move,' Lawson said.

'They've gone, Johnny.' Reuven Weissberg hunched down beside him.

'Who has, sir?'

'All of them, the bastards.'

'Has Mr Goldmann gone, sir?'

'All of them. I went to where he was, and where Mikhail was. They were gone.'

'Yes, sir.'

'I am betrayed, Johnny, as my grandmother was. It is a place of betrayal.'

'Why would they do that, sir?'

'It is a place for traitors, Johnny.'

And the light flashed.

Carrick started up. His feet slipped on the

mud's sheen. He found his balance. He stood.

It was downstream of them. Perhaps two hundred metres along the far bank from the point opposite. Four short flashes, then killed.

'Do you have the torch, sir, or did they?'

'Goldmann had the torch. The pig. He goes in concrete. First I strangle him, then the concrete. I—'

'You have a lighter, sir.'

'You think well, Johnny. Good.'

He felt the movements beside him, then heard the click. The lighter flame was shielded in Reuven Weissberg's hands, and Carrick helped him protect it.

The darkness came again. It was behind them and in front of them, but the moonlight on the water was splitting the darkness. Carrick went back and scrambled up the bank to where the boat was. He threw the coil of rope into it. At the end of the rope was the device – he was proud of it – that he had fashioned in the last hour. It was a broken-off branch, two inches thick, and protruding from it was a slighter branch, which he had snapped six inches from the main stem. Inverted, the branch was lashed with string to the rope. He had made a hook. He saw the light again. It had moved so slowly, but had come along the far bank and upstream, had halved the distance to the point across the water from them. Reuven Weissberg had to protect the lighter flame, and the wind off the river guttered it.

Carrick took hold of the front of the boat. He heaved it free from where it had settled against birch trunks. He levered the boat down the steep bank, and lost control of it. It cannoned into his shins, and the pain ran rich. He arrested its slithering fall. He worked it down, short pace by short pace, towards the waterline. Took an age. In his ears was the rumble of the river, and its roar seemed louder to him now, keener. He brought the boat to the edge.

The back end had gone into the water. He held it there – had he not, it would have slid down and been taken.

'You are with me, Johnny?'

'Yes, sir.'

'Will not betray me? Are not them? Traitors all.' The words came with spittle on the breath.

'Will not, sir.'

He saw the light again, four flashes. It was across the river from them. Now Reuven Weissberg called, but Carrick didn't understand. Over the water's roar, at this narrow point, came a croaked, feeble response, then a hacked cough, but from near enough for Carrick to hear it clearly. A second shout from Reuven Weissberg, an instruction. Carrick took the rope with the improvised hook he had made, gave it. Didn't know whether the rope could be thrown far enough. He had the boat further into the water, clung to it, and saw Reuven Weissberg pirouette as he hurled the rope across the water towards the far trees and saw it snake out. Willed it . . . Another shout from the far bank, and the rope went taut. He tested it, and Reuven Weissberg did.

A moment. Reuven Weissberg reached out, snatched at Carrick's neck, held it and kissed him. They were in the boat. Then they were launched.

Chapter 20: 16 April 2008

Carrick clung to the rope, arms high above his head, hands clenched on it. Had his grip failed when they had pushed off, or when they were at the mid-point of the river, or at the moment when the boat's front end hit the far bank, they would have been lost. He had taken the weight of the boat. In front of him, Reuven Weissberg was too short-built to use both hands on the rope and have his feet wedged against the sides. He had used the rope as kids did in an adventure playground, hand over hand and swinging, desperate to keep his feet in the boat and to guide it. The worst had been when a tree trunk – might have been thirty feet long – had hit the back end when they were beyond mid-stream but where the current had a fiercer thrust. The boat had rocked with the impact but stayed up.

They had scraped against sunken branches, had had to heave on the rope to get through them, and had reached the bank.

Weissberg skipped off. Carrick groped, found a tree root and heaved at it to test its strength, then used the cord hooked to the boat to moor – did that one-handed, then let the rope go free and swing up.

He heard, 'Stay close to me, Johnny.'

'Yes, sir.'

'You have your weapon?'

'Yes, sir.'

'Be careful of them.'

'Yes, sir.'

'Dangerous and desperate, these people, and thieves.'

'Yes, sir.'

They went up the bank, Reuven Weissberg first, then Carrick. He was on his hands and knees, grappling with mud, when he came to the top. Branches slashed at his face. He crawled forward, then the foot ahead of him, unseen in the black darkness below a mat of branches and tall weeds, kicked against his chin. He did not call out.

He cleared the rim of the bank, and the torch came on.

Carrick blinked. For a moment he was blinded. He thought it was held less than fifteen feet ahead of him. He screwed his eyes shut to lose the brightness. The beam shook, as if the hand holding it could not keep steady. There was a bad cough from behind the torch, which made the beam shake worse. He heard a question called, and Reuven Weissberg answered it. The beam was lowered.

Where was he? Where he had not been before. Why was he there? He had no idea. Who was he? He didn't know.

He saw them. Each had a hand on a young tree and used it as a support. The torchbeam flared out and showed enough of them. Two old men. Two old men with stubble and filth on their faces. Two old men with mud-smeared, torn clothes. Two old men, and one gasped for breath while the other was bent half double with coughing. He saw that one, the shorter, had lost a shoe. His sock was sodden and ripped, and blood seeped into the mud round it; it was the other who coughed and couldn't spit out what was lodged in his lungs. He had thought they would be young, aggressive and athletic, the same as Viktor and Mikhail, would have the same flat, thin fair hair and smooth skins and . . . Between them was the canister.

He realized then that two old men had dragged it across country to meet the rendezvous. Carrick thought it would have been the same on that side of the river as what they had trekked through, coming past the Sobibor camp, to reach the Bug. Already the canister was settled in the mud and had the weight to make a puddle round its base. The torch-beam shook because the hand of the taller man trembled. They were both, Carrick reckoned, on the point of collapse.

It was like a dance, but the artists were exhausted and clumsy.

Reuven Weissberg advanced on the canister and reached for one of its side straps.

The taller one, holding the torch, used his second hand to pull the thing back.

The shorter one inserted himself between Reuven Weissberg and the canister.

Argument broke out. Reuven Weissberg told Carrick, low voice, that they wanted money. Where was it? Carrick was told there was no money until the content was verified. Had they not known there would be no money paid to them for delivery? He was told it didn't matter what they had believed: they would get money on verification. They were two old men, not *mafiya*. They couldn't have fought

549

with Reuven Weissberg, and Carrick saw no weapons. He could tell from their faces that they had come expecting to be paid. He could see fragments of writing stencilled, black on olive green, on the canister's canvas cover. The voices were raised but Carrick turned away.

He went back down the bank to the water.

He took a handkerchief from his pocket, dipped it and felt the chill water flowing against his arm.

Carrick climbed the bank and walked back to them. The dispute cascaded around him. The old men couldn't win it. Each would be broken, as a matchstick was snapped after use. He pushed past the one who blocked Reuven Weissberg, bent in front of the canister, wiped hard and saw the letters and numbers. He couldn't read Cyrillic. He cleared the dirt off the canvas. It was obvious to him that the letters and numbers represented a batch number, or a serial number, or designated a weapon type. Two old men had gone through hell, many shades of it, to bring the thing to the Bug. Reuven Weissberg had come from Berlin and Josef Goldmann had travelled from the soft comfort of London to collect it but Goldmann, Mikhail and Viktor had copped out, as if the thing were too big, too dangerous . . . He saw them. They were crowded into the long cabin of the narrowboat. They had lassoed and corralled him, then bloody exploited him. Wouldn't have done it for a sack of grenades, wouldn't have hazarded him for a drum of Kalashnikovs, RPGs or even Stinger ground-to-air jobs. Carrick looked up.

He was near to the one without the shoe. He saw the face, its weariness and despair. He broke into the argument. 'How much do they get?'

Surprise at the boldness of his demand for an answer. 'What? Not your business.'

'How much?'

'They get a million American when it is verified. It is a good price – but not your business.'

'Yes, sir.'

He knew what was that size, what was worth two old men carting a canister to the Bug river, what a weapon worth a million American could do to a city. Carrick hung his head and the argument resumed.

'We were never told. I was not, Igor was not.'

'If Oleg had known, and I, we would never have come.'

'You're a cheat.'

'It's trickery, deceit. We were told we would be paid.'

Molenkov led. He had no fear, which surprised him. 'We did everything as we had said we would. We've come, we've brought it. We were promised we would be paid when we delivered. We have delivered. Do you have no honour? Does your word mean nothing?'

Old sensitivities ran through him. In front of him was the squat little bastard in the old leather jacket, a *mafiya* tsar. He thought of how it would have been for this pig if he had worn his uniform and been in his office, had owned the power and influence that sustained a ranking political officer. He tried to ape who he once was, who he had once been. The bastard, the pig, did not react. The torchbeam shone into the man's face. Alongside him Yashkin babbled in near-incoherence. Lightly, but with malice, he kicked Yashkin's ankle. There was more chatter about a 'new life', about 'sunshine' and about a 'future', so Molenkov kicked Yashkin again, harder, and it was sufficient to silence him.

He had no fear, not after what they had endured – the trauma of the frontier, the beating by the thieves, the exhaustion of dragging the canister through the forest – but he had a view of reality. So many of the scientists, chief technicians and prominent engineers at Arzamas-16 had been Jews, and at other secret cities where there were fewer of them the complex was called – had the sneered name – 'Egypt'. He had never been able to read them; they were separate, apart and aloof.

The *mafiya* Jew heard him out, then snapped his fingers. 'It will go for verification. If it is what you say, it will be paid for. You will be told the address of a bank and an account number. It will be in Cyprus. My word is as strong as my arm.'

Finish. What could he do? End. Could he and Yashkin fight for possession of it and take it back? It was the moment that a dream ended. The torchbeam showed the strength of the Jew, the muscle power of his shoulders and the great size of his hands. Another man hovered behind him, but had not intervened and watched, observed, but when the light fell on his face, it was impassive.

Molenkov made the gesture. He took out his wallet, shone the torch on to it, showed it was empty and replaced it. Then he put his hands into his trouser pockets and pulled out the insides to show what they held: a sodden handkerchief, a ring with keys, a few coins that were almost worthless. He had tried to fight and failed. He pleaded. They had been robbed. They had no money. They had no fuel in the vehicle. He had imagined they would be big men, each with a half-share of a million American dollars, each able to purchase a view of the sea. They had nothing.

From his hip pocket, the Jew took a wad of notes,

peeled some off and gave them as though it were a charity thing. Molenkov took what he was offered and hid the anger. The Jew waved for the man behind him to come forward. Each took a holding strap, and they turned their backs. They went past the point where the hook was lodged secure among a mass of birches, went under the rope that stretched away over the water and down to their boat.

He felt, almost, an affection for the fucking thing. They carried it easily as if the weight were a trifle. He had the torch on it. It was lifted into the boat. There had been no handshake, no hug, no kiss. They were gone and with them was the dream. It was hoisted into the boat.

'Can you do without a shoe, Yashkin?'

'I can,' Yashkin said. His voice was a murmur under the roar of the flooded Bug. 'Perhaps, in a week, they will tell us that the money is lodged.'

'I want to go home,' Molenkov said. 'Perhaps they will tell us.'

Neither looked back as they took their first steps into the darkness of the forest.

A few feet from the bank, Lawson stood erect, tall and proud. Beside him was Deadeye who had his rifle up to his shoulder and whose right eye was lodged against the aperture of his image-intensifier sight. Deadeye gave him the whispered commentary. Lawson had no need of it now. All he had required to know was that an object, near to waist height and with the thickness of a stout torso, had been man-handled aboard. The boat and the two figures were a dark blur against the silver of the water. There were soft voices behind him. He could imagine the triumph awaiting him. Might just, and he'd fight damn hard to achieve it, get the covering off the thing – after the boffins had cleared it for contamination – and walk it back along the corridors of VBX and show it to them in Non-Proliferation, then take it up in the lift, dump it on the floor of Pettigrew's office and have a drink with him. Yes, he allowed himself the luxury of imagination.

Rather them. The black shape of his agent, his target, their boat and its cargo inched out towards the river's main flow. The rope that was tied to the tree root was near to him and shivered with the strain it took. He fell back on more immediate imagination. Two men stood upright in that small battered craft and dragged themselves across, hand over hand, on the rope. He could see, now, the white water swept back from the shape and it poisoned the cleanliness of the silver. He thought that every muscle in their bodies was strained with the effort of holding the rope and bringing the boat across.

'How are they doing?'

'So far so good, Mr Lawson, is how they're doing.'

'No misunderstandings, Deadeye. The target comes ashore, is bumped and taken.'

'Of course, Mr Lawson.'

'If he fights, he's dead.'

'Yes, Mr Lawson.'

Always a regret, never a life without a regret to harbour. He wished Clipper had been there. Clipper Reade might have enjoyed this rather substantially. He thought they were close to halfway across and the wind sang on the rope's tightness. When it bucked, Lawson saw that one or other of them was changing hands and pulling harder to make progress against the flow. It would be a triumph, his vindication.

* * *

The rope burned Carrick's palms. He thought his arms were being dragged slowly, inexorably, from his shoulders. He took more of the strain because he was taller than Reuven Weissberg.

He had been the confidant who was told the story of the extermination camp and of an escape from that place. Had been the chosen man of Reuven Weissberg when the other rats had fled. Had been the bodyguard of Josef Goldmann, money-launderer. Johnny Carrick had been, also, an officer of the Serious Crime Directorate 10, and had sworn the oath. His knees were clamped on a weapon of massive killing power. He took the Makharov pistol out of the pancake holster, clung one-handed to the rope, twisted and called for Reuven Weissberg to watch him. There was sufficient moonlight. He held up the pistol, where it was seen. He waved it in front of Reuven Weissberg's eyes, a few inches from them. He threw it, and white spray bounced from the silver, feathered up, then was lost. Again, both hands were on the rope and he dragged the boat closer to the black wall that was the bank. He thought he had seen, against the trees, a man standing but could not have sworn to it; thought he had seen the moonlight flash momentarily on metal, a rifle's barrel. It was a nuclear weapon and it had jolted the skin off him.

Carrick shouted, 'Can you hear me?'

'Why you do that? Why? I hear you.'

'I am a lie, live one and act one. Time for truth.'

'What?'

'Wearing the gun was a lie.'

'You talk shit.'

'Truth says I'm a police officer. I'm a police officer

seconded to an intelligence agency. I targeted Josef Goldmann for criminal investigation. I came here to live a lie, to betray you.'

'Not you, Johnny – not you?' He thought he heard agony, as if a scream was raised, like the owls' shriek, like branches grating together when a gale blows. 'Not you? Tell me, not you?'

They were at the mid-point where the strain on arms, shoulders, hips and knees was greatest. The boat juddered and was turned half round. The big log hit it, seemed to snag it, brought water in and freed itself. He pulled the boat nearer to that bank, yard by yard.

'It's the truth. When we get there you'll be arrested. Men are there who have tracked you. I'm bringing you to them, Reuven Weissberg. If it hadn't been for the weapon it wouldn't have happened, but the weapon's there. It'll be cordoned and there will be guns. Sir, I understand about the camp and I'm sorry.'

The yell cut the night, was over the Bug's roar. Reuven Weissberg shrieked, 'We owe them nothing. Everything was betrayal. An officer rode a horse beside them and said they would be shipped to the east. It was betrayal. An officer in a white coat pretended to be a doctor as he led them to the death chambers and betrayed innocence. A man seemed to come from God and led them from the camp, then abandoned them and betrayed trust. A child found them and betrayed them to his father. Nobody, because of what was done, is owed anything.'

I had been in the forest for two weeks and had eaten only decomposing berries, chewed roots, and drunk rainwater from puddles. I was deep in the forest and heard no man, nor saw one. It was because I was asleep that I hadn't run. I was found by men from a partisan unit. They were Jewish, of the Chil group, and their leader was Yechiel Greenspan. When they woke me, I thought at first they were Polish Christians and tried to fight them. There were too many and I was too weak. They took me back to their camp, far into the Parczew forest.

When we came to where the sentries were they gave a password. It was 'Amcha', the password of our people when they fought the Syrians two thousand years before. I learned that it had survived, used through history by Jews in flight. I learned also that their principal enemy was the men of the Armia Krajowa. They said that more of the escapers had been killed by the Armia Krajowa than by the Germans.

I lived with them.

I became a fighter with them.

I killed with them and hunted for food with them.

They were people I trusted, but no other man or woman.

The child grew in me.

My son was born on 22 July, two weeks late. The pain of the birth was worse than anything I had experienced. I called him Jakob, which was the name of our sub-unit commander. The same day that I gave birth we heard the sounds of artillery and tank fire. The noise of the fighting came from outside where we were, in the most dense and remote part of the forest, but still within six hours' walk of where the camp had been.

It was impossible for me to go. Others went.

On the day after the Red Army had gone through Sobibor and had advanced towards Chelm, Hańsk, Sawin and Cycow, a patrol of the Chil partisans set off to find out what had happened at the camp, to make contact with the rear echelon of the Red Army, and to beg for food.

They were gone at dawn and were back in the long evening before the late dusk. They had not met Russians but they had seen men of the Armia Krajowa strutting in the street at Suchawa and Okuninka. They had hidden from them. One sat down with me and told me of what he had found at the death camp of Sobibor. He said there were many Poles there.

There were farm peasants, forest workers and women from Osowa and Kosyn. There were shopkeepers from Wlodawa, and some had brought their families. They were all Catholic Poles. With them they had carried abandoned shells and mortar bombs, which had been left by the Germans as they had retreated back from the river Bug, and they had brought a very small amount of dynamite from a quarry, only a small amount was necessary, a few grams, and fuse cord. While I suckled my baby, he told me what he had seen from the cover of the trees.

In the hours after the escape, the Germans had shot dead all the prisoners who had not escaped, shot dead all the wounded and all of those recaptured in the forest. They were shot, in their clothes, above a pit and their bodies fell into it. The Germans covered the pit.

The camp was then closed, abandoned, destroyed and made to look like a farm. The huts were taken down. Work parties were brought to Sobibor, shifted more soil into the pit and levelled the ground. By the next summer it was impossible to know where the pit was, where some four hundred Jews were buried.

Those people who came, whom he saw, did not know where the bodies were.

As he watched, hidden, the people buried the shells and bombs, with the small amounts of dynamite to help the explosion, and they lit the fuse cords. They blew up the shells and bombs, then searched in the craters for Jews' bodies.

When they found corpses, rotting, stinking, they stripped off the clothes and hunted for gold and jewellery that might have been stitched into them. They believed, those people, that all Jews had money and valuables. And they looked in the jaws of the dead for the teeth.

Even the dead of Sobibor were betrayed.

You should never forget the betrayal of your people, of your blood. You owe no man, no woman, no child anything.

After Sobibor, softness was dead, love and kindness with it.

'My God, my God, why have You forsaken me?'

'Hear, O Israel, the Lord our God, the Lord is one.'

Remember what I have told you, dear Reuven. Remember it well.

The boat bucked, rocked.

Reuven Weissberg hung on the rope and launched the kick towards the turned spine of the man he had believed loyal.

He heard, against the thunder of the water and the moan of the wind, the click that was metal on metal. It carried to him over what remained of the river to be crossed, and he knew that a weapon was armed. A sight would now be focused on him and the cross-hairs would be over his chest.

He had wanted a clear kick with the maximum impact and the greatest surprise.

The bastard held on to the rope, had it and rode the flow. The boat shook and the shape of the thing slithered in bilge water along the planks, came to rest against his feet, and he could not make the second kick.

At that moment what was Reuven Weissberg's plan? There was none. His life and his power were built on the twin foundations that came from careful planning. Fury consumed him.

They were twenty metres from the blackness of the far bank. He hung, now, with one hand on the rope, and with the other he groped forward for Johnny Carrick's throat. If he found the throat of the man who had betrayed him, he would break the neck bones, crush and snap them. He felt flesh but didn't have a good hold.

The boat shook and the river water slopped into it and lapped around the cargo.

A hand tried to free his, but could not.

Lawson hissed in his ear, 'Shoot, damn you. Take him out.'

In the sight, the cross-hairs bounced on two pastel shapes in a washed-out green that were against a background of a harsher green, that of lawn grass after rain. But the shapes had merged. The boat seemed to Deadeye to be marooned out there in the river, but the flow force struggled to break it free and the white water powered round it. He was not there to watch pretty pictures of the wake the boat created or to see the balletic dance of the figures, those shapes. Yes, safety was off. Yes, the lever was on 'single' and not automatic. Yes, his right index finger was off the guard and on the trigger. Yes, it rested there gently, without pressure. No, he had no damn target. What made it harder was following the shapes with the water behind and in front of them because the moonlight reflected back up off the surface and flared.

'Can't separate them.'

'You have to take out Weissberg.'

It was an old rule for marksmen. He – true for any marksman – could not be ordered by a superior to shoot. His decision. No man, whatever his seniority, made the decision for him. His finger stayed on the trigger bar and the pressure was not applied. They were together. The shapes were one, writhing and moving, heaving and shaking, but indivisible.

'For God's sake, Deadeye, do it.'

'Fuck off . . .' afterthought '. . . sir.'

Stress mounted in Deadeye. They were locked together, and the dazzle came off the water, spoiling the quality of his view. He held off. Inside the sight, with the cross-hairs, was the range finder, and the digits showed the figure 30. Thirty metres range. The stress surged. He thought it a struggle for life. His mind wobbled, shouldn't have done, and he saw the man come fast, rat speed, across the pavement – six days before – and seemed to feel the barged weight of him in the moments that he'd fired two blank rounds. He heard the girl, whom Lawson called 'the little cuckoo', murmur that if their man went into the water he was gone, lost. Didn't need to be told it, knew it.

He couldn't buck the stress.

Deadeye waited for the heads to come apart, not the bodies. He thought, from what the sight showed him, that water came into the boat. They each had one hand on the rope and fought with the other, and he saw each of the punches thrown and each of the flailing kicks. He leaned hard against a sapling tree, used it for support, and had the cross-hairs wavering on their heads. At that range, with the image intensifier's magnification, he could see half of the snarled face of his target. Needed the whole of the damned face.

Had it, squeezed, went for it.

Deadeye felt the recoil belt his shoulder joint.

They flinched. They ducked. Any man with a

561

high-velocity bullet blasting over his head would flinch and duck. The two hands came off the rope.

Fucking missed. When had he last missed? Top scores always on a range. Didn't understand. Had missed.

The rope, without the weight on it, leaped up, seeming to shimmer and shiver, then went slack.

They had balance for a moment, but briefly.

Two seconds, or three. The rope was now high above them. Either man, to have caught the rope again, would have had to reach up and leave himself defenceless. If Carrick had done it, stretched his arm towards the rope, his stomach and head would have been open . . . and the chance was gone. The river took the boat.

Again, Reuven Weissberg came at him. Fingers gouged at his eyes and a knee came into the pit of his stomach. Carrick gasped. They were rolling.

They were lost, gone, and he knew it. He fought back, had to. Had to free himself and the water surged round him and he felt it round his legs. They went in.

Still struggling, hands now on his clothing. Reuven Weissberg's head was inches from Carrick's and water was spat from it. Carrick could not have said where his strength came from. Fingers found Reuven Weissberg's eyes. A little choked gasp of pain. Carrick was free. The great current tugged and the undertow sucked at him.

He could no longer see Reuven Weissberg or the boat, or what the boat had carried.

A branch cannoned into his back. He snatched it, but it lacked the buoyancy to hold him up. The water went round him.

Darkness closed on him.

'Who's going in?' Lawson faced them.

In chorus: 'Waste of time. Can't swim, never have. Bloody suicide. Nothing lives in that.'

He did not identify the voices. It seemed clear-cut. A kaleidoscope of sights and thoughts rampaged in him. He was God, the relic of the Good Old Days. *Sorry, and all that, Clipper, but I'm stepping out of line.* Lawson kicked off his good brogues and heaved down the zip of the waxed coat. He thought of the Spree river, the agent who had been Foxglove and the great open water by the Oberbaumbrücke, and himself waiting in the cold, stamping to keep his feet warm. He loosened his tie, went forward in his stockinged feet, slipped down the bank. No one tried to stop him, funny that. Had they, he would have pushed them away. Seemed to see the searchlights and hear the rattle of gunfire, machine-guns using three- or four-round bursts with tracer. One was using a flashlight and it played over the water's surface and caught a branch. There might have been the top of a head but it was moving too fast for him to focus on and retain. And Foxglove had screamed, a shrill, piercing call for help. Then his tube had been holed, its buoyancy gone. He'd not seen Foxglove for a full minute before the body had tangled in one of the nets that ran down the river. He'd lived with it so damned long, and made a pretence that what happened to an agent was all part of the game – greater good of the greater number. *God, Clipper, it's bloody cold* . . . The water was at his knees and the eddy by the bank drew him out and into the flow. Then his feet lost contact with the bottom. He started to swim, used the combination of breaststroke and dog-paddle he'd learned at school.

He was guided by shouts from behind him and by the direction in which the torchbeam was aimed. He might have seen a head bob up, and what was ahead of him might have been the bottom of the little boat or it might have been another of those wretched trees coming down the river.

I remember what you said, Clipper. 'An agent is lost and you go find another.' Good counsel. And you said, 'Get close and sentimental to an agent and you get to be useless.' It's what I am, Clipper, bloody useless. What he had thought might have been the bottom of the boat was indeed a log, and when the swell surge carried him closer to what might have been a head, the torchbeam showed a deflated football.

He was beyond the reach of the torchbeam. They'd be running along the bank to get ahead of him and light the river again. They would.

So damn tired, and cold.

You quit when you were ahead, Clipper. Best thing you could have done . . . But heh, Clipper, it was there, it was coming. Not any more. They can't take that away from . . .

The water was foul-tasting. It was in his eyes, up his nose and inside his ears. Each time he tried to spit it out, more of the Bug water slopped into Lawson's mouth.

He thought himself free.

He believed the curse lifted.

The dog sat patient on the floor and watched him. Tadeuz Komiski stepped up on to the seat of the wooden chair and reached for the noose. He felt no fear. Guilt had been purged and a grave would go undisturbed.

* * *

The Crow said, 'It is time. We leave.'

Sak asked, 'What could have happened? Why didn't they come?'

'Do you think it is easy to fight? Go home. Forget you were ever here. Erase from your mind the image of my face. Ask no questions and you will be safe. Talk of this and you will be dead. They did not come, but the struggle stays alive.'

Two cars pulled away from a picnic site on the Lüneburger Heide. One would head for Hamburg, and the first flight in the morning would take a school-laboratory technician back to his home in the West Midlands of Britain. The other would be driven to Cologne and, en route, a device for testing a man-portable nuclear weapon for confirmed and heavy plutonium presence would be discarded in a rubbish bin. Before the next evening a deal prepared carefully and secretively with a *hawaldar* banker would be cancelled. Cranes would beckon that man and the fierceness of the Gulf's sun would shine on him.

And later . . .

> LAWSON, Christopher (late of the Diplomatic Service). Drowned in a boating accident while abroad. Aged 61. Beloved husband of Lavinia and father of Harry. Will be sadly missed by all who knew him. Private funeral, but donations may be made to English Heritage (Church Restoration Fund). A memorial service will follow.

It was a summer's day, pleasantly warm. He had thought it necessary to be there. The church was between the Clapham Road and the Lambeth Road and had an association with the VBX building, he was told by an usher. It was not only appropriate but convenient as it was at most a five-minute walk from that awful green and cream and tinted-glass edifice. He had been late to arrive and had squeezed into a pew near to the back, but he'd been noticed, and he'd heard a little murmur run down the nave. He'd been stared at and identified by pointing fingers. There had been a photograph on a table in front of the altar of the man – he'd never known his name until he was handed the order of the service – who had dragooned him on the narrowboat, and a candle had burned beside it. The service had started with a bizarre touch: a mobile phone had rung and its call jingle had been 'Deutschland Über Alles' and there had been a ripple of laughter he'd not understood. Then there had been an address from a big cat and a reading by a young man he'd presumed to be Lawson's son. Two hymns – 'I Vow to Thee My Country' and 'Amazing Grace' – brief prayers and, after a bare half-hour, they spilled out of the church into the sunshine. There were to be sandwiches and drinks in the hall adjoining it, but people seemed reluctant to wander there and milled around. He realized then that two confused queues had formed. One waited to shake the widow's hand, and her son's, but the second was near to him. It was as though his queue waited for a man of importance to break the ice.

That man came. 'You're Johnny Carrick. I'm Pettigrew, the director. Most in there would have had to swallow their bile for the length of the pro- ceedings. Christopher Lawson was cordially detested by the huge majority of his colleagues, but not by me. Without him, this city or another would be in dire danger. A few hours before he died he spoke on his phone to me and praised you to the hilt. I'll miss him, not that others will. Anyway, well done. Haystack was one of our better efforts. You didn't see him in the water, did you? No, I didn't think you would have. Must press on.'

He recognized the next in line, the young man who had been with Lawson on the narrowboat and whom he had seen under the wall of Warsaw's old quarter, holding Katie Jennings tightly.

'I'm Luke Davies. When you made it to the bank, it was me who dragged you out of that bloody river. Sorry and all that about the other side of the coin. I suppose you've realized Katie and I are together, and she's transferred out of that unit you were with. I think it's the sort of thing that happens in a stress situation – it was, you know, stressful for us. Anyway, the best of luck. I suppose at the end of the day it was a good result. Not that it'll matter to you but I've been promoted on the back of it. Keep safe.'

The next in line had a tangled mess of hair and a cheerful smile.

'I had the job of pumping your chest, getting all that sewer water from the Bug out of your lungs. Remember, the psychologist, Shrinks? Did you act on my advice, get the counselling bit in? Very important for someone who's been exposed to the syndrome, as you have. Did you?'

He shook his head. Yes, he remembered being dragged up the bank and having his chest beaten, and then he'd been left while they'd scoured the river's edge. He looked over the man's shoulder, like people did at parties when they were searching for a more interesting guest. He was rewarded.

'Hello, I'm Giles Banham. I was running the crisis desk that night, and was short-handed because we didn't actually believe it was real.

Anyway . . . Look, this is confidential, Official Secrets and that guff, but you've the right to know. Josef Goldmann came fast back to London, then quickly did the flit. We think he's in Israel, and the word is that his family hate it, and that he's chucked a pretty considerable bung at the government, and they'll give him citizenship and protection. The thugs, the two of them, ended up in northern Cyprus and are training the locals in security. Extradition isn't done from there. Reuven Weissberg made it out of the river, back to Berlin. There's CCTV of him at his apartment, going in and still looking like a semi-drowned rodent. He was there half an hour and exited with his grandmother – bizarre, but all they had was basic hand baggage, and what looked like a picture wrapped in news-paper. Must have been something important. There was a report that they'd showed up in Moldova, and another that said their refuge was Paraguay, but we don't have confirmation. The two old men you met on the Bug's far side we haven't heard of. The good thing out of it all is, when it suits us, we'll shove a sanitized part of the file to the FSB, just to cause some keen embarrassment. All of them – Weissberg, Goldmann and the thugs – will spend the rest of their days looking over their shoulders, and being pretty damn careful what they drink and eat. We'll leave them for a bit in their new homes, then exert some civilized pressure. I expect they'll turn and answers to our questions will be provided. We're short of who was the purchaser, who the device would ultimately have been sold to, but we'll get there, believe me.'

He recalled them all. He saw the hostility of Viktor, the malice of Mikhail. He could hear the respect and gratitude of Josef and Esther

Goldmann. He could feel the bear-hug, before the anger, and the warmth of Reuven Weissberg. He could picture the painting of a forest's trees. An older man with wispy grey hair that had been allowed to grow beyond tidiness came forward.

'Good to meet you, Mr Carrick. I don't have a name, not one that you need, anyway. In a quiet corner, I do threat analysis. Excessive rainfall this spring in central Ukraine, floodplains rising and riverbanks bursting, but all manner of silt and filth carried down the main arteries. We think, from your description of it, that the weapon was in the RA series, man-portable and dating from the seventies – not big but giving a useful bang for the buck, enough to destroy the heart of an urban mass, a deep-buried command post or a missile silo, to demolish a strategic bridge – and we think, also, it went down into the Bug, would have been tumbled along the bed then snagged. Probably covered within an hour and well buried by the following morning. By the end of the week it would have been under four or five feet of muck. The chance of it going on downstream and eventually into the Vistula or even the Baltic is – we estimate – remote. Best place for it, buried and forgotten. It could not of itself have exploded. It would have needed a precursor agent, commercial or military dynamite, to be activated. Then it would have contaminated the centre of a city, New York, Los Angeles, Paris, Berlin or – most probably – London. One of those cities, spattered with plutonium, would have been poisoned for all time. No centre of population could survive such an attack. So, we won this time but in a difficult world we have to win every time. Good to have met you.'

He had not seen him before, not in the church or

in the garden between the door and the street gate. He was bent, his weight was suspended over two hospital sticks, and the clothes hung loose on him. Must have been a big man once but was shrunken now.

'Won't hold you, young man. I'm told you did a fine job, beyond the duty call . . . These guys hated his guts because he was a stickler for detail and commitment, and had a bad way with idiots. These guys, goddam hypocrites all of them, and doing the hand-wringing . . . They told me a little of what happened – I envy you. I have a powerful amount of envy for you for being there and having done it well. He's better where he is than where I am. A retirement home, Delray Beach in Florida, is a degree of hell. Won't keep you . . . Ever in Delray Beach, ever on Angelo Drive, ever by the Corpus Christi Retirement Home, come see me and we'll go get a beer. My privilege to have met you, sir.'

A young woman had her hand outstretched. 'My name's Alison and I'm from the crowd on the other side of the river. No one wanted to come because Mr Lawson was loathed so I picked up the ticket. I didn't turn up because of him, it was you I wanted to meet. I think I owe you an apology, Mr Carrick, a big one.'

'Do you?'

'I do liaison between our lot and theirs. We helped with the background stuff right at the beginning, and your name came up as a staffer for Goldmann. Then our computers threw out that you were funny – the National Insurance and the driving licence had been doctored. Our gear can do that. I told Mr Lawson you were an undercover, SCD10. I chucked you in it. Isn't that worth an apology?'

'Maybe, maybe not.'

'Are you about through here?'

'Leave's finished, and I'm due back in my office. First time back there after . . . Yes, I could be finished here.'

'Going to walk over the bridge?'

'Sounds right.'

In the line was the man he had kicked in the groin on the City pavement, and three others who had been on the banks of the Bug. He went past them, as if they didn't exist, and up the side-street that led to the bridge.

The sun was on his back and it warmed his face. He slipped off his coat and hitched it over his shoulder. He didn't think he needed an apology. He told her, Alison, as they walked across the river bridge, about a forest of birches and pines, and of the place where a revolt had been fashioned. He spoke of a camp that was demolished and how the fences and watchtowers, minefields and barracks huts had been buried and hidden, and of the darkness under the trees, the despair that still lived, and the hate. He did not talk about the events and incidents of Haystack, but of a track called the Road to Heaven that ran between newly planted pines, and of the plank-faced homes that had once been the Swallow's Nest and the Merry Flea, and of a great mound that was formed of incinerated bodies.

Carrick said, 'If you haven't been there and haven't heard the stories, it isn't possible to understand the present. It's about the camp, the killing there and the escape. What happened is rooted in that past. So, I go back to work. I forget it. I forget where I was and who I was with, and what person I became. I have to. I was there and thought I walked and ran with them.'

They were at the end of the bridge. He realized then that she had hold of his hand and his cheeks were wet.

'Will you be all right?'

'I'll be fine. It never happened. I don't need your apology.'

She loosed his hand, and went right, along the Embankment and towards the Box 500 building. Carrick blinked, wiped his face on his sleeve, and set out with a good stride towards his Pimlico office. He killed the faces that had clamoured in his mind. Best to believe it had never happened.

THE END

A Journey to Sobibor

by Gerald Seymour

The birds do sing in the forests at Sobibor.

It is a common fiction writer's cliché that where there has been horrendous barbarity and brutality on a scale that is barely comprehensible, and on a site where evil was practised with enthusiasm and expertise, the birds don't sing, not ever. Wrong ... chaffinches and thrushes and tits and blackbirds chirrup happily in the pines and birches that cover the Second World War extermination camp.

Nothing, not even songbirds with their innocence of events sixty-five years ago, can remove the sense of catastrophe and misery at a place where a quarter of a million Jews were put to death in the space of seventeen months.

Then, trains brought the condemned off

the branch line and into a siding close to the Sobibor gate, and within two hours of arrival all those who stepped down onto the platform would be dead. The process of killing was described at his post-war trial by SS-*Oberscharfuhrer* Kurt Bolender.

'Before the Jews undressed, *Oberscharfuhrer* Hermann Michel made a speech to them. On these occasions he used to wear a white coat to give the impression he was a physician. Michel announced to the Jews that they would be sent to work. But before this they would have to take baths and undergo disinfection, so as to prevent the spread of diseases. After undressing, the Jews were taken through the "Tube", by an SS man leading the way, with five or six Ukrainians at the back hastening the Jews along.' (The Tube was an open-air corridor flanked by wire fencing, closely woven into which were fronds of pine so that no view of the permanent camp was possible to those who first dumped their bags, then were made to strip naked, then were rushed forward the last hundred yards.) 'When the Jews had entered the gas chambers, the Ukrainians closed the doors. The motor of a truck, with the exhaust fumes piped to the chambers, was switched on by the Ukrainian Emil Kostenko and by the German driver Erich Bauer from Berlin. After the gassing, the doors were opened and the corpses were removed by Jewish workers.' The capacity of the chambers permitted some nine hundred men and women and children to be suffocated at a time. The final spasms of life sometimes lasted as much as twenty-five minutes.

Now, in the endless forest of pipe and birch there is a clearing. In the centre of the clearing is a great shallow mound, created from ashes, that is some seventy metres in diameter. It is all that remains as a stark memorial to the tens of thousands of Polish, Czech, German, Austrian, Lithuanian, French and Dutch Jews sent to Sobibor. This is not Dachau or Belsen or Auschwitz. No buses come here with school children, and precious few visitors make the long journey. There is so little to see here: the concrete base foundations of a central watchtower; a building, used today by a Polish forestry manager, which was the home of the commandant, Franz Reichsleiter. Another timbered building was the Happy Flea and occupied by the SS personnel as an officers' mess, where the younger and prettier Jewesses could gain a few hours more of life by providing entertainment. And, the platform onto which the unsuspecting Jews were dumped with their little suitcases is still there, with the wood of the buffers slowly rotting, and the wagons now are loaded with pine wood pit props destined for the coal mines in the south.

The camp was sustained by six hundred Jewish prisoners who worked at the sifting of the clothes and possessions of the condemned arriving on the train transports and took the bodies from the killing chambers for burning in pits, and in return – a pact with the devil – their lives were eked out for a few more weeks. All of them knew that when the usefulness of the camp was exhausted, they too would be herded along the Tube, have the doors slammed and fastened behind them, and the truck engine would be switched on. The workers had none of the ignorance of many of those brought on the trains. They knew what awaited them.

The Germans destroyed Sobibor, tried to erase the memory of the camp's existence, after the shock of the first major armed breakout from a death camp.

A charismatic Red Army lieutenant – a Jew – had been sent to the camp as a worker. He was an obvious leader. Leon Feldhendler, the worker inmates' escape committee chief, recognized the exceptional qualities of Sasha Pechersky, then aged thirty-one, and gave him full authority and backing to organize a mass escape. Was it possible? Could a few hundred exhausted, half starved and terrorized men and women overwhelm a garrison manned by well-armed German SS men and their Ukrainian mercenaries? Around the camp were perimeter fences topped with barbed wire, in the watchtowers above them the guards were issued with machine guns, and beyond the wire was a densely sown mine field.

Without the magnetic personality of Pechersky, they would have gone meekly, in a week or a month, up the well trodden track that was the Tube, hurried on their way by whips and leaping dogs and rifle butts.

Here, on 14 October 1943, in the late afternoon, a desperate break for freedom – unique in the savage and brutal histories of the networks of camps – began. The plan of Pechersky was launched. As many SS men as wandered the camp, unsuspecting, were grabbed, then were clubbed or stabbed to death – but not enough. And insufficient weapons were taken from the armoury to silence the machine guns in the watch-towers. Three hundred wretched, emaciated, hungry men and women dared to try to flee and clambered up the wire fences. Half of them were shot down or were blown up by the exploding mines. An estimated one hundred and fifty reached the cover of the forest, and ran and blundered through the trees in the growing darkness.

I walked down the Tube, where those men and women would have been herded if they had not summoned the courage to fight. I met some German radicals who were defining the route to death by planting pines along the track that links the railway platform to the great circular mound of whitened ashes where the death chambers were: they were fresh faced, young, articulate and earnest, and only one was Jewish. The Jew's elderly father, Kurt Gutmann, had been left in the loggers' office to rest. I met him and heard his extraordinary story. He only discovered two years ago that his mother and his eldest brother had been gassed at Sobibor. He had been shipped to Britain in 1938 and fostered by a family on the Isle of Arran, as a sallow and puny eleven-year-old. At the minimum age permitted he had volunteered for the Coldstream Guards, been accepted, and had left that remote and storm swept west coast of Scotland. He had served, after the capitulation, in occupied Berlin where he now lives. His family were already dead several months before the breakout. I found a man who did not harbour bitterness, but who was overwhelmed by the sadness of what had happened here to his blood relatives. He had more interest in the 250,000 who were killed at Sobibor than the 150 who had reached the cover of the forest on that October night.

I left him – have never met him again – and walked in to the forest to try and imagine how it was on that night.

There are no museums at Sobibor, no audio and visual experiences created by clever young people. The memorials are the heap of ashes and a solitary figure carved in red sandstone whose image has become blurred with weather erosion. Only imagination is available to the visitor, and the accounts of the few – very few – survivors.

The Russian group, led by Pechersky, reached the Bug river, struggled across its fierce flow and eventually reached the Soviet lines further east. He had decided that his responsibilities to the other survivors had ended when he led the escape clear of the wire and the mines. He abandoned them, and his small team came safely through.

A recurring theme from other survivors is: 'The Germans were bad, the Poles were worse'. The civilians, left to survive or die in the forests, did not have the military experience of the Russians, nor their strength, nor Pechersky's dynamism to drive them. There were blocks on bridges and roads, spotter aircraft overhead, and the forests were combed by mounted police. Some escapees wandered in lost circles close to the camp, and then went in desperation – no food and nothing to drink, cold and soaked, and not knowing where they were – to the homes of woodsmen and farmers. Some were betrayed to the German searchers for as little reward as a kilo bag of sugar; some were slaughtered by Catholic Polish partisans; some were shown no charity by the local people – some were helped by the great bravery of a handful of Poles and were fed and hidden. Only fifty still lived from the three hundred who had dared when the Soviet tanks forded the Bug and reached the forests in the following spring.

Amongst the trees, walking in silence on the old composted leaves and the pine needles, there is nothing to see. Great treachery and great courage, and an indomitable human spirit were acted out here. The fugitives would have been like hunted animals in the depths of tiredness and weakness; what they achieved was the redress of that humiliating image of lines of men and women and children, with their suitcases, queuing with docility before being murdered. In the forests around Sobibor they fought, and only our imagination can be their witness.

I came back each day for a week. I searched for the signs, the evidence, of the malevolent evil done. I have read the accounts of the survivors from Thomas Toivi Blatt's emotionally draining and excellent *The Forgotten Revolt*, and have stared down at the photographs of men such as *Gasmeister* Bauer who received a life sentence, and many others – Lachman, Shutt, Juhrs, Zierke – who had been charged and were then freed. But it is the quiet of the forest and what we see in our minds that opens up the images of flight and pursuit, and of inhuman cruelty and bestiality. An example – one of so many: thirty teenage girls held back after the rest of their transport had been slaughtered, left in the reception area of the Tube for thirty-six hours, kept corralled there, so that *Reichsfuhrer* Heinrich Himmler when he visited Sobibor could watch at first-hand the sport of killing. Now, you cannot find the place where those terrified children spent their last night of life – nor can you find where Himmler stood – but you can see it in your mind, and you tremble with the shared fear, and you almost vomit with disgust at what was done.

With thoroughness, after the escape and the massacre of those who had not chosen to go to the wire, the camp was closed. The site was bulldozed and the ground was ploughed and Ukrainian farmers were settled on the area behind the Swallow's Nest, the Commandant's house. It is bare and lifeless ground on to which the forest has never encroached, and until recently there were brightly coloured swings and slides there for the woodsmen's children to play on. I believe it adds to the massive dignity of Sobibor that the memorial symbols are sparing and that a state-of-the-art tourist centre has never been built.

At the end of the Tube, near to the mound of ashes, I thought of the sounds of this small corner of an actual hell. Bauer's engine would have coughed into action, the Jews squashed into the six chambers would have realized the deception and chanted, muffled: *Schma Israel! Adonai Elohaynu! Adonai Ehad* (Hear, O Israel! The Lord is our God! The Lord is One). A flock of geese are chased round an enclosure by a young Jew, kept alive for this daily job, and they squawk and scream to mask the noise of death ... It is a humbling place to have visited. Some amongst those who survived the camp and the escape said they could never laugh or love again, however long they lived.

There is a simple stone at the head of the Tube and I paused there at the end of my final visit. Engraved on the stone, from the Book of Job, is *Earth Conceal not my Blood*. Big words, good words, and fitting. I pondered on them and mercifully – as a gift from God – I heard the sweetness of the cries of the songbirds, and their purity.

Gerald Seymour
August, 2008

RAT RUN
By Gerald Seymour

Cowardice is the dirtiest word in the military
lexicon. When Malachy Kitchen, an intelligence
officer in Iraq, is accused of running away in the
face of enemy fire, his career is left in tatters.

Kicked out of the army, Malachy sinks into
despair. He becomes an isolated recluse in a
drug-infested London estate. But the mugging
of an elderly widow by addicts draws him into
a fight to regain his lost pride. His target is
the network of narcotics traders.

Pushers, dealers and suppliers all form part
of that network, and at their head is Ricky Capel,
a crime baron responsible for importing hard
drugs into the UK. Untouchable up to now,
Capel will have to confront an enemy more
driven than any of the policemen he has
so far successfully outwitted . . .

'The finest thriller writer
in the world today'
Daily Telegraph

9780552153423

CORGI BOOKS

THE UNTOUCHABLE
By Gerald Seymour

Albert William Packer is the supreme baron of London crime. He rules his manor with a cruel, ruthless fist. To those around him, on whatever side of the law, he is the Untouchable.

When another criminal case against him collapses, Packer turns his attention to expanding his heroin empire abroad. Where better to cut out the middle man than at the historic smuggling crossroads of Europe, the Balkans?

New men and women are drafted into the Customs & Excise unit dedicated to convicting Packer. Only one from the old team survives: the most junior, Joey Cann, retained solely for his obsessional knowledge of the man who calls himself 'Mister'. When Packer leaves for Sarajevo, it is inevitable that Cann be sent after him for 'intrusive surveillance'. The brief: to bring back the evidence that will nail Packer to the wall, whatever it takes.

In London, it would have been no contest. But here on the war-torn streets of a city where justice is enforced by gangster warlords, Packer is far from home and from what he knows. Here, who will be the Untouchable, who will walk away?

'A clever, informed and worldly cynical story about arrogance, obsession and tragedy'
The Times

'A genuinely exciting epic . . . the novel has a truly memorable final chapter . . . entertaining'
Daily Telegraph

9780552148160

CORGI BOOKS

THE WALKING DEAD
By Gerald Seymour

A young man starts a journey from a dusty village
in Saudi Arabia. He believes it will end with his
death in faraway England. If his mission succeeds,
he will go to his god a martyr – and many
innocents will die with him.

For David Banks, an armed protection officer charged
with neutralizing the growing menace to London's
safety, the certainties that rule his thinking are no
longer black and white. Banks has begun to realize
that one man's terrorist is another man's freedom
fighter. Never have those distinctions been more
dangerous to a police officer with his finger on the
trigger – and to those who depend upon him.

On a bright spring morning the two men's paths will
cross. The suicide bomber and the policeman will
have equal cause to question the roads they've taken.
Win or lose, neither will be the same again . . .

'[Seymour is] the master . . . on every possible count'
Sunday Times

'One of the best plotters in the business'
Time Out

'A brilliant storyteller'
Sunday Express

9780552155182

CORGI BOOKS

THE UNKNOWN SOLDIER
By Gerald Seymour

Hidden in the world's greatest desert a
tiny caravan of fugitives and camels inches
towards its goal. It is a place where only the
strongest and most determined men will
survive. In the caravan one man stands out.
His strength, self-imposed discipline and
leadership mark him. He is an Outsider
whose past is blanked from his memory.
And his loyalty to the leadership is total.

Searching for him in the limitless dunes
are American and British experts in counter-
terrorism with a full range of sophisticated
electronics at hand. Hunting him from above
is the unmanned Predator aircraft, invisible
in the cloudless skies, carrying the Hellfire
missiles. But he is no easy prey.

If they fail to find and kill him, if he reaches
his family and receives his orders, the
Outsider will disappear again, before
re-emerging in a teeming western city
with a suitcase that will wreak havoc,
mass murder when it is detonated . . .

'A superb feat of storytelling
by a master of his craft'
The Times

9780552151733

CORGI BOOKS

TRAITOR'S KISS
By Gerald Seymour

An English trawler strays into Russian waters.
When it returns, the captain has a package to
deliver to British intelligence. For the next
four years a high-ranked Russian naval officer,
Viktor Archenko, passes valuable information
to MI6. Suddenly the flow of information
stops. His contacts in London know nothing
about him – but they know that he's under
suspicion. The time has come to get him out.

But the new breed now playing the spy game
have no interest in irrelevant Cold War
sparring or the risk of a spy scandal. There are
deals to be done, alliances to be made. They
would rather leave Archenko to fend for
himself. Only one veteran agent realises that
there is much more at stake than one man's
life. Only he dares ask the question: if the war
is over, who will fight the peace?

'The finest thriller writer in the world today'
Daily Telegraph

9780552150439

CORGI BOOKS

HOLDING THE ZERO
By Gerald Seymour

Gus Peake should have kept his job and stayed at home, but an old family debt of friendship draws him to the remote wastes of Northern Iraq and to a savage forgotten war between Kurdish guerillas and Saddam Hussein's military strength.

To the brutal, no-quarter combat, Peake can bring the skills he has learned as a marksman. But there is no room for mistakes on the field of battle and he must quickly learn to deal out random death at long distance, and help the guerillas to reach their goal, the city of Kirkuk, the old capital of the Kurdish people.

From Baghdad, Iraq sends Major Karim Aziz, the most dedicated and professional sniper in Saddam's army. For both men their duel, from which only one can walk away, becomes an obsession. And it will only take one shot, echoing in the mountains and valleys, to settle the score . . .

'As good as ever on dusty forgotten battles . . . has what the likes of Richard North Patterson lack: a singular voice and the gift of making the reader read on'
Guardian

'Bears all the hallmarks of a master writer'
Daily Telegraph

'Mesmerizing' *Sunday Times*

'A brilliant storyteller' *Sunday Express*

'Refreshingly original . . . Another gem from the master of the modern adventure story'
The Times

9780552146661

CORGI BOOKS